BIRTHRIGHT

By Phillip Finch

BIRTHRIGHT

PHILLIP FINCH

Seaview Books

NEW YORK

C. 2

Library of Congress Cataloging in Publication Data

Finch, Phillip.
    Birthright.

    1. Virginia City, Nev.—History—Fiction.   2. Washo
Indians—Fiction.   I. Title.
PZ4.F4925Bi [PS3556.I456]   813'.5'4   79–15047
ISBN 0–87223–528–9

To my mother and my father

BIRTHRIGHT

Disinherited by his wealthy Boston
family, Joshua Belden, a professional
gambler, heads West to Virginia City
where, with a half-breed Indian and
a prostitute, he plans to con one of
the city's richest and most obnoxious
mine owners.

PROLOGUE

From up on the bare mountainside the wind bucks and rolls into Virginia City. It buffets the buildings that stand in its way and whistles down the corridors formed by structures lining the east-west streets. The wind is an afternoon constant in Virginia City, Nevada Territory. Now it is November, and with the dark thumb of Sun Mountain's shadow pressing down on the city, there is the chill, too, assaulting Joshua Belden as he climbs Taylor Street, hands shoved into the pockets of his woolen greatcoat, neck and head withdrawn to the shelter of the collar, bent at the waist against the force of the wind and squinting through the tears its sting brings to his eyes.

These days he knows how to walk with the wind. His first week in Virginia, a gust caught him unready as he was crossing C Street and dumped him into the dust and pulverized droppings. A miner walking behind him stopped and looked down at him, full of pitying reproach, before extending an arm to help Joshua to his feet.

"Weren't," the man said, "but a middlin' Washoe Zephyr."

On a good day a Washoe Zephyr can topple stovepipes, can strip shingles, can raise a dust storm to dull and pit a freshly painted wall in two minutes, and blast it bare in ten, can rattle windows and slam doors, can snatch away dozens of hats, send them flying down into Six-Mile Canyon, depositing them there with all the debris and detritus that has not been fastened down. Like the heat of the summer and the cold of winter and the foul drinking water and the outrageous expenses of living and the marauders on the Divide, the wind and its effects are a source of some perverse civic pride in a city that is itself a monument to perverse stubbornness. Terraced into the steep brown slope of Sun Mountain, the town is a clinging foreign growth that finds its form in angularities of wood and brick and tin. That is its physical appearance, but in spirit it is a sucking parasite that will not be shaken loose from its leech's hold on the precious metals that lie beneath it.

Joshua stops at the corner of B Street to let two carriages pass by. Then he runs in front of another carriage, takes long strides for another half block, and turns into a narrow alley that connects Taylor and Union. He walks down the alley past three doors, pushes open a fourth, and walks into French Louie Florin's billiard hall. The wind swoops past him, and the men clumped around the tables glare for a moment at Joshua, until he closes the door and shuts off the chill blast.

Only Florin still looks at him then. Stares and purses his lips, brings his hands together slowly at his waist and clutches them together, fingers working. He looks around the room.

"Belden," he whispers.

The two men at the table closest to them glance up at the sound.

"Hello, Louie," Joshua says. He walks across the room to the corner where Florin stands. There is a black barrel-shaped stove in the corner, so Joshua unbuttons his greatcoat to take in the warmth from the fire. He extends his arms and faces his palms toward the heat.

"What the hell you doing here?" Florin says.

"I got cold and I knew you had a fire in here. I didn't want my hands to freeze. Least of all my hands."

Florin's eyes move across the room, not so much in a sweep as in a series of darting moves, settling for an instant in a spot and then jumping to another: here, here, here.

"You should not be here. Should not."

"You worry too much. Nobody saw me come in. These boys don't care, and anyway, where is the crime in two poker friends exchanging a few amiable words?"

Florin is short and running to pudgy, with a pencil-line moustache and a rounded hook of a nose. He kneads his hands one moment more, then separates them and runs one across a bald forescalp and a thin covering of brown hair, combed straight back and slick with oil.

He lets his eyes settle finally on Joshua. The click of two ivory balls and a susurrus of muted conversation fill the silence.

"So okay," he says. "So what you want?"

"McGee is getting the back room at Almack's. He is having a game tonight, and he wants you."

Florin shrugs.

"I told him not tonight," he says. "No cards tonight."

"He wants me there, too."

"No, Belden. No more. Too dangerous. I don't want no more of this trouble."

"This trouble may make you a rich man if you don't let yourself get too frightened. We have been devilishly lucky, and now he is set up right. He is mad and he figures your streak won't hold and tonight is his night.

"Where is the risk to you, Louie? I rig the cards. You have nothing to do but to lay in that crimp, then sit back and watch the money slide over to your corner of the table like the room was tilted that way. I don't call that such a chore."

Joshua has known French Louie Florin for three months. They met first across a faro table when Joshua was dealing at the Occidental, and once again at a back-room session of *vingt-et-un*, and a third time in a private poker game in one of the big houses up on the hill. It was on that occasion that Joshua Belden—of the Beacon Hill, Harvard, and India Wharf Beldens; son of Matthew, who once owned the third, sixth, seventh, and eleventh largest ships in the Massachusetts merchant fleet; grandson of Ezra, who survived the loss of one of his own packets off Tierra del Fuego by grasping an empty water keg and riding it to shore, to lie battered and senseless on the beach at Cape Horn until he was discovered; great-grandson of Elisha, who, upon falling heir to the family's sixteen-acre homestead farm in a section of northeastern Vermont that seemed to heave forth a new crop of plow-chipping rocks under cover of snow each winter, sold the place, used the proceeds to purchase an old two-masted schooner, and within fifteen years had six ships working the East India trade—this Joshua Belden spotted French Louie Florin trying to deal himself winners off the bottom of the deck.

Joshua said nothing at the moment. He threw in his hand, but when the game was finished he followed Florin out into the street. He walked behind him and tapped him on one shoulder. The little man twisted around, startled. He had been a big winner and he was carrying a lot of money.

"I want to tell you," Joshua said, "that you won't get away with it one of these nights. If you keep trying what you pulled tonight, at least wait until they are plenty drunk. Then you might have at least a wildcat chance of living to see your next birthday."

"I did nothing."

"You did nothing the way it was supposed to be done. You slopped the bottom card and half the time you had to go back to pick it up. Plain missed it the first time around. Even a drunk is going to spot that soon enough. My advice to you is that if you can't cheat right, best not try it at all."

Florin straightened his back and squared his shoulders.

"You insult me," he said. "I am a man of honor. I do not cheat."

"Good. It will be useful, this little act of yours. You will need it soon, I promise you."

"You have no proof," Florin said. But the stiffness was leaving his body as quickly as it had come, and his voice was beginning to quaver. "This is only your opinion."

"Now don't give up so easy, Frenchman. Keep lying right to the end, is the way I was told, and it was good advice. Not that it would matter much in this instance. Look, I am Joshua Belden. Among the people who know me at the card table, and there are more than a few of those, my word has some currency. If I say I've spotted you working some kind of blind, I'll be believed. No proof needed."

"Do not. Please."

"If I wanted to, do you think I'd have waited until now to stand here discussing it with you? I'm hoping that we may be able to do some business. You ought to be grateful, considering that I have warned you off a certain death at the poker table one night not too far down the line."

Joshua always had use for a partner, someone else to win extravagantly while he maintained his reputation as only a modestly successful player. He could work the blind and Florin could win and keep one third of his winnings.

Both men were regulars in the poker society of Virginia City, and three times in the next two weeks they were invited separately to the same private game. Each time, Florin sat to Joshua's immediate right. Joshua could run up the deck and deal seconds or do whatever else was necessary to get Florin a big winning hand two or three times a night. (Any more would have been greedy.) Florin had only to play the winning cards and, when cutting the deck, at a signal from Joshua, to lightly crease a bridge into the packet of cards he removed from the top. The crimp was all Joshua needed to restore the deck to its original arranged order with a neat little one-handed change he had learned one night a few years earlier in the texas of a Mississippi riverboat.

Henry McGee played in each of these three games. McGee: loud, swaggering, a little vain about poker. Usually he won. He bet heavily into Florin's winners each of these three nights, though, and took the losses first impassively and then, in succession, with grim frowns, grumbling, ejaculations of astonishment, and a loud promise that this crap was going to end soon.

"Not McGee," Florin says. "Maybe we start with somebody else. Not McGee."

"We can't turn our backs on the gift of good fortune, Louie. It was nothing but luck that put us in this spot, him showing up at three games in a row and then betting in such a strong-headed fashion, so sure that he couldn't be beat. You wouldn't push *une jolie fille* out of your bed if she wandered there by mistake, would you, Louie? Why should you want to do the same with McGee?"

"He scares me, Belden. That gun. Like the fifth leg of a mule."

"Yes. He enjoys walking about with five pounds of iron

bouncing on his hip. But not once have I seen him make the effort to drag that thing from its holster. Anyway you don't want to let the size get to you. That forty-four won't make a man any more dead than a ball from a thirty-six or even a thirty-two. I would personally prefer to see somebody try to use that big cannon when he was trying to kill me. By the time he got it drawed and steady I'll have had time to stroll halfway to Carson City."

"No, Belden. No more with McGee."

"If you don't play tonight, Louie, you'll never play another hand of poker as long as I'm in this town. If I see you at a table I will wait and then call you down for a cheat the first time you touch the deck. You know I'll be believed. People are always ready to think the worst. If you're losing they'll think you're trying to get even, and if you're ahead of the game they'll be sure you got that way by cheating. I promise that I'll do this if you try to squeeze clear of me now."

Florin says nothing. The fire in the black stove hisses and pops; the wood is manzanita and pinyon that Florin buys from Chinese and Paiutes, one dollar for an armload of splintery faggots. There is good pine and fir to the west, in the Sierras, but that is sawed for lumber or squared and sent down into the mines. Already there is enough pine timber in the mines to keep every stove in Virginia burning for a century.

"*Bien*," Florin says finally. "But tonight only. Tonight and that is the end of our partnership, yes?"

"Sure enough, pard," Joshua says. "If that is the way you want it. But we string up McGee good and proper tonight."

The wind is at his back as Joshua steps down Taylor, walking down the hill now. At C Street a crowd has gathered, hooting and laughing. A freight wagon has slipped a wheel into a mudhole, up to the axle, and the bystanders shout as the teamster tries to pull the wagon clear, standing in mud halfway up his calves, straining at the wheel as he grasps the wooden spokes. The oxen struggle and shake their thick necks (creating a shower of tinkling from the bells stitched to their yokes), but the wheel does not budge. When Joshua reaches the corner, a second wagon comes alongside. This one is full of Copperheads in chains, seated face to face on two rows of benches. The driver and the rifle-carrying guard who sits in the wagon both wear the blue uniform of the Virginia volunteer militia.

"These Seceshes are headed for Fort Churchill to do some sand packing," the driver yells down to the teamster, "but I don't suppose a slight delay will inconvenience them."

The guard pulls free the chains, the prisoners surround the wagon on both sides, and with the teamster putting the whip to the animals, the wagon is pulled free of the muck. The Copperheads climb onto the benches and the guard fastens the chains again. No complaints from them. This time tomorrow they will be in the middle of a desert, carrying fifty-pound sacks of sand back and forth across a prison yard for having spoken too loudly, maybe, in the wrong place to the wrong person about what will happen to Abe Lincoln when Robert E. Lee marches into Washington City. Virginia has its Rebels, but they do not often show the flag nor brag about Chancellorsville or Manassas. This is a Union town, proud that its silver and gold help keep Lincoln's armies warm and armed and fed.

The bystanders clap and cheer as the wagon is lifted free—in winter, almost any break in routine is a moment to be touched and scuffed and worn down to bare warp and woof before being reluctantly discarded—and when they are slow in dispersing, Joshua uses his shoulder to carve a path through them and down to D Street.

In her room in the white bungalow on the west side of D, Liz Burgess stands before a mirror and lets her brush melt down through her long auburn hair. It *is* fetching this way, falling down to the shoulders. Joshua prefers it long and loose, too. She studies her face in the mirror as she draws the brush up to the back of her head and starts it down again. A miracle of no mean proportions: She is still beautiful. Enough men tell her so with enough fervor that she knows it to be true. She has been fortunate. Most women seem to age three years for every one they live as a mining-camp whore. But Liz's face is still unlined, her body still trim and firm.

She sees Joshua reflected in the mirror, standing framed in the doorway, smiling the same uncertain boyish way he did the first time he walked into this room. In the weeks since then she has doubted the innocence of the smile. She has seen nothing else in his life that is not calculated for effect, and she knows enough to realize that there is no reason why his actions with her should be different. But she is no innocent herself, and there is no denying the tenderness and the passion of his lovemaking. He is attentive and considerate, most times. She has never loved before, and, having committed herself to this course, she will need overwhelming reasons to swerve from it. When you take a man, she tells herself, you take all of him. Besides, when he talks to her of marriage he makes her believe that this could be possible. Her, married! She could love him just for this, for using his beguiling ways and mesmeric words to create for her this dream out of nothing, to make it so real and palpable that she might handle it and study it and regard it with all the awe that it deserves.

"Please don't comb it so much that you pull it all out. I like it just as it is," he says. "It is perfect right now, like the rest of you."

They are together in the middle of the room, embracing, kissing.

"I've been missing you," she says. "It was past time that you were here."

"Business," he says. "You understand."

He has shut the door behind him, and now, as he kisses her, his hands work at the hooks of her dress, running the length of her spine. He is adept, those fingers so nimble and precise. Quicker than if she had done it herself, she is down to a camisole and he is all over her, hands, mouth, flat pressing stomach.

Some minutes later they are still, lying beside each other in the bed, beneath blankets and comforter. Joshua is drowsy. He is half asleep when a rhythmic series of sharp thumps sound in the wall behind the bed.

"Damn them," he says.

"It is Caroline, entertaining. I told her to move the bed away from the wall, that the headboard strikes the wall when it is too close. But she paid no mind."

The wall is thin. Joshua can hear a man's explosive grunts, and a pause, and a low moaning groan.

"Enough of this," he says. "I will have you out of here soon, I hope, as soon as I have the money."

"The money is not so important."

"The money is important to me," he says.

"You usually tell me that when you are going to leave me alone for the evening."

"Not long tonight. Midnight, no later."

"The cards again?"

"Of course the cards. What else do I know? What other means do I have to get you out of here, have us together as husband and wife?"

When she does not reply he says: "Not that I should feel compelled to apologize. I have a skill and I use it to my advantage. This is what I do best. I'll go now and get dinner in a restaurant, if you wish, but you know I'd prefer to eat here with you."

After they have dressed, Liz goes to the kitchen to prepare the meal. Joshua follows her, and as she salts a roast and boils potatoes, he sits with a pack of cards before him. He has been working on a one-hand bottom deal, difficult but with a beauty of purpose that delights him. Nobody will be looking for a bottom deal with the right hand alone so casually flicking the cards across the table. The action of the hand in flipping the card covers the action of the thumb pulling back the top card and the third finger sliding out the bottom one. A beautiful move. He almost has it right and when he does he will use it often.

They eat with little conversation. Liz is sorry now to have scolded him. She tries to coax him into talk. Did you see DeQuille's bit of nonsense today in the *Enterprise* about the ugly Gold Hill mules? Ours are much handsomer and bray more melodiously, he says. And the rumor is that Artemus Ward will come to lecture at Maguire's next month. The talk is that Tom Maguire wired him asking what he would want for forty nights. He cabled back "brandy and water." I know you think he is obvious and puerile, Josh, but I would like to see him if he comes. May we? Please?

Joshua eats quickly and pushes away from the table. In Liz's room he changes to a clean suit of clothes that he keeps in her closet. An absurd outfit—swallowtail coat, charcoal trousers, and a starched white shirt with a stiff front and a black cravat. He will be overdressed for the game, but to be otherwise would disappoint his acquaintances. He has culti- vated a reputation as a gentleman with a flair, and he will play the role so long as it benefits him; better a fop than a sharp. He pulls on the greatcoat, kisses Liz on the cheek as she sits in the kitchen, then walks out into the night. One block up the hill and two down C Street brings him to Almack's Saloon. He walks in, through the bar and into a back room. In the small compartment is a card table with six chairs about it, the light cast by an oil lamp hanging from the ceiling and another on one wall. Good. Less light the better when he goes to work.

McGee is there already, telling two others that tonight he will slice up the fat little Frenchman. A fifth arrives, and there is some grumbling that this is enough waiting, time to play cards now, but McGee refuses. This is my game, he says, and we will wait for Florin. Maybe a drink at the bar while we wait, Joshua puts in. He wants to keep them standing until Florin arrives, so that he can take the seat at Florin's left arm, to give him the cut on his deal. They are agreeing to this when Florin comes into the room, full of apologies, glancing at Joshua. He takes off his overcoat, and as he stretches to hang the coat on a hook, Joshua sees a metallic flash, a nickel-plated revolver stuck into Florin's waistband and hidden beneath his suit coat. Damn fool, Joshua thinks. He carries a gun when he need only lay in that crimp three or four times. Best we have no more to do together after tonight.

The players drift to the table, and Joshua takes the seat he wants at Florin's left. They play. Pure luck is with Florin. He takes three hands in the first half hour without help from Joshua, and Henry McGee stays to the last call each time. After he loses the third hand he stares across the table at Florin, unblinking. The smoke from his cigarette, clamped in his mouth, curls up into his eyes.

So he is ready, Joshua thinks. He takes in the discards as he waits for his turn to deal. A glance down at them as the hand is played. He finds two pair, queens and sixes, for McGee. For Florin, three deuces. He adds the stocked cards to the deck and keeps them in position with an overhand shuffle—McGee's to be coming off the bottom—and before he slides the shuffled deck to Florin for the cut, he moves his right leg to tap the Frenchman on the foot, the signal. He notices Florin's right hand trembling slightly while reaching for the deck, the movement so slight, though, that it will escape anyone who is not watching for it. When Joshua reaches for the deck from Florin, his fingers find the crimp, the bridge more pronounced than it ought to be, but still there, anyway, and he covers the easy change by leaning in toward the table. Then it is done, except for dealing McGee's two pair off the bottom.

The one-handed deal. Why not? Felt good tonight in the kitchen. He is shooting the cards around for the fourth time, has slipped McGee's fourth card from the bottom and sent it skidding across the table, when he hears a heavy hand hit the table. It is McGee. He has picked the card off the table and looked at it, and now he shouts: "Goddamn cheating bastard!"

He caught a flash of that bottom card, Joshua thinks. Saw it one moment at the bottom of the deck and next it is in his hand. So he knows. But the others, they don't. Joshua can look at their faces, startled up from studying their own cards, and he sees that they do not comprehend.

"Lousy sharping son of a bitch," McGee says, less loudly but with more venom.

If it is him alone I can talk my way out of it, Joshua thinks. Not if he gets the others behind him, but him alone I can handle. Then, beside him, Joshua notices Florin. Florin with frightened eyes, staring at McGee, leaning away from the table. He sees Florin's hand disappear beneath his jacket, making for his waistband. Sees Florin fumbling, yanking at the gun but being unable to pull it out, the butt and handle, shining trigger, now plain to all. Joshua is fixed on Florin pulling at the gun, so the movement across the table registers only subliminally. And it is through unconscious reaction that Joshua begins to fall back, turning away, trying to put distance between himself and Florin.

The sound of McGee's big pistol fills the room, fills Joshua's head. First there is the sound, and then the instant pall of gray powder smoke it expels from the barrel. Joshua, falling back, is aware of a fine, misty wet spray across his face, and of Florin being thrust backward, slamming into the back wall as though kicked by a mule, and of McGee, knocked off balance by the recoil of the Colt, scuffling and wrestling with the men on each side of him.

Joshua is on his knees. He shouts for someone to pick up McGee's gun, take it beyond his reach. Then he looks to Florin. The little man's eyes are open but expressionless. He is slumped against the wall, and in his forehead is a penny-sized neat red hole. As Joshua watches, a trickle of blood wells up in the hole, then slides out and down Florin's nose. On his knees, Joshua takes one step forward and sees that the back of Florin's head is gone, replaced by a cavity, white-rimmed with skull bone at the edges.

McGee is down and quiet by the time the constable arrives, glances down at the body, takes statements from the witness. Yessir, Henry called the Frenchman a cheat, and maybe he was right, 'cause the Frenchman went for that pistol there in his pantaloons and Henry just popped him one, is the way it happened. Well, Henry, he was ready to use his gun, I 'spect, but it was Louie that drawed first. Now who'd have spotted the Frenchman for a sharper? Don't know what he was doin', but he acted guilty enough. Look at that, now. I wondered what took Louie so long gettin' that pistol out in the open. Blade sight caught in his trousers, hung up there, and he couldn't get it free.

"How about it, Henry?" the constable says. "Is that the way? He was going for you first? You got him cheating and when you called him down he went for the pistol?"

McGee is standing up now, but weak-kneed, eyes fixed on the body against the wall.

"Yes," he says. "Right." His eyes meet Joshua's and then move down to Florin's body again. "That's the way it was."

The constable is looking at Joshua now.

"You'll want to clean yourself up," he says, and only then does Joshua look down at his clothes and his hands. They are speckled with pinprick spots of blood and bits of tissue and flesh and shards of bone. He puts the back of a hand to his cheek and feels more of it there. He is covered with the stuff. He brushes off what he can and takes his greatcoat and hurries into the street.

The door of the bungalow is not locked. He walks in, and one of the girls tells him Lizzie was tired, she has gone to sleep already. He goes to the kitchen and pours water into a basin and then splashes the water on face, neck, hands. It is dark in her room, so he needs only to take off the swallowtail coat and his trousers and white shirt, to roll them into a ball and throw them into a corner, from which he can retrieve them tomorrow before she sees them.

He slides into the sheets, naked.

"You're early," she said. "I didn't expect you for some time. Did you do well?"

"Not so well," he says. "I had something of a setback tonight."

She turns to kiss him on the side of his head.

"I'm sorry," she says.

"There'll be another game," he says.

CHAPTER ONE

Joshua Belden was born in August, 1834, heir to a wealth of ambition, confident direction, and material possessions.

His father was third generation of a line of merchant shippers and traders, the first who had not commanded a vessel of the family fleet. He was thickset, heavy through waist and hip and thigh, and disposed to much contemplative sucking on a meerschaum that had once belonged to his grandfather. He spoke few words, but his austere eyes over the bowl of the pipe were expressive. He could scold, could haggle, could flagellate with those eyes. As a boy, Joshua learned to read those eyes and know the power in them to elevate or to dismiss, to redeem or to doom.

The day of the boy's birth was hot and humid. In the same walnut four-poster bed where she had given birth to three other children—only one of them still alive by this time— Amanda Belden strained and heaved to bring forth another, the sheets of the bed clammy against her skin. He weighed five pounds two ounces at birth, and he was not a robust child as he grew. But he had delicate fine features, his bearing was straight, and his face remained unmarked by pox scars.

The family lived in a three-story home on Belknap Street in the Beacon Hill section of Boston. The exterior of the place was plain, with the roof slight in pitch and edged by a stone balustrade. There were no gables, no filigree, only the rail and posts that ringed the edges of the roof, the green-painted shutters on each window (four each per side per floor, stacked one atop the other), and the black iron fence around the property. The sole break in the imposing vista of straight lines and right angles was the arched doorway that opened into a long central hall. Hanging from the ceiling beyond the entrance was a crystal chandelier that tinkled in a draft. The floors were maple, polished to a gloss, but rugs covered most of the floor area in most of the rooms. On the walls were paintings by Copley and Gericault and landscapes by Constable and J. M. W. Turner. In all of these reality was slightly skewed, the colors deeper and richer, the contrasts slightly more striking than they would be in life.

Joshua's mother was a loving woman, but the love made way for a fear from which she was never quite free. She had seen one daughter die of pneumonia and one son claimed by a fever. Her grief was great, and the pain stayed with her in her memory. Twice she had been unprepared for it, and it had devastated her because she had let it surprise her. That will not happen again, she told herself, so she woke each day telling herself that one or both of her sons might be gone from her by the end of the day. Each night she whispered a grateful prayer that she had been spared this time, yet still she knew that sorrow lay inevitable before her in the future, and she wondered whether, for all her awareness, she would be able to stand up against the grief, whether it might not crush her with its weight despite all she had done to brace herself against the impact. She took precautions: When her husband insisted on sleigh rides after dinner on winter evenings, the boys were bundled into warm clothing so thick that they were practically immobile. They had to totter out to the sled, leaning on their parents' arms. And she insisted that they sleep in fine woolen drawers and shirts—flannel was for the masses—because she was convinced that these would protect the boys from chill and infection. That the boys remained remarkably healthy vindicated all her fussing, but did not allay her fears.

And yet she was in other ways a strong and bold person.

She was an Abolitionist, attended meetings in the homes of sympathizers, and persuaded her husband to contribute to the cause. He did so, but anonymously; he had close business contacts in the South.

John and Joshua Belden did not attend school. They had a tutor. Besides Latin and mathematics, penmanship, history, English grammar and literature (Joshua's favorites were Cooper and Scott), the tutor stressed geography and foreign languages. This was at their father's insistence, for he knew these would be helpful when his boys became partners in the business. Both John and Joshua learned Spanish and French.

Yet most of what the child Joshua knew about the world and his place in it he learned as he sat at the great oak table in the family's dining room. His father was a merchant shipper. Sometimes his captains, back from a voyage, came to dinner. Sometimes it was a competitor, though a competitor in his father's business was more like a comrade in arms. As they told stories Joshua imagined his father's power and influence spreading out like tendrils from a vine, reaching, reaching, across oceans and continents.

The stories! He listened when the men spoke. Later he went to his father's library to look for the names of the places on the lacquered globe there. When he found Java Head or Canton or Fayal or Liverpool he would slowly trace the path from Boston. He would imagine the expanses of ocean and land. And he glowed with the knowledge that in these places, so far away, there were men who knew of his father, who bought and sold goods that were stacked in his father's warehouses on India Wharf.

Spreading. Reaching. One day he would own the world.

It was a captain named Bradley who first told him about Houqua, the Chinese merchant. Never signs a contract. His word's his life, the captain said one night. Has these factories, calls them *hongs*. Has hundreds of the heathen Chinee working for him. They kowtow to him, you bet. (*Kowtow*. That's a Chinese word. Means they know who's boss.) You bring gold when you trade with him. But that is the way it has to be, boy. You want to trade in China, you do your trading with Houqua. He has what you want, and wants what you got.

That night Joshua Belden ran to find Canton on the globe. There was a man there with some of his father's gold.

He heard about the Azores from a captain named Burke, who worked for another company. Burke had muttonchop whiskers and liked good wine, and his stories became more florid and descriptive with each glass he drank. He had returned from a voyage to Ponta Delgada in the Azores two nights earlier. The sidewalks there, they are sort of mosaic, he said. Black and white tiles in the most intricate patterns. Quite a sight. But still it is nothing compared to the countryside. We were there just as the hydrangeas were coming into bloom. The farmers, they use them for fences, y'know. Long rows of them, sprawling over the countryside for miles and miles. All pink and blue. Oh, it is something to see.

The Azores. His father sent packets there every month. He imagined his father's packets, which he saw tied up at the wharf, with sails full against a backdrop of green hills broken by long rows of pink and blue flowers.

When other merchants came to dinner they liked to tell stories of success. These were supposed to be for the benefit of Joshua and his older brother, but the men liked to fondle these familiar, comforting touchstones of their way of life.

Frederic Tudor, he was their favorite. Tudor, who had dared to ship ice from frozen ponds in Massachusetts to Martinique. He had had a ready market in Martinique because of the yellow fever there. Doctors used it to cool the fire that raged in a victim's head.

And was he a success, boy, do you suppose? Was that a profitable venture?

John Belden was seven years older than his brother. He already knew the answer. He let Joshua speak up first.

"Yes, sir!" Joshua said. After all, the Tudors were rich.

No. The ice melted. What do you expect ice to do, boy, sitting on a pier in the tropics?

And there was deep laughter from the men at the great oak dinner table. Truly, this was their favorite story.

But the point is, boy, that Frederic Tudor did not stick his tail 'tween his legs like some whipped pup. He built icehouses on the wharves. He bought a machine that would cut the ice in blocks from the pond. He put sawdust between the blocks so they would not melt on the voyage. Now you might figure that a warm winter would mean the end of his business, but it wasn't so, Joshua. He sent crews and ships to the seas off Newfoundland and cut chunks off icebergs to fill the demand.

Frederic Tudor and his ice. Ginseng to Canton. Sandalwood and rubber, copra and quinine. Cowhide and coffee, tobacco and tea. The men sat back in their chairs and beamed at the words as they rolled them off their tongues. Calcutta and peppercorns and Java and cocoa and Zanzibar and pewter. Listen to these names, the merchants seemed to tell Joshua. They tell of the kind of men we are, the kind of man you will be. As a farmer plants his fields, we sail to these ports. We make something from nothing. We give people what they did not know they needed. There is nothing too difficult for us to do. We ship ice to Calcutta; this is who we are.

And Joshua Belden sat at the table, sat at the great oak table in the house on Beacon Hill, imagining the tendrils of power and money stretching, reaching, in all directions.

He was eleven years old in the spring of 1845, when his brother left on his first voyage for the Belden Merchant Company. John had been graduated from Harvard. Now he was sailing as supercargo on one of his father's packets, bound for the Azores.

"You will have no problem if you remember that they are anxious to have the coffee and the cotton," Matthew Belden told his son. "They can take or leave the sugar and the brass lamps. But they will give us our price on those if they know that is the only way they can get the coffee and the cotton."

John was going to sail with the outgoing tide before daybreak the next morning. Except when Matthew Belden spoke, there was only the subdued click of silverware against the china as they ate. Joshua knew that his mother did not want John to go sailing to the Azores. But it was the practice for the sons of merchants to begin their career in the business by working as supercargo. Things were done that way, and having a son ready to do this made Matthew Belden proud.

"Will I be able to see John at the dock tomorrow?" Joshua said.

"I will be there," his father said. "You may ride to the dock with me, if you would like. But I shall spend my morning at the countinghouse. You might be bored."

"No," said his mother. "There will be a chill in the air, so early tomorrow. And Joshua is a sickly child. You know that, Matthew. You know that he is inclined to illness."

"I know nothing like that," Matthew Belden said. "If that is so, perhaps it is because he is not exposed often enough to exercise and the elements. You may come with me to-morrow, Joshua, if you will spend the rest of the morning with me at the countinghouse."

They all assumed that Amanda Belden would not be at the dock when the ship cast off.

"One thing more, John," Matthew Belden said. "These are good hard traders. They have been at their business for a long time. But we have what they want and they will give us our price if you hold to it."

"I understand," John Belden said.

Amanda Belden pushed her chair away from the table. She put a handkerchief to her face and walked stiffly from the room. They all watched her, watched her form receding out of the range of the candles that lit the table.

"She ought to understand," John Belden said.

"She is a woman," their father said. "She would have you here in this house forever. She would have me home from the wharf and the countinghouse every day before noon, if she had her way. She does not understand what we are about, the business of our lives.

"Listen to me," said Matthew Belden. "Listen to what I have to say."

The dining-room table would seat twelve. The four of them had been sitting together at one end, the rest of the table empty. So Matthew Belden was able to reach across the corner of the table and hold his older son's left shoulder with one hand.

"I want you to understand this. I want you to understand what we are doing. There is nobody in the world like us," he said. "There is nobody who can do what we are doing as well as we. This country is special. It was born to do great things. It is the finest nation on this earth. And we are the finest of the finest."

Though he had been gone less than three weeks, there was a feast in the big house on Belknap Street the evening John Belden returned home. His father had studied the ledgers and was pleased. His mother wanted to hold him close and be thankful. They ate beef filets in pastry crust, with heavy rich sauce on the side; and drank Bordeaux wine; and ate chocolate mousse. John excused himself early; he said that he had become accustomed to going to his cabin soon after sundown, and he was tired now. Joshua waited a minute and then followed him up the stairs to the bedroom. His brother was there, sitting on the edge of his bed with bare feet. Joshua sat opposite him in a chair.

"Tell me about your voyage," Joshua Belden said.

"It was a good ship. We made good time. I did everything that I was supposed to do and the company made money."

"Tell me, John."

"Really, there is very little to tell. The Azores were as green as you have heard from the stories. Ponta Delgada is a small city, clean and neat. From the boat I could see roads leading out of the city, up and over the hills behind it. I wasn't able to follow the roads, though I would have liked to have been able to do that. Maybe another time."

"You sound like one of father's captains. That's not what I want to know."

"There was one moment that I shall not forget soon. Until you have been to sea you will not know the sensation of being out there on the water from morning to night and through the night to another morning, for days on end. And then to see land, to see your destination, first as simply a dark wrinkle on the horizon and then as a solid spot of earth— well, that is memorable."

"Yes. You said so at dinner," Joshua Belden said. "John, you know that in not too many years I shall be doing the same thing you are now. I want to know about it."

"That is fair enough, I suppose," his brother said. "I will

tell you the truth. I was nervous but full of anticipation when we arrived at Ponta Delgada. A trader had come alone to the ship and wanted to come aboard. He had heard that we were carrying the cotton and coffee that he needed.

"I told the second mate that he should send the man to my cabin. I went there, and as I waited I told myself that I was about to experience one of the most important moments of my life. This was the first step in the career to which I was born, for which I had trained, and at which I would spend the rest of my life.

"Brother, I have always been afflicted by an enlarged sense of myself and what I was about. One can overdo these things, you know. But I felt that the next few minutes, when I confronted my adversary in our bargaining match, would be something that I would remember, a legitimate milepost in my life. And more than that. I had even frightened myself into believing that my future as a trader would be determined by the outcome of these negotiations, that if I failed I would be marked forever and might never recover from the setback."

"Well?" Joshua Belden said.

"The man was an idiot. You could have gotten the price Father wanted for the shipment. That is no exaggeration, Joshua, but plain truth. And really, his qualities as a trader were almost moot. He needed what we had in the hold, we both knew that, and nothing he said could change that."

"Perhaps the next voyage will be different," Joshua Belden said.

"Perhaps. But I have my doubts. Our father and our grandfather did their work well, Joshua. They created the markets. They matched sellers on one continent to buyers on another. They plowed the ground and sowed the seed and tended the field. Now the crop is coming in."

And if that is true, John Belden thought, then I am the farm boy mechanically swinging the scythe, bringing in the harvest. Nothing more.

"You won't be a supercargo forever. Father was pleased tonight. You made him proud."

"I know. At first I wanted to tell him how easy it had all been, but I didn't want to spoil his moment, or mine.

"Now you know. But don't trust my word, little brother. Study hard and listen to what Father has to tell you. Maybe, on your first voyage, you will have to peddle an entire shipful of brass lamps that nobody wants. The man across the table from you will turn cold and look at you with flinty eyes. You will remember this conversation and think that your brother was the greatest fool who ever lived.

"Now I am tired," John Belden said. "I want to sleep."

His brother left the room, and John Belden was alone.

It is going to be so easy, he thought. So easy.

CHAPTER TWO

The Maker provided. It was an article of faith. What the Wa-She-Shu needed, the Maker made available. Because they needed shelter, He provided the reeds and willows along riverbanks. Because they had enemies, He provided strong men with hearts that beat full in the chest, men who would stand tall and shoot straight to defend what was theirs. Because they were only men, and subject to the awesome powers, He put among them healers and dreamers, men who knew and understood the spirits and the ways of the earth. Because they hungered, He provided deer and antelope; and pinyon trees, roots, and seed-bearing grasses; and streams thick with fish in the spring; and hillocks that teemed with fat jack rabbit in the fall. And He put among them men who knew the ways of these creatures and plants, who could predict migrations and ripenings and resting places. What the Wa-She-Shu needed, He provided.

So it happened that a boy child like no other was born to a woman of the tribe. He was born on the fourth day of *gumsabye*, when all the different bunches had gathered together as they did every autumn in the arid scrub hills that lay in the southeast of the range of the people. They had come together, all the scattered bunches, to sing and to dance and to gather from the trees the pinyon nuts that would feed the people throughout the winter.

The mother felt the pains and she knew that she would gather no pine nuts this year. Her own mother was dead, but two of her mother's sisters were there for *gumsabye*. The woman sent her husband to find them, to tell them that her time was near.

He found them giggling like girls as they shuffled the circle dance in the light of a campfire. *Gumsabye* was like that, a time for laughing. They listened to what he told them and left with him in the darkness to find the willow shelter where their niece lay.

The baby was coming early. The mother had not yet finished the laying basket for her child, so they sent her first-born son for one of the winnowing baskets that they had brought to prepare the pine nuts. The baby was brought into the world in due course. His father, waiting outside, whispered a prayer of thanks when he heard the squeal. He waited until he was summoned by the old women. Then he stepped into the shelter. His wife and his son lay together under a blanket of rabbit pelts. The shelter seemed suffused with warmth; his body felt ready to burst, too small to contain the feelings that swelled within him.

The boy was healthy. His father was a fine hunter, and when the time came for celebration and gift giving, he provided a fat deer and all the rabbit that the bunch could eat. The mother ate none of this. She was forbidden meat for some time after giving birth. But she gobbled elderberries and broth and a paste made from the cooked pinyon nuts. She was full of milk for her child. After a time she rose to her feet. Her insides had healed, she told her aunts, and she was able again. And about this time the baby boy was moved to a cradleboard that hung on the wall of their winter dwelling. Mother and father laughed at the way he balled his hand into a fist and then opened his hand and then made a fist again. His brother watched and laughed, too, and he began calling the infant Crooked Fingers. It would become the child's first name.

That winter was long and hard, as most of them were. On the west side of the mountains was a man named Jedediah Smith. He and a party of adventurers had crossed the Southwestern regions, passing through the area that became Arizona and New Mexico, to arrive in Spanish California. He and his companions left Mission San Gabriel in January of 1826, striking out north and then east until they reached a snow-covered barrier of mountains. They tried to cross, and had to retreat or else die of starvation. They waited until May to try a second time, and still the snow lay several feet deep in the passes.

The father of Crooked Fingers and two other men from the bunch were on the ridges that day when Jedediah Smith and his companions pushed across the crest of the mountains. These were the first white men to cross the Sierra mountains, and the three Wa-She-Shu hid behind boulders to marvel at the spectacle. The pack animals floundered in drifts of snow. The trappers tried to stay on crusty sections of snow, but sometimes the crust gave way and the men fell chest-high in the snow. After the trappers had gone, their shouts and curses still carrying in the air, the Wa-She-Shu came down from the ridges to study the marks of their passing. They knelt to peer closer at the tracks that the strangers had left in the snow.

That night they gathered in the dwelling of Crooked Fingers's father to discuss what they had seen.

"Do you suppose they were men?" one of them said.

"There was hair on their faces," another said. "They had hairy bodies, too. What kind of man is this?"

"And what kind of animal," said the father of Crooked Fingers, "that strips off its fur as it pleases?"

It had been a sunny day. The trappers had pulled off their fur coats and slung them over the packs of the mules.

"Let me remind you," said the second, "of the tracks they left in the snow."

They all remembered the impression left by the stiff soles and the heels of the trappers' boots.

"Like hooves of a horse," said the first, "pointed in opposite directions."

Then another who had been listening to all this spoke for the first time.

"My grandfather," he said, "told me that long ago there were strange men in this region. I am sure that you have all heard those tales. The men spoke a strange language, from which we took some words to use as our own. They rode horses, like the Paiute. They covered their bodies, too, as these men did today. They captured some of our people and forced them to dig deep in the ground. Then they left and we were alone again in this land, as we have been for so long.

"I remind you of these things so that you will keep in mind that in this world there may be many things of which we have no knowledge. I mean birds that do not fly in our sky here, and animals that leave tracks which baffle us. Men may wander by chance into our regions and pass through. I believe that these, these"—here he struggled for a phrase before finally selecting one: *Da Gashu Weti,* meaning White Faces —"these White Faces have lost their way and are attempting to return to their proper place. They will find it, I hope, for their sake. But really we need not be concerned. There is nothing for them here. This is not their place. In the next day and the day after that, they will be out of the deep snow. I am sure that then they will travel quickly to their place, wherever that is. They will be gone from our region, and I will have a story of my own to tell my grandson."

While the men talked, the baby burbled happily in his cradleboard on the wall.

For the Maker always provided.

CHAPTER THREE

The Sierra Nevada mountains rise, primeval and imposing, along four hundred miles of what is now the eastern border of the state of California. Bounded on one side by a desert basin and on the other by a fertile valley, the range exists unto itself as a world of special textures, light, smells, and climate. It is, more precisely, a collection of distinct worlds, each owing its own peculiar properties to the effects of a change in elevation of two or three thousand feet. The range is an uplifted mass of granite (spattered occasionally by outcroppings of volcanic rock) tilted in such a fashion that it rises gradually, almost imperceptibly, from the west and abruptly from the east. On the western side it is segmented by a series of watersheds that gradually have cut deep canyons. There are thick forests of both deciduous and evergreen trees, and from a viewpoint atop one of the lateral ridges the appearance is that of a blue-green sea moving toward shore in a series of rolling heaves and undulations. In the Carolinas or Vermont or Tennessee these ridges would be called mountains. Here, given the sobering perspective of size and grandeur provided by the peaks that lay within sight to the east, they are simply foothills.

On the eastern side the rise from level ground is abrupt and more awesome. Here, in the lee of the moisture-bearing westerly winds, the earth is dry and bare. A day's climb from the desert will take a hiker through at least three zones of vegetation and animal life. But never is the plant growth as thick and lush as on the western slopes that catch the water in eastbound storms and eventually return it to the Pacific Ocean. The east slope is an enigma of rough edges and gritty sand; soft steep hillsides; earth stained red and brown in spots by oxides; sagebrush and high narrow canyons; hawks and eagles that wheel in instinctive circles along the edges of rising convective currents, movement without motion; and treasures of tiny streams that start as seepage from a rock face, then splash down rocky streambeds. It fails normal standards of beauty, for these are based on commonly experienced and accepted qualities. The eastern slope rejects such considerations. Its elements are not rare or exotic, yet their proportions and juxtaposition are such as to render them almost unidentifiable, like a familiar face in an unexpected context. Judgments of beauty, grace, or utility are as useless here as a cutaway formal in an Amazon village. As useless and as silly, for the east slope plays by its own rules.

Between benign west and bizarre east is the crest of the range, a narrow band of extravagant peaks and crags. Here the mountains are highest and most imperious. Here the snow piles in huge drifts, whipped and packed hard by gale-force winds. Here the granite is bare, sharp-cleft, gray, and cold. Here the few footpaths wind around boulder fields and scattered tiny clear lakes. Here the slab-side monoliths glow orange at dusk and dawn. Here the wind blows unobstructed, and accelerates venturi-fashion between narrow gaps in the crest. Here, too, can still be found the solitude and the majesty and special psychic sway that every bit of the Sierras once held. Even after a century and a half of pervasive human influence, this part of the Sierras remains a remote and magic and sometimes deadly and terrifying place.

White civilization penetrated the mountains with the wagon trains of the California settlers, but these pioneer transients left little mark, and the eastern slope with its unfriendly topography effectively resisted settling for a long time. But the western side gave way more easily. The central valley of the state was a staging area for one assault after another of settlements, towns, roads, and cleared land.

The most considerable outpost of white men and their ways was the fort of John Sutter along the confluence of the American and Sacramento Rivers.

Sutter had been a splendid failure. He was a dreamer of great dreams, though never once had his dreams been equal to reality. But California was going to be different. He built a fort in the Sacramento Valley and trained a militia of Mokelumne Indians that he outfitted in cast-off Russian uniforms; he believed himself a born military leader. He had a forty-nine-thousand-acre fiefdom. He had holdings in wheat and livestock and a distillery. He bought and sold and traded. He ran a river launch up and down the Sacramento.

Always he needed lumber. His settlement was growing. He hired a man named John Marshall to build and manage a sawmill on the south fork of the American in the Sierra foothills. It was an enormous undertaking, for the foothills were wilderness then, and the sawmill was to be forty miles from Sutter's fort. The logs were cut and drawn and hewn by hand. The iron parts were forged at the fort. Marshall and his men used oxen and dynamite to deepen a dry channel beside a bar in the river. He planned to dam the river and divert the water into the channel. This would be the millrace. The mill was supposed to straddle the channel to take the energy out of the rushing water and use it to power the saw. In the middle of January, 1848, Marshall sent water coursing into the channel so that he could test the mill. He saw that the channel would have to be broadened and deepened.

Every morning, Marshall inspected the channel. One morning in January, as he walked downstream from the mill, he used a pocketknife to dig some shining scraps of metal out of the bedrock of the channel. The metal was gold. Marshall brought his samples to Sutter, and the two men tested the metal according to the criteria listed in an encyclopedia. But Sutter's fort was a gathering place, Sutter could not keep his secret, and it is legend that not long after Marshall dug his gold out of the bedrock, a maverick Mormon trader named Samuel Brannan walked into San Francisco brandishing nuggets in a jar.

Among Brannan's commercial ventures was a newspaper, the California *Star*. It was one of two newspapers competing for readership among a literate population of fewer than five hundred people. Yet for a month not a word of the strike appeared in either publication, though men left daily for Coloma, one hundred fifty miles away. Finally Brannan's *Star* was scooped by the rival *Alta California,* which used a one-paragraph notice on page two reading, in full:

GOLD MINE FOUND—In the newly made raceway of the Saw Mill recently erected by Captain Sutter, on the American Fork, gold has been found in considerable quantities. One person brought thirty dollars' worth to New Helvetia, gathered there in a short time. California, no doubt, is rich in mineral wealth, great chances here for scientific capitalists. Gold has been found in almost every part of the country.

Brannan's *Star* did not report the news for another ten days, when it granted the story a few desultory lines. But they galvanized the nation. To boost circulation, the *Star* had been sending two thousand copies of each issue on an overland mule train to the East. Seven months after John Marshall picked the first nugget out of the American River, the New York *Herald* reprinted the story. Aside from rumor, it was the first notice in the East of the discovery.

Marshall, having fulfilled his contract to Sutter, went prospecting. He would die penniless. Sutter saw his colony collapse as workmen left the fields and plundered his stocks for the goods that they would need.

The sawmill on the American River, after operating for a month, was abandoned.

CHAPTER FOUR

It was the old man's idea to go see the whites. Talks Soft had seen them in a dream, camping in the Pine Nut hills.

"Always we have hid when the White Faces approached. So we know little of him, and he knows little of us. Now I want to see these creatures and to talk with them if that is possible," he said.

So he took two of his grandsons, Mouse and Fingers, and they walked off together to the place the old man had seen in the dream.

After Jedediah Smith's crossing of the Sierras, a few years had passed before the next whites came to Washo territory. There had been a trapping party and then the first wagon train. Now every year for the last four years there had been at least one wagon party hauling through the canyons toward the summit. There was no established route yet, and each party simply picked a promising path up into the mountains that lay between them and Sutter's Fort. The Washo—this was the way the whites one day would name them—watched their progress from the cover of boulders and brush. They were close enough to hear the shouts of the teamsters, so that they heard the whites' names for the pack animals: Geehaw and Goddamn. Some foolhardy young man might prove his courage by stealing a horse or an ox from the camp at night, then slaughtering it. But the taste of that strange flesh sickened most of them. A year earlier, one Washo had been shot in such a raid. There was a story that some whites had killed many Paiute in a battle, but that did not especially alarm most of the Washo. The Paiute, Talks Soft reminded his bunch, were a belligerent people and probably deserved all that they got from the whites that day.

The two cousins by now were young men, and their grandfather had aged so that he could no longer walk with a full stride as he once had. Their pace was slow, and they rested often. But still they had no doubt that they would find the whites where he had dreamed them. His visions were more strong than ever.

Fingers had been a puny child, and he was now a slight young man. He had not distinguished himself in battle, and he was not an especially capable hunter. His cousin, Mouse, had killed his first deer at age fourteen, and the buck had been so big that Mouse was able to crawl through its rack of antlers. Now Mouse was squat and powerful, an accomplished stalker who could throw a deerskin over his body, tie a stripped manzanita bush to his head to simulate antlers, and then mimic a buck so well that he would get a point-blank shot with his bow. Fingers could not even approach such ability. For a while he feared that he had somehow offended the deer and the rabbits, because none of them would stand still for him to kill them as they did for his cousin. But when the bunch went on a rabbit drive the animals sometimes jumped into the net where Fingers held it. They did not seem to care that he was there then. His grandfather reminded him gently that prayer and reverence alone were not enough. Maybe, the old man had suggested, Crooked Fingers was simply not skilled at the hunt.

He had one talent. He could speak the language of the Miwok over the mountains, with whom the bunch traded every autumn. The transaction was simple and traditional: baskets of pine nuts for a like amount of acorns. Fingers's father had brought him on the trip for the first time when the boy was nine years old. Within two seasons, the boy was able to converse with the Miwok in their villages as the goods were being exchanged. Most Washo knew a few Mi-

wok words, but the boy's facility was greater than that. He
spoke easily and without hesitation. This was from only
three different trips into the Miwok camp, of no more than
two or three days apiece.

"He has a gift," the old man said when he heard this. "The
son of my son has a gift."

And yet it seemed an arcane skill, for the two people had
little to say to one another that could not be said without
signs and each's laughable attempts at the other's tongue.
But the next season, when Fingers was thirteen, the Washo
returned from the other side of the mountain with twelve
baskets of acorns, though they had brought only ten of
pine nuts. The boy had talked with the Miwok, argued with
them, in their language. He had told them, he said, that
their acorns seemed of poorer quality than usual this year,
while the pine nuts the Wa-She-Shu had brought were
especially good. And eventually he had gotten twelve baskets of acorns instead of the usual ten. He did the same
thing the next year and the year after, and finally he did not
have to argue any more. Both sides accepted that Miwok
acorns were inferior to Washo pine nuts, so the Washo always took away more than they had brought with them.

To the place where Talks Soft had dreamed the whites
was two days' walk at the old man's pace. It was winter, and
the bunch was camped in the valley as always, and the two
cousins and their grandfather each wore a rabbitskin robe.

They found the whites by the smoke of a campfire. There
were as many as in Talks Soft's bunch, but all men, gathered about the big fire. They had horses and mules, and
tents and guns, and crates of supplies. The old man took
all this in and marveled that so few men would have so many
belongings.

The Washo had approached the camp without notice.
They stood behind a small hillock, peered over the top, and
watched and listened. Talks Soft was suddenly afraid.
These whites, they seemed so different. But though their
words were harsh to his ears, their voices sounded human.
They seemed to need the fire, just like a human being.
Take away the horses and all the trappings, strip off the
heavy coats and the boots, make their skins red, remove the

hair on their faces . . . they could be Wa-She-Shu, he thought. Maybe they are not so different after all.

He drew a deep breath and stepped forward. He reached the top of the hill and started down toward the fire, his two grandsons a step behind him. When they were full-figure against the horizon, one of the whites looked up from the fire and saw them. He pointed. Heads turned. Hands reached for guns.

The old man did not know guns, but he recognized the aggression in the gesture and the fright in the eyes of some of the whites. So, he thought, they are afraid of us, too. His throat tightened, but he forced his legs to keep stepping forward.

He stopped a few feet from the fire and looked at them. The whites had gathered in a clump. One came forward a step and spoke a few words of bad Paiute.

"We are not Paiute," the old man said in his own language. The whites seemed not to understand. So the old man held out a buckskin pouch, and one of the whites took it, opened it, spilled the contents into a cupped hand.

They were pine nuts. The whites tried them, and smiled. One of them found a red scrap of bandana, another a blue-and-gold cavalry scarf and a soft shapeless felt hat, and they passed these across to the Washo.

In not too many minutes whites and the Washo were squatting together by the fire. One of the whites was scraping a diagram in the dirt with the pointed end of a stick and then pointing toward the mountains lying to the west.

"Grandfather," Fingers said, "I believe these men want to cross the mountains."

"Now? They want to do this now?"

"That is what I understand from his picture."

First the old man wanted to laugh. Then he felt an anger building inside him. No! he found himself shouting. No, this is wrong. Men do not belong there now. This is wrong.

The whites did not understand.

"We must tell them, Fingers, tell them that what they want to do cannot be done during these hard months."

Snow had begun to fall. Fingers reached out and let flakes fall into his palm. He pointed at the flakes, and slowly he said the word.

"Snow," he said in his own language. He repeated it again, slowly, as though enunciating the two syllables— *tah vay, tah vay,* was what he said—would help them to comprehend.

The whites chattered among themselves. Then they looked back at him, nodding.

Fingers bent to pick up a heavy round stone.

"Rock," he said, again using his people's word. "Rock."

Again the whites nodded.

He pointed toward the mountains, where storm clouds were roiling, dark and ugly, around the peaks.

"Rock on rock," Fingers said. "Rock on rock. Snow on snow."

They understood that, he was sure. And yet the man who had first stepped forward only shook his head, swept his arm around the group, and pointed back up toward the mountains.

They stood silent for some time while the wind-driven snow pelted and stung their faces. Talks Soft stared into the face of the man who had first stepped forward, who had motioned so foolishly and so confidently toward the mountains, as though crossing would be no more effort than the sweep of an arm. But the eyes yielded up no secrets. And when the whites took out food, the three Washo stayed there beside the fire and ate. The beans were pleasing to them, and the whites' jerky was not unlike their own strips of dried rabbit and venison. But they spat out the dry, lumpy hardtack.

When they had finished the meal, the white who seemed to speak for them all jabbed his stick down at the drawing in the dirt and then in the direction of the mountains again.

They will not give up this madness, the old man thought. They have this idea and they are like badgers, the way they hold on to it.

"Fingers, you know the way across to the other side," he said. "You have been there on trading trips. I have thought about this and I believe we should show these men the way."

"Yes," Mouse said. "When they are there they will see that crossing is impossible until the end of the winter, and they will return."

"No," Fingers said. "They will get up there and they will

die. They are foolish. They will keep trying to get across and they will die. And the father of our fathers feels that such fools deserve such an end. Isn't that so, Grandfather?"

The old man huddled under his robe and said nothing.

Washo and whites walked together for two days. They skirted the encampments in the valley—Talks Soft was not sure that he wanted these whites around women and children—and when they reached the place where the path led up into the mountains, Mouse and his grandfather left the party and Fingers was alone with the whites.

The first day the skies were clear and the snow on the ground was not so thick as to impede them. By the afternoon of the second day they had climbed through a narrow canyon and into a valley where the snow was deeper. Men and horses struggled and stumbled, and the sky was full of clouds that became gradually darker and thicker and closer to the ground.

That night snow fell, and the next morning and most of the next day. They stayed in tents anchored by the snow that collected around the bases and advanced up the sloping sides. The animals milled outside in a restless knot. When the storm passed the sky was clear, the air so cold that a breath drawn incautiously through the mouth would rasp at the back of the throat. There was no time to travel that afternoon, so they slept in the tents again that night and struck out early the next morning through powder snow. Horses and mules sank in up to their shoulders, the men to waist level. In groups of three they took fifteen-minute turns at breaking a path through the snow. By the end of that time they were spent, and others moved to the front. Still they covered only three miles that day.

The next morning there was more snow. This time they stayed in camp the day after the storm ended, while the leader of the party and four others set off to the gap in the otherwise unbroken profile of peaks to which Fingers pointed them. After they had left, those who stayed behind gathered tree limbs and rushes from the side of a frozen stream nearby. From these they fashioned snowshoes.

After two days, one of the five returned. He gave orders, and the others struck camp, loaded the animals, and began to stamp a path out of the valley and toward the pass. They moved in a phalanx, the front row falling back after some time so that others could replace them. Each wave of men flattened the snow and hardened it so that the pack would support the weight of the animals. After a while the men began to sing, the chanting rhythms a challenge to the cold and the snow and the vastness that surrounded them.

Fingers saw all this and was struck with wonder. The Washo might work together for a common purpose, as when all the members of a bunch would cooperate on a rabbit drive, with some beating the brush and others holding the long net, then all joining in the killing. Several bunches might gather at an arranged place and time to do battle with Miwok or Paiute. But none of that had prepared him for the single-minded, purposeful way these whites worked together. Every man fell in line, everyone stamped and sang, and Fingers could see that they were not individual men any longer but parts of a creature that pushed forward with a single idea. He followed them through that afternoon, and though their progress was slow, he saw that they were on their way to the top. That evening after they had made camp and settled down to sleep, Fingers left them. He walked away in the night, traveled down the high valley, and finally lay beside a fallen log that sheltered him from the wind. But he could not sleep. His mind was full of these White Faces and their ways. He closed his eyes and tried to shove them out of his mind, but their words kept surfacing in his consciousness, like bubbles rising to the top of murky water. At first the sounds had been difficult for him. But he had repeated the syllables aloud, and when the whites had understood what he was trying to do they helped him. Such words: Coffee. Carson. Bastard. Lake. Fitzpatrick. Horse. Foot. Shit. As he lay with his robe wrapped around him now, he mouthed them again. Deer. Water. February. Eat. Maryland. Piss. Indian. He had learned that one the second day he was alone with them. He had been listening to them, had heard the word several times. Then he realized that they glanced at him sometimes when they said it. They had given him a name. He was Indian.

Fingers had his own snowshoes, made with less haste

and more care than the whites'. The next morning he left the low end of the valley and climbed down the canyon, and by evening he was in the camp again. The old man wanted to see him, somebody told him after he had been greeted and welcomed. So he crawled into Talks Soft's shelter, and the two of them were alone there.

"There is a reason I asked you to go with the White Faces," the old man said. "First, I wanted the whites to leave our territory. What I have seen of them disturbs me much. Others in the bunch know the way to the other side, but I wanted you to go because of the way you are, son of my son. You can know a man by observing him. You are not inclined to foolish bravery, and you use good sense. You are cautious and reasonable. When you were children, your cousin Mouse was always first to jump into a hole in the river. But you, Fingers, you would go to the edge and look about you and then walk in slowly.

"So I asked you to go because I thought you might be able to tell me something about these strangers."

Fingers had so much to tell the old man and so few words to use. How could he explain the baffling, strange things he had seen?

"Father of my father," he began, "the White Faces are like us. And yet they are different from us. I don't know whether they are human beings. I mean, they eat and sleep and crap just the way we do. They shiver at night and they get tired. But still they are different."

He was quiet, knowing that his words must sound ridiculous.

"They have eyes, father of my father, which seem to see things that we do not see. Yet they are blind to things that are obvious to us. They walk over the earth but they do not touch it or feel it. They draw in air but they do not taste it."

He found his voice rising, and he was saying things that he had only dimly sensed before. Yet these things were true, he believed that.

"They have a boss," he went on. "His name was Free-mont. But he was not a boss like you. He had no dreams, as far as I know. He was not any wiser than the rest of them. But all the others respected him and obeyed him. I did not understand this, but that is the way they were."

Talks Soft, squatting on his haunches, listened to all this without comment. He rocked almost imperceptibly back and forth, and he said nothing for some time after his grandson had finished speaking.

Then the old man said: "Fingers, every night since I met those White Faces I have had the same dream. It scares me because I don't know what it means, and because I don't know what I can do about it. Let me tell you about it.

"In my dream this land where we roam has been changed. Trees have been pulled down. There are open fields where there used to be forest. But not open like a meadow. I mean the land has been cut up into pieces. And in these pieces are plants I have never seen before. I see dwellings on this land, made from fallen trees stacked together. There are long pieces of heavy string across the paths we have always used. It is heavier than the heaviest bowstring and it has thorns that prick and scratch.

"But the worst part is that so many of the places where we hunt and gather food have been changed, destroyed. The pine nut trees are gone and the land there is bare. The deer have been chased back into the high country that they always leave every fall. The rabbit have been killed.

"I don't know what has caused all this. I don't see any people. But I am afraid that this is the White Faces' doing, and since you have been with them these past days I thought you might understand the meaning of this dream."

Crooked Fingers thought, and then he answered.

"I did not see any string like you said, father of my father. I did not see them cut up any land."

But then he thought of how the whites had stood shoulder to shoulder against the wind and the snow, had stamped out a way to the top of the pass while they sang their defiant song.

"But they are capable of many things, all the same. That much I know."

CHAPTER FIVE

From where he sat on his stool, in the front window of the building where he kept store, Tom Burgess could watch the Ohio River flow past Stoat's Landing, Kentucky. He had grown up in the town, and when he had been a boy he had known no finer hours than those he spent on or beside the river. It meant something to him then. He understood it and he loved it. He thought and wondered about where the water had come from and where it was going and what lay beyond the next bend downstream.

Then for a while he stopped wondering about what was downstream and he no longer thought much about the river. He stopped seeing it as something special. He stopped seeing it at all. He would have laughed at the idea of the river having moods or a character. He was a busy man, with a wife and a family and a grocery store that he had inherited from his father.

Now he was forty-two years old and watching the river again. He sat on the stool at the far end of a counter and watched the river flow by. There were buildings across the street from the store and buildings on either side, so he did not get much of a view of the river. But still he watched and wondered about the places the river passed after it left Stoat's Landing.

The bell on the door rang as a customer walked in from outside. Tom Burgess was easing himself off the stool when his new stock boy, the first help he had ever hired, came around from the back to greet her.

He was all smiles and eagerness, this boy. (He had been on the job six weeks now.) Help you, ma'am? Yes, ma'am, the potaters is good and solid, no soft spots. Ten pounds of flour? Yes, ma'am, comin' right up. Apples? None yet, ma'am, but I 'spect we'll be seein' some any day now. He scurried behind the counter, back and forth along the shelves, plucking out the items she read from a list, putting them together in a spot near the cash register, then hurrying off again to the shelves as though her words were a military command.

Hiring help had been his wife's idea. She has plenty of those, Tom thought, plenty of ideas about what I ought to do. You ought to hire some young man to assist you, she had said. Tom junior is too young to be much help even when he is not in school, and anyway, you can afford a half dozen helpers. You are a man of substance, she had told him. It is demeaning for you to be seen sweeping the sidewalk in front of the store or cleaning windows. At first he had resisted her. But one day while making change he had dropped a penny on the floor behind the counter and reached down to pick it up. Then he had noticed the shallow rut that was worn into the wooden floor. The rut ran the length of the walkway behind the counter. He had retrieved the penny and thanked the customer. Then he had bent down on one knee to run a hand, wonderingly, over the depression. I remember when this floor was new, he thought. That was not so long ago, was it? Strange that I have not noticed this rut before. Surely it didn't just appear overnight. How many of my footsteps did it take to make this rut, I wonder, he thought. How many trips up and down the counter with an armful of goods, being jerked back and forth like a marionette by the words of my customers?

At that moment he decided to hire a stock boy. Somebody else can go to work on that rut, he thought. He hired a boy named Hank, nineteen years old and engaged to be married. Hank stocked the shelves, swept and cleaned, and waited on customers. Tom Burgess found himself despising the boy for being so willing to take on every bit of drudgery that was offered up to him. He wanted to tell him, Listen, you are nineteen years old, strong and not stupid. You could be doing anything now. You could get into a raft and float down to the Gulf of Mexico if you wanted.

At least I had a reason for getting tied down to a grocery store, he told himself. His father owned the store and young Tom Burgess knew the business would be his own one day. His father had founded the business, having built it on land that his own father had homesteaded. The bluff where the business section of the town stood now had been on a far corner of the hundred twenty acres Tom Burgess's grandfather had hacked clear of virgin timber so dense that the floor of the forest had been covered in the summer by thick green moss and liverwort and lush fern.

The bluff was too steep for farming, but it was a good place to put a town out of reach of the spring floods. Tom Burgess's father put a store there when he was twenty years old. He did not care for farming, but he thought that with settlements appearing up and down the banks of the Ohio he might be able to make some money with a trading post. A man named Stoat bought an acre along the riverbank and built a pier there. For a while Arthur Burgess's post was the only commercial enterprise for thirty miles along the Ohio. Eventually Arthur Burgess divided the bluffs into lots and sold one to a man who wanted to open a hardware store. Arthur Burgess gave up his line of hardware in his own store. There followed an apothecary and a haberdasher and a gunsmith. Arthur Burgess happily gave up all those lines, too. He realized that the people who were settling along the Ohio now were different from his father, who had come here because he could be alone here and might live as he pleased. These newcomers, they wanted to be close to others like themselves. They wanted to be near a place that had shops and a doctor and a church and a school. Arthur Burgess gladly gave up all his sidelines to his competitors so that he might be able to sell groceries to all the newcomers.

In the summer of 1848, six thousand people lived within five miles of the town, and half that number lived within the

city limits. Arthur Burgess was ten years dead. Tom Burgess
supposed that his grandfather was long dead, too, but nobody in the family knew when or of what cause. About five
years after his son had opened the post, he had walked inside with a flintlock rifle on his shoulder and a fringed buckskin pack on his back. He had looked around the place,
stared down his nose at a family of new settlers, and spat
deliberately on the floor. Then he had turned and walked
westward into the forest and had never returned.

That had been in 1818. Now thirty years had passed, and
his grandson was spending his days in the front window of
his grocery store, watching the Ohio River flow past.

Dinner was waiting for Tom Burgess when he reached
home. It was chicken with gravy and biscuits. Dessert was
cherry pie, heavy with lard shortening. Tom Burgess's wife
talked about a farming family named Collins that was
building a new home in town, moving off the farm and leaving an overseer to run the place. The new home would have
indoor toilets flushed from a cistern, she said. And gaslight,
too, was the rumor, though she herself considered it dangerous and gaudy.

"The foundation is in already," she said. "Mary Borden
has seen it and she says it could be for a barn, the place will
be so large. It will definitely shame anything else in Stoat's
Landing."

"They must have a large family," he said.

"Four children. Not so large."

"I don't see the sense of such a large place, then," he said.

"Thomas," she said, "we ought to work on our plans some
more. We could have a new home. No reason why not."

Six months earlier, they had talked of building a new
home on acreage still left in the family, not yet sold off to
newcomers. Most of the rest of Arthur Burgess's settlement
had been divided into parcels, sold, and used as building
sites. They had talked about the new home, and he had even
sat down to sketch out the floor plan. But after he had
thought about the idea for a while he had shoved the plan
into a drawer.

"We have the money," she said. "We have the land. We
could order new furniture from St. Louis."

"Nothing wrong with this home. I grew up in this house. Anyway, it suits our needs."

"I know there was a time when this house was the most elegant in the town," she said. "But there are a dozen as fine now, and they are in better repair."

He said nothing.

"You seem to forget sometimes that you are an important man in this community," she said. "You seem bent on disguising the fact, as though you are ashamed of it."

He chewed a biscuit and stared down at the food on his plate.

"Maybe I'll try to find those plans when I have a chance," he said without looking up.

After dinner he sat, as he almost always did after large meals, in an armchair in their parlor. The cherry pie crust and the biscuits were giving him dyspepsia. His meal sat stonelike in his stomach, so he sat quietly and listened to his daughter read Longfellow. As she spoke the words she affected a kind of trill. Tom Burgess knew nothing about poetry but he was sure that he would prefer these lines if Elizabeth would speak them naturally. She had a lovely voice, clear and distinct and pleasing. Besides all that, she was becoming a beautiful woman. Just as her voice was leaving behind the sharp edges of childhood, becoming fuller and deeper, so was her body taking on its mature form. Like her mother, she was tall and erect, with high cheekbones, slender fingers, and auburn hair that dropped to her shoulders in cascading curls those rare times when she let it fall free. The ideal of the era tended to fleshiness: thick proportions through bust, hips, thighs, calves, and ankles. Neither Livvie Burgess nor her daughter qualified. Yet Tom Burgess knew they were beautiful women. And he knew that his daughter, this one who could cook a soufflé and recite poetry, could sew a gown and arrange a flower setting, would be married and gone too soon from his home.

When she had finished reading, Tom Burgess picked up the Cincinnati newspaper that his son had brought into the parlor, read, and discarded. Tom Burgess began to leaf through the pages. He was turning a page, ready to scan the next one, when a small headline at the bottom of the previous page caught him and he turned back.

The headline said simply:

GOLD IN CALIFORNIA

He read the story once quickly. There was a river called the American and people were taking gold out of it. Parties were leaving San Francisco to search for the precious stuff.

He read the story through a second time. Then he turned the page and read a story about a lyceum lecture.

His next few days passed as all the recent ones had. Tom Burgess sat on his stool and watched the river. He made excuses for failing to find the plans he had sketched for the family's new home. Word of the gold strike was spreading, and there was gossip that two of the town's unmarried men were planning to leave their homes, winter in St. Joseph, and head overland with the first wagons of the coming spring. This summer was too far gone for anyone to consider crossing the Rockies and the Sierras before the onset of winter.

One evening after dinner Tom Burgess asked his son to follow him outside, to a log cabin that sat behind the main house. The cabin was used mostly for storage now. Tom Burgess moved boxes and shuffled clutter until he found what he wanted. In one corner was an axe. He lifted it in his hands, feeling the pleasing heft of the thick handle.

"My grandpa," he said, "used this axe to build the cabin we are in. He built this cabin for his family, including my own father, your grandfather. Later my father paid a carpenter to build the home we live in now. Here, let me show you some more."

He held a lantern above a wooden crate, reached inside, and pulled out a rusted blade with a wooden handle on each end.

"This is a drawknife. He used it to strip the bark off the logs. He showed me all these things when I was young, no older than you are. This here is a scribe"—he was holding a tool that resembled a draftsman's compass—"that he used to mark his notches.

"That is another thing. I want you to come close to the corner of the building and look at this. I want you to look at the way one log locks into another. These V-notches took a lot of careful cutting. There are easier ways of doing the job, but they have their faults. Some of them, they leave a place for the rainwater to collect after it seeps in. Before too long, the ends of the logs rot and the cabin is ruined.

"But he used that V-notch, the carved top of one log fitting into the notched bottom of another, you see, and the cabin is solid after forty years.

"He did all this with his hands and with his head. You had to know what you were about—a strong back wasn't sufficient. He built this cabin and cleared land for a farm and raised a family. He made something out of nothing, and that is why this town is here today."

The lantern's light pulsed against the rough-hewn walls.

"Men could do that then," he said.

That night Tom Burgess lay beside his wife in their bed. He listened to the crickets outside, felt a breeze stir the curtains at the open window. His wife was quiet but he knew that she was not asleep.

"Tom, are you bothered?" she said after a while.

"No."

"You seem so distant," she said. "As though your thoughts were somewhere else, not here in this house with us."

"No," he said. Then, after a long moment:

"In truth, I have not been happy for some time."

"The business is healthy," she said.

"Oh, yes."

"Your own health? Tom, are you ill?"

"No," he said. "My back aches in the evening, and somehow I have gained thirty pounds without once noticing that it was happening, but that by itself would be nothing."

"Then you are unhappy with me."

He turned to face her for the first time, found himself reaching for her, holding her against his body.

"No," he said. "I love you. You are all that a wife could be. You have made my life what it is, a good life, and if I am not satisfied with that then the fault is in me."

"I don't understand," she said.

"Lately," he said, "I've been a stranger to myself. The things that used to mean so much to me, my business and my home, mean nothing. I'm no longer happy where I am, doing what I have done for so many years.

"All these years," he said, "I have sought order and certainty. I have valued them. I surrounded myself with them and they made me warm and secure. Suddenly I detest them. I built walls around myself, and now I hate the walls because they are keeping me trapped."

"We could leave the town," she said. "Go to a bigger place. St. Louis even. You are a good businessman. You could open a store elsewhere and be a success. I know that."

"No. Not St. Louis."

He pulled back from her so that his arms would be free. He made a grasping gesture in the air.

"I want to do something with my hands," he said. "I want to do something that somebody else has not done. I want to make something of my own so that when my back aches at night and my legs are dead I will know that my energy has gone into doing something that I want to do, something of my own."

"The business is yours."

"No," he said, his voice abrupt and certain. "The store was my father's first. Then it became mine when he was finished with it. That's not right. I didn't have a choice about what I was going to do, what was going to be mine. I will remember that with young Tom when the time comes for him to take over what is mine. He will have a choice."

"Then what do you want to do?" she said.

"I've spent more than half my life running a store. That's what I know. So I think I ought to start a business somewhere."

"Where?"

"California," he said.

"California. California is wilderness. California is across the continent, across mountains and deserts, I've heard. Why California, Thomas?"

"For all those reasons. People will be needing stores. There will be thousands leaving the States to try to find gold, and some of them will stay on. I can sell them what they need and it will be different from the store now. It will be something that I did, alone."

"I don't understand why you are doing this. I don't understand you at all," she said.

"I don't understand either, Livvie. But I know this. I have tried to ignore these feelings, tried to pretend that they didn't exist. But they are in me all the same and will not be denied. I have to follow my heart. Will you do the same? Will you come with me?"

"It's not fair," she said.

"I don't know what you mean."

"I mean from the time I was a girl I was taught to make a home and to please my husband. I tried to do that with you. And one night after so many years you tell me that all I have done is a waste."

She stopped to draw a long breath. She had never spoken to him this way before.

"The fault's in me, not you," he said.

"All the same," she said.

"Livvie, will you come? Will you come with me and see me through this?"

"I will," she said. "Of course I will."

CHAPTER SIX

Amanda Belden shook herself loose from a restless sleep, stared up into the darkness above her bed, and threw off the blankets and comforter that covered her. The air was frigid; so much the better, for the sleep that had not really been sleep at all had left her groggy and wooden. She climbed from the bed, wrapped a robe tight against her body, and looked at the clock on the wall. Five-twenty. In the window the bay was silver with moonlight.

She poured water from a pitcher into the porcelain basin on her dresser. This morning her eldest son was going to California. Strangely, the prospect did not alarm her. He was sailing to California, and that meant a perilous trip around Cape Horn—"Cape Stiff," she had heard her husband's captains call it. But any trip across the ocean was full of potential peril. True, California was an unknown. But the same could be said of most of the ports to which Matthew's ships sailed. So really California was no different from any other place. As long as she could not have him there beside her, under her careful influence, then one faraway destination was the same as another. And in truth she had felt pride rising in her that evening when he told her and Matthew that he was leaving the family business for a while to go after gold in California. Something she had seen in him at that moment, his forthrightness, maybe, or his determination, had brought a flush to her cheeks with the thought: So this is my son. He is a man. We have done well, Matthew and I.

But Matthew had exploded. Never had she seen him react this way. He had shouted at John, cursed his impudence and stupidity. An idiot unworthy of the family name, he had said, while John stood before him tall and unshaken and silent.

I hope you don't expect us to pay for your passage, boy, he had said. Because if you do you will be a long time getting to California.

He had joined a company, John said. A cooperative of other young men in Boston. They had bought a ship and stores and equipment. They had agreed to work together in California and share equally in the proceeds. His share in the company was one thousand dollars.

A thousand! his father had shouted. You're not touching your inheritance. From this night on, you have no inheritance.

And then John told him that the money was paid already. He had invested his salary from his father's company for the last six months and had turned a reasonable profit, enough to buy into the gold company.

His father had glowered—Amanda saw the rage building in him—and then had left the room, stalking out and slamming the door of his library behind him.

Amanda Belden dried her face with a towel and began to dress. She had needed all of her influence to persuade Matthew that John should stay in the house until he left for California. Matthew would have had him in a rooming house, alone. Even so, the two had not spoken to each other since that night. John ate alone, in the kitchen. Much of his time he spent with the other members of the company. (They were young men, most of them; Amanda had gone with John to a meeting. And good men, too, some of Boston's best: an Adams, two Whipples, and a Cabot among them.) When he and his father were at home, John stayed in his room, Matthew in his library. They had met only once that she knew of, passing in the hall, with each returning the other's studied indifference.

Her husband was awake now, she knew. The two of them had laid together silently, one or the other of them occasionally lapsing into sleep but mostly awake with nothing to say. She felt a gulf between herself and her husband, something that had never been there before. That frightened her. Matthew had changed somehow since the night with John. He spent twelve, fourteen hours a day at the docks, withdrawing into his world the way a wounded animal seeks safe shelter. Death and its effects she expected, but the slow disintegration of a family was different, even more horrible in its way. She could see her child grow sick and die. That happened. One sent for a doctor, followed his instructions. No more could be done. The rest was to fate. But to see her husband and her son turn into strangers to each other, to see her husband changed and hardened, to be in the midst of all this and still be unable to prevent it, was to know true helplessness. Somehow calamity was easier to accept.

She fastened the last button of her dress, took a coat from the closet, and left the bedroom without a word, feeling Matthew's eyes on her back. Down the hall she walked to Joshua's room. She opened the door and found him nearly dressed. John had already roused him, he told her.

Downstairs she saw John's bags beside the front door. He was in the kitchen, drinking tea. He smiled at her, rose to hold her and kiss her.

He seems so happy today, she thought. This must be right, this trip. This must be what he should do.

"I'm pleased that you're coming," he said. "I want you to be there, and I want to have the chance to explain myself."

"No need to explain, John."

"I want to tell somebody. I'm not sure Joshua would understand. Father won't listen. So I have to tell you and hope that you will be able to tell them both someday.

"I didn't want to hurt anyone. I didn't want to make Father angry. But I need to do something of my own. Gold isn't so important to me. I have money here. But if I go off on my own and find gold and become rich in a few years, then that will be different from staying here in Father's business and making money. Can you understand that? Can you see the difference?"

She nodded slowly, tentatively.

"If I stay here and perpetuate the business, then I will never know. I will sit in Father's countinghouse office fifty years from now, and look at all the company ships tied up at the dock and see all the company goods piled in the warehouses, and know in my head the fine state of the company accounts. And I will never know how much of it was because of me and how much of it was inevitable and would have happened without me or in spite of me.

"And most of all, I will never know what I could have done on my own. Never know what I might have been capable of doing. I think of myself sitting alone there in that office fifty years from now and I am frightened, Mother. Do you see me there? Do you comprehend why it terrifies me so?"

She reached for his right hand and held it.

"We are so different," she said. "But I think so. I think I understand."

"Then please tell Father when he will listen. Though I'm not sure that he will ever understand. He never had such concerns, I suppose. If he did, he would be more sympathetic, I know. He would have known why I'm doing this."

She said nothing to that.

They rode together down to the wharves, with a servant driving the carriage. There was still an hour yet before the crest of the outbound tide, so Amanda and Joshua walked with John up aboard the ship. The men of the company— they were calling themselves the B..y State–California Mining and Exploration Joint Stock Corporation—had gathered on the foredeck, some of them blowing into their bare hands or clapping arms against chests for warmth on the February morning, some of them talking and some laughing but hushed in the predawn. Then they all were silent when a figure stood on the fo'c's'le, a black silhouette against the pink sky to the east, and raised one hand above his head. There was a puff of breeze; his cape rustled.

"Brethren, young men," he began when they had all knelt on the bare wood of the deck, "you have asked me for a benediction as you begin your journey."

In a strong and clear voice the minister blessed them. He exhorted them to keep whole their ideals and beliefs. He forbade them to drink to excess, to commune with unholy persons, to gamble, or to take in vain the name of the Lord. He warned them against pervasive greed. He urged them to keep holy the Sabbath. And finally he raised both arms above his head and beseeched the Almighty to look with favor upon these young men, these adventurers, to reward their industry.

"Amen," he said in a breathless whisper.

John kissed his mother. He put an arm around Joshua's shoulders and held him tight to his side. Then Joshua and Amanda climbed down to the dock and watched as John stripped off his coat to join the crew, helping to cast off the mooring lines.

Amanda Belden turned away as the ship drifted from the dock.

"We should go home," she said. "Your father is alone there."

He had already left by the time they returned. But he was home again not long after lunch—since the argument with John, he had been staying away so long he missed supper— and he kissed Amanda briskly on the cheek when she greeted him. Then he wanted to speak to Joshua's tutor, ordered him sent to the library.

"Joshua is doing well with his studies?" Matthew wanted to know.

"Yes, sir. Admirably."

"He is an apt student, then? So far a match for anything to which you have exposed him?"

"Oh, absolutely, sir. He is a genuinely intelligent child."

"Good. Excellent. Then the progress of his learning should not suffer unduly when he begins to spend his mornings with me."

"Sir?"

"I believe the time has come for his education to take a more practical bent," Matthew Belden said. He leaned back in his stuffed armchair. "Now, book learning is essential, a sine qua non, one might say. In fact, my own father stressed my own education, and I am ever grateful. Yet, for all that," —here he made a vague dissatisfied motion with one hand, as if absentmindedly swatting backhand at a bothersome insect—"a young man can learn only so much from books. Once the foundation of general knowledge has been established, then the superstructure, the frame and flooring and finishing of practical experience, must begin.

"Joshua is going to be a merchant trader. That is ordained. And since you have done your job so well, I myself can now begin the process of teaching the boy the practical aspects of my business.

"Not that your role is finished. Far from it. I know that some polishing and refinement remains. So you will have him in the afternoons, after he has passed his mornings with me."

And of course the tutor could only agree.

So from the next morning on, Joshua rose at the same time as his father, and they ate breakfast together and rode down together to the wharf. It was not an unpleasant way to spend a morning. He had always enjoyed the warehouses, pungent with spices and stacked high with bales and boxes and cartons. Now the clerks and captains and dockmasters nodded solemnly, deferentially, at him as he stood as his father's side. He took his place among the other merchants when they warmed their hands over the potbellied stove on the top floor of his father's countinghouse, or when they sipped brandy or rum and told stories at Topliffe's. And learning his father's business was far simpler than conjugating irregular verbs, or working problems in geometry, or writing compositions in French. He discovered to his own delight that while he might be alone with his own limitations in puzzling out a pluperfect subjunctive or figuring the volume of a cylinder, there were always people in his father's office to be responsible for troublesome details and tedious jobs. His father's task, he discovered, consisted mostly of ensuring that everyone in the offices and warehouses, on the docks and ships, performed as he was paid to do. Really, this was simpler than book work.

Before too many weeks he knew the business. He understood the columns of figures in the leather-bound ledger books, grasped that they were not empty numbers but graphic representations of the goods in the warehouses and in the holds of the ships, and of the wealth and standing of his family. When the traders gathered at the Merchants' Exchange in their gold-buttoned broadcloth coats, white beaver hats, and black stockings to talk of their dealings, he understood what they said and he knew how that affected his father's business. When he heard one merchant complain of a poor crop of coffee, he was not surprised to hear his father raise prices on the tons of the stuff that already sat on his own dock. He would have done the same himself if the decision had been put to him.

In the afternoons he studied with the tutor, the words in the books seeming somehow insignificant and a little silly compared to the dealings he saw so casually transacted every day, thousands of dollars changing hands at a nod. About once a week, after his father had shut himself in his library, his mother called Joshua to her room. Then they would sit together on the edge of her bed to read the latest from John in California. He mailed the letters to a neighbor, who delivered them to Amanda.

Joshua was happy. He walked proud beside his father in the mornings. He saw his future in the countinghouse. Following his father seemed a good and natural thing to do, and though he loved his brother, he thought him something of a fool for abandoning his share of this.

Life was good. The illusion of changeless solidity that the big house on Belknap Street had once imparted had been restored in the months after his brother's departure. John was safe and alive, and there was still love and warmth in the family. That would always be the same. Joshua was so sure of it that he never considered any other possibility.

In December of 1850, Matthew and Joshua and Amanda Belden joined the rest of Boston's merchant princes and a crowd of ten thousand others to watch the launching of Donald McKay's newest clipper ship. The day was bitterly cold; that night Amanda Belden went to bed early with a sore throat. Four days later she was dead of pneumonia.

CHAPTER SEVEN

Tom Burgess and his wife and two children stepped off a riverboat at the St. Joe landing the first week of January, 1849. He had sold his grocery for less money than it should have brought, for he had bragged about his plans, and buyers knew that he would be anxious to sell and leave. He had sold his home, too, and his land, having convinced himself that every penny of capital put into the venture would be multiplied many times over in California. They sold at auction all their goods and furnishings and belongings except those that could be carried by hand aboard the Ohio River steamboat. Olivia Burgess, having decided to follow her husband, matched his own fervid energy. She organized the auction of their belongings, and spoke up sharply several times when the bidding flagged on one or another especially prized piece.

Their son boasted for weeks about his father's plans. He kept a scrapbook of newspaper clippings about California.

But Elizabeth had sat silent for a few minutes at the dinner table the night that Tom Burgess told his children what he intended to do. Then she bolted to her room and cried. She had many friends in Stoat's Landing. Young men met her after church on Sunday, and came to visit after supper. She had her vision of the future: a husband (whose face in her imaginings was different from one week to another) and a small home (which in her imaginings was always cleaner and somehow warmer and more inviting than those around it). Sometimes she saw herself pregnant, sometimes with a baby suckling at her breast. She imagined herself shopping downtown in the afternoons, chatting as an equal with the women she met in the stores or along the walks. In all their variations, these dreams had one constant: Always she was in Stoat's Landing. This had always been her home, and would be for a long time, she had assumed. To see this happening in some other town was difficult; in California, preposterous.

So she cried that night and again the next day, and for some time after that she sulked. But still her father went about his self-appointed job of cutting loose from the town and making ready to leave, and her mother did the same. When she saw that she could change nothing, she stopped sulking. It was hard work, anyway, and a waste of time if it accomplished nothing. Knowing that she would be leaving it soon let her look at the town and its people with a certain detachment, and for the first time she could appraise it as a part of her imaginings. The boys her own age were hopeless prospects for marriage, of course, and of those older than she was, the handsomest and best spoken, those with the good jobs and good reputations, seemed already married or engaged. The remainder were to a man dull, shiftless, or unappealing. She looked at them all with a suddenly hypercritical eye, and she could not find one whose features she would like to see in her own child.

The women to whose company she had once aspired seemed to be hopeless drudges now, their chatter monotonous and inane. As for the rest, the child and the perfect white house, they did not depend on Stoat's Landing. She could have those anywhere, even in the wilderness of California.

Free of these fantasies, which now seemed so childish, she could accept her father's venture with what she thought was a woman's stoicism. No girl now, she thought. I am a woman, and life is not always easy for women. But we survive. We find a way.

Still, she had to give way to the sob that began to swell inside her as they left the house for the last time, that fought against her throat as they rode in a friend's carriage away from the house and down River Street, past the grocery down to the dock, that finally burst out against all her efforts at containing it as the four of them stood at the rail of the steamboat and watched the town recede.

She tried to choke back the tears. Then she saw that her mother was holding a handkerchief to her own face and her father was kneading the rail, his face grim. Even young Tom was looking out bleakly at the disappearing town.

But when the town was beyond sight there was nothing to sustain the sadness. Tom Burgess and his wife found another family bound for St. Joe and California. Tom junior left to visit the wheelhouse. Elizabeth found a chair on the forward deck—the day was not uncomfortably cold—not far from a young man who stood straight-backed and handsome, like some square-jawed figurehead, against the rail. They flirted all that afternoon and the next day.

The family stayed overnight in Cairo before the short hop up to St. Louis, then a half day there before changing boats again for the trip up the Missouri to St. Joe.

In St. Louis they left behind the last lingering residue of regret and doubt. Many of their fellow passengers on the Missouri riverboat were bound for the jumping-off spots like Independence and St. Joe, so the family felt part of a fellowship of adventurers. Those who were staying in the States, for whatever reason, seemed envious of the gold seekers. So when the steamboat put into the St. Joe landing that day in January, the Burgess family walked off with heads high, buoyed by a feeling of being a part of a great movement, priding themselves on being in the front ranks of the great surge west.

St. Joe that winter was a welter of muddy streets and screeching mules, rumor and boast and gold lust, an uneasy convention of whores and quacks; high-booted pickpans and hungry-eyed sharpers; frightened farm boys seeing a city for the first time and city boys who swaggered into saloons with Colt's Dragoons stuck into their waistbands; teamsters with the laconic look of men holding a pat hand, knowing they would be in demand, and bearded mountain men in buckskin and rough fur, who reigned above all because they had been *out there*, out on the broad plain that lay beyond the Missouri out to the Rockies and the big basin and the Sierras even, out there to places that the rest of them knew only from books and stories. And all of these people watched the low winter skies and cursed the cold rain as they fidgeted and drank and smoked and played cards and whored, waiting for spring and the chance to be gone for California.

Tom Burgess had arranged for rooms at the Edgar House, two rooms and board at twelve dollars per room per week. And even at that outrageous price he had to bribe the manager ten dollars to give up the rooms. He tried not to think about what twenty-four dollars would buy elsewhere, and how hard he had worked for that money. He reminded himself that St. Joe and all the other places touched by gold fever had no connection with the rest of the world. They operated by their own rules, with their own economies. He told himself that he had to be here, had to be ready for an early spring, had to make preparations.

The alternatives were unthinkable: take cramped quarters in one of the less reputable boardinghouses, or else join the squatters out in the flats below the town, who had pitched their tents and thrown up shelters in a sea of mud and filth. At least the Edgar was clean.

Besides, he had money, a thick roll of cash that represented the family fortune. The morning after they arrived he stuck the money into his right boot, wedging the wad between leg and leather, and walked out into the streets of St. Joe.

And into the turmoil.

Men jostled his shoulders or brushed him aside when he tried to walk at a normal pace. That was not good enough for them, for the town seemed to be trying to burn off its excess energy in a frenzy of barter and speculation. Everyone had someplace to go; nobody wanted to be caught short. A foolish few had tried the trail in midwinter, and had returned a couple of weeks later thoroughly broken and beaten, lucky to have reclaimed their wagons from the muck. The road was impassable in this weather, so there was no possibility of getting an early start. The city swelled every day with men and women, and they all needed teams and wagons, provisions and equipment.

Tom Burgess needed that, and more. He had heard that supplies of all kinds were short in California. He looked around him, knowing that for each impatient adventurer he saw in St. Joe, a thousand would come eventually. So he had decided to buy goods in Missouri and take them with him to California. He would be able to sell them for ten times what he had paid. He was sure of that.

Oxen were preferred for teams, and through the winter their price rose from fifty to ninety dollars per yoke. Tom Burgess spent several days visiting the stock lots, watching other men buy the animals. Oxen were bought quickly; even unbroken mules sold fast. After three days, Tom Burgess could wait no longer. He paid seven hundred fifty dollars for nine yoke, then paid in advance to board the animals at the lot until he would need them.

Good wagons were just as rare. He spent four more days —now pushing and cursing with the rest, hurrying from a smith's shop to a carpenter's to a wagon wholesaler's— searching for suitable wagons. They had to be well built: beds caulked, iron braces on the stakes, half-springs strong and heavy, tops of heavy canvas that could be pulled tight with a drawstring, and beefy axles. Good wagons brought good money, but Tom Burgess convinced himself that nothing but the best would suffice if he was to get his family and his goods across the continent.

He found his teamsters the same afternoon he bought his first two wagons at an auction. He knew little about wagons, but the bidding on each of these two had seemed spirited, and he had decided to outbid everyone else on them. Now he was inspecting another at a livery yard. He was walking around the wagon. It looked good—wood solid and seasoned, no cracks, running gear hefty and whole. He stepped back a few paces to gaze on it, though he did not exactly know what he should be looking for. He had already decided to buy the wagon, but he did not want to seem hasty.

"What do you think of that piece of work?" a man's voice said behind him.

Tom Burgess turned to face a man bent forward, arms crossed, his weight against the top rail of the log fence that bounded the yard.

"I'm considering it," Tom Burgess said.

The onlooker grunted.

"He is askin' too much," the stranger said after a few moments.

"Oh, I don't know," said Tom Burgess. "It looks like a solid wagon to me."

"I s'pose it is. But it ain't worth the money he wants, that thief."

Tom Burgess glanced around. The owner of the livery yard was busy, seemed not to have heard.

"Don't get me wrong, mister," the stranger said. "I ain't sayin' that it ain't a better wagon than some that will make the trip come spring. But it ain't exactly right, neither."

Tom Burgess could not argue. The man could be right, for all he knew.

"Take them rims. Out on the trail they will get loose when the spokes get to rubbin' into the hubs. But there ain't no way to tighten 'em. And the stakes is too short. Come time to ford a river, you want to be able to raise that bed up high so she will float across. But that un won't do it."

Tom Burgess walked over to the man.

"You know wagons?" he said.

"Me and my brother run freight in Illinois three years. Conestogas. Heavier'n these."

Tom Burgess looked at him. The man was squat and homely, with a crooked nose and small brown eyes that looked out, porcinelike, through low lids and over heavy cheeks. His neck was thick and muscular, his forearms the same under his red flannel shirt, and he spoke with the easy assurance of a man who knows what he is about.

"Is your brother here in St. Joe?"

"Yep. Me and him are fixin' to go to Californy."

"So am I. As you can see."

Tom Burgess held out his right hand and spoke his name. The other did the same.

"Alvah Perkins," he said. "My brother is Joseph. I got him makin' the rounds of the stables, same as me, lookin' for somebody that has got a wagon an' needs a couple a handy men with a team."

"I have nine yoke of oxen and two wagons," Tom Burgess said. "I still need a third."

"For the price he wants for that un, I know another. Long ways a better wagon."

They left together to see this wagon. It was, as Alvah Perkins had promised, a better wagon. The rims were adjustable by nut and bolt, the box could be raised high on the stakes, and the spokes were of high-grade oak.

Tom Burgess bought the wagon. Then he tried to hire Alvah Perkins and his brother to drive the teams.

"I'll provide you with supplies. You can have space in one of the wagons for your own belongings if you wish. And I will give you a hundred each when we reach California."

Perkins listened to the proposition. He scratched the toe of one rough boot in the wet earth.

"Now me and my brother, we want to get to Californy, for sure," he said. "But let me tell you. A fella we know, he went to Californy a couple a years ago, before the gold. Now he writes to his kin an' he says that a dollar out there just ain't what it is here, even in St. Joe. I mean it just will not buy the same stuff there that it will here. A hunnerd is a heap a money here but maybe not so much there.

"Now he says that for all the gold, one thing they ain't got there is wagons. Me and Joseph, we figger that a couple a teamsters with a couple a good wagons could do all right out there. So maybe instead a the two hunnerd we will take two wagons and six yoke a oxen at th' other end. We lose one wagon an' team on the way, that is your loss. We still get the two that is left. We lose two, then we are both out, but we take the one that is left. Lose all three an' we don't need to worry about who gets what."

The wagons and the teams were expensive. But Tom Burgess did not know how much they would bring in California. He would not need them, at least not all three.

"I want to leave as soon as possible," Tom Burgess said.

"That suits us fine, me and Joseph."

So he had teams and teamsters. Still there was work to be done. He had to buy provisions and stock. Their personal wants could wait, but the wholesalers in St. Joe needed at least three weeks' notice for large orders. He had decided on coffee and sugar, tobacco, rice, and hardware essentials: axes, shovels and picks, ammunition. None of these things, he was sure, would go wasting in California, and if the wholesaler gouged him here in St. Joe, well, he would get it back triple the first day his gloriously loaded wagons creaked into a mining camp.

One blustery evening in February he stood on a bluff above the river and looked out at the sun setting beside broken gray clouds. The land goes on forever out there, he thought, and he knew that even when they reached the edge of the horizon as he saw it now they would hardly have begun their journey. He wondered at his own temerity, leaving his home and business for such an undertaking. I will be out there soon, he realized, out beyond the horizon, seeing places and things that I cannot imagine now. These boots that I am wearing will walk in California soil. I am going to do it. But not alone.

So he decided to join with a wagon company. Finding one was easy. They were forming every day in saloons and on street corners. A man with a convincing manner and a loud voice could draw a crowd and put together a company in an afternoon. But the haphazard informality of that method bothered Tom Burgess. Most of the men he met on the streets and saw in the bars and gambling rooms would be poor companions on the trail, he thought.

One day as he passed the post office, though, he read a printed broadside tacked on the wall next to the door of the main post office, the busiest building in all the town.

Set in four different elaborate typefaces, it read:

ATTENTION ARGONAUTS

A company of gold seekers from the State of Kentucky are searching for a choice like few to accompany them on the Great Trek to the mining precincts of California, for purposes of mutual protection, succor and congenial society. Only the best-outfitted parties will be considered.

NO STRAGGLERS
NO PICKPANS
NO OUTLAWS
Mules must be broke.
ABLE-BODIED CHRISTIANS ONLY

There would be a meeting the next evening at a nearby stable, the flier added.

Tom Burgess thought this was more promising. A group of his peers, sober and serious men, these would be proper companions during the journey.

At the specified time and place, Tom Burgess found himself among a group of nearly a hundred men who had taken shelter from a chill rain inside a barn. They perched on wagons, leaned against walls, sat on piles of hay. A drone of conversation simmered inside the barn, and Tom Burgess realized with delight that the snatches of talk that he caught from one side or the other could have come from his friends and neighbors back in Stoat's Landing. These are my people, he thought. They talk like me, surely think like me, too. I belong with them.

Three men clambered atop a flatbed wagon, and one of them swung a cowbell over his head. That stopped the chatter. Then a second man on the wagon spoke.

Frank Jackson, he said his name was. The man with the cowbell was his brother Benjamin, the third his friend Ezra Wheat. They were all from Frankfort, he said. Now they were looking for other Kentuckians to join them on the trip.

They asked each man in the barn to say his name and describe his outfit. One by one they spoke. They were from Louisville and Bowling Green and Owensboro and Somerset and Clover Bottom and Mitchellsburg and Beaver Dam. They had ox-drawn wagons and horses and mule teams and pony carts. Sometimes the men on the wagon asked questions: You with the mules, are they Missouri mules? Are they good and broke? Are you carrying grain for the horses? Can you shoot? Do you have provisions? Is your wife healthy? One of the men on the wagon wrote the names into a book, and sometimes made notations as each man answered the questions put to him.

When his turn came Tom Burgess tried to speak loudly and clearly.

Thomas Burgess, formerly a storekeeper, from Stoat's Landing, he said. Three wagons of goods drawn by three yoke of oxen apiece. Two hired teamsters. A family of four, including his healthy wife and two children, each well disciplined. Carrying ample supplies for five months of travel.

He was about to sit down. The three on the wagon seemed to have no questions. But before the man to his left could stand, Tom Burgess was on his feet again, shouting emphatically now: "And looking for a few good men to make the trip with me!"

The men on the wagon grinned. Others in the barn clapped and shouted. And when all the men had spoken and the three on the wagon had huddled together over the book, "Tom Burgess" was among the names they called to stay behind and join the company.

Now it was a smaller and more intimate circle of men that gathered together around the wagon after the others had left. They were strangers no longer, but partners. There was much ahead of them, but they would face it together now.

"Boys," Frank Jackson said, "you are the best of a good bunch and we are proud to have you with us. I will tell you now that we aim to do this good and proper. First thing we need is a name. I propose the Bluegrass Rangers, but if anyone has anything better, I will listen."

Nobody spoke. He continued.

"Then the Bluegrass Rangers it is. Next we need a constitution, and a covenant of some sort so that we all know the rules. Things will be strict and proper. That is the best way."

They talked four hours that night, gathered again the next morning and talked through that afternoon. When they were finished, they had thirty pages of constitution and by-laws in Ezra Wheat's careful longhand, specifying such details as compulsory church services every Sunday morning, division of common duties among all the men of the party, minimum supplies to be carried for each member of each party, and a hierarchy of command, military fashion, with

Frank Jackson being captain of the company and thus responsible for all decisions involving the group.

His first order was for thrice-weekly marching drills and target practice. They were sure to encounter hostile Indians, he said, and must learn to skirmish in military fashion.

So Tom Burgess's days were hardly empty. While his family stayed in their rooms at the Edgar, he marched with the rest of the Rangers, donning the navy-blue uniform with its epaulettes and braid that the company had accepted, or walked to the dock to await his shipment of goods, or passed the afternoon with some of the other Rangers in speculation about the weather and the most propitious time to leave. This was not an insignificant matter. They wanted to be on the trail as soon as possible, of course; everyone did. But the road had to be dry and the grass had to be high enough to feed the stock. But to wait too long meant that all the grass might be gone.

At night he sat studying the two-bit guidebooks that peddlers hawked on the streets. Each purported to be the final word on the route and its dangers. Tom Burgess read them all by the light of an oil lamp while his wife lay alone in bed, and when he finally slept, it was with the images that he had formed from the books' descriptions still etched clear in his mind.

Winter broke the first week of April that year, with four days of uninterrupted sunshine. Grass sprouted in the lawns and the buds of cherry trees showed white. St. Joe reacted tentatively at first, as though unwilling to play the fool for winter's caprices. Gray skies and a hard rain the fifth day seemed to justify that wariness, but the next day there was sunshine, and the day after that, and by the middle of the month St. Joe had cast off the last of its reserve and was throwing itself headlong onto the California Trail.

Tom Burgess went out to buy his family's provisions, and found prices higher, stocks dwindling. In Stoat's Landing he could have stocked his grocery for two months on what he paid for the necessities: flour and cornmeal, ham and bacon, baking soda, dried apples, rice and beans and spices, cooking pots and pans, lanterns and patent medicines.

His wholesale goods had finally arrived in March. Now

Tom Burgess loaded them onto the wagons at the warehouse where he had paid to store them. It was a snug fit, and the Perkins brothers insisted that at least one of the wagons was overloaded, that the oxen would not pull such a load all the way to California. In one wagon he laid hinged sideboards over the cargo. These could be folded up and stored during the day, then unfolded at night so that he and his family would not have to sleep on cold, wet earth.

The Rangers gathered just outside St. Joe in the first hour after dawn, May 1, 1849. They wanted their first day on the trail to be a full one. They formed the wagons into a line, two by two, and the men in their uniforms marched beside their teams, rifles shouldered. The procession was short; it ended a half mile from the river crossing. The water was deep and swift, and the only way across was on one of the two old scow ferries. So the Rangers joined the small army of wagons, unhappy men, mewling children, and restless animals gathered on the east bank of the river, waiting to use the ferry. The rising sun took the last chill from the air. Soon the day was hot. The Rangers' uniforms were wool—that had seemed so much more practical than cotton when they drilled in February, but now the shirts irritated sweaty backs. By mid-afternoon almost all the braid and royal blue had been packed away, and the Rangers' neat formation had disintegrated. Now the company was indistinguishable from the rest of the anxious milling group that seemed to grow on the riverbank no matter how tightly packed the ferries were and how frequent their shuttle. That afternoon there were pistol shots somewhere ahead of the Rangers; a few minutes later, men carried past them the bodies of two teamsters who had argued over a place in line. By late evening the Rangers had advanced as far as the crossing. Tom Burgess was one of perhaps a dozen of the company whose wagons were on the last trip of the day. When he stepped off the scow and onto Kansas soil he was in foreign territory, outside the United States for the first time in his life.

CHAPTER EIGHT

The university-educated stockholders of the Bay State–California Company had renamed their ship the *Argo*. Most of the vessels taken to California that year and the next were the dregs of the merchant fleet, cast-off and surplus. It was assumed that crews would desert and that the ship would be abandoned anyway, so for most of the ships that voyage was their last.

But the *Argo* was strong and swift, more than just serviceable. The sons of Boston's first families did not go to sea in creaking rattraps. Their voyage to San Francisco was ninety-four days, shorter than most, and they were lucky, too. When they tried to round the Horn the westerlies were not as strong as they had been, and would be; the skipper tracked far south and then beat around. It required a mere eight days. Later, other ships would be held up for weeks.

It was not an unpleasant voyage. The ship put in first at Rio de Janeiro, then at Valparaiso after the trip round the Horn. Other companies delayed the voyage at this point to travel to Lima for sightseeing. But these young men were after gold, in as short and efficient order as possible. Next landfall was San Francisco.

There was a string quartet on board, and a couple of thespians who gave readings from Shakespeare. Most men carried books, and traded them. It was eighteen days before the first deck of cards appeared, but they were commonly seen thereafter. The men of the company took shifts at crewing the ship, besides, for they had hired only a skipper and a first mate. Most of them had been to sea before. No need to carry some seaman to the gold fields, and pay him for the privilege, when they could haul line and trim sail as well as any. So even if the string quartet did play to deaf ears after a while, and even though the thespians did get hooted into silence after one tried the *Hamlet* soliloquy for the fourth time in a month, the passage was not as tedious as it might have been. Finally, for the last three days there was the coastline of California off starboard, blue-green and hilly and hazy in the distance, full of promise.

The last morning on the ocean, the *Argo* was engulfed by a fog bank. The captain tacked toward shore; he could out-run the stuff if it was not moving too fast, he said. And after an hour they did break into the sunshine. They were not a mile from shore, and from where the ship rocked in a patch of choppy water they could see a notch in the shoreline where the San Francisco Bay was supposed to be.

The Golden Gate was guarded by rock cliffs on the south side, stained and streaked white by generations of bird droppings. At the northern end of the entrance the hills were less precipitous, and greener, though upcoast there was a high mountain that fell directly to the sea on its western side.

The city is a few miles within, one of the more knowledge-able said. (They were all standing on the top deck now.) Starboard side. Just across from the shit-laden island with all the birds.

They passed a small brick fort tucked into the foot of the rocks near the southern point of the entrance. There was a stretch of uninhabited hills, mostly sand, and beyond these the land rumpled even more. Somebody with a glass spotted tents pitched on the side of one of these rises, and then the *Argo* put about and the city was before them, a city of tents and shanties that planted itself firmly along the waterfront and then tentatively up the hills behind it like moss up the side of a fallen tree.

Men gathered about the ship as it docked at the long pier

on the north edge of the harbor. Later that summer the piers would be so clogged with abandoned ships that new arrivals would drop anchor in the bay and row to shore. Did they carry mail? None. Newspapers, then? As a courtesy, someone went below to gather up a handful of three-month-old Boston papers. He found the men on dock bidding six bits or a dollar apiece for these treasures.

When the ship was secure, the men of the company walked down the gangplank—the curious crowd beginning to dissolve now—then along the pier and into the city. Somebody remarked on the wind and the dust, another on the skins and clothes of the people in the streets: white and black, mundane and bizarre, with infinite variations. A third laughed at the sidewalks—sides of crates, discarded buckets turned upside down for steppingstones, planks and barrelheads—that gave footing in streets that otherwise were deeply rutted. None of the newcomers failed to notice the stench of entrails that had been tossed out by a butcher and left to sit in the sun.

And they laughed at the ridiculous, burlesque version of homes and buildings. A frame structure of unpainted clapboard was something of a palace here. Rough planks and lagging nailed to a crooked frame was above standard; canvas tacked to four-by-four uprights was the rule. And this place has the pretension to call itself a *city,* one of the company howled.

And yet John Belden thought it was an admirable place in its way. The streets and buildings were undeniably absurd, but the physical setting was magnificent. Probably the place will wither as the gold runs out, John thought. It seems to have no other function than depot and supply place for the mines. But still, it would be a striking spot for a city. He could imagine Boston spread out over these hills with the wild green shoreline across the whitecapped bay.

The people were different, too. He had seen some ports in half a year's sailing on his father's ships, and this was unlike any other. He sensed a splendid isolation. There was an ocean to one side of them and more than a thousand miles of wilderness at the other. These people were cut off from all that they had known. They were alone.

Then it struck him: Every man who walked these streets had traveled here. The Mexicans and the Kanakas, the Yankees and Dutch and the Frenchmen, they were all here because they wanted to be. None had been born here, to be trapped by inertia and circumstances. They were adventurers, every one, who had heard the call and come a long way to be here. They were different. They were special.

The surge of traffic on the sidewalks brought the company, inevitably, to Portsmouth Square and the customhouse. Within five blocks the flow toward the old Mexican Plaza was almost irresistible. The young men from Boston had no destination, so they allowed themselves to be picked up and carried along like flotsam in a wild stream. Three blocks away they heard music, a discordant and formless song poorly played. As they drew closer the sound was more distinct, not a single song at all but several tunes that filtered from different buildings and shanties that looked onto the square.

Gambling houses, somebody in the group said.

From one of the places came piano chords, from another the frantic strumming of a poorly tuned banjo, from a third the tinny plinking and tooting of a mechanical orchestrion. At first the men of the *Argo* gathered together in a tight bunch in the middle of the square, as far as possible from the gambling dens. Then one of them and another detached himself from the bunch, and a group of seven or eight punched through the crowd and into a two-story frame building with wide double doors. One of them came running back a few seconds later. Gold! he shouted. Gold in piles everywhere. Men were dumping it onto the gaming tables from linen pouches and leather purses. It was being shoved back and forth with every turn of the cards.

That brought them all inside. One of the Whipples was already at a faro table, calling the turn as casually as if he were buying a newspaper. Some of John's friends were reaching into their pockets; others were already holding their money and watching the games, the coins clicking and rattling in their hands.

John and the rest who had just walked in from the square shifted eyes from the little heaps and mounds of gold on the tables to the paintings on the wall—fleshy nudes in recumbent poses—then back to the gold again. It was different from what you saw in jewelry, one of them said. So, so *golden*. That was the word, but they hadn't really grasped its meaning until now. *Golden* would always have meaning to them now, and they would surely recognize this stuff when they saw traces of it amidst sand and gravel from a riverbank.

John left alone when all the others stayed to play faro or chuck-a-luck or roulette. His funds were short, and he alone of all the young men of the *Argo* could not count on a family fortune if he failed here and returned to Boston. The others could fail here and call it a lark. He was without alternatives or choice.

On Kearney Street he stopped at a restaurant. A menu chalked on a board showed beefsteak at five dollars, eggs a dollar each. And this in a place with rough-sawn board planking for floors, long benches, and packing-crate tables. The smell of steak and potatoes sizzling in a pan came at him as he peered through a window. Not since Valparaiso had he eaten fresh meat, and he was hungry.

Not for five dollars, he thought. Maybe there was a difference between Boston dollars and San Francisco dollars, but five was still a lot to him now. So instead he stopped at a bakery and paid six bits for a loaf of bread, trying to forget that it would have cost no more than a nickel in Boston. The *Argo* was deserted when he climbed aboard, not a sign of the four who had been left behind to guard the cargo. John Belden lit a candle and looked down into the hold. He let his eyes grow accustomed to the dimness. Then the shapes became more distinct. The boxes and bales were all as they should have been. No problem. But he would have to bring the matter up anyway. Those four were supposed to have stayed on board. That was their job, and they all would have their jobs in the next few weeks. All would work, and all would share. They had agreed. He would have to bring it up.

He found some fishing line, baited a hook with cheese from the galley, tossed it over the side. Twice he lost the bait when he missed the strike. Third time he yanked hard, felt pleasing resistance as he pulled the line in hand over hand. On the end of the line was a rockfish, small but pan-size. In a few minutes it was cooked and he was eating it with chunks that he tore whole out of the fresh loaf. By that time day was done. Evening was cool, the winds of the afternoon had ended, and the ship rocked gently at its berth. On impulse, he climbed up the rigging of the mainmast, swung one leg over the topmost spar, and took in the view with a slow sweep of the head. The sky above the city's hills held a pale pink tinge. From this cove he could not see the ocean or the entrance to the bay, but he knew that the sun was dissolving into the water somewhere out there. Lights were glimmering in the settlement. As he watched he saw two, three, four of them flicker alive. Night in that place. That would be something. At that moment he wanted to be gone, wanted to be in the mines and working a claim. No place for a poor man in San Francisco, and he was that, for the first time. I would like to come back here with my pockets heavy with gold, he thought. That would be the way to walk these streets.

He went below, stretched out in his bunk, and read by the light of a lantern. He had brought from Boston five books: a Bible, Boswell's *Life of Johnson*, a thick and heavy complete collection of Shakespeare's works set in ponderous gray blocks of nonpareil type. Those were from the library of the house on Belknap Street. The other two he had found in a bookstore off Harvard Square. One, the thicker of the two, was in Latin. *De Re Metallica*. Though the original edition had been published nearly three hundred years earlier, the text was still the most current explanation of mining methods available. The other he had found buried in a stack of scientific manuals, piled in a corner of the shop. *A Report on the Development of Mining Techniques in the State of Georgia, 1809–1840.*

He had read them both in Boston, and again during the voyage. Now he was reading the Latin text once more. He had tried to interest his shipmates in them. They had laughed. You need a book, do you, Belden, to shake gold out of grass roots?

He was reading when the others began to return, laughing, loud, some of them drunk. The four who were supposed to have stayed behind came in talking about the *señoritas* in their tents at the foot of Telegraph Hill. The locals called them greasers, they said. And they had charged thirty dollars. Thirty! For a dark-skinned whore! But they had paid anyway.

They stayed two days in San Francisco, then sailed again up the San Joaquin River. They docked at Stockton, assessed each man ten dollars to buy a few mules, then loaded their supplies and began the slow march across the San Joaquin Valley and into the foothills. After two days' hikes they began to follow Sutter's Creek. Along its banks men were panning or working rockers, some shoveling gravel. Their pants and shirts were dirty, faces streaked by sweat. Some of them looked up from digging when the company passed, nodded wearily, wiped sweat from their foreheads, maybe smiled at the fresh clothes of the newcomers. But most paid no notice at all. There was work to be done, and every day brought different faces.

So they were in gold country now, though they hadn't seen anyone digging out streaks of gold with a penknife, or reaching into the water to pull out a fistful of nuggets. The night of the third day, gathered around a campfire, they voted to stake a claim the next morning. Any open ground along the river would do, they figured. One spot was as good as another.

They staked the next unclaimed bar the next morning. Some of them knelt in the water with pans and tried to imitate the prospectors they had seen working the creek. Finally somebody yelled that he had color. They gathered for a look, saw a few flecks of gold in black sand. And that was good enough. Some of them were detailed to unpack the mules and pitch camp—they had elected the Adams boy captain, and he was giving orders now—and the others were to begin setting up cradles that they had bought in Boston and carried with them. They had eight, nine hours of daylight yet. So they swung picks and heaved gravel, putting their backs into the work, joyously tearing into the earth. Gold in every spadeful! one of them shouted. Bear that in mind, boys!

And the gravel flew.

A bucket brigade kept water flowing into the cradles. They chucked gravel onto a sieve at the top end of the cradle to screen out the big stones; then they needed water to wash the fine gravel down the cradle and over the cleats on the side. The gold, being heavier than sand, was supposed to sink and gather along the upper side of the cleats.

They shoveled and dumped water for fifteen minutes, then could contain themselves no longer. They were sure that the gold must be clogging the bottoms of the rockers. So they stopped work and gathered around while young Adams used a penknife to scrape the sediment from the top cleat of the first rocker.

He dumped it onto a piece of paper, then prodded it with the tip of the blade, a blackish lump that would have fit neatly into a thimble. There was some muttering. This was supposed to be gold. Then Adams smeared it on the paper, and they caught a dull glow from a couple of specks. That was gold, and about time. He scraped the side of every cleat in each of the three rockers. There were no nuggets, no pure streaks of color.

Well, it takes time, somebody said. Those little flakes, they add up. It won't happen all at once.

They went back to digging, and this time they worked nearly a half hour before stopping so that Adams could scrape the cleats. They stopped again a half hour later, not so much to gather the residue as to rest tired backs and blistering hands. This was hard work, and the day was hot.

By evening they had filled one quarter of a pickle jar with the scrapings from the cleats. Most of it was black sand. They had to figure some way of getting the gold out of that damn sand. You could sift it, somebody said. Pan it, said another. Pan it like it was just gravel from a stream. No, said another. He had heard how they did it in this region. You dry it and wait for a good breeze, and then you toss it up in a blanket. The wind will catch the sand and blow it away. The gold will fall down into the blanket, and there you have it.

"You need mercury," John Belden said when they had all spoken.

They all turned to look at him.

"Gold has an affinity for mercury," he said. "The black sand doesn't. You heat the mercury until it boils away and all you've got left is gold.

"It's in my books," he said.

They didn't have mercury, but they would find some, by God. They had worked and sweated a day, and they wanted some gold to look at for their effort.

By the end of the third day they had thirty ounces of gold, worth nearly five hundred dollars. But with thirty of them sharing, they had been working for less than six dollars a day.

This news brought shouting to the evening meal. It was time to move on, some of them yelled. This bar was worked out already. Others claimed that they hadn't been lucky yet, that they hadn't yet found the pay dirt that was bound to be somewhere on this bar.

John Belden left the group and walked out of camp, into the darkness. He thought: So it is happening already. They will break up soon, sure as sunrise. Problem was, you didn't need thirty men to run three rockers. He had seen other miners working a rocker alone, though it was slow work. Two or three men was plenty if you paced yourself. Now, there was nothing wrong with five hundred for three days' work. But it was not much when you divided it up like this among men born rich, who wouldn't chase six bucks back in Boston if they had to run to catch it.

He walked until he could not hear the shouting. It was not an aimless stroll. For two days he had been wanting to look at the rocky outcropping of this hill west of camp. Now he saw it up close for the first time. He ran a hand over a ledge of loose quartz, its hard flat facets reflecting the moonlight.

The company moved upstream two days later. They worked another spot for three days and cleared less than four hundred. By unanimous vote, the company was dissolved that evening. The assets were distributed. John Belden got a pick and shovel, cooking utensils, and food for three days. He traded his share in the *Argo* for another ration of food, so that he had nearly enough for a week. His share of the gold was just over two ounces.

Some of the others were forming into groups of three or four to work the rockers, or to prospect remote areas. But John Belden walked alone from the camp, shaking hands with every one of the others, wishing them luck.

He walked to the hillside near their original camp, the

hillside he had first explored by moonlight, and in the early morning a day later. He pulled brush out from the side of the hill to expose the outcropping. This is as good a place as any to start, he thought.

Now the gold has to come from somewhere, he had told himself. Just like the sand in the riverbeds. It comes from somewhere. From the hillsides, just like this one. The water runs down the hillside and it carries part of that hillside away. Mostly sand, quartz sand like this quartz rock. But there is gold there in the streams and it has to come from hillsides and croppings like these.

And this is as likely a place as any.

He swung, and loose rock crumbled under the point of the pick.

Besides. It says so in the books.

CHAPTER NINE

Years later, when she thought about her journey overland to California, Elizabeth Burgess would remark that there was no middle ground, no in-between. She would recall days of mind-numbing boredom, each one so much like the next that to remember just one moment of bone-weariness, of choking on dust while the brain chafed against the constant creaking of the wheels and wagon bed, of hot sun baking the canvas that rocked back and forth as the wagon dipped in and out of potholes and over rocks, was to remember a million moments exactly like it. Her only other impression was of sorrow and shock so great that after so many years every detail was still sharp, and she could feel it again just as she had then on the trail.

And that was all, the boredom and then the pain that made her hurt so much she had yearned for the anesthetic monotony. No in-between. And that wasn't fair, she would tell herself later. It had been a long and difficult trip, something to be proud of. It must have been full of small joys and pleasures, moments of pride and disappointment and accomplishment. But she could recall almost none of these. The two extremes had left room for nothing else.

The Bluegrass Rangers covered thirteen miles the first day out of St. Joe, with Elizabeth and her mother riding inside the family wagon, while Tom Burgess walked alongside the oxen, with young Tom beside him, until his feet ached. Alvah Perkins and his brother each drove one of the two wagons loaded with stores.

The trail that first day was more like a highway. There was not a single path but a wide series of parallel wagon tracks. The company broke out of orderly double file and traveled three or four abreast. Thirteen miles was nothing special, Tom Burgess admitted to his wife that night. To cross the mountains in California before first snow, they would need to average sixteen or seventeen per day, and some days they would have to struggle to do half that. But they were getting the feel of the trail, he said, the men learning the habits of their teams and the oxen unlimbering their legs after the winter's confinement.

Also, they had made camp earlier than they would normally. Frank Jackson—he still wore the blue woolen uniform shirt, and puffed noticeably when addressed by his rank— had ordered a camp drill that first afternoon, so as to be able to pitch and strike camp quickly. They would want to use as much daylight as possible for traveling.

They saw their first Indian that day. He was a skinny Sac who stood beside the road a few miles from St. Joe, looking at them blankly as they passed. He was not armed, did not menace them, and seemed not much different from the city-spoiled Indians who walked the streets of St. Joe. But he was the real article, Jackson told them all, a wild red man. And they were in *his* territory now, he added. So he ordered the wagons drawn up in a circle that night, the tongue of one hitched to the rear of the next. He designated squads of four men each to keep a night watch at three-hour intervals between sundown and dawn.

They made fifteen miles the next day, and nineteen the day after that, and nineteen again. Elizabeth Burgess sat in the wagon, sometimes dozing, sometimes trying to read the books she had brought from Stoat's Landing. The days began to melt into one another as the wagons trundled west over the billowing prairie. The Rangers rose before dawn, ate, packed the wagons and hitched the oxen. They trudged on until midday, rested an hour, and then rolled again until evening. They forded creeks, rolled in and out of gullies, and wound around bluffs. Sometimes Elizabeth sat in the back of the wagon. There was a young man, son of one of the other families, and single. He had large brown eyes and a bashful smile. She was the only girl of her age in the company, and after she had been peeking out the back of the wagon at him for two days, he followed her down to a creek one evening to carry back the bucket she had filled.

Owen Mason was his name, he said. From Louisville, a city boy. He was nineteen years old.

He looked away from her when he said this. She thought he had been watching her while she sat in the back of the wagon and he traipsed beside his family's mule team. But she had never caught him at it, and he had not once looked directly into her face. Now, this evening, the courage to make the introduction had fallen short of helping him through talk. He said nothing else as they walked back to the camp.

It has been a powerful hot day, she said. But look at those storm clouds. I reckon they will break the spell.

I reckon so, he mumbled.

I keep expecting Indians, she said. Not the beggars we have seen so far, I mean. But marauders, Pawnee. Everybody says they are killers.

That roused him. No worry, he said, we will fight them off. I can shoot straight, and there ain't an Indian alive that is a match for a white man defendin' his womenfolk. You can put that worry out a your head.

Oh, I will, she said. I will indeed.

He said nothing, but on the edge of her vision she saw him smiling, proud and a little awkward, like a colt that is just growing into its long legs.

She put him into her musings that night, gave his face to the man she saw sitting across from her at the dinner table in her perfect white fantasy home. He had rough edges, of course. Silent and inward was fine for a man, but she would like to see more confidence. With time, she told herself, with time. And they had time. They would be together for weeks. It could happen, a courtship on the plains.

It gave her something to do, anyway, as the company struggled on. Every morning he contrived to pull his family's

wagon directly behind the one in which she rode. She sometimes leaned against the hindgate and looked back at him,
so it was almost impossible for him to avoid conversation
above the wagon's creak and the fall of the animals' hooves.
He opened up gradually. She had him: no running away
from her, and he had to keep looking straight ahead. So he
told her about Louisville and what he was going to do in
California and how he would spend his share of the gold
they would surely find. She encouraged him. She wanted
him to claim her. Maybe it would discourage Alvah Perkins,
with his narrow eyes following her steadily, evenly, whenever
she was near him.

Three days out of St. Joe the company saw the first grave
on the trail. They appeared more frequently after that, some
of them unmarked, some with wooden headboards. There
were Indian bodies, too, tied in branches or atop platforms
if there were no trees. But the whites' graves bothered them
more, naturally, because they proved the stories they had
heard of cholera decimating the trains. The Bluegrass
Rangers' first casualty, though, was an accident. A man
named Jenkins jumped down from his wagon when one
wheel hung up on a rock while they were fording the Big
Blue, ten days out of St. Joe. In heaving against the wagon,
he slipped and fell, and drowned. A day later Frank Jackson's
brother, driving a lead wagon, saw a party of five Pawnee
on a rise beside the trail and tried to pull his rifle from the
wagon, barrel first. The trigger caught. He lost most of his
right arm, and died three days later from the ensuing infection. Outside Fort Kearny cholera claimed its first victim
of the company, a man about forty who had signed on as a
teamster the day before the party left St. Joe. The others
knew only his first name.

And yet the Rangers went on, because the train and its
progress were life now, and the train stopped only for sleep,
the Sabbath, and burials that became successively less elaborate. The routine saved them, the comforting regularity of
rising, moving, then finding a good camp spot again, with
decent water and grass. Though there was hardly a mile
along the Platte without a single fresh grave, Elizabeth and
most of the others seemed to ignore death after a while.

Probably it was unavoidable, and certainly it was too momentous to bear much consideration. The nuisances occupied them far more. There was the dust that rose from each train in tall plumes now that they had left behind moist Kansas and the frequent May thundershowers. Those who waded in the Platte at evening were by the next midday streaked and coated with dust, and many abandoned bathing as a waste of time. Animals and wagons wore the yellow dust perpetually between rains. Still, they would have taken twice the dust if they could have been rid of the Indians. The violent assaults that the Rangers had been promised never materialized. They would have almost preferred that, a pitched battle with casualties. Instead, the Indians begged, and stole when they could, so that the guard had to be doubled at night.

When the family spoke over dinner at night, then, the conversation was most likely to be of the swarming insects or the poor quality of the Platte's water or the difficulty of fording the stream that afternoon. Twenty miles out of Fort Laramie, Owen Mason went to sleep with a sore throat and stomach cramps and never awoke. It was cholera, his parents said, and when they buried him that morning, Elizabeth drifted over to the grave only long enough to pray that the coyotes would not dig up his grave, as they did so many of the others. A month earlier she would have been devastated by the loss of someone she had known, cut down so fast. But it happens, she told herself now. It happened to everyone; the graves sprouting beside the road like dandelions said so.

That night at dinner the first topic of conversation was the cast-off goods that littered the trail toward Fort Laramie.

"I counted four iron cookstoves today alone," Olivia Burgess said. "Why someone would bring them in the first place is past me. Sides of bacon that have spoiled. Books. We ought to stop and let you pick through the books sometime, Elizabeth. Did you notice, Tom, that lovely embroidered settee we passed this afternoon?"

Tom Burgess said nothing. He had been pensive, almost sullen, for the last couple of days. There had been shouting one morning before they broke camp, he and Frank Jackson exchanging words so loud and bitter that everyone else had turned away, the talk too raw for polite eavesdropping.

"They oughtn't to throw away the bad bacon," young Tom said. "It is good for the mules when they get poisoned by alkali. So I've heard."

They ate for a while, and then Olivia Burgess said that she would be grateful to reach Fort Laramie, just a couple of miles distant now.

"The talk is that the chol'ra does not strike past Laramie," she said.

"Must be the altitude," the boy said. "The elevation."

"I pray the water will be more pure. This Platte so far is liquid filth. The shallow wells are no better, just Platte water with a bit less mud. I have heard that boiling the water makes it better, but I don't see how. It kills the little wiggle-tails, is all the difference that I can see.

"We have been fortunate, to judge from the graves I've seen beside the road. That boy who passed this morning, he will be our last, I hope. It was so quick. If it hadn't been so quick, we might have saved him. With so many dying in St. Joe this winter, the talk was that a dose of laudanum with peppermint or camphor would effect a cure, as long as there were no sweaty chills. But chol'ra is too quick some-times. We never had a chance with that poor boy. You know, I didn't even know his name."

"It was Owen," Elizabeth said. "Owen Mason."

"Mason. Yes, that is the family's name, I recall. You knew him, Elizabeth? Why, of course, you used to talk, he at the lead of his team and you in our wagon. Wasn't that the boy? Such a pity. Such a pity."

Tom Burgess looked up from the smoldering fire for the first time.

"He would have me reach California empty-handed," he said.

The others looked at him, uncomprehending.

"Jackson, I mean. He and the others have decided that I should give up some of my coffee and sugar and tobacco to the thieving redskins. They can't spare any of their own, they say, and I have plenty. Never mind that my life's fortune is riding in those two wagons.

"He claims that he has given a brother to the cause of the company's security and that no sacrifice I make can be as great. His brother. A clumsy fool. Now I should give up my

future profits because he and the others are afraid of having
a few stray arrows loosed at us. I won't do it, Olivia."

"How much could it be?" she said. "A handful here or
there, will we miss it so?"

He spat into the fire.

"Let me tell you. In California those goods will be as
valuable as gold. I mean that. Some man will come to me
for six ounces of coffee and he will give me six ounces of
gold in payment."

"Now, Thomas," she said. She used a gently chiding tone
she had developed over the years.

"No," he said. "I know this. Pound for pound, that wagon
is carrying gold. He would have me dip into it and favor every
itinerant savage with a handful or two. Why not just throw it
to the wind while I am about it? No. No. I will not do it."

The boy Tom looked at his father.

"Can they make you do that, Father? They can't do that,
can they?"

"They will have to load their rifles and point them at my
head before I do," he said. His voice became softer. "But
they can make us leave the train."

"They would do that?" Olivia Burgess said.

"They have," Tom Burgess said, his voice even softer now
as he stared into the fire, ignoring their eyes on his face
as he spoke. "After I set Jackson straight this morning, he
gathered the others. They took his side, of course. Said that if
I didn't let loose of some of my goods, they would drive me
from the company."

"We will have to do as they say, then."

"No. We don't need them. They are holding us back, anyways. They and their ill-bred mules and their burials. We
could be fifty miles farther up the trail now if we were on
our own.

"And it's not as though we will be alone. We still have
Alvah and Joseph to split the watches with me until we find
a few strays like ourselves."

His wife said nothing. His eyes, now lifted from the fire,
skipped from one face to another before he spoke again.

"Now let me show you," he said. "As I drove the team
today, I thought about the guidebooks I bought in St. Joe. I

found them this evening"—he reached behind his back for a few of these pamphlets, paperbound and carelessly stitched, that he had stuck into his waistband—"and I looked through them to be sure I remembered right."

He opened one, then another, to pages that he had marked with a turned-down corner.

"We will have to follow the same trail as all the others from Laramie to South Pass. No alternative. But at the other side of the pass there is a road that leads west and south past Fort Bridger and through Salt Lake. It makes more sense, really. We will need to go south from the pass anyway, but the main trail leads north to Fort Hall. So if we take this cutoff we will save miles. This one says two-ninety. At the least, that is two weeks on the trail, two weeks faster to California. So this is a blessing, I think. With our strong oxen and this cutoff, we will be in California before the company has crossed Forty-Mile Desert."

He paused, held out the open guidebooks for them.

"If this is such a fine route, Tom, why isn't everyone using it?"

"Well, it has its hazards, of course. But every route does. Someone with a poor team, or an overloaded wagon, might have his problems. But there is time to be made here if the traveler is prepared. Those are the words, the exact words, mind you, here in this book."

"This alternate route, does it have a name?"

"The books call it the Hastings Cutoff," he said.

"Pa—that was the Donners' route," the boy said.

"Tom!"

"That was three years ago, a long time. There have been plenty of wagons over the route since. The Donners, they were making their own trails, meandering back and forth. But the route is straightforward now, the books say."

"It seems such a chance, Tom. Such a chance, when we could follow the main road, and know we will be among others. Two weeks more or less, does it matter so much?"

"It matters. I don't want to share this trail with all these others, not any longer than I must. And I want to be waiting there in California, halfway to being a rich man, when they arrive. That is important to me."

There was no budging him once he had decided. The two teamsters took the news and shrugged. So much the better if they could save a few days. The boy saw it as a great adventure, and Elizabeth found herself trusting her father. He was no longer a storekeeper. He was a man who had ideas and ambitions and could make them come to pass. Why, he had brought them here so far. From Stoat's Landing to Fort Laramie, Wyoming, he had been right. He had been able to make things happen. Could one section of trail be so much different from another? Olivia still was unhappy, and a year earlier she might have been able to change his mind, to make him understand her fears and accede to them. But he was a different man now from what he had been. And she had to concede that maybe he was right, maybe was drawing on resources of strength and judgment she had never suspected.

In the last couple of miles to Fort Laramie, where the cast-off articles made the trail a virtual rubbish heap, Elizabeth scavenged a pair of boy's boots that fit her feet. In Stoat's Landing she would never have worn anything but slippers or her delicate pointed-toe shoes. But their thin soles and elevated heels made hard walking impossible, and she was tired of riding inside the wagon. Now she could walk at least a few miles a day in these heavy brogans. They were graceless and ugly, but the emigrants had thrown off their notions of style along with all the other burdensome luxuries many miles back on the trail. These boots were useful, and thus admirable.

Fort Laramie was a decrepit, decaying adobe settlement. The Army had moved into the place just a week before the Rangers arrived expecting a garrison and finding a poorly maintained trading post that now housed a few platoons of soldiers instead of merchants. Still, it was civilization, the last permanent trace of white men for hundreds of miles to the west. Here the Rangers and Tom Burgess parted. The company wanted to visit a blacksmith at the fort for repairs, but his three wagons rolled past the buildings and on down the trail, his face set straight ahead as he passed the others.

The fort lay surrounded by hills, and beyond the hills were mountains. Topographically and symbolically, this was the end of the Great Plains and the start of the mountains.

Beyond the mountains was the Great Basin, and beyond that the Sierra Nevada, so there would be little easy going from here on. The cast-off goods on the trail to the fort represented a grudging capitulation to realism.

Beyond the fort the hills were steeper and more frequent than they had been before. For the first time Tom Burgess saw wagons broken and abandoned. The foot of each incline would be marked by a mound of debris, others who had gone before having shed all but the most essential goods so that the wagon could be hauled to the top of the grade. Usually it was a futile gesture, for the stock animals were predictably exhausted by having hauled the overload more than seven hundred miles, and circling vultures marked the bottom of each ascent as they circled slowly over the bodies of dead stock.

Tom Burgess's oxen were strong yet. The first steep hill had taught the family to tie down everything in the wagon. The problem was not in climbing but in descending, when loose items would pitch forward out of the wagon and into the feet of oxen already struggling for purchase in the steep ground, the weight of the wagon nudging them forward. The party traveled alone, for Tom Burgess was driving them from first light to nightfall, leaving camp earlier in the morning and then staying on the trail longer than any of the stray teams they met on the trail. Though he knew he must have left the Rangers far behind, he still looked backward from every promontory, as though fearful that they were gaining on him and he would have to endure the indignity of having them pass him on the trail.

Six days out of Fort Laramie, they left behind the Platte and followed the course of the Sweetwater. At Independence Rock Tom Burgess stopped long enough for the boy to scratch their four names into the granite. Here and at Devil's Gate, and at Split Rock and Three Crossings farther down the trail, the road was more congested than it had been before. In some spots there was room for no more than one wagon, with no place to pass, and at one point for five hours Tom Burgess found his three wagons behind a single ambling mule and a pushcart. He cursed the man who led the mule and cart, damned his impertinence at constricting the public byways with such miserable equipment, prophesied doom for such a ridiculous outfit in the rough going that lay ahead.

Eleven days out of Fort Laramie and an even fifty after crossing the Missouri River from St. Joe, Tom Burgess and his family and three wagons stood in the broad saddle that marked the Great Divide. The ascent to the top was gradual and easy, and the pass was in just one in a series of low rounded hills. But this was the Divide, Tom Burgess said when they paused a moment at the top. Spit in a stream facing one way and it will end up in the Mississippi and finally flow into the Gulf. Turn the other direction and your spit will flow west into the Pacific.

The party camped just beyond the pass that night and started early down the west side of the grade. Ahead were the Rockies and the Wind River Mountains, hazy blue and white in the distance. A dozen miles beyond the pass the road forked: to the right, Sublette's cutoff across the desert, and eventually to Fort Hall; to the left, the trail less well defined, the road to Fort Bridger and Salt Lake City.

Tom Burgess, driving the lead team, did not hesitate. He yelled, "Haw," in a clear voice and flicked his long-handled whip at the first two oxen. For the next few days they marked time by stream crossings. The Green River. Ham's Fork. Black's Fork. One after another, they appeared and rolled beneath the wagons' wheels as the guidebooks had said. The trail was near empty, but no matter. That meant plenty of feed for the oxen. And the going was good. Three days in a row they put twenty miles or more behind them. Tom Burgess was happy, relaxed. The third night on the trail, he asked Elizabeth to read to him from a book of poetry. That same night he hummed a song and danced with Olivia, swinging her around the campfire. Every night for six nights they found water and grass and firewood. There were camps at Fort Bridger, too. Tom Burgess laid by for a day so that a blacksmith there could tighten and repair the wheels of one of the wagons. Going was tougher beyond the fort. Tom Burgess knew that, told his family so. But they were ready, he said.

Two days beyond Fort Bridger, the trail descended into a narrow canyon, then across a stream and up the other side.

Elizabeth Burgess climbed out of the wagon and stood on the rim. Beneath her the canyon was dark in shadows and the stream flowed silently, so far distant. She would walk down behind the last wagon. On steep grades like these the two teamsters and her father handled the wagons one at a time, Tom Burgess inside watching the load while Alvah Perkins and his brother took the lead yoke by hand to steady them down.

First down was one of the freight wagons. The trail was narrow, with a half dozen switchbacks, so that it doubled back beneath itself as it dropped to the bottom of the gorge. Twice on its way down the first freight wagon scraped sides against the rock wall of the canyon. High on the trail the wheels dislodged stones that fell from the edge and down to the path below. When they reached the bottom of the canyon the men left the wagon and walked back to the top.

The second freight wagon went down, and again the three men climbed the grade. It was mid-afternoon, the day hot. Tom Burgess and his two teamsters were sweating, their shirts wet, as they rested in the shade cast by the third wagon, the Burgess's family wagon. They rose slowly after a while. Tom Burgess climbed aboard the wagon and sat facing the rear, so that he might catch any stray part of that load that worked loose during the descent. Olivia Burgess sat on the front board seat, where she had spent much of the journey; no walk down a canyon for her. Young Tom was stretched out in the back, where he had gone to nap while the men led down the first two wagons. He opened his eyes as the wagon creaked and moved. He sat up and looked out at Elizabeth walking behind the wagon, and grinned foolishly and stuck his tongue out at her.

This wagon, too, scraped the canyon wall in one spot before the first switchback. Again, loose rocks broke away and plummeted.

What happened next, Elizabeth saw, and would see for the rest of her life, in a dreamlike slow motion, a nightmare that she witnessed but could not affect. The wagon rumbled around the second switchback. Gravel crunched beneath the wheels. The sideboard on the right scraped against a bulge in the canyon wall.

That wheel is close to the edge, she thought. She walked

and said nothing. *That wheel is terribly close to the edge.*

The left rear wheel dropped as the gravel at the edge of the trail fell away from it. Young Tom leaned out over the hindgate, saw the wheel drop over the edge, saw the road fall away in chunks and slabs.

Elizabeth's mind, lulled by the heat and by her regular pace behind the wagon, assessed the sight idly, as though at half speed. Drop? No. It can't possibly.

Her voice registered dimly in her ears. She was shouting, but the sound seemed distant. Tom. Jump, Tom. Oh, Ma, she was crying. Oh, Pa. Jump, Tom.

The men at the lead yoke looked back, startled by her voice and by the sound of the crumbling roadbed sliding and beginning to smack into the trail below it. One yanked hard at the oxen. The animals twisted. The wagon sagged down into the sudden cavity. The rear axle hung for a moment on the crescent edge, until that dropped away too and there was nothing to hold the weight.

Young Tom was in the air, jumping. The wagon was falling, having broken free of the animals. It was tumbling. It was rolling and falling and tumbling.

The drop to the next section of road below was more than one hundred feet. The wagon hit there in the pile of loose gravel from the slide, and burst. Elizabeth Burgess could see splintered boards flying free before the dust rose from the rubble. She heard the tortured rending of joints and splices. Then there was no sound until a splash from the river, and when the wind blew away the dust she saw the wagon gone from the road below her and (her eyes sweeping downward slowly, fearfully) lying in a broken heap in the streambed, the tattered canvas top playing out in the current.

She ran to where Tom lay in the road. When she saw the boy raising himself from the ground, she ran past him, past the two teamsters, and down the trail. She ran past a pile of calico halfway down the trail until she remembered that her mother had been wearing a dress of that material. She was turning back to it when she saw a limp blood-streaked leg in one of the folds.

The thought registered: No. Can't face that. So she

turned back down the trail, drew in shallow desperate breaths, ran headlong down the trail until she reached the bottom. There she found her father's body in the jumble of ruptured barrels, boxes, scattered clothing, split and broken planks of the wagon. White flour from one of the burst casks blew across the wreckage. No. Too much, too much. There was weight, a physical weight, on her shoulders. She felt her knees giving way. But Tom was coming down the trail. She found strength, turned to hold him so that he would not see. They sagged against each other and cried until the two teamsters drew down the trail with the wagon's three yoke of oxen in tow, her mother's body draped across one of them. Then Elizabeth blinked back the tears and stood straight to face them.

"I don't know what happened," the one called Joseph said to her. "Don't know. The road give way. The wagon busted loose. That shouldn't a happened, the pin snappin' that way."

"It weren't our fault," his brother said. "The road give way and the pin broke. That is all. It shouldn't a happened, but it did."

She stared at them. She felt a fury rising in her. This wasn't her fault, and not young Tom's. So the blame must be theirs. She let the anger build. It felt good, because it blocked out the terrible desolate bleakness that made her knees start to buckle. This anger, it made her strong. She savored it and held it inside, pent up, until she knew she could contain it no longer. Then she lunged at Alvah Perkins, knocked him backward and into the sand. She clawed at his face, tried to dig her fingers into his eyes. Those eyes. Those awful pig eyes that had followed her. And he had killed her father.

Joseph Perkins grabbed her by the waist, lifted her off. Alvah was starting to his feet when she broke loose and came at him again. This time he caught her by the shoulders, held one of her arms, and twisted it so that he was behind her.

"I'm sorry," he said in her ear. "They are dead and that is all. Nobody's fault. Nothin' I could a done to change that. It happened, is all."

He pushed her away. She walked a few steps and saw a

gleam of cutlery inside the wreckage. She looked back. No fury now, but calculation. The two teamsters were ignoring her. Alvah Perkins had turned away, and his brother was peering close at the scratches she had made in Alvah's face. So they did not see her pick up the knife, hold it in the folds of her skirt. They don't see, she thought. Tom, he knows. But Tom won't stop me. He watched her with fearful eyes but he did not speak, did not move. She walked toward the two teamsters, steps even and light, right hand and knife by her side. Joseph Perkins glanced at her, looked back at his brother's face. So close now she could see the grime on the back of Alvah's neck. She thought: Where is the heart? Left side? Right? Her steps quickening, she raised the knife and stumbled forward. Alvah's head jerked around at the sound of her steps, and the knife was plunging down toward his neck when Joseph raised a hand from his shoulder, met the blade with the meat of his palm, and knocked it aside, so that it ripped red flannel without leaving a mark on skin.

This time they both grabbed her, swung her off her feet and down to the ground. Alvah twisted the knife from her hand.

"No more!" he shouted. "No more! You'd kill me, I believe."

"In God's name, I would, you and your brother both, if I could."

Alvah Perkins looked away from her, at his brother, but he kept his head cocked so that she was at the periphery of his sight.

"Your hand?"

"Not bad." Joseph Perkins had the cut at his mouth, took it away to examine it, wiped it on his shirt. "Just a kitchen knife. But sharp enough, all the same."

"We are leavin'. I would stay to dig graves, but not my own."

He walked to the wrecked wagon, found a length of rope, walked behind Elizabeth Burgess, and tied her hands.

"Do you suppose you want to go on to Californy?" he said when he was finished.

"Not with you. You killed my ma and my pa."

"I didn't. Think a spell and you'll know that. I won't stay

waitin' for you to regain your sense, though. My brother and me, we are bound to see the elephant and we don't have the time to wait on you. All right, then. I am going over to that wagon to pick out a few supplies. We will leave you plenty for yourselves. Your pa agreed to give me two wagon and six yoke a oxen at trip's end. I suppose one wagon and the goods in it and four yoke will make us square. That leaves you a wagon and goods and five yoke. You'll make out on that."

He turned away, walked to the wreckage, began filling an arm with food. He threw that load into the first freight wagon, halved a side of bacon and took one piece and tossed that into the wagon, too. He pushed aside debris in the wreckage to come up with her father's rifle, a small cask of powder, a box of caps.

"I am taking this because I figger you will have no use for it," he said. "I took a barrel of cornmeal, left you a full barrel of flour. You won't starve, anyways."

Joseph was unhitching a yoke from the loose team of oxen. He tied the two animals to the back of the first wagon, climbed inside at a motion from his brother. Alvah walked a few steps toward the wagon, stopped, and looked back at her.

"It ain't the best thing I ever done," he said, "leaving you and the boy here this way. But I won't have a knife stuck in my back."

He picked up his whip from the front seat of the wagon, walked to the lead team. The wagon moved across the shallow stream and up the canyonside.

She watched them leave, and began to cry hard for the first time. Young Tom came to her, held her.

"I'll cut you free, Liz. But don't try to kill them. Don't do that."

"No. I won't." She thought: I don't care what they do to me, but the boy would be in some fix then.

They hugged and cried until the wagon was up the canyon trail, on the rim, and finally gone from sight.

"We have graves to dig," she said finally.

First they laid the bodies out together, pulling their mother off the ox and Tom Burgess out of the broken wagon.

Together they found a spot of solid earth away from the

sand and gravel at the canyon floor. Here they dug. The grave would have to be deep so that the coyotes and Indians would be discouraged, and wide enough for the two bodies. They dug until the hole was as deep as Elizabeth was tall, so that she had to fling the dirt over her head and out of the hole. Then they laid the bodies as gently as they could into the grave, side by side. She draped what remained of the canvas top over them, and found pieces of boards from the wagon. These she wedged beside the bodies and over the canvas, for coyotes dug sideways as well as straight down when they were after meat. She prayed, murmuring a litany, as she and Tom tossed the earth back into the hole.

By this time darkness was closing in. She sent Tom to gather wood scraps and matches to start a fire. With the sun far gone from the canyon floor, she was cold, so they sat together under a blanket, staring at the flames of the fire.

The boy began to cry again.

"Please don't," she said. "I got to think, Tom."

"Liz, I can't stand it. It hurts too much. I want to die."

"I know. But it doesn't last like this. Ma told me so when Gramma Allen died. She said it hurts so bad you want to die yourself so it will end. But after a while it is not so bad. It's true, Tom. It has to be."

"I don't care."

"I do. Somebody has to. I fixed us good, Tom. I tried to kill the only two people we had to help us, and now we are alone."

"Somebody will come."

"Sure, somebody will come along," she said. But she thought: We didn't pass a wagon from the time we left Fort Bridger. Not one.

"When I go to sleep tonight," he said, "I ain't waking up. I know that."

"You don't think so. But you will. I know how it will be, Tommy. We will wake up early in the morning, and for a couple of seconds we won't remember where we are or what happened to us today. Then we'll look around and see this canyon and it will come back to us. But not quite so bad as it is tonight. Bad. But not quite so bad as it is right now."

She held him, her right arm around his shoulders. I have to take care of this boy, she thought. He and I, we are all that is left of Stoat's Landing and our house there and the life we had. We must keep alive.

Tomorrow I will make up my mind about some things. Go to California, go back to Kentucky. We will see how things work out. Maybe we will have to take what God gives us in that matter. Now, I will have to try to make it through the night. Not enough that I watched my parents die. I had to try to kill a man, too. It happened so easy. Seeing myself do that, it was like having light shed all of a sudden in some black hole and seeing for the first time what it holds. It is in me. Whatever it is that made me do it has been there all along. It will always be there, ready to come out again.

And knowing that is the worst part of all.

CHAPTER TEN

The boy has a right sharp eye for a deal, was the way they put it at Topliffe's Reading Room and in the countinghouses on India Wharf. He has fuzzy cheeks yet, but he can run a trading company. Mind you, he is no Frederic Tudor. But what was Tudor at seventeen?

When he returned home after his wife's funeral, Matthew Belden walked into his library alone and shut the door behind him. He did not emerge for two days, having asked that his meals be brought to him there. He ordered his clothes moved from the bedroom he and Amanda had shared, and only then did he leave the library to sleep. After that he divided his time between bed and library, spending hours and sometimes days in those rooms. Joshua saw him only when he came to the dining table for his meals. Then they ate silently, his father haggard and distracted. When three weeks had passed since the funeral, the office manager at the countinghouse, a man named Rutherford, came knocking at the door. Joshua met him there, brought him into the drawing room. The man stood there with his hat in his hands, glancing around the room and fidgeting.

"Master Belden," he began, "my condolences to you both. I pray that I am not intruding on your hour of grief. But there are matters in need of immediate attention. I thought it best to bring them here personally. Not much, really, a few signatures. You know that I wouldn't do this if it were not so urgent."

No, his father was not available, Joshua said. But if he could have the papers he would see that his father acted on them.

Joshua leafed through the stack that Rutherford left with him. Payroll. Vouchers. Accounts payable. A few drafts. And a dunning notice, after only three weeks, from a cordage company. That one he would not forget for a while.

He took the papers to his father in the library. Matthew looked up from a book that he had spread on his desk. He seemed surprised and a little wary, frowned at the papers, but signed them without a glance. Joshua took the papers, and his father bent over the book again.

"Father," Joshua said. "Are you well?"

"Am I well? Yes, of course I am well."

"Will you be going to the wharf tomorrow?"

Matthew peered at him steadily for a moment, then looked away.

"No. Not tomorrow, I don't believe."

"It would do you well, I think, to leave the house for an hour or two, to see the sun again."

"I'm sure that your opinion is most valuable. But I want to be alone. I want to think. Understood?"

That night Joshua pinned a black band to a sleeve of his overcoat and ordered a carriage ready for him the next morning. He rode down to the wharf, visited the offices, scanned the account books. He tried to pacify a ship's master who had been in port two weeks now without orders, who complained that he was losing his crew. In the warehouses he tried tallying the inventory. All the time Rutherford was by his side, anxious, nervous. The man has held things together, Joshua thought. Or maybe a creation of this size and complexity does not collapse in three weeks, but in slow stages.

"I thank you for your good work. You've taken on a lot of responsibility, Rutherford, I can see that," Joshua said before he left that afternoon. "I will tell my father. He'll be pleased, I know."

"Will he be returning soon, Master Belden?"

"I don't know. I hope so."

Rutherford considered that.

"And you, Master Joshua?"

"I shall be here tomorrow."

Rutherford reached for Joshua's right hand, clutched it. "I'm glad, sir. Truly I am. We're in need of a steady hand at the helm."

A month passed and still Matthew did not visit the office, or even mention the business. Joshua brought him the bills and drafts that needed his signature. For a while he tried to draw Matthew into conversation: Rutherford hired a new accounts clerk today. The *Pride of Plymouth* returned from Rio today, full of that Brazilian coffee; should have smelled it in the warehouse, so deep and strong and rich. There is a glut of sperm candles at the moment, so I am holding back our stock on hand; others are doing the same, so I am sure that the price will be where it belongs before long.

To any of this Matthew Belden would nod without a word, or else tell Joshua: "Fine, boy. Yes, you did right, son." After a month of this, seven weeks having elapsed since his mother's death, with Matthew still dividing his time between library and bedroom, Joshua asked Rutherford for the bank forms that he would need to write drafts on the company account. He presented these to his father at the bottom of the weekly stack of documents.

"With this the bank will honor my signature as well as yours, father," Joshua said. "I hope you approve. Sometimes it is an inconvenience to bring these papers home to you. This will make the job slightly easier."

Matthew stared at the form, dipped his pen in the inkwell, looked up at his son, down at the paper again.

Then he said: "Yes, yes, it will." And he put his pen to the paper.

From that time on, Joshua ran the company. He was not brilliant. He engineered no coups, expanded cautiously, relied on proven trade staples and routes. The gambles and master strokes that merchants might talk about over dinner fifty years later, these would come in time, he told himself. He was happy to show a profit every quarter, to keep the company ships sailing around the world as they had for three generations before him.

It was not an especially arduous task. He discovered a

dozen men like Rutherford on the payroll, who knew their jobs and cared about the company. They understood the business better than he, but, as Rutherford had in those first few weeks after the funeral, they froze short of making decisions. So Joshua made them. He listened to the men, heard their advice, and, sometimes once a day, sometimes once a week, issued a command that made them all happy because it gave them direction and relieved them of the responsibility. Sometimes he wondered whether the particulars of a decision were as important as the fact that a decision had been made. It was the firmness, the illusion of control, that counted. The great machine trundled forward always, perhaps not quite so quickly or efficiently as it might have under more skilled hands, but it moved along anyway, and quite happily, as long as there was someone to point it and hold it on course.

Matthew visited the offices only once, on a summer day about six months after Amanda's death. Joshua was in the countinghouse, bending over ledgers. He looked up and saw one clerk and then another rise slowly at his desk, pushing away his chair. They were looking behind Joshua. He turned and saw Matthew standing at the door, hesitant. Joshua got up from his books and went across the room to meet him. Seeing him here in these surroundings, Joshua knew that his father had changed. He seemed somehow shrunk and diminished. He stood in the doorway now not as the plenipotentiary he had once been but as a polite visitor. The fire was gone from his eyes. And Joshua knew at that moment that his father was finished with the business, that somehow in his grief he had released his grasp on it and would never try to reclaim it.

When Joshua reached his father, he held him for a moment and then stepped back to let the others come forward, shake his hand, murmur their own words of welcome. To each of them Matthew extended a hand and spoke a few perfunctory words:

Yes, Hawkins, how are you? How have you been? Your wife and children are well?

Williams. Your lumbago is no worse, I hope. Yes, happy to see you, too.

The words were polite, but his mien was distant, as though

the connection between himself and this place, these people, was eluding him. He smiled genially, almost paternally, but without feeling. When he had greeted them all he walked with Joshua to the ledgers. He turned the pages and ran a finger across the lines of figures for perhaps two minutes. He looked up at Joshua and told him, "Well, my boy, everything seems in order."

"I've worked hard to keep everything right, Father. And everyone here has helped immensely, too."

"I'm sure. Are you drawing a salary?"

"Fifty a week."

"Fifty? Not much, Joshua. You deserve more."

"I get what I need from the household accounts. I want to keep company expenses down as much as possible."

"Well said. You have the makings of a fine businessman. You will do well. I always knew that you would."

They walked together to the door.

"We can go to the warehouses, Father. The *Chimera* is in port; we can go aboard after we've toured the warehouses."

Matthew put up a hand to stop him.

"No need," he said. "I can see that the business is healthy. A businessman has a sense for these things, you know. He can feel the vitality of success or the putrid smell of failure. No need for a complete audit to tell him what he already perceives. I know that all is well."

He raised his voice so that the rest of the room could hear him.

"You have all served me well. You know that I am grateful. I have been most fortunate."

He walked alone down the stairs and outside, a suddenly small and melancholy man.

He is gone, Joshua thought. The father I had once is gone, and has left this tired old man in his place. I don't know whether he has changed so much or I have grown. But we will never be strong father and subservient son again.

Several days later Joshua returned home from the wharf to find his father gone. Out to pass the evening with friends, a servant explained. He did not return until almost midnight, and was gone the next evening, too. Matthew was changing. He was smiling occasionally. He walked purposefully. He was out of the house as often as not in the next few weeks. One night his father sat beside him as Joshua ate a late supper, shared a bottle of wine with him, spoke offhand of the weather, of a new Copley that he had decided to buy, of stout Dan'l Webster's efforts at holding together the Union, of the sensationalist new book called, what was it, *Uncle Tom's House*?

Yes, Joshua told him, the nights had been snappy of late. Ought to be seeing some color in the trees any day now. He admired Copley, of course. They would have to find room for this new one. Webster was one of a kind, all right. The name of the book was *Uncle Tom's Cabin*, he thought. One of the clerks had brought a copy to the countinghouse and had sat reading it when he should have been eating lunch.

"And tell me," Matthew Belden said when Joshua had finished his meal and had drained the last wine from his glass, "are you acquainted with Spurzheim?"

Spurzheim. He has made quite a sensation here of late. Teaches phrenology. Bit of a crank, some say.

"No," Matthew Belden said. "He is a genius, in fact. And phrenology has answers for us all. I'm very impressed, Joshua. Very much so. I've done a good deal of reading in the past several weeks, and I must say I'm impressed. This is no passing fancy, Joshua, but an established science. I wish you could meet some of the people with whom I've become acquainted at Spurzheim's lectures. They are stable, honest, and most intelligent. I only wish that I had become familiar with phrenology much earlier. The applications to business and to personal life, my boy, are simply staggering. I could have avoided so many mistakes, Joshua."

Joshua thought: I've not seen such passion in him since Mother died. But at least he cares again. At least there is something alive in him yet.

"Well, Father, I must say that I've been busy and don't know a great deal about Spurzheim or his theories. Some highly esteemed people think a great deal of him, though, I will admit."

"I want you to meet him."

"Father, I'm not sure that I have time."

"He is coming here tomorrow night. He and some of my

friends from the lectures are coming to dinner, and then he will favor us with a discourse."

He would try, Joshua said. Time permitting, he would be there.

He left the countinghouse early the next afternoon to return home. If it meant that much to his father, then he would be here. It would be good to see the chairs in the dining room filled, to hear talk and chatter in the parlor.

The guests came in carriages, most of them. Their clothes were expensive, their bearing easy in this big house with its fine furnishings. All this surprised Joshua. These were not ignorant or weak people. Yet when Spurzheim spoke during dinner, conversation stopped around the rest of the table, and later, when he stood in the middle of the parlor to address them, referring now and again to charts and diagrams on an easel beside him, they drew up chairs around him and listened, intent, nodding as he talked of faculties and propensities and subclassifications. He was an evangelist, and he spoke with an evangelical pride and fervor that left no room for doubt or alternatives. He seemed to say: This is the way things are, and this is why we behave as we do.

When he finished speaking, they all applauded, and he drew a crowd swarming around him, full of questions and congratulations. Matthew Belden shook his hand (Spurzheim taking the hand with both of his own, then bowing slightly at the waist), then withdrew and whispered to a woman who stood at the fringe of the crowd. They walked together to where Joshua stood in a corner.

Her name was Emily Lancaster. They had met at one of Spurzheim's lyceum lectures and become friends, his father said. Good friends, he said, and she blushed and reached to lay a gloved hand on his forearm.

She was plump and pretty, about thirty-five years old. Not as pretty as Mother, though, Joshua felt himself thinking. And it is coarse the way she raises her voice nearly an octave when she talks of Spurzheim.

A great man, is he not? she said. A great thinker. He will be remembered. His work is staggering. She herself had been one of his first adherents. She had always been receptive to advanced ideas. Mesmerism, for example. Could anyone seriously dispute the existence of animal magnetism? Was he familiar with the writings of Fourier? Of Owen? Of Noyes? He was a healer, Noyes. He had worked miracles in Putney, Vermont, not many years ago.

She came to dinner often after that, and went with Matthew to lectures, and brought him books. One night she coaxed Joshua into sitting for a phrenological reading. Her hands wandered over his skull. A strong organ of amativeness, she said; he would have to deal with that propensity. Likewise concentrativeness and adhesiveness. He was lacking in combativeness but had strong tendencies to acquisitiveness and constructiveness. As for the lower sentiments, his self-esteem was high, but not his love of approbation. ("He was never one to beg a compliment, for a fact," his father murmured at that.) Of the higher sentiments he was amply blessed in benevolence, conscientiousness, and firmness.

When she was finished, Matthew sat beaming. Yes, I have a fine son, he said. A fine son.

One night they brought a guest to dinner. He was a poet and a philosopher, they said. His name was Henry Gault. He was hardly older than Joshua, with eyes dark and set deep in his head, his hair longer than the fashion and falling into his eyes, thick and black. He spoke little; he interrupted the conversation at one point to quote a passage from Revelations, and when he had finished he went back to his meal.

He left alone in a carriage.

"That is a great man. A brilliant man," Matthew Belden said as he and Emily and Joshua sat in the drawing room.

"A man of vision," Emily Lancaster said. "He sees ahead. The rest of us are blind to what he sees."

"He did not seem to have much to say tonight," Joshua Belden said.

"No. His mind is occupied with things that are beyond us," Matthew said. "We are concerned with life's trivia, and he has no time for such things."

"A poet, you say?"

"A poet," Matthew said. "But not principally. In truth, he is a holy man."

"A preacher?"

"More than that," Matthew said.

"He has a vision of the new order that will be upon us soon," Emily said.

"Some say he is a prophet," Matthew said.

"But we like to think that he is a Messiah," Emily said.

CHAPTER ELEVEN

As she slept, her mind churned with alternating visions of childhood afternoons and slowly tumbling wagons, a summer picnic beside the Ohio and broken bodies lying at the bottom of a dark grave, one image dissolving into another with a terrible logical continuity. She was never far from consciousness, and when she was not dreaming she lay with her eyes open to the strip of stars that showed above the canyon, and tried to grapple with the decision she would have to make soon.

Kentucky. California. She told herself that there should be no choice, no decision. She had kin back East, her mother's two sisters and their families. In times of trouble, you turn to family. They were not wealthy people, so probably she and Tom would be split between them. Still, that would be the thing to do, try to get back to Kentucky to find family.

But this trip had changed her. She found a part of herself ready to rise up and walk up the other end of the canyon and go on to California. She was part of the movement now, and it was not easily resisted. It is understandable, she told herself as she lay in the darkness. When you have traveled a thousand miles in one direction, your next step is naturally in that same direction. You do not just face about and start back toward where you began. More than that. She was all that was left of her father and his dreams now, and even if she did not share them or understand them, they were part of her. It would be hard to bury them out here with all the rest of him.

And one more thing. He said that they had a fortune sitting in their wagons, same as gold pound for pound if they could get it to California. In Kentucky it would be just another wagonful of common goods. That was something to think on.

In any case, they would need money. As daylight broke and began to filter down into the depths of the canyon, she remembered that her father had hidden his roll of bank notes in a tea tin inside the wagon. It was a lot of money; she had seen it the day they arrived in St. Joe, when he had shoved it into a boot to go shopping for teams and wagons.

She scrambled up and ran to the wreckage. The teamsters, they couldn't have taken it by mistake. Couldn't have. She pawed through the wreckage until she found the tin under a dirty blanket. She pried open the top, reached inside to pull out the wad of paper. It was not as thick as she had remembered, but when she turned the tin upside down some gold double eagles fell out into the sand. She stacked them, fourteen of them. She counted out nine fives in the paper money and twenty-two ones. That was two hundred eighty in coin, sixty-seven in paper. Three hundred forty-seven dollars.

This is my fortune, she thought. My dowry and my inheritance. Some oxen and a loaded wagon, three hundred forty-seven dollars, and this urge to keep moving on to California. This is what you have left me, Papa.

She was kneeling there in the sand beside the wreckage when she sensed movement up on the canyon's rim. First she saw dark silhouettes against the sun, but when the shapes began to descend the trail she saw them more distinctly: a small wagon pulled by two mules, with one figure leading the mules and two others trailing the wagon; and a man with a cart leading them down, bracing his body against the weight of the cart as the trail steepened. She watched them stop at the place in the trail where the road had fallen away. The cart went past, and the man chocked its wheels

with stones. Then he stood on the lip of the cavity. Mules
and wagon eased forward, the bed dipped, the man seemed
to dig his feet into the loose earth of the slide. He grabbed
the bed of the wagon, lifting it up and pushing it, with the
dirt sliding out from under his feet. He lifted and pushed
until the mules had dragged the rear wheels past the edge
of the hole and onto solid trail again. Then he climbed out,
the gravel still tumbling out from beneath his foothold. He
kicked the rocks out from under the wheels of his cart, and
they all followed the trail as it wound down.

Elizabeth watched them as they reached the canyon floor
and approached. The man with the cart was black, the dark
smooth skin of his face slick with sweat. His shoulders were
broad, the muscles hard and sharply defined where they
sloped down from the neck and flowed beneath the collar.
He stopped a short distance from her and bent to let the
cart's long twin handles come to rest on the earth. Elizabeth
stood up as the figure at the head of the wagon walked toward her. He was dressed in man's clothes, ill-fitting denim
pants, loose flannel shirt. But the gait was strange. They
stood facing each other for a moment. Elizabeth noticed
smooth fleshy cheeks and a curve in the hips that wrinkled
blue denim did not hide. This was no man.

"Child, what has happened here?" a woman's voice said.

Elizabeth found herself unable to speak. What are the
words, she thought, for what we have been through?

"Where are your folks?"

"There," Elizabeth said. "Buried there in that grave. This
wagon, it fell off the trail above us. And they were killed."

"You're alone?"

"Me and my brother." Tom was waking now, looking at
these people with half-conscious eyes.

"Are you hurt?"

"No. We didn't fall. I thought Indians might kill us last
night, but we didn't see a one."

The two from behind the wagon were coming up now.
They were women, too, in men's rough clothes.

"They're not alone, Jenny?" one of them said.

"They are. Folks dead, they say. You ain't Mormons, are
you, young lady?"

"No, ma'am. Are you?"

The three women laughed at that. The black man, waiting beside his cart, smiled.

"No, we ain't Mormons, dear. We ain't Mormons by any means. I am only asking because I thought we might help you get to Salt Lake City if that is where you were bound. But you are off to Californy, I s'pose."

"Yes, ma'am."

"You got people back East? Folks to take you in?"

"Two aunts."

"Then you are going to Salt Lake after all, I reckon. There're plenty of Mormons leaving there and headed back to the States. They are strange people, but kind enough, I guess. You will find someone to help you back East if you look hard enough. Especially as you have your own wagon and mule."

The woman named Jenny looked over her shoulder at the black man.

"Can we do that, Ezekiel? Can we get these young'uns and their wagon down the road a piece to Salt Lake?"

"We can do it," he said.

"The mules can use the rest anyways. We can hitch these spare oxen to the wagon. That would do, won't you say?

"Do you want to come with us, child? We are not the biggest and best-armed and best-stocked company on the trail, but we have made it this far. We will get you to Salt Lake."

Elizabeth felt tears in her eyes.

"I just want to leave here," she said. "I want to be away from this place."

"Then let us gather up whatever food is there in that pile. Ezekiel is a dead shot, but we have little enough in the way of provisions aside from the meat he brings to the fire. You don't have to share if you don't want, but we will at least have to ask you to provide your own essentials. We ain't flint-hearted, but our larder is low already. Oh, and you will have to walk most of the way. There is room for one to ride in the wagon and another up front, so we have been taking turns riding and walking. Except for Ezekiel. He has dragged his cart the distance. You can take regular turns riding. Sometimes it is easier to be on your feet than in that wagon, anyways."

Tom and Elizabeth walked with Jenny behind the wagons and the mules, which now followed on a tether. Jenny talked. The others were called Deirdre and Anne, short for Annabelle. They were off to California, same as half the rest of the world. No, they were not sisters, but friends, good friends. No, not married, none of them. Not exactly off to California to find husbands, and no, not to find gold. Well, not directly. Not by prospecting. But there ought to be plenty of it around, she said. Ezekiel, he was a free nigger from Missouri. Found him in Independence ready to set out with the cart and a pick and shovel and a shotgun and not much else. They'd staked him to food in return for his help in making the trip. Three women alone wouldn't be able to do it, they knew.

"Don't let his skin blind you, girl," Jenny said. "There is more heart in that man pulling his cart than in any ten white men you can pick out of a crowd. He paid for his food the first week, getting us out of scrapes. If the mules will not make a grade, he puts his shoulder to the wagon and pushes it and them both up to the top."

They walked on for a while, feet scraping in the dust. Then Jenny spoke again, her voice softer this time.

"They would not let us travel with them, any of the comp'-nies," she said. "It was bad enough, three women alone without husbands or family. The wives would not have it. Then to bring a nigger along on top of it, that was too much. They would have none of us. He has a wife in Alabama, Ezekiel does. He wants only enough gold to buy her freedom. When he has it he is going to leave California, he says. I believe him."

They were six or seven days out of Salt Lake, Ezekiel said when they made camp that evening. The next day they met a Mormon party going in the other direction. They would not take Elizabeth and Tom, not even with a wagon and extra oxen. Another eastbound party the next day said the same, but plainer: no Gentiles in their company.

That evening they ate two rabbits that Ezekiel had shot. He cut a long branch for a spit, and the two carcasses sizzled over a fire of smoky green cedar branches.

"We will have to do something," Jenny said as they sat about the fire, watching the meat cook. "We will have to lie, tell them that you are Mormons. They will quiz you, maybe. How much do you know about the religion, Liz? Do you suppose we could get away with it?"

"Not likely."

"Something has to be done. I will feel awful leaving you in Salt Lake without prospects of getting home this summer."

The fire popped and sent an ember arcing into the darkness.

"I want to go to California," Elizabeth said.

"Girl, don't be foolish," the one named Deirdre said.

"You have nothing in California," Jenny said. "It will be no place for you and the boy. You have next to nothing, and that is not a place to have nothing. Believe me. Your family was prosperous, judging from the way you talk, your clothes, that wagon. Prob'ly you've never done without. I have. It is nothing you ever want to know, being poor. You go back to Kentucky. You have people who love you there, and that is nothing to throw away for California."

"Tell her about the wagon, Liz," the boy said.

"Yes. The wagon. I want to get those goods to California. My papa died trying to do that. He said we would be rich if we did that. I can sell the goods and sail home. We have enough provisions for ourselves and some to share. Ezekiel can throw his cart in the wagon and lead the oxen. We can do it."

"There are other things to consider," Jenny said. "Things you don't know."

Nobody spoke.

"Tom, you go down to the creek for a spell," Deirdre said. "Go down there and wait till we call you to come."

When he had gone, Jenny spoke.

"We are harlots," she said. "Do you know the word?"

"From the Bible."

"You know what it means?"

"It means a bad woman. But you aren't bad, I know that."

"Not exactly, it don't. It means, ummm, it means we satisfy men for money. Do you understand that? I mean in the way a wife satisfies her husband. Now do you understand?"

"Yes."

"People do not think well of us. It would be wrong for you to go with us, girl. Now, I don't think we are bad, but there are those who do. Your mama and papa would be among 'em, I guess, if they were alive. A few days to Salt Lake, that is one thing. But more than six weeks to California is different. People will think it is wrong. Ezekiel and us, we are outcasts. You are traveling in bad company, Liz."

Then the black man spoke. His voice was deep and strong. He had been staring into the fire as though detached from the conversation, but now he held them all with his eyes and his tone.

"You think we are bad? Anythin' wrong with us?"

"No," Elizabeth said.

"I mean all a you. We bad people?"

"We know we ain't bad," Annabelle said.

"Different, but not bad," Deirdre said.

"Others do, Ezekiel, and you know it. People have their ideas. They say there is them and there is us. They make the rules, and that is the way of the world. Them and us. This girl and her brother belong with them."

"To hell with them. This girl ain't dumb. You tol' her what you was and she still want to go to Californy wit' us. Ain't that so, girl? She see us for who we are, not what we s'pose to be. Now if she know what we are an' she still want to go to Californy wit' us, then she can go. Hell. We can use th' oxen, anyways."

Three days later they passed Salt Lake City without stopping.

CHAPTER TWELVE

Matthew Belden married Emily Lancaster in the autumn of 1854. First they spoke their vows before a judge who was an acquaintance of Matthew's. An hour later, they stood in front of Henry Gault in their drawing room to repeat the vows. The double ceremony was necessary since Gault was not an ordained minister. But it was his recognition they sought, his approval of their union that they coveted. In the past year, Matthew had become both devoted disciple of and generous benefactor to Gault. His money had financed a speaking tour of New England, a new hall and home for Gault in Boston.

Gault stood on a dais in the drawing room and spread his arms beneath a royal-purple robe while bride and groom knelt at his feet. There were about two dozen guests, most of them strangers to Joshua. The few that he recognized were members of Gault's congregation whom he had met when they visited the home. Though a small organ sat in one corner of the room, there was no music, only Gault spreading his arms with the full sleeves of the robe draped from them like wings, holding that posture for at least a minute without a cough or a rustle from the audience, then speaking, at first in a whisper that somehow filled the room, each syllable distinct and fully enunciated:

"My friends. We are gathered here to bear *witness* to the marriage vows of our beloved *sister* and *brother,* Emily and Matthew. Let it be *known*"—by a rising pitch and intensity, Gault was emphasizing certain words, as much for rhythm as for meaning—"that we do *countenance* this union, that we do *grant* our blessing to Emily and Matthew. This is a *right* and proper thing that they do, brethren, for they *bring* to this marriage a *knowledge* and a belief in the new *order* of the universe, for they *consecrate* their bond with a com- mitment to one another, and to the purity and the *righteous- ness* of heart that we must have *within* ourselves to survive the cataclysm that is upon us."

Now the voice became louder, and Gault dropped one hand to his side while forming the other into a fist that he shook as he spoke.

"Emily and Matthew, brethren, have *chosen* to stand side by side against the iniquity that threatens us from all quar- ters. They have *chosen,* brethren, to stand together for mutual support against the vengeful upheavals to come. They have *chosen,* oh dear ones, to huddle together in the darkness that is upon us, thus to keep warm and alive the ideals of goodness that must survive."

Again the whisper.

"I tell you now. Let it be done. Let . . . it . . . be . . . done."

The fist relaxed and dropped. Gault bowed his head and was silent for a moment. When he raised his head he spoke in almost businesslike tones.

"Do you, Emily," he said, "take this man, Matthew, for your husband and spiritual partner, to keep pure your heart and mind, to resist with him evil, to keep him strong and up- right against the terrors of the inevitable Apocalypse, and to join with him in establishing the new order in a world purged of its evil?"

"I do," Emily said.

"And do you, Matthew, take this woman, Emily, for your wife and spiritual partner, to resist with her insidious evil, to shelter her against the raging storm, to accept her assist- ance in establishing the new order in a world purged of its evil?"

"I do," Matthew said.

Gault smiled benignly.

"I now pronounce you man and wife," he said, "and partners in the struggle."

This Gault believed: that the world man had created was evil, and offensive to the Lord; that He would destroy it soon, in a purgative cataclysm; that only a very few virtuous people who had prepared themselves for the holy upheaval would survive it; that these few would be charged with the sacred duty of regenerating the earth and instituting a new order that would leave no room for evil. All this had been revealed to him in visions, he said. He even knew the date on which the Apocalypse would begin—August 19, 1858, in the early-morning hours, though it might come sooner if the Lord lost patience with man's perfidy and venality.

For a few months Matthew and Emily lived in the house on Belknap Street. When Joshua saw them they spoke constantly of Gault, and speculated about the nature of the coming disaster (whether fire or rain or earthquake), and, as confidently as an architect describing the configuration of a half-built house, discussed the way of life under Gault's new order.

They were worried about Joshua. They loved him, and they wanted him with them when the world began anew. But unless he changed he would not have a chance. He would surely perish in the cataclysm. Oh, he was not a bad young man, not at all bad. But the absence of fault was not enough, Matthew told him a dozen times. He must make positive steps. He must align himself with the forces of right.

Always, Joshua thanked them for their concern. But he did not believe, he told them. He would have to look after his soul in his own way. They shook their heads sadly at that.

Business was good. He was becoming more confident and assured now, and had commissioned a new clipper ship for the Far East trade. It would be the biggest ship in the fleet, certainly the fastest, and once he had seen its trim lines in the wooden skeleton as it sat in the shipyard, he contracted for another. The company could afford it.

He visited their banker to make the arrangements. No

problem with the second ship, the bank president told him. Certainly the company's credit was outstanding, and Joshua had managed to keep up the capital reserves.

But there was one matter, the banker said. A personal matter, nothing to do with the company's accounts. Probably Joshua knew already, and probably it was a breach of professional ethics to discuss it, even with Joshua. But he would risk the breach, the banker said. He thought Joshua ought to be aware that his father was drawing heavily on his own personal accounts.

Joshua said that his father had always spent well: paintings, carriages, horses, clothes. He liked to spend.

But never this way, the banker said. At least ten thousand a month from his accounts for each of the last six months. He was far exceeding the interest payments. There was still some left, but at this rate it would be gone in a couple of years. And most of the money had gone into drafts endorsed to one man. Henry Gault was the name.

That night he spoke to his father.

Yes, he had been contributing to Gault for some time. Gault was building a community outside Waltham, and he needed money.

"But that is a great deal of money, Father," Joshua said. "Do you think it is wise to spend it so freely?"

His father smiled just as he had once when Joshua, as a child, had asked an especially naive and amusing question about the shipping business.

"We will have no need of it," Matthew said. "No amount of money will buy safety once the Apocalypse arrives, and there will be no place for personal fortunes under the new order. We might as well get some use from it, and Gault's work is certainly deserving. There is so little time left now, and Gault wants to provide a sanctuary against the storm for all of his faithful followers. We must survive, you know, my boy. We must be ready to do Gault's work. The time is so short. I wish you were one of us, Joshua."

There was little else for Joshua to say. The money was his father's to spend. He extracted a promise that Matthew would not touch the company capital. Matthew agreed, again with that same bemused smile.

Joshua took a carriage to visit Gault in his new home the

next day. He stood at the front door of the place while an attendant delivered his calling card. The master would see him, the attendant said when he returned a few moments later. He led Joshua to the office where Gault waited. It had a domed ceiling and high translucent windows, through which sunlight broke and slashed into the room in long diagonal patterns.

Joshua took a seat across a broad teakwood desk from Gault.

"I want my father back," Joshua said.

"I am not detaining your father in any way. He seems to be a free and happy man, by all standards."

"He is under your control. You know that. Your word is literally gospel to him. I'm appealing to you. Let him go."

"He does respect me, it is true. I'm proud of that, Belden. It means a great deal to me that a man of your father's strong will should believe what I have to say. But I can't do what you say. His commitment is to my words, not to myself. I have put forth ideas and he believes them."

"I will pay you well, if that is what you want," Joshua said.

"I cannot do what you ask."

Joshua leaned across the desk.

"I want you to tell me one thing. The answer is for me alone. But I want to know. Are you a madman or merely a charlatan?"

Gault laughed, loudly. The sound echoed against the high white walls of the room.

"You have given me quite a choice," he said. "Madman or charlatan? No other alternatives, Belden? No other possibilities? I can't answer, but I will put a question to you. Is your father less happy now than he ever has been? Is he less satisfied with his life now than he was when he went every morning to his countinghouse?"

"He is not the same man now that he was then. It is a mean and petty thing that you are doing, Gault. He was a tired, lonely man, and you took advantage of that."

Gault took this without reaction. He stood up at his chair and walked to one of the high slit windows and looked outside as he spoke.

"My own father was a poor man," he said. "I mention this because it makes us different. It is not simply a distinction of material wealth, Belden, but of a man's standing in the world. With money goes confidence and assurance. You take this for granted, because you are a rich man and you move like a star in predictable celestial patterns with other rich men, so high above the rest of us that you are hardly aware of our presence beneath you. You're distressed now because you see your father weak and easily swayed, vulnerable. That was my father from the first day I ever looked at him and judged him.

"Money can make up for so much. It is an insulator, I think, that shields the rich from so many of the disasters that terrorize others. It can buy warm houses and good food, competent surgeons and justice in the courts. It will buy the approbation of the world, too. Probably you have never thought about these things. They have been yours as long as you remember, and you expect that they will always be yours. But the poor are different. They are mice in a pantry, going through life with a minimum of disturbance, hoping to stay overlooked but always expecting the single stroke of unreasonable fortune that can end their life. My father literally walked softly, as though he were afraid of upsetting the delicate tenuous balance on which his existence rested. It was no way to live.

"The irony is that this is the poor man's one advantage. He knows that as men we are vulnerable. He accepts life's rude shocks without complaints. The rich man who thinks that he is immune to disaster is far less able to accept fate. Your father endured the death of two children and the desertion of another by submerging himself in his business. He refused to acknowledge that these things occurred, I think, and that got him through. But the loss of his wife was too great. He realized then that there is a limit to what his money can buy. He saw that he could not bribe death, and from that time on he had no use for his business or for his money.

"Now he is only too willing to give part of his fortune to me. It is of no value to him anymore. When I talk of disasters before us, he understands what I mean. And when

I tell him that he can survive disaster, he listens. He wants to believe that. There are many like him, too."

Not much later, Matthew and Emily left the Beacon Hill home to live in Gault's new community near Waltham. It was built on one hundred sixty acres surrounded by a high stone fence. Inside the fence were a church, gardens and cultivated fields, a blacksmith's shop, barns, warehouses, a commissary, and a circle of identical white bungalows surrounding the larger white house that was Gault's home and office.

The community was supposed to be self-supporting. It was his Ark, Gault said. The residents would feed and clothe one another now, because when the cataclysm arrived there would be nobody else to supply them. Matthew worked in the fields and was learning carpentry. Emily was a seamstress. Joshua went to visit them once. They served him a dinner of vegetables and boiled potatoes. Joshua noticed calluses on his father's hands; he wore overalls, and Emily a drab, shapeless cotton dress.

They were strangers to him. They talked of people whom he did not know, prattled on about Gault and the new order. Matthew's life and his had only the chance biological connection of birth; Matthew had produced the seed that had let Joshua grow in Amanda's womb. It was all they had in common any more.

In September of 1856 Matthew and Emily left with Gault when he began a speaking tour of Great Britain. They traveled with him a month. When he decided to continue his tour on the Continent, they prepared to return home, at his request. He trusted them and wanted them to oversee the community in Waltham in his extended absence. They sailed home. In fog and heavy seas their ship foundered off Gloucester with the loss of all aboard.

The funeral was a small Presbyterian service. Matthew Belden was buried at noon, and an hour later Joshua was in the office of the family lawyer for the reading of the will. He sat in a plush leather-covered chair across from the lawyer's desk. There was one other chair beside this one, and in a minute that was filled by a man whom Joshua had seen once before, at Matthew's wedding to Emily. The lawyer appeared behind him, his leather shoes squeaking. He sat behind the desk, reached for an envelope that sat in front of him, held it in his left hand while with his right he picked up a silver letter opener and deftly inserted it under the flap and broke the blue wax seal.

He withdrew a single stiff piece of foolscap, folded once. He opened the document and looked at Joshua for the first time. Then his eyes shifted quickly, furtively, back to the paper, and at that moment Joshua knew that something was wrong.

He heard the words only dimly:

"The document is dated the nineteenth day of November, year of Our Lord 1854," the lawyer was saying. "It reads: 'Being of sound mind and body, I, Matthew John Belden, do hereby bequeath all of my worldly possessions, including my business with all its stocks, fixtures, and improvements; my home with all its furnishings; my other real estate holdings, a list of which is kept current by my attorney; and all of the monies contained in my business and personal accounts, to the holy man Henry Gault, that he may continue his good work.' The document is signed by Matthew John Belden and properly witnessed."

Joshua rose to his feet, fell forward, and caught himself with a hand on the lawyer's desk. In one ear the man from Gault's congregation was telling Joshua that they did not want to inconvenience him, that he could have a few days to pack his personal belongings, but that of course a representative of the congregation would be in the home immediately to inspect everything removed from the house, that Joshua would not need to return to the countinghouse again. And the lawyer was apologizing, telling Joshua that he had argued with Matthew, had tried without success to dissuade him from this reckless course. But it was his duty to execute the will as ordered, the lawyer said. He hoped Joshua would understand.

Joshua was standing, pushing them both aside. Joshua was running, stumbling, out of the lawyer's office and into the street.

CHAPTER THIRTEEN

〰〰〰〰〰〰〰〰〰〰〰〰〰〰〰〰〰〰〰〰〰〰〰〰〰

Every summer there were more whites than there ever had been before, until one summer they came in a flood, their long trains of wagons working like segmented serpents up the twisting canyons and through boulder fields. By that time they were barely a curiosity. Hardly a Washo had not stood atop a ridge to hear their shouts filter up from the trails they had cut for their wagons. The whites' strange clothes and their oxen and the trash they left behind had long since ceased to amaze, though the whites were still a prime topic of conversation and controversy. From Miwok and Maidu had come the answer to the question of where these strangers were going. They were crossing the mountains and settling in the lowlands, cutting down trees, damming creeks and putting up dwellings, as though they intended to stay for a while. But still nobody knew their source. The Paiute disclaimed them. There was even a story on its way to becoming legend about some whites eating the flesh of their dead when they were trapped one winter in high snow. Most Washo generally discounted it as a gruesome fable. But if it were true, they agreed, the question of whether the whites were actually human would certainly no longer be in doubt.

Then one summer the whites came in an endless stream,

and the Washos' life was never the same. This is the way
it happened. Most of the whites passed through, but a few
stayed behind. A log stockade went up in the big valley at
the very foot of a high mountain. There was a corral and
stock inside, and soon the whites had begun to cut and
harvest the tall grass in the valley, and to fence off other
sections so that the animals could graze. Not long after that
came a store and several houses. The Washo left the high
country that winter and went to live in camps that they
moved from the whites' settlement on the river. When they
returned the next spring they found whites there ahead of
them already, the axes thumping into tall trees that crumpled to the ground like deer pierced through the heart. The
whites' settlements did not extend high into the mountains,
and then only in the valleys and meadows. But it was in
the valleys and the meadows that the Washo gathered much
of their forage.

The Washo, as they almost always had, reacted individu-
ally or in small groups. There was no concerted effort against
the whites. One bunch might grow belligerent and drag off
horses or oxen. Another might simply retreat from the settlements and find other places to search for food. Some whites
shot at Washo they found stealing their stock, and a few
Washo attacked isolated whites. The year after the whites
began to settle the valleys and the meadows was a bad one
for the Washo. They searched twice as hard for half as much
food. The pine nut harvest was mediocre, and the winter
was long. They dug deep into their baskets for the last bits
of pine nut flour and dried rabbit, and still winter was not
finished. A few of them starved to death, but others survived by raiding the whites' garbage heaps. They found
much there that was useful, not only food but scraps of
clothing and wood that they could use for shelter. Curiously,
these whites who cut loose stinging birdshot at Washo they
found near their stock would leave out plates of food when
they saw these same Washo poking through valuable garbage dumps. Really, these people were unfathomable.

Talks Soft had passed over a year before the torrential
arrival of the California-bound whites. His son, the father
of Mouse, was respected for his intelligence and humility,

so when the old man went over to the other side they began to consult Grub—so called because, like a Paiute, he had developed a taste for soft pulpy mealworms—on matters of community life. He predicted for them the gatherings of deer and rabbit, the ripening of the wild forage that sustained them through the summer. He was not a dreamer as his father had been, had not managed to gather any special power about him yet, so naturally his advice was not as sound as his father's. But he gave counsel sparingly, almost reluctantly, and only when asked. The others appreciated this trait, and in time Grub became accepted as the leader of the bunch, though he never once exercised the authority that went with the position.

They were awakened one summer night by faraway shouts. The noise came from down a canyon where they had camped to harvest ripe chokecherries. As the bunch rose, the shouts became louder, mingled with the sound of careless rustling of the thickets of brush where the chokecherries grew in the moist bed of a trickling stream.

Two young men of the bunch stumbled out of the bushes.

"The savages have Mouse," one of them gasped. They stood panting in the moonlight, chests heaving. "We ran all the way to tell you."

Grub stepped forward.

"Tell me how this happened," he said.

"We went to take some horses. We were running away with them when the White Faces met us on the trail. They chased us. Mouse told us to run with the horses. He stayed to fight them. He fought bravely, Grub. But they were too many for one man. They pushed him down and captured him. We tried to ride the horses when the whites started to chase us, but those animals are impossible. So we left them and ran up here."

"Did they hurt him?" Grub said.

"I don't think so. He was still trying to fight when they carried him away."

"Why did you do this?" a woman said. "We have always tried to avoid the whites until now."

"Mouse wanted to do it. He said the whites were living in a meadow where he kills a buck every year. He said that if he could make the whites leave then maybe the deer would come back."

"Will the whites come here?" somebody said.

"They lost us."

"We must do something," Grub said.

"We can fight them. There were four of them. If we surprise them, we can take Mouse away before they hurt him.'"

No one spoke for a moment. Then Fingers heard himself talking.

"I can go down there," he said. "I can speak with them."

"The whites don't know our words," Grub said.

"I know theirs. I can talk to them."

Grub walked toward him until they were face to face.

"I would rather not make enemies of these strangers," he said. "They seem to be here to stay for a long time. I don't like that, but it seems we should learn to live with them. If you will do this, Fingers, and bring back my son, then we would all be grateful."

Fingers walked alone out of the canyon and down toward the valley. He knew the meadow where Mouse always killed a buck. As he walked, he mouthed aloud the words he would say. We Are. Sorry. Please. Give. Me. Man. For three years he had listened to the whites talk. He had squatted for hours in the rushes beside the camps, listening to the whites speak as they sat beside their campfires. He had strained to hear the stream of unfamiliar syllables. Before too long he could isolate one word from another. Soon he was recognizing words that they repeated often and then connecting the words to an object or an idea. Sugar. He heard the word, saw them spoon the stuff into their food, and the next morning after they had left he went to the spot, found some sugar where they had dropped it, and put it to his lips. Several times he heard *sweet* used with sugar, so that was a new idea. Sugar is sweet. The first few dozen words were tough, but the others came easier. The more words he knew, the more he learned. Within a year he squatted silently in the brush a few yards from the camps and understood most of the words. Much of what he did not know, he could guess.

But talking was different. Now, for the first time, he would have to speak the white man's words. He had not tried that for years, since his first few ridiculous attempts with the man Free-mont. Whispering them to himself, trying to imitate the whites, was poor training for what he would have to do now.

Let the words be right, he prayed as he walked in the darkness. The son of my father's brother needs me. The bunch has put its faith in me. Let the words be right.

A half mile from the settlement he found one of the whites' horses wandering in a stand of trees, still wearing a rope halter. The horse shied at first, but Fingers grabbed the rope and pulled, and then the animal trotted willingly beside him. There was light in the window of one of the whites' dwelling, and as he came closer he could hear muffled voices. Once a figure crossed the window. The noise of the voices rose and crested, dropped and grew louder again. Fingers stopped short of the door, holding the horse. He waited. He drew several deep breaths to slow the beating of his heart, and then he raised his voice and shouted at the cabin.

"White people. Come. Talk."

The voices inside the cabin were silent. A face came to the window, with a hand up beside it to shut out the light inside. But there was no answer, and he shouted again.

"White people. Please. I want talk."

This time the door opened. A man's form was silhouetted in the light. Fingers spoke again, less loudly.

"White people. Your horse. Take. We are sorry. Please. Give me man. Give Indian man. Please."

"Frank," the man in the door said, "this bastard speaks English."

Two more figures appeared as the door swung open wider.

"It's okay. He's alone. I heard him, I tell you. The bastard speaks English."

He took a step down from the door.

"Indian. Bring the horse. *Comprende*? Bring. The. Horse."

Fingers walked forward a few steps with the horse and stopped and let go of the reins. The horse trotted forward.

"He ⟨ ⟩s understand, by God," another voice said at the

door. "Hey, Digger. Garbage-eater. You're a worthless piece of shit. You understand that, Indian?"

They laughed.

"Frank, hush," a woman's voice said. "You ought to be ashamed. Such language, even if he is an Indian."

"I understand," Fingers said. "Please. Give Indian man. We are sorry. Please."

"Now it ain't that easy," the first man said. "You Indians can't go on stealing our horses and our oxen. You understand that?"

"Yes. I understand."

"Good. We've been putting up with your thieving long enough. We won't take it any more."

"Please. Give Indian man. I give deer. Please."

"He wants to swap, Frank," the first man said. "One deer for one ornery Indian. What do you say?"

"He is stinking up the barn anyways."

"Okay. Indian, we give you man. But you tell your Indian pardners, no more steal. Understand? No more steal. Next time we kill. Understand?"

"Understand."

"Now where is that deer?"

"Tomorrow," Fingers said. "Bring tomorrow, two, three day."

"A promise from an Indian. I reckon I won't take that to the bank. Two, three day. I bet, two, three day."

Two men went to a barn behind the house and returned with Mouse between them, his hands tied behind his back, face sullen. He jerked his arms free when one of the whites cut the rope, and he walked ahead with his face set forward, past Fingers and into the darkness.

"We go," Fingers said to the whites. "Give deer, two, three day. Good bye."

Fingers hurried to catch his cousin. Then they walked together to the camp in the canyon, Mouse's stride long and angry.

"Mouse, are you hurt?"

"No."

"I need help. I promised the whites a deer."

"No. Not for those savages."

"I said I would give them a deer. I'm not a hunter."

The bunch ran to embrace Mouse when they reached the camp. While they gathered around his cousin, Fingers stood off to the side, alone, until Grub came to him.

"My brother's son, you have done well. You have a gift. It is true. My father said so and he was right. You have a gift of words. I thought my son was dead, but you talked him away from the whites.

"My father said that we would need you one day. He said that you had been given a gift to help the Wa-She-Shu out of a special difficulty. I didn't know what he meant then, but now I do. Fingers, you are a word boss. Always we have had a rabbit boss to help us find food. Now we need a word boss and we find you among us."

Mouse refused to kill a deer for the whites. It was Fingers's promise, not his, he said. So Fingers went out alone the next day. He went upstream from the camp to a spring at the head of the canyon. He saw deer tracks in the mud. There was a trail beside the stream, and Fingers followed it until it bent away. At the bend was a clump of thick brush. He tossed a pinch of dust into the air, saw that the slight breeze was into his face. That was good. He crouched behind the brush and waited. Through the afternoon he waited, his mouth becoming parched and dry, his muscles aching. But it had to be this way. He would never be able to stalk the way Mouse did.

He saw nothing that evening. He slept at the spot, and awoke the next morning with the eastern sky still dark. The wind was again right. He crouched again, holding the bow before him. As the sun was rising, two does and two fawns poked their heads around the bend, stopped, sniffed, and then walked past Fingers. The wind was stronger now and blowing in his face. A few minutes later a buck followed them. Fingers drew back the bowstring slowly as the buck paused in the trail. Farther back on the string with the notched arrow. Then raising the bow, sighting, just as the buck turned its side to him.

The arrow thunked into the buck's brown hide a few inches behind the shoulder. The animal reared, drawing its two front legs up off the ground for a moment, then plunged into the brush. Fingers rose slowly from his crouch. He walked to the bend in the trail and stopped to pick up the arrow shaft that the deer had broken off with its convulsive movement. There was blood on the shaft.

Patience, his grandfather had taught him. An arrow behind the shoulder will do its work but you must be patient. Fingers walked through the brush, gathering dried grass and twigs. He found a small flat rock; that would do well. With a chipping stone and a few wispy strands of dried grass he started a smoldering fire. When the blaze had gone out, he smeared the blood from the arrowhead into his palm, spat on it, and mixed blood with saliva. He let the mixture drip down onto the hot rock. It sizzled and steamed. As he did this he prayed: Let the deer lie down and die. Let his life blow away like this steam. Lie down, deer. Close your eyes and sleep. When the last drop of bloody saliva had sizzled away, he stood up and notched another arrow onto the bowstring and started into the brush where the deer had fled.

Tracking the deer was easy. It had left splotches of blood, now drying dark in the morning sun, every few feet on ground or on brush. Soon Fingers found the deer, dead, in the middle of a small clearing.

When he had bled the animal and covered up the blood, Fingers bent down and grabbed the buck and wrestled the body across his own shoulders. It was not a big deer, but he was not a big man. Through the morning he carried the deer on his shoulders down to the meadow where the whites lived.

Adam Longstreet was splitting fence rails when he saw the skinny Indian struggling and sweating beneath the buck. He ran to him and grabbed the back legs of the deer, and the two of them carried the carcass into the barn.

"I'll be damned," he said. "You did it. You brought the damn deer."

"I said bring deer, two, three days."

"You did, all right. What is your name, fella?"

Fingers spoke his name in Washo.

"That won't do. I'll never be able to call you if we don't give you another. You want water?"

"Yes."

"I have a spring out back. Good cold water for a hot day like today. Listen, how much of my lingo do you understand, anyway?"

"Lingo?"

"My talk. English."

"Understand good. Speak not good."

"Not bad. I have heard worse from white men. I have known hardheaded Dutch that could not speak a word of English two years off the boat. Too dumb or too stubborn, I don't know which. You are a curiosity for sure, Injun."

They drank water from the spring box behind the barn, and then Adam Longstreet reached into the high grass around the wooden frame. He pulled out a crockery jug stopped with a cork.

"You know whiskey, fella?"

"No."

" 'Bout time you did. I been swingin' an axe all mornin', and I earned me a swig."

He pulled out the cork with his teeth, spat it to the ground, and lifted the jug to his lips.

"Hooee. That is the real article, boy. Kentucky sour mash. Give it a whirl. But take it easy at first."

Fingers lifted the jug and let the stuff flow into his mouth. It stung his mouth, and he swallowed quickly. Then it burned. He stuck his face into the spring box and drank the cool water.

"Yeah. It is a revelation, though, ain't it?"

The white man pulled again at the jug, his throat working. He threw back his head and expelled air up at the sky. Fingers watched this white who had spoken so harshly two nights earlier, but there seemed to be no acrimony now.

"You want another? No? You are a smart un. Well, I believe I will indulge myself."

When he had swallowed another mouthful, he spoke again.

"Injun, you will have to talk to your chief. Get him to cut out this stealin'. It don't do nobody no good. Red man and white, we ought to get along better."

"I don't know chief."

"Why, sure. Chief. A big boss, y'know. The fella that gives you all orders, tell you all what to do."

"Wa-She-Shu got nobody like that."

"Sure you do. All Injuns got chiefs. It is a known fact. You don't, you ought to get yourself one. Tell you what. We will make you one. You'll be a captain, okay? A white man's chief. Now you'll need a Christian name. Let's see. I got a cousin named James. He is an ornery son of a bitch. He will fry when I tell him that I have give his name to a Digger. Jim it is, then. You are Captain Jim of the Diggers now. I do here christen you."

He dipped a cupped hand into the spring box, splashed water on Fingers's head. Then he tilted the jug back again.

"I been thinkin'. As I said, Jim, you are quite a curiosity. A curiosity of some magnitude indeed. Now, people will pay money to see curiosities. My wife, she paid two bits back in Pennsylvania to see a diorama of the Hudson Valley. Wax figgers, wild animals, people will pay money to see them. Now do you suppose a Digger that speaks the white man's tongue is any less worthy? Not your city-spoilt Injun, mind you, but a wild Digger. Jim, there ought to be some way we can make money off of you."

"What is money?"

"Money? Why, money, Jim, is the life's blood of our system. Money is what keeps us goin', Jim. Money is the point a all this here."

He swept an arm around the cabins, the barn, the clearing, the fences.

"Understand, Jim?"

"No. You got money?"

"I got some. Not enough, by far. Oh. You mean to see. Money to show. I got some inside, but at the moment I am rather fixed to this spot. But I can tell you about it. Some of it is pieces of paper, Jim. Special paper. That is greenbacks, but they ain't worth much out here. Other money is coins. Bits of shiny metal, gold and silver. You got enough of that stuff, there is nothin' you can't buy. Money is amazin' stuff, Jim."

"What does money do?"

"Do? It don't do nothin', Jim. It just is. Say I got a few head a cattle that the fella next door wants. Chances are, Jim, he will give me money for it. Now I can take that money an' give it to another fella for a gun or a wagon, whatever it is I need. Then that fella has the money to buy what he wants. See how it works, Jim? The trick is to have more money comin' in than goin' out."

They talked some more, and Adam Longstreet drank until his wife found them and scolded him for neglecting his work. Fingers left, but Longstreet made him promise to return. He did, two evenings later. Adam Longstreet brought him venison from the dinner table, and Fingers chewed it as he sat on the front doorstep of the cabin. Longstreet came out with a lantern and a book and sat beside him.

"This is a book, Jim." He opened it and tilted it so that the lantern's light fell on the open pages. "These are words. Words like we speak, the same ones, only writ down. Like this one here. That word is *lake*. You know that one, don't you? This word on paper means the same as sayin' it. Readin' a book is like havin' somebody talkin' to you, same thing, 'cept what is in a book is gen'rally of a high class or a more elegant nature, if you follow my meanin'.

"I had in mind to teach you to read. That was my first thought. We will get to that one of these days, but I got another idea I can do quicker. This is gonna astonish them, for certain. What I want you to do, Jim, is to remember the words I read and then say them after me. You got that? Just remember what I say and say it back. If we come to a word you don't know, we'll skip over it for the moment an' come back to it later."

Not far from Adam Longstreet's cabin was a trading post that catered to the emigrants. There they could buy hay and provisions for the last leg of the trip, up and over the mountains. They could also find the first whiskey west of Fort Bridger, in a small lean-to shack built against the side of the main building.

One evening Adam Longstreet and Fingers walked into the lean-to. There were more than a dozen men drinking inside, and Adam Longstreet shouted to be heard above them.

"Gents," he said, "I have come to provide entertainment for you tonight. There is no charge, but I know you will be liberal with your contributions when you see the unique aspect of this diversion. For your pleasure, gentlemen of the trail, I present Captain Jim of the California Diggers."

Longstreet pointed to a whiskey cask beside one wall, motioned for Fingers to stand up on it. Fingers did. He felt awkward among all these whites. They were all looking at him through blue-white tobacco smoke that stung his eyes. Longstreet had made him smear his face with clay and ashes—war paint, the white man had called it—and had told him to carry a hatchet in one hand. Fingers felt silly.

"Go on, Jim," Longstreet was whispering. "Don't freeze up on me now, fella. Do it jus' the way we been workin' on it."

Fingers cleared his throat of the phlegm that had formed there from the smoke.

"Hunting Song," he said. "By Sir Walter Scott."

"Louder!" somebody yelled in the back of the room.

Fingers raised his voice.

"Waken, lords and ladies gay," he said. "On the mountain dawns the day, All the jolly chase is here, with hawk and horse and hunting-spear."

There was silence in the room. He spoke again, more confidently. His tongue seemed born to the words, these white men's words that had been so awkward to him before. When he finished, the men in the lean-to were throwing coins at him—Longstreet had told him to expect this—and yelling for more.

Within a month Captain Jim was doing readings from Shakespeare. Within two he was finished with *McGuffey's First Reader* and had begun the second, and he walked the street of the settlement wearing a Mormon-style hat, a white shirt with a celluloid collar, and cotton pants with money clinking in the pockets.

CHAPTER FOURTEEN

The servants clustered around Joshua when he returned home from the lawyer's office. Something was wrong, they said. A man who claimed to be one of Gault's people had come in, called them together, discharged them and paid them from the household cash. The house belonged to Gault now and would shortly be sold, he had said. Was this true? How could it be?

It was too true, Joshua told them. He wished them luck and then pulled away from them, went up the big staircase to his room. Gault's man followed him up, stood in the doorway without a word to watch him pack. Joshua filled a trunk with clothes, decided to leave the rest. He would have to leave his books, too. Probably he would be traveling, he thought. The man in the doorway stepped in closer to watch when Joshua took a miniature from his bureau and put it atop the clothes in the trunk. It was his own, Joshua told him. Every other painting in the place had belonged to his father. This one was about worthless anyway, he said: a portrait of his mother. In a quarter of an hour he had finished. Gault had retained a carriage driver from the staff, and he would take Joshua anyplace in the city.

Joshua left the house on Belknap Street without looking back and took a room in a hotel in Cambridge. For a few days he did little, thought little. He rose at his accustomed hour, ate breakfast, then walked most of the day. He saw most of Boston, some of it for the first time, but avoided the waterfront. Of course, word of his father's will would have reached the countinghouses quickly. Joshua was not to blame for his father's imbalance, but the other merchants would look at him with pity, displaced as he was from the company he had rescued, cheated of his birthright. He could not take the pity, so he stayed away from the wharves.

After a few days he began to think while he wandered. He had been drawing a salary for four years, fifty dollars a week. He had spent little of it, had never had the time to spend much money. So now he had it all in a bank, and though it was nothing beside his father's fortune, it was still more than most men ever put together.

He was more than twenty years old now, but different from any other man his age he knew. They were just beginning careers; he had commanded a company. But for all his experience in business, he felt he had been sheltered by the job. While he had been trading goods across continents, others his age had been learning to dance on the spring-floor hall at Papanti's, talking to girls, playing games. There was so much he had not done. He had known as he packed a few days earlier that he would be traveling. So travel it will be, he told himself one afternoon as he looked in the shop windows on Tremont Street. He had time and he had money. New York would be a good place to start. He had never been there.

On a whim, he left Boston by the railroad. It had a reputation for being uncomfortable and dangerous. True, the cinders did blow in through an open window, and the sheer speed was discomforting at first. The wicker seat was merciless, but at the train's first stop out of Boston he leaned from the window and bought a cushion from one of the vendors on the platform, and then the trip was not so bad. He had relaxed enough to be sleepy, close his eyes, and let his head tilt as the wheels clattered beneath him, when a voice spoke beside him.

"You can sleep on a moving rail-car, I see," the voice said.

Joshua opened his eyes and turned. The voice, high and

piping, came from a midget who had sat beside him while
he dozed. The man was the size of a small child, perfectly
formed and proportioned. He was about forty years old,
Joshua guessed from the lines at the corners of his eyes and
the scalp that showed through the hair on the top of his
head. He wore a red velvet suit with ruffled collar and cuffs,
and his legs dangled above the floor.

"Some people can do it," the midget said. "The regular
motion of the car as it sways on its undercarriage is irresistible for some, as is the staccato clicking of the wheels on
the track. Yet those same qualities make sleep impossible
for others. Their conscious mind is fearful and will not relax
its grip as long as there is the slightest suggestion of motion.
You seem to be one of the lucky ones, as I am."

Joshua yawned, and the midget beamed at him, as though
immensely pleased with his own observation.

"Burgess Putnam, professional entertainer and amateur
student of human nature," he said. He had been holding
between the fingers of his right hand a cigar nearly the size
of his own forearm, and he stuck it into his mouth to offer
his hand. Joshua took it in a handshake; the palm and tiny
fingers were swallowed up in Joshua's hand, but the midget
shook vigorously anyway.

"You are a first-time traveler," Putnam said.

"I am. How did you know?"

"Your carpetbag is still new. Not a crease, a scar, or a
stain. Either you are needing one for the first time or you
already have worn out one and needed another for this
journey."

The bag *was* new. Joshua had bought it and some shirts
and underwear the day before.

"I hope," Putnam said, "it is not a calamity that makes
you travel for the first time."

"No calamity."

"Some unexpected turn in your life, then?"

"Well. To some extent," Joshua said.

"Let me explain. You are about of university age. But this
is the middle of the term, so if you were a student you
would be attending class now. Of course you are financially
able to attend a university. Your clothes are very expensive.

Tailor-made, too, since you have no crease in your pantaloons. Only shelf pants have creases.

"You are no longer in school, and therefore you should be learning a business, putting your education to work. The first autumn on a new job is hardly the time to vacation. Yet here you are. You are not in school and you are not in business and you are not traveling because of an emergency. You do not follow the norm. Ergo, your life has taken an unusual turn."

"Very good," Joshua said. The midget had spoken loudly, and people were staring. Not enough that he should be three feet tall and dress in red velvet, Joshua thought, but he must speak like a professor as well. But Putnam seemed oblivious to the attention. He crossed his legs, leaned back in the seat, puffed at the cigar, tilted back his head, and released the smoke in a series of perfect rings that drifted up to the ceiling of the coach.

"I'm grateful that you've indulged me my little display," the midget said. "Probably you have guessed already: I am not simply Burgess Putnam. That is my born name, of course, but you likely know me as Bob Thimble."

"No," Joshua said, "I'm sorry."

"Bob Thimble. The Lilliputian Nostradamus."

"I don't think so."

"Damn!" Putnam spoke so loudly that heads turned in the car. "It's that damn Stratton."

"Pardon?"

"The General," Putnam said. And finally, spitting out the words when he saw that Joshua still did not understand: "Tom Thumb, damn it."

"Oh. I have heard of him."

"No doubt every soul on this train has. It is an accident of birth, young man. A matter of a couple of inches, a few pounds. Also, he has Barnum, and I, God help me, have Hemingway. Charles Stratton, therefore, is the toast of continents. Burgess Putnam toils in obscurity, his gifts wasted. Diminutive though we are, there seems room in the public heart and mind for only one of us little people. Charlie Stratton has gotten there ahead of me and isn't likely to relinquish his comfortable position."

Again he puffed at the cigar, released the smoke slowly
with his head thrown back.

"Outrageous fortune. Slings and arrows, young man. You
know. Still, I endure, and even prosper on a limited scale."
He chewed the end of the cigar and spoke around it. "I
am traveling with a touring company. Charles Hemingway's
Florentine Caravan, Menagerie, and Museum of Natural
Oddities. To be more precise, I *am* the touring company.
Oh, we have a strongman and a sleight-of-hand artist and a
few mangy animals, but I am the one that holds the show
together.

"First I sing and dance. Not like the General. I have real
talent. My voice lacks the proper range, but my breathing is
good and I can hit a note and hold it. Stratton is different.
Barnum trots him out in some cute uniform, he takes a few
bows, squeaks a little ditty, and is finished. But I have talent.
And Stratton doesn't even try what I do next. My mentalist
routine. You already have had a short demonstration. I am
not saying that I don't get some help from confederates, but
an observant eye will go a long way. I size them up when
they rise up in the audience. One look and I know a lot. I
can tell you what they think of Buchanan and whether
they eat eggs for breakfast and how long they have been
married.

"It is all observation, young fellow, and after a while it
is practically intuitive. Happens without a conscious thought.
Now and again I even get flashes that I can't explain. Aug-
mented perception, I call it. Second sight. Most folks, they
think it is all from that. They think I am a seer. Fine. I don't
discourage the impression, though in fact observation and
deductive reasoning are far more impressive to me. All I
tell them is, sometimes we little people are born with special
gifts to make up for our physical deficiencies. They all suppose I mean second sight. That is how I came up with my
title. The Lilliputian Nostradamus."

"I'd like to see your performance," Joshua said.

"Not bound for Bridgeport, by any chance?"

"No. New York."

"That is a shame. We are playing Bridgeport tomorrow.
You've heard of Barnum's place, Iranistan. We have engaged

the vacant lot across the street from it in Bridgeport. We will fill the tent for every performance if we have to give away tickets. Barnum will have a conniption fit. If you are on an extended tour, perhaps you could see us elsewhere. We are in Albany for two days after Bridgeport, then White Plains. In a week or so we will begin working our way down and across Pennsylvania. I can find you an itinerary if you know your plans."

"I have no plans except to go to New York for a while."

Putnam grinned.

"Trying the life of a vagabond?" he said.

"I suppose so."

"Expensive clothes. Obviously well bred. Suddenly at liberty. You've had business reverses, maybe?"

"Only in a roundabout fashion."

"What did you do?"

"I managed a shipping company."

"A bit young for that, aren't you?"

"Old enough."

Putnam said nothing for a few moments. He looked around the coach, as though avoiding Joshua. He whistled a tune softly. He kicked his legs in short erratic arcs under his seat, as a child might. Then he looked again at Joshua.

"What happened to the business?"

"My father gave it away."

"It was worth so little?"

"It was worth a great deal."

Putnam nodded thoughtfully.

"We could give you a job," he said. "I see you are ready to decline already without even hearing the proposition. It is not so important a job as managing a shipping company, but we are not going to give away the business, either, Hemingway and I."

Joshua said nothing.

"Perhaps you do not need a job."

"Not immediately."

"You want to travel, evidently. You would travel a great deal in this position. Wherever the rails will take us, sooner or later. Hemingway has even spoken of a European tour. No promises there, however."

"I don't know," Joshua said. "I'm not certain why you would offer a job to a stranger."

"Why, young fellow, I already know a great deal about you. You've been kind enough to suffer the pomposity of an embarrassing little freak. No, no, let me say it. I know what I am and how people look at me when I am not on a stage. Almost nobody would have the courage to tell someone of my unusual stature to go away, at least not directly in front of other strangers. But you suffered me with good grace and without obvious discomfort. That is good. You say that you managed a large business. The truth of that will be evident or not very quickly, so we'll have lost very little by offering you the job."

Putnam puffed on the cigar.

"If you are inept," he said cheerfully, "why, we'll discharge you and it will have cost us just a day or two in salary to find out. But if you are as qualified as you say, you'll be more than suitable for the position.

"Besides," he said, "I am desperate. I am willing to try any measure. Including speaking to strangers on a train."

"One of these days I'll need a job," Joshua said.

"You won't find one to rival this one in variety, if not monetary compensation. And we do travel a lot."

"What is the job?"

"We need a business manager. Come, follow me back to our car. Hemingway and I travel in a private car and the others take seats in the regular coaches. We carry the tent and equipment and animals in our own burthen car, besides. Come back and talk to Hemingway, and I'll describe the job."

He hopped down to the floor. Joshua rose and followed the midget down the aisle.

"The show used to be Hemingway's. It was a total failure. About ten years ago he found me performing in a museum in St. Louis and tried to persuade me to join his troupe. After Stratton, every museum and traveling show needed some dwarf or other if it could hope to attract an audience. I told Hemingway that I would join him for no less than twenty percent of the business and a like share of the profits, plus room and board. He agreed readily. Anything to keep his expenses down, and this way he could avoid adding a name to the payroll. Over the years I have threatened to quit the troupe unless Hemingway increased my share. My ploy was invariably successful, since in quitting the show I would merely be giving up my share of a nearly worthless business. He, on the other hand, would be losing *me*. By that means I have gradually acquired a half share of the business and the profits for as long as I perform."

They left the car, and Putnam nimbly leaped the space over to the next. Inside that coach, the members of the troupe sat together: a thick-necked weightlifter, an armless man, and a magician, who (Putnam explained as they passed by) also ate fire and lectured on mesmerism.

"Two months ago we lost our manager. His nose was bit off by our Bactrian camel and he decided to retire from show business. Hemingway has been doing the job in the interim, but that is unsatisfactory from every aspect. First, he is not a very good businessman. He is a middling good advance booster, though. We could have used him in Bridgeport the last two or three days, bribing the newspapers for coverage, posting notices, raising banners, and generally inciting the public interest. That sort of thing isn't always necessary, but it is helpful for important engagements of several days' duration or more. In smaller towns we create interest by our very presence.

"But now Hemingway is traveling with the troupe, because he must handle the business matters. The worst part is that he again has the opportunity to cheat me of my profits. While I am sweating onstage, he is in the ticket booth, taking in the money. I have only his word of the proceeds, and though I try to count the house myself, that's not reliable since we give away so many passes.

"You see then, young fellow, that I need someone I can trust. Hemingway won't go back on the road in advance of us for a while, but he might if he eventually believes you are impartial. We need you, young man."

They had reached the door at one end of the troupe's private coach. Putnam had a hand on the doorknob when he turned.

"What the hell is your name, by the way?" he said.

"Joshua Belden."

Putnam swung open the door.

"Charlie Hemingway," he shouted, "meet Joshua Belden! Joshua is our new business manager. You hear that, you miserable old bastard?"

CHAPTER FIFTEEN

When he had dressed, Captain Jim left the barn and walked
to the back door of the Longstreets' cabin. His breakfast
was there as usual, where Mrs. Longstreet always left it.
Today it was mush and corn muffins. He sat on the halved
section of log that served as a back step and he ate. He
thought it was delicious, as most white people's food was.

When he had eaten it all he rapped on the back door and
handed the dishes to Mrs. Longstreet. He walked away
whistling "Oh! Susannah." Adam had nothing for him to do
today or tomorrow, so Jim had decided to visit the bunch.
They would be camping at the lake now. He walked down
the street of the settlement. The town was growing: two
new homes in the last three months. And everybody knew
Jim. As he walked down the street, women smiled at him
from inside the houses and men waved from horseback. He
basked in their approval. The white man was a good friend
to have, and they were Jim's friends. You can get along with
an Indian like Jim, they said.

Longstreet was his best friend of all. Adam let him sleep
in the barn. Adam bought him clothes and fed him. And
Adam took him traveling by wagon over the mountains into
the diggings so Jim could do his recitals. The miners were
hungry for diversion, and Jim was something special. They

paid two bits apiece to crowd into Longstreet's canvas tent to hear Jim do readings from the Bible, a recitation of *Rime of the Ancient Mariner*, maybe or poetry by Spenser, Percy Shelley, Robert Browning. A Scot who had given the Woodfords—this was the name the settlers had given the community of an inn, a sawmill, and a few homes that held a first tentative step up the side of the east slope—had taught Jim to read Burns with an accent. Now he could mimic it flawlessly, and was perfecting his imitations of Germans and Irish and Chinese, too.

He did all this in war paint, carrying the hatchet that was supposed to be a tomahawk, wearing a headdress of magpie feathers that Longstreet had made and a bone breastplate that one of the miners had taken off the body of an Indian on the trip across the plains. His finale, since there were always those who were sure that what they were seeing was impossible and there must be some trick, was to offer to read anything that the audience might send up to him. Longstreet always suggested letters from home. "Some missive from a loved one" was the way he put it. More often than not it was an unopened envelope that was passed forward first. A miner unable to read might hoard them for months, keeping them in a shirt pocket close to his chest, tied with a ribbon, maybe, the whole package becoming grimy and sweat-stained while the man refused to trust the secrets in the letters to any of his literate acquaintances. His friends would know this, would wrestle him down, pluck the package from his shirt, and toss it up to Jim to read. This happened often. No telling what was in these letters, but it was guaranteed to have them laughing when it came from the mouth of a wild red man. When Jim recognized that the script was in a woman's hand (and usually it was), he affected a falsetto. Sometimes even the victim of the prank could not resist a smile, then a grin and a smirk, at so ludicrous a spectacle. When the show was finished and Jim had done his encore, usually a rendition of one or another familiar minstrel song, Longstreet passed a hat, and though they had already paid an admission, the miners were always generous. A couple of hours with Jim was worth a sight more than fifty cents, they agreed. Jim and Adam were still splitting the proceeds, though Jim didn't see much of his money. Adam was keeping it for him and was doling out an allowance. At that, Jim was still the richest Indian in the state, maybe in the whole damn country. He had two pairs of pants, three shirts, a hat, a pair of boots that he had bought two sizes too large, since he was sure that would make them easier to wear, five red bandanas and five blue ones, a six-bladed Barlow, and a pocket watch. He had learned to tell time.

There was a road now up the canyon where he had led Fremont. The emigrants had hauled their wagons up the canyon, fording the river three times in seven miles to take advantage of slightly more forgiving terrain on one side or another. The up-canyon pitch had been steep, the canyon narrow and strewn with boulders, some of them taller than the wagons. The whites had laid trees side by side across the more difficult fords, had pushed and levered the boulders aside when they were not too heavy, or blasted them into more manageable size. Now the road up the canyon could be negotiated by wagon in less than three hours. It had been a daylong job in '49.

Jim walked on the side of the road, acknowledging the occasional greetings from teamsters and stage drivers who recognized him. The boots flopped around on his feet, almost independent of his stride. But he would not take them off. Never barefoot for him again. He reached the camp beside the lake with a couple hours' daylight remaining. His legs ached. That had never happened before. He had always been able to walk all day without a problem, but today he had to stop to rest, catch his breath. Now a boy playing beside the trail saw him, ran yelling into the camp. The bunch was there to meet him, his parents, his friends, Grub. Mouse stood at the fringes of the pack.

"Fingers, come. Sit here with us and eat some fish." This was Grub talking. "Your father was telling the story about the rabbit drive near Double Springs, the time you tripped carrying the net and fell into the ants' nest, the one full of those big black ants. I know you must remember that."

He remembered. His father told again the story they had all heard before, showed how his son had flopped onto the anthill, laid still, then felt the ants crawl on his body and jumped up screaming as the insects began to bite, flapping his arms and trying to shake off the ants, finally rolling and writhing in the dirt to get rid of them.

The bunch laughed. This was a good story, told by a good storyteller.

"I would never have been bitten if I had been covered by the white man's *clothes* as I am now," Jim said.

"Tell me, Fingers," Mouse said. "What is the use of those things?"

"You forget that I have taken a new name. My name is Jim. Captain Jim."

"I forget. Jim. Tell me why you cover your body this way."

"This is the way the white men dress. They have *money* and they *buy* clothes. When they see me wearing these things they know that I also have money. Besides, other Wa-She-Shu wear such clothes, but not as good as these."

"I don't understand," his mother said. "What are these words our son uses? *Buy? Money?*"

"The last time I was with you. . ." Jim began.

"Yes, you must remember," Mouse said. "He explained it all to us then. All about *money* and *buy*. All about the white man's ways."

"Boys, don't argue," Grub said. "Here, have some more fish. We have had a good catch this time, Jim. The fish are fat and there are plenty of them."

Jim chewed for a moment.

"It is good," he said. "But let me tell you about a meal the white women cook. *Chicken* and *dumplings* with *gravy*. My mouth gets wet when I think about it."

Mouse stood, spat out his food, threw the fish he had been eating into the brush.

"That is enough!" he shouted. "Two full moons go by before we see you, and when you do come all we hear is about the white man. I can't tolerate this."

Grub spoke loudly.

"Son, come back. Here, sit with us here. My brother's son says things that we ought to hear. He understands the white man. We can learn from him. There is much that we don't know, and maybe he can help us."

Mouse returned to the circle without looking at Jim.

"Son," Jim's father said, "we are happy that you have returned to visit us. There are things we all want to know."

"Yes. We will all speak quietly," Grub said. "Help us, Jim."

"You are my family and my friends. You know that I'll help."

"Good," Grub said. "We want to know the white man better. Can you tell us why he doesn't like us?"

"That's not true."

"Jim," said his father, "they laugh at us when we pass by. They throw stones at us. We are nothing to them."

"They don't understand us," Jim said. "They think we're different. If you all would change your habits, wear *clothes* like these and learn to speak the white man's language as I did, things would be different. You should learn to live like the whites."

"We want to live like the people that we are," Mouse said.

"The whites live well, Mouse. In all the time I have been with them I have never seen one of them go hungry for a day. When the snow falls they don't shiver; their homes are as warm as a summer afternoon. The whites are powerful. If something is not the way they want, they change it. That is the kind of people they are."

"I think you must be white now," Mouse said.

"No fights," Grub said. "We will listen to what Jim says. Jim, we want you to do this. We want you to go to the whites and tell them that they are ruining our land. They are destroying the forests. Their animals are chewing up the meadows where we used to gather food. They are taking all the fish out of the streams. Tell them that they are killing us, Jim. Tell them that they must stop."

"They will not stop," Jim said.

"They are killing us."

"The white man wants this land. He has taken it already. Whatever is left you have only because the white man doesn't want it yet."

"We'll all die," Grub said. "We must have our land to live."

"You should get some *money*," Jim said. "With *money* anything is possible."

"How can we do this?"

"The whites have plenty, Grub. I don't mean that you should try to steal it. You must get them to give you some."

Nobody spoke. They had never considered this idea before.

"This is why I have come here," Jim said. "Even though I live with the white man, I'm still Wa-She-Shu. My thoughts are with you often. I worry about you. I know that you all aren't as fortunate as I. So I have a plan. You will have plenty of food this winter, and maybe the whites will understand you better."

The next day Jim walked back to Woodfords from the camp at the lake. He told Adam that he had an idea and he wanted help. A week later, on a Saturday night, white families from as far as twenty miles away came to the yard of the lumber mill at Woodfords. At about that time, the Washo began to emerge from the forest to gather at the yard. The wood had been piled to one side, and some white musicians stood on it to play a reel on banjo, guitar, fiddle. The whites clumped together at one end of the yard, began to dance. The Washo did the same, at Jim's urging, trying to adapt their circle dance to the bouncing rhythms of the music. When the musicians were tired, Adam stood up to give a speech which Jim translated for the Washo. Jim translated for the whites when one of the Washo spoke. That night there were no unfriendly words.

After the speeches were spoken, whites and Washo exchanged gifts. It had been understood that each white family would bring a sack of flour to the gathering. Each Washo was to have brought a deerskin. The goods were brought into the yard and piled together. Slowly at first, but then more eagerly, each group went forward to claim its portion of the gifts.

The dance was spoken of often for the next few months in both white and Washo households. The Washo remarked how clever that boy who called himself Jim had been. The flour from the whites would feed them through the winter. Nobody would starve this year. Whites, too, remarked that Jim was a clever one. They didn't mind a good scheme now and then, most of them. They had been taken, all right, but good. You have to give that Indian credit. Flour, after all, cost eight dollars a sack. A deerskin would fetch no more than a single dollar, if you could find someone to buy it.

CHAPTER SIXTEEN

In the end, it was Ezekiel who pulled them through, in some spots literally pulled them across the desert and into California. And still it was not so much his physical strength that got them through in the end as his courage and single-mindedness. They would not fail. Ezekiel would not let them fail. Others were making California, and they would too. They were as good as anybody on this trail.

Elizabeth and the others joined the mainstream of the emigrants near Humboldt Wells, in what is now north-eastern Nevada, on the trail that followed the ever-diminishing Humboldt River deeper into the desert. Here the dust was unlike any other they had encountered: fine as flour, rising at the slightest motion into clouds that obscured vision beyond fifteen or twenty feet. It was bitter with alkali and blistered the lips. Ezekiel tied a handkerchief around his nose and his mouth and trudged on through it, a spectral apparition coated with dust so thick that it covered the black of his skin.

The only water was in the Humboldt or in the hundreds of potholes along the route. At first the Humboldt ran a perceptible course and the water from the river was not too bad. But as they got closer to the Humboldt Sink the water was stagnant and the river was really nothing more than a marshy path marked by a line of rushes and tall grass. Ezekiel had to fight the oxen and the mules at every watering stop so that they would not drink too much. They needed some, even if it was bad water, but too much would kill them, and they would have drunk themselves dead if he had not dragged them and kicked them away from the holes. As it was, they eventually lost two oxen to poison, another to Paiute arrows one night (the Paiute would scavenge the carcass when it was left behind), and one more to the rigors of the trip. It simply dropped dead in the yoke.

Ezekiel pushed the group forward. If they wept at night from the desolation and the putrid water and the heat, he would speak softly to them at first and then begin to shout. We will do it, woman. We cain't let it beat us. If others can do it, we can too. There ain't none better than us. He seemed tireless. He walked ahead of them, heaved the wagons out of gullies, wrestled the stock, and at night he waded into the mire of the river to cut grass.

For the first time, they began to pass parties and companies better equipped than they were. What she saw and heard those days between Humboldt Wells and the Carson River changed Elizabeth forever. The desert was beating some, but they themselves were pushing on, at least fighting it to a standoff. Strong men were giving up. Men with better wagons and healthier animals were stopping in the desert to lie down and die. Ezekiel might puke up his breakfast from having had a sip too much of the bad water, but he would wipe his mouth, maybe even smile through swollen lips, then walk forward again. One night a man came into their camp, asking for some cream of tartar. It was supposed to neutralize the alkali in the water. They had none, they told him.

"I don't know what I'm going to do," he said. "Every day the oxen get weaker and we cover less ground. We covered nine miles today and will be lucky to do seven tomorrow. At that rate we won't make the Carson. When we can't go on we'll die, I suppose. That'll be the end."

It doesn't have to be that way, Elizabeth thought. You don't have to die. You can make it if only you will do the things that have to be done no matter how painful or how hard they are. She knew that now. You do what you have to do. You don't give in to bad times.

At the end of the Humboldt Sink lay the Forty-Mile Desert. Beyond that was the Carson River, which flowed out of the Sierras, and it was supposed to be good and pure. They set out across the Forty-Mile Desert in late afternoon. Ezekiel had made them ready. He had soaked the wagon wheels to swell them tight, had filled the canteens and water casks that they had been salvaging from abandoned wagons, had fed and watered the animals. They traveled through the night, the desert quiet and somber, the alkali stains purple in the moonlight. They rested for a few hours at daybreak and then walked on again. At about midday Elizabeth, riding in her father's wagon, saw a fringe of green on the horizon. For a minute she said nothing, but when it became more distinct she spoke up. They had not seen green in weeks.

Out of the wagons, Ezekiel commanded them. The animals will run when they smell the water, and I cain't hold both teams. The mules broke first, churning through the heavy sand and dragging the wagon behind them. Ezekiel put his weight against the oxen and they held, fighting against him but holding anyway, until they were within sight of the water. Then he stopped them and loosed the rigging so that, one after another, the oxen plunged down the embankment and into the stream. Elizabeth and Tom and the women ran down and knelt beside the animals in the shallow water. Ezekiel was the last to enter. After he had set loose the last yoke of oxen he stood alone on the embankment and stared down at the running water for a while before he walked slowly, almost stiffly, down the bank, then into the water.

This place was called Ragtown for all the cast-off clothes that blew in from the desert. They stayed a day beside the river and then followed its course toward the Sierras. They could see the mountains ahead of them as they wound around stands of cottonwood trees and patches of chest-high grass along the riverbanks, and every day the mountains grew closer and larger. Finally the travelers camped in the Carson Valley, at the foot of the tallest peaks, where the wild grass and clover made a thick mat beneath them when they slept. Ezekiel decided that they should rest here three or four days before beginning the ascent. The days were still warm, so there was no danger of an early-season snow. They could give the oxen time to recover.

When they finally joined the stream in struggling up the eastern slope, it was Ezekiel, again, who made the difference. Sheer strength this time, lifting the wagons over boulders, grasping on a rope and pulling the wagons up grades too steep for the animals alone. They broke out of evergreen forests and into bare steep ridges as they climbed. The wind was cold and unbroken, and at night Elizabeth and Tom and the women fanned out to gather scraps of weathered wood for a campfire. They were three days in that high country and three more descending the west slope, where the trail broke off into a hundred different branches, each leading to one or another gold camp. Followed to its conclusion, the road led to Hangtown. It was supposed to be a good-sized camp with a rowdy reputation, so Jenny had decided to start business there. They were about ten miles away, had stopped for lunch at a fork in the road, and expected to make Hangtown by that evening, when Ezekiel lifted his handcart from the big wagon.

"Time to say goodbye," he said to the others.

"You're going?"

"I want to stay away from the big diggin's. I hear they are tough on niggers. Maybe it will not be so bad if I can find a little spot off to myself."

The women rose from where they had been eating, gathered around him. Jenny put her arms around him, and then the others closed in to touch him.

"You can get these wagons the last few miles into town. I wouldn't leave you if you couldn't."

Elizabeth was among them, pressing in close to him.

"You all let me go now. I got to be moving on." He shrugged, and they stepped back as if he had shed them.

"You be good," he said. He smiled. "As good as you can be an' still get by. You too, girl. An' you, Tom. You get yourself a high price for them goods."

He walked to the cart, bent at the knees to find the

handles, turned down the narrow path at one side of the
fork, and was gone.

They finished their lunch and walked beside the wagons
the last few miles into Hangtown. And the next day they
went to find a trader to buy Elizabeth's goods.

Hangtown—later to be called Placerville—had been created from nothing within a year after the discovery of rich
alluvial gold deposits. Like every other gold camp at that
time, it was hastily built and utterly disposable. Stone buildings would come later in the few camps that survived:
typically, a Wells, Fargo office, a bank, a Mason lodge. Now
it was a human version of an anthill or a hornets' nest, con-
structed mostly out of the materials of nature, mud and
fallen logs, holding together whatever stray man-made
materials happened to be at hand. A. J. Peckinpaugh kept
the store in a hovel that backed against a dirt bank. A tunnel
in the bank was storage, and bedroom, and the bank served
as a back wall into which Peckinpaugh had dug long shallow
depressions that served as shelves. Unpeeled lodgepole logs
for corner posts, plates, and purlins supported a roof of
evergreen boughs. The walls of logs and earth extended to
waist level on two sides. The front of the place was totally
open.

Elizabeth and Jenny and the others led oxen and wagon
into the camp. They got directions to Peckinpaugh's place
from a miner with arms full of supplies. The four women
and Tom walked into the place together.

Peckinpaugh stood behind a counter of planks supported
by barrels at each end.

"Help you?"

"I have some goods," Elizabeth said. "Brought overland
from the States. I will sell you as many as you can afford
to buy."

Peckinpaugh was about thirty-five, plump, bald across the
top of his skull. He squinted at Elizabeth.

"What sort of goods?" he said.

"Tobacco and rice, mostly." Her voice was proud. "It was
a tough job hauling them here, I'll tell you."

"And a thankless one, too."

Jenny spoke up first.

"Don't try to take advantage of us, mister. We'll sell these goods off the wagon if we have to."

"My papa said these goods would be valuable out here. He said this would make us rich."

Peckinpaugh laughed.

"Your papa was prob'ly right when he said that. This spring you'd have had men killing each other for a chance to buy tobacco and rice. But things change quick around here. Two months ago, four boatloads of rice arrived in San Francisco within a week of one another. Each one was worth less than the one before it. The fourth was scuttled in the middle of the bay. Wasn't even worth unloading. Tobacco, the same. April or May, I could get a bag of gold dust for a bag of snuff, no complaints. Now I've heard they are throwing the stuff into the holes in the streets in San Francisco. I ain't saying I got everything I need. Eggs, fresh vegetables, wheat, I'll take all I can get. But rice and tobacco I got plenty. So does every other trader in these camps."

"I don't believe you," Elizabeth said.

"Girl, let me tell you. When there ain't enough of something to go around here, these men will pay about any price if it's something they need. It's just gold to them. Maybe that sounds silly to you, you havin' just crossed the mountains and bein' new here. But they get it out a the ground every day, and those that don't find it right away figure they will find it soon enough. So it is just gold, and they will gladly give it up for something they need and can't find no place else.

"So if you had what I could sell, I would pay you plenty for it. But you don't. Problem is that there are other traders in this camp to keep me honest. They will tell you the same about your tobacco and your rice. Don't suppose you have anything else on that wagon?"

"I do," she said. "Gunpowder and caps and picks and shovels."

"That I can use. Maybe we can make a deal after all. I will take whatever you have."

"We have a barrel of powder. Several gross of caps. Maybe eighteen, twenty picks, and about the same number of shovels."

"Let's take a look," he said. They walked out to the wagon together, Peckinpaugh carrying a small slate and a piece of chalk. He squinted again into the wagon.

"That's twenty-five pounds of powder. I could use a hogshead if you had it." He made some marks on the slate, then counted the hardware. "That's ten shovels, thirteen picks." Again he scratched on the slate. With one hand he picked up the box of caps. "This says four gross. That's five hundred seventy-six, minus a few gone from this broke-open box. A couple of thousand would've done just fine. Ain't that always the way?" The chalk clicked again on the slate.

"We have more broke-down oxen than we can use in this territory, and these don't look much better. But the wagon is good. I can take the rig and maybe use it to pay for my freight costs next time I get a shipment. I'll give you a hundred for the wagon and the team." He was reading from the slate as he spoke. "I'll give sixty, no, seventy for the powder. Five cents each for the caps is twenty-nine dollars. I'll make it thirty. Ten each for the picks and shovels. That is four hundred thirty. I'll speculate and offer you seventy-five for the lot of tobacco and rice. It'll keep for some time, and maybe the price will go up on it. If not, I'll take a loss. The total is five hundred and five dollars. Being new here, you ought to understand that gold is worth sixteen an ounce anywhere, and eighteen if you haggle good and hard. I'll split the difference, make it seventeen."

He pursed his lips and worked at the slate once more. "You can check my long division if you'd like, but I make that out to be twenty-nine ounces and a fraction. I'll say thirty for the mess as it sits here."

"It seems so little," she said, "compared to what we expected."

"There are three other traders in the camp. Brashears is in a tent quarter mile down this direction. Atkins is across the draw in a falling-down cabin that nearly washed away in the rains last winter. Everett is behind him a ways. Go talk to 'em, girl. See if they don't tell you the same. Maybe you'll get an ounce or two more out of one of 'em, dependin' on how bad they want the powder and the hardware. If you don't, come on back here. My offer stands. Thirty ounces.

But that's for the lot. I don't want to see you come back with a wagon full of nothin' but rice and tobacco."

Brashears would go only twenty-nine ounces, Atkins thirty-two. When Everett offered just twenty-eight, they went back to Atkins, and he measured the gold out on a balance that he, like all the other storekeepers, kept on the counter. He emptied it into a cloth sack, which Elizabeth carried out of the store in one hand. When she was outside, she began to cry.

"Don't," Jenny said. "We did the best we could. We got the most we were going to get."

"I'm not crying for me. The money doesn't really matter. You understand that? It's my papa. He was so sure. So sure that these goods would make him rich. You see?"

"Yes. Well, it will get you back home, anyway. I don't know for sure but I think this money will buy you passage back East."

"I'm not going back East."

"This is no place for you," Jenny said.

"That gold won't last long here," Deirdre said.

"I want to join up with you."

"Hush, Liz," Annabelle said. "You hush with that talk. Tommy, you run off so you don't hear this."

"No, he can stay. He'll know soon enough. I thought about it some that night we crossed Forty-Mile Desert. I thought, you are the best friends I ever had. Whatever you are, whatever you do, it can't be as bad as people say or you wouldn't be who you are.

"I thought about it some more when we left that first store. I hoped that man was trying to cheat me, but I didn't think so. I knew then that I wasn't going to get rich from that wagon load. I knew I'd have to do something else. And there's not much I can do to make money."

"You can go home," Jenny said. "You can do that. You can go home to your kin in Kentucky."

Elizabeth smiled. Her mouth trembled and her eyes were still wet, but she held the smile.

"No. Tom and I have traveled too much, for one thing. I want to set down in one place. I'm tired of seeing the world, and I can't face a long trip for a while. But most of all, I've done too much and seen too much to go back there. They will want me to be a sixteen-year-old girl like I was when we left St. Joe this spring, but it can't be. I can't set aside these weeks, the things that have happened to me. I think back to what I was this spring and I don't hardly recognize that girl. I know she is me but I have to laugh at her. She's ridiculous. She's empty-headed. She knows nothing like what I know now. I can't be that girl again, and my kin won't take me for what I am now. They wouldn't know what to do with me."

The three women said nothing.

"I can make money, can't I? Enough to see that Tommy has a decent home?"

"Well, yes. There is money to be made. But you don't realize what you're getting into. You have no conception," Jenny said.

"This is a bad life," Deirdre said. "You don't know."

"No," Elizabeth said. "I don't know. But whatever it is, I can do it. I know that. I am dead certain of that."

CHAPTER SEVENTEEN

Charles Hemingway's traveling show needed just two hours, a railroad siding, and an empty lot to unfold itself in all its self-conscious gaudiness. Hemingway employed three roustabouts who also did a tumbling act. They and every other able-bodied member of the crew carried the big canvas tent out of the baggage car and hoisted it on its twenty-foot centerpole in the nearest available spot. The site didn't have to be large; two hundred people in the tent left barely enough room in one corner for the performers. For a long time every show had played to standing room only, as there were no seats. Finally Hemingway gave in to his partner's urging and bought grandstands that would accommodate perhaps thirty. He charged a nickel extra for the use of this luxury. When the seats had been pulled off the car and set up in the tent, the true disgorgement began: a llama, a wrestling black bear, a camel, a parrot, two small monkeys, a raccoon, and a barnyard goat with beard dyed red and coat streaked green, which Hemingway tried to pass off as a variety of Andean mountain goat. All these creatures shared a pen at one end of the car and had learned from necessity to exist in peace. After the animals came a ticket booth, large painted flats as high as the tent that depicted each attraction of the show, then the magician's apparatus, wardrobe crates, a smaller tent to house the animals (admission extra). Last out was a cheesecloth painting furled on a pole that was hung from the tent roof. At the climax of each performance, the master of ceremonies, one of the roustabouts, would announce in heavy tones that the pachyderm which had traveled with the show for years had died just a few days earlier. The cheesecloth was then pulled open to show a painting of an elephant, actually Barnum's Jumbo copied from a poster. Our elephant is dead, the speech went, but at least he is with us in memory. In fact there never had been an elephant. They were too expensive for Hemingway.

With all this unpacked and set in the proper places, one part of the car still was crammed with Hemingway's oddities. These included stuffed birds, a carved bas-relief representation of the signing of the Declaration of Independence, a variety of rough peasant shirts and blankets from Mexico, a rusted musket that purportedly had fired the first shot of the Revolutionary War, a detailed graphic explanation of the photographic process. The roustabouts first swept the hay and droppings from the animals' end of the car, dismantled the pen, and then arranged the oddities so as to fill the interior. That left the final chore of attaching another canvas enclosure to the open door on one side of the baggage car, then arranging within it a system of sliding mirrors by which a placid and apparently normal young man (any one of the ubiquitous roustabouts) was seen to transform himself into a snarling hairy animal of vaguely human form (yet another roustabout, in costume). This miraculous change took place during breaks in the roustabouts' other duties, for an audience that had paid an extra nickel to slip behind the curtain draped across the door. Since the mirrors were hidden, and slid silently on oiled bearings, the change was most startling and realistic, especially in the dark, cramped enclosure. When the beast growled and swiped a hairy paw out at the audience in the small attached tent, men often ran, frightened, from the exhibit. Their shrieks and blanched faces invariably swelled the audience at the next showing.

Joshua kept the accounts, booked engagements, made the payroll, and negotiated with the railroads from his office in the private car. Hemingway taught him to be a barker. He felt ridiculous at first, but recited the spiel mechanically anyway. In time, by watching the crowd and sensing the effect of his words, he could tailor his pitch to the collective mood. He got a certain satisfaction from this, from being able to step to his podium beside the ticket booth, survey the curious and the smug and the bored people who milled in front of him, judge that crowd as the unique individual organism that it always was, and then work it by getting its attention, arousing its interest, jabbing it with words to tease humor and compliance and sometimes the beginnings of anger out of it, then coaxing it into the tent and into the car the way an animal trainer might do with wild cats. They were never the same, the crowds. Never one alike. The size of the crowd and the weather and the time of day all affected them. Geography had its effect too, though a bumpkin crowd one night could be totally different from a bumpkin crowd the next night ten miles down the tracks. You have to respect them, Joshua told himself eventually. You have to take each one as it comes and know that it is not like any other crowd you ever worked. You don't play to just one or two people, because people are different in a crowd than they would be if you got them off alone. But just the same, you can pick out a few people and know that if those people move toward the tent then the rest of the crowd will, too. No explanation for that. It is just the way crowds are.

In time he became a good barker. Hemingway said so. Hemingway also scrutinized the ledgers and the receipts, and one day pronounced himself ready to leave the troupe to begin working in advance of the show on selected engagements. Joshua, he said, was sufficiently strong-willed to resist the influence of Putnam for at least a few days in his absence. So Joshua conducted business and worked the crowds, lived with the freaks and the performers, and traveled. He saw the faces of the country staring up at him as he yelled from the podium.

The troupe's magician was named Jack Murdoch, billed as the Amazing Merlini. In major cities, magicians were following the lead of a French innovator named Robert-Houdin, who performed in evening clothes. Murdoch, though, found the traditional dress of the trade more effective with his small-town audiences. Murdoch used stage paint to deepen the creases in his face, and he wore a long gray wig. His costume was a high pointed hat and a loose black robe adorned with cabalistic symbols stitched in gold. This fitted the less sophisticated public's image of a conjurer, and the capacious sleeves of the outfit served as both distraction and cover for some of his bolder moves.

Murdoch's repertoire of effects was standard for the time. Milk, water, and red wine would shift mysteriously from one goblet to another; a bouquet of roses would materialize in a handkerchief-covered vase; a live baby chick or rabbit would be plucked from a pan in which Merlini had been preparing an omelette; a card selected by a member of the audience, having been torn up and burned, would appear at the tip of a candle that had been in plain view of the audience throughout the performance; a skull sitting on a plate glass would nod answers to simple questions posed by the audience. All these effects were accomplished either by drugstore chemicals, cranky mechanical devices, or a hidden assistant. After a few years Murdoch had come to despise his routine and his audience. When he drank too much he would rail against them in the private car: Gullible idiots. Fools. Cretins. Nincompoops. They will swallow anything.

He was contemptuous of them because they were most impressed by effects which required the least skill. In his early weeks with the troupe he had included a few sleight-of-hand tricks with the mechanical effects, but was frustrated to find that the sleights which had required hundreds of hours of work in front of a mirror—a one-handed card change, maybe, or an especially difficult coin pass—produced only polite applause. For setting in motion a clockwork mechanism or standing off to the side while one of the roustabouts tugged a black thread lost against a black backdrop, he got loud cheers and fervent applause. Finally his working stage repertoire was pared of the sleight-of-hand material until it included only one moderately difficult effect: a trick called the Miser's Dream, during which he apparently plucked coins out of the air and tossed them into a bucket. There were several mechanical devices to accomplish the effect, but Murdoch stubbornly relied on sleight-of-hand methods.

He was happiest when he was offstage, performing for the troupe as the train clattered from one point to the next. He still devoted hours to his sleight of hand, perfecting techniques, polishing trick shuffles and passes, sometimes inventing new methods for standard tricks. Once or twice a month the performers of the troupe became his audience, and then Murdoch was a happy man, fulfilled. He had people to watch him do what he did best. They wanted to see him be the artist that he was. And more than that. They knew that what he did was difficult, and they appreciated him all the more for that.

Joshua, like all the others, gathered around him one afternoon on the train for one of his performances. They had played an engagement outside Baltimore, and now the car was rattling through the Maryland countryside. Murdoch had some new effects to show: banging a saltshaker through a tabletop, vanishing a silver dollar from a plain matchbox that Joshua held clasped in his hand and then sending it into Putnam's vest pocket. When he had finished these new tricks he resurrected a few old ones: a routine with the cups and balls that he claimed to have learned from a man who had learned it from the great Bartolomeo Bosco, and a series of card sleights that ended with what he called the Persistent Jack.

"I have the jack of diamonds in my hand. I put it very carefully into the deck. Very carefully. Look. I want you to watch. Into the middle of the deck. Now I lay the deck in the middle of the table. No strings, gentlefolk. No wires. Now you, Joshua, you're close. Turn over the top card of the deck."

Joshua did. It was the jack of diamonds.

"You see? That's my problem. The jack refuses to stay put. I think we have a pretender to the throne, because no matter where I place the fellow"—again the card was shoved into the deck—"he instantly works his way to the top." And again the jack of diamonds was the top card in the deck. A half dozen times this happened. Sometimes it was Murdoch inserting the card into the deck, and sometimes it was

Putnam or the weightlifter or a roustabout. They all took turns turning over the top card, and yet always it was the jack of diamonds, and each time the jack was exposed, the performers clustered around Murdoch shook their heads or furrowed their brows or drew in an involuntary gasping breath. No polite affectation for their friend's benefit. They had all seen the trick before, and yet they were still baffled, still impressed. This time, as he always did, Murdoch ended the trick by fanning the cards face up on the table about the time that they had all convinced themselves that this was a deck composed solely of jacks of diamonds. And of course it was a normal deck, except that there was no jack of diamonds at all.

When he had finished he spread his hands palms up and smiled. End of performance. The troupe thanked him, clapped him on the back, made the usual jokes about making Hemingway disappear for good, if he was such a wizard. Murdoch was gathering his simple props, tossing them into a valise, when Joshua approached him.

"Quite a show, Jack," he said.

"Thanks, Josh. My pleasure."

"Jack, I want you to show me that trick. The one with the jack of diamonds."

Murdoch looked at him and smiled.

"Can't do that, Josh. Necromancer's oath. Strange and terrible misfortunes will be visited upon me if I reveal the dark secrets of the trade."

"Just this one, Jack."

Putnam had been standing off to the side. Now he spoke.

"You don't want to know," he said. "That would spoil it all for you. You can watch it now and be thrilled. It would never be the same again if you know."

"Besides," Murdoch said, "if I told you how, you wouldn't believe me. You wouldn't think it possible."

"I still want to know. I watched close and there isn't a way you could do it, but still I know there must be."

"There is. And it's tough."

"Teach me, then. If you won't show me, then teach me how to do it myself."

"It ain't like playing the banjo. You don't just pick it up

and start doing it. But, Josh-you-way, pal of mine, I'll teach you if you really care."

"I care."

"Not good enough. You'll have to prove it. Have to buy your ticket inside the tent like everybody else."

He handed Joshua the pack of cards from the top of the table.

"You take this deck and go off by yourself. This is what I want you to do: figure out a way of shuffling the cards so that you can keep track of the ace of spades. Put it in the pack, shuffle six or eight times, and still be able to cut to that ace anytime I ask you to. And make it look natural when you shuffle. You do that, I'll show you the jack trick and more. At least you'll be able to appreciate what I do, because you'll have sweated out a few hours with these devilish things yourself, trying to make them do what you want them to do.

"What do you say, Burgess? Shouldn't take him more than twenty years, wouldn't you say?"

Putnam laughed.

"He ought to be ready for that jack trick about the time that Hemingway becomes a philanthropist."

Joshua took the cards to a seat. He found the ace of spades, held it, rubbed it between the fingers of his right hand. Shouldn't be too hard, he thought. Person of normal intelligence, normal dexterity, ought to be able to figure a way of doing this. Hold the pack this way, the ace this way, shuffle . . . The cards sprayed into the air, and Joshua heard Burgess and Jack Murdoch laughing behind him.

For three or four days the cards were his enemy. They resisted him. They felt awkward in his hands. Though he had played cards before, he had never struggled against them the way he did now. But then he had never tried to do these things with cards. He had held them but he had never felt them, never before had given all his concentration to touching and feeling and manipulating.

He had always used an overhead shuffle playing cards, so he started with that. Okay. Ace of spades on top. You throw some cards on top of that and it is . . . lost. So you have to separate the cards on top from the ace. You could jog them out a little. Just so much. No. When they shift you've lost the ace again. You could bend one corner of the ace. But if you bend it enough to make a difference then it bulges, and Murdoch had said to make it look natural.

After a few days he could at least keep the pack square without thinking about it. The cards responded to his touch. They felt right cradled in his hand. Murdoch and Putnam no longer laughed at him as he sat alone, working with the cards, shuffling, thinking, shuffling some more. Accidentally he found a way of keeping track of the ace, and then it was only a matter of practice, practice, make it right, make it look natural. His little finger had gotten in the way of a packet of cards when he threw them down on the ace and there had been a separation. It was too big, too obvious, but that was his start.

He went to Murdoch one evening after a performance.

"I'm ready for that jack trick."

"You think you're ready for your test? No marks on the back? Just the cards and your two hands?"

The two of them went to the private car and sat across from each other at a table.

"Okay, here is a deck. Let me pick a card, doesn't have to be the ace. Here, fan 'em and hold 'em out there for me to pick one. Let's see. Three of clubs. Now suppose I want to put the card in the deck myself. Will that work? Good. Then hold the deck out and let me slide it in here. Here, right about the middle. Now you shuffle."

Joshua shuffled until Murdoch told him to stop. Then he cut the deck and dropped the top card from the cut deck. It flipped over in midair and landed face up on the table: the three of clubs.

"Hindoo shuffle. Not bad, Josh. Who taught you that?"

"Nobody."

"You figured it out by yourself? You did good, boy. I ain't saying that you could fool a three-year-old with it right now. It's awful rough. You could drive this train through the break you made with your finger. But just to think of it and get it that far is damn good. Look, let me show you something. 'Stead of that little finger that's hidin' out there for all to see, you use your second finger, in such a way. Shuffle, keep the cards movin', and nobody will notice the break. When you stop shufflin' you clamp down hard on the cards, not so hard that your knuckles get white and you squeeze your finger out of the break, but hard enough that you squeeze out whatever gap shows in front. You see?"

"I understand."

"Here, Josh, give me your hands, fingers spread."

Murdoch bent close to Joshua's hands, turned them palm up, ran fingers over his skin.

"You never done a day's work with your hands. Not a day's hard work in your life. Don't be ashamed. I ain't either, an' don't intend to. Soft skin makes it easier to feel. I don't mean touch, but feel. You keep up with this, you'll know the difference soon enough, if you don't already."

Murdoch dug into his pocket for a snap purse. He opened it and emptied the coins into one hand, then threw back all but several pennies. These he stacked and held in one hand.

"Close your eyes, Josh. Now take these pennies. Right here, 'tween thumb and forefinger. Don't move 'em, just feel and tell me how many."

Joshua took the coins.

"Four," he said.

"Five. Give 'em back. Now try this."

"Three."

"Three it is. And this."

"That's four."

"Right once more. Now this."

"Six. No, five."

"Yes. You can open your eyes now. Oh, you got the equipment for this dodge, boy, no doubt of that. You got nice long fingers and plenty of meat there at the base of your thumb an' along the heel of the hand. Here an' in here, you see? That's good, all that. Most of all, you got the feel. You could be good, boy. You got the hands. The question is whether you got the desire."

"I do, Jack. I want to learn that jack trick."

Murdoch laughed.

"That trick. It ain't a trick at all, as much as seven or eight different ways of gettin' a card up to the top of the deck without anybody knowin', none of 'em easy. But if you learn what I can teach you, Josh, you'll do it just like I do, more as an amusement than anything."

"You want to teach me these things?"

"You want to learn?"

"I never thought about it. Never thought I had much chance. Never saw myself doing all the things you do, Jack. What you do is special. It's magic, Jack."

"It is hard work. For you it might not be as hard as for others. Look, boy. I'm sixty years old. In cold weather, last few winters, the joints of my fingers have ached. My hands, they don't do what they used to do, 'least not as fast and smooth as they used to. Fast ain't all that important, and so far I have got by on savvy. But it can't last forever.

"Josh, I'm an old man and I feel it. I make a living of sorts in this third-rate diversion, foolin' fools with gimcracks and geegaws the way you'd distract a puppy with a shiny bauble. I ain't rich. I ain't famous. I got no family. All I got are my hands and the know-how in my head to use 'em. What I'm saying, boy, is that what I got in this head is all I got to give an' I wouldn't mind givin' it to you. If you worked hard at it. If you took it as serious and cared for it as much as I do."

Joshua spread his fingers, stared down at his hands for a moment.

"They don't look special to me. But what you do is special. If you'd teach me, I'd try all right."

Murdoch nodded.

"Good," he said. "We can do cards, coins, the cups and balls, all the same. As you learn one, you'll find the others will come easier. The moves are only half of it, though. You have to know people to know what you can get away with, and when. That'll come in time. Right now we'll learn how to deal an' shuffle. Jus' a straight deal an' shuffle. Don't look so disappointed. There's a right way, an' you got to do it right straight 'fore you can do it crooked. Besides, this'll get you closer to the cards so you feel 'em the way you'll have to. When you can shuffle an' deal I'll teach you a palm. That's a straight magical move.

"I used to be a gambler. Used to be a crooked gambler. There is a difference b'tween gamblin' moves and pure magical moves. Gamblin' moves can be easier but they got to be perfect. I was perfect, for a while. About twenty years ago, I started feelin' a knot in my stomach when I knew I'd have to make a crooked move in a card game. My hands would get clammy, I'd find myself drummin' my fingers on the tabletop. I started hearin' a voice inside me, sayin' 'You can't fool these people.' The bad part was I started believin' the voice, an' it took all the quick talk I had inside me to get out alive. So I stopped bein' a gambler.

"Josh-you-way, I'll teach you the moves an' make you work till you can't see what you're doing when you do it. What you got inside of you in the line of little voices, that is another matter. But we'll see, boy."

CHAPTER EIGHTEEN

Grub stood and straightened his back, a slow and painful unlimbering of bone and muscle. He had been stooping for more than an hour. He looked about him now and saw infinite uniform rows of cornstalks. Hidden as they hunched in between the rows were Washo from his bunch, their hands working quickly and deftly in among the stalks, yanking weeds and tossing them aside to die. The day was hot. Grub was sweating. There was shade in between the rows, but no wind penetrated there, and he had risen hoping for a slight breeze. For a moment the air was still, but then a gust ruffled the green leaves of the corn and cooled his face. Grub let the moving air caress his face and his bare chest, and he remembered an afternoon like this one, not many years ago, when these fields had been covered with wild grass that had rippled like a lake when a breath of wind moved across it.

This was their second year of working in the whites' cultivated fields. They'd had to do something. Another winter like the one before last and there would be none of them left. First Grub had failed to find the big droves of rabbits. The deer kill had been spotty, for the whites with their rifles had killed four deer for every one the Washo had taken. The pine nut harvest had been mediocre, and the whites had even chased them off the traditional fishing camps at the lake. So they had gone into the winter with few stores, and the winter had been a hard one. The children had become emaciated and then grotesquely bloated. They had chewed on strips of deerskin for nourishment. Finally Grub himself had gone down into the settlement to find Jim, discovered him in a shed on Longstreet's property that he had taken for his own home. There had been a fire in an iron stove; Grub had sat close to the warmth while Jim brought him bread and meat and honey. Only when his stomach was full and he had stopped shivering did he tell Jim why he had come. The bunch was dying. Wa-She-Shu everywhere were dying. Something had to be done.

That was how they had come to work the whites' fields. The white man will take care of you, Jim said, but you have to give in return. Come down from the hills and live here in town. In the spring you can work the land and plant, and for now the women can work in the homes. The white women will use help cleaning and cooking. In return you will have food. But you have to *earn* what you get. You will have to give up these crazy old wandering ways, because it makes the white man nervous when you are here one day and gone the next. You will have to start dressing like the white man, in *decent* fashion, and learning his words. This is a good life the white man has here. You can have it and share it. But you will have to realize that the old life is gone forever. You'll have to change and become more like the white man, as I have done, so that he will trust you.

Leave it to me, Jim had said. I know the whites. I will find places for you all.

Most of the bunch followed Grub out of the hills and down to the town. Jim said that he could keep them from starving, and that was good enough for them. They found that Jim had spoken true. He had gotten barns and sheds for all of them. The women had gone to work in the homes, and then in the spring they had all gone out into the fields. It was a miserable time, but none of them had starved after they had moved into the town, and none of them had frozen to death.

The bunch was not really a bunch any more. They lived apart from each other some of the time, and though they still had gathered together last autumn to drive rabbits and to have *gumsabye* with the others in the Pine Nut hills, the spirit was gone. They had no leader. Grub was just another one of them now, for though they had followed his advice about going to live with the whites, that had been the last time his word carried any weight. They no longer needed him, for the white man ordered their lives, through Jim. Jim was boss now, not just for this bunch but for Washo all over the hills. Jim knew the whites, and the whites fed them now and gave them shelter. To know Jim was to have a guide through an otherwise impenetrable white society.

In two years, babies had been born who would never know the days when the Washo listened to the advice of a sage and then roamed far and free over the land. Some of the Washo were taking the names of the white families who had sheltered them and fed them, were dressing in whites' clothes and trying the language. They still followed all the old rituals and ceremonies, but most of those were pointless now. No woman, when unclean, would yet eat meat that had been killed by someone she knew, for that would ruin the hunter's chances the next time he went stalking. But most of the men worked in the fields these days and had little time for hunting, so the ritual had lost its meaning.

Not all of them had left the mountains. Mouse had stayed behind when his father had led the bunch down into the settlement. He had a wife and a baby boy, and he shouted that he would rather see them dead than living beside the whites. Somehow they had survived. Now Mouse had a bunch of his own formed from obstinate ones who would not give in. They stayed in the high country most of the time, and were rarely seen by whites. At the last *gumsabye* they had camped apart from the others, for they wanted no part of the whites' clothes, words, or smells that the others had brought with them.

The breeze in the cornfield died. Grub waited for it to revive. When it did not, and the leaves on the stalks lay limp and still, he went back to work. He took a last look up at the mountains beyond the fields, and he thought of his son and his grandson roaming up there. Then he stooped, buried himself in the green stalks, and reached for a sprouting weed.

CHAPTER NINETEEN

They were playing a three-day engagement in Canton, Ohio. Jack happened to know Canton, and had found a game there a few years before. Most nights, he said, the local sports used to get together in the back room of a tailor shop. Maybe we should see what we can scare up, Josh-you-way.

They found the tailor shop, Jack and Joshua and Burgess Putnam. Jack rapped three times, sharply, on the rear entrance, and that got him inside, to where four men sat playing *vingt-et-un* and four more sat at a cutting table with poker hands held close to their chests. Somebody remembered Jack. A real 'leg, one of them said. Lost sixty one night and then treated the house to breakfast the next morning. He would sit this one out, Jack said. He was a magician now and didn't want hard feelings. But these other two, they wouldn't mind catching a few hands.

Joshua had been working with Jack Murdoch for more than a year now. He was good, Jack said. He had learned ungodly fast. He had gotten the magic stuff fast enough, and was a positive wizard with the cups and balls. Murdoch had taught him early to second-deal for some magic tricks, and that became his first gambler's move. But doing it at a card table was different. He had to learn to do it without the top card whispering when he pulled the second. He had to do it with his hands out in front of him and the cards in plain view. None of this shading the deck with the fingers the way you could get away with in magic. When he could do that, Jack showed him the bottom deal just as a matter of reference. But soon as you learn it, he said, you can just disremember it, because the bottom deal is the first thing the rubes will be expecting from a blackleg. Joshua learned to item himself a hand when the deal came around, gathering in the discards and then contriving to put together a winning hand as his turn came to deal. Then you had to know how to restore a deck after the cut. It could be done but it took nerve, because it had to happen there on the table, the quick one-handed change covered by the more obvious motion as the arm pulled the cards back in for the deal. There were other things that Joshua was supposed to know and then forget. Like daubing. Some sharps wore hollow cufflinks that contained stains to match the inks of the printed backs of the major brands of cards; a bit of paint on the thumbnail went a long way, and if you put it in the right place you could mark every court card in the deck after just a few hands. Like crimping corners. Like notching aces with a sharp fingernail. Like wearing a shiner, a broad ring, on one finger of the dealing hand, the ring reflecting the face of each card as it came off the top of the deck.

And when Joshua had learned all these things, then Jack Murdoch taught him to play cards. No sleights, no moves. Just the percentages and a feel for the game. Know the game and likely you won't have to cheat. Or at most you will have to nudge the averages around a little bit to let you break even with the canniest player and the luckiest streak.

For a few months now he had been trying to find games in the towns they played, to give Joshua a feel for the action. Sometimes Burgess Putnam sat in too, but Murdoch sat aside so that he could concentrate on Joshua. You can't roll a bluff past the kid, he said. He looks at you and it's like he can see straight into your head. But he can raise you three times with deuces high and scare you off, the way he smiles and leans back in his chair and hardly listens to your raise, like he had four aces and couldn't care what you said.

This night in Canton Joshua took a fourteen-dollar pot

early and then was caught twice trying to buy small hands. By midnight he was up eight dollars. By two he was up seventeen. We ought to break at three, somebody said, and there was general assent to that. Joshua's deal came at three minutes before three. He had dropped out of the previous hand, so he had time to stack the discards and shuffle them absent-mindedly as he watched the hand being played.

Four others were left at the table when he dealt the hand: Putnam, the tailor, a thick-fingered farmer who spoke with a Swedish accent, and a drummer who had spent much of the night describing his line of men's footwear. The tailor squinted at his cards as he picked them up one by one from the table. He opened for a half dollar. Putnam raised. The farmer threw in his cards and the drummer called and Joshua called, and when the tailor raised again for a dollar, the raise was good around the table.

"Cards," Joshua said.

"Pat," said the tailor.

"One," said Putnam.

The farmer hooted. "Got a hell of a hand, boys, a hell of a hand going here."

The drummer took one card and Joshua stood pat. This time the bets and the raises went around the table three times, with more than forty dollars in the pot.

"Call," Joshua said at last.

"Straight," said Joshua. "Ten high."

"Beats my two pair, aces," the drummer said.

"Straight," said the tailor. "King high." He laid the cards out in an even crescent in front of him and reached to scoop in the pot.

"I think four deuces takes the pot," Putnam said, and one at a time he flipped them out onto the table. "My arms are lacking a bit in length. Maybe one of you gents will be so kind as to shove the spondulix in my direction."

When they left the shop they walked down dark, silent streets. They said nothing for a while, and then Putnam spoke.

"By Jupiter, he did it again."

"Yep. He does it every time, it seems."

In every game they found in every small town, Putnam

had won a large pot on Joshua's last deal. It was safest that way, Murdoch and Joshua had decided. Nobody was going to argue with a midget even if there were any suspicion. Nobody would have the nerve to do it.

"You can give me the twelve I threw in and then split the rest," Joshua said.

"I'm tempted to say I'll give it all up if you'll tell me how you did it. You itemed your hand. I know that. There is no way you could have put together hands like that unless you stocked them. Has to be."

They had found an alley off the road and now were sitting against a wall, with Putnam counting out the money.

"Yes. He had to item them," Jack said. He was looking at Joshua.

"But I don't understand one thing. You had to item four different hands," Putnam said. "Now how did he keep track of them all, deal them all out the way he was supposed to?"

"Three," Joshua said. "Just three hands."

"You never saw his hand," Jack said. "He threw in and never showed his cards."

"Three. Correct. But how the hell did he handle even three?"

"I've been wondering myself," Jack said.

Putnam had counted out the last of the money. Joshua dropped the coins into a pocket and folded the paper money.

"One on the top. That was the tailor's. One on the bottom. That was yours, Putnam. Everybody was getting tired, and I figured I could get the bottom deal past them."

"That still leaves one," Murdoch said.

"I sideslipped it, Jack. Kept a break and dealt out of the middle. That was the drummer's."

"Hell," Jack said.

"Something wrong?" Putnam said.

"No. Except there ain't ten sharpers in the country that can middle-deal, and I only heard about them. Never saw anybody do it myself."

"You saw one tonight. I've been working on it awhile. It felt good the last few times I did it alone, so I decided to try it tonight, if I could put the hands together. I found three good hands in the throwaways, so I did it. Made the pot nice and fat. We haven't seen one like that for a while. Not since the last time we played Cairo, remember?"

"I never saw it," Putnam said.

"You know you're not supposed to."

"But a middle deal."

"How else? Except to cold-deck them, and you know I didn't do that."

"No. You didn't."

"I won't say it was easy. But I kept at it."

"So you did. And there is just one more thing. You itemed them hands without looking at the faces," Putnam said.

"Readers. Somebody rang in a cold deck of readers after the deal had gone around a couple of times," Joshua said.

"Readers," said Murdoch. "I never caught 'em."

"The farmer. That big old Swede," Putnam said. "I never once bluffed him all night long."

"The farmer," Joshua said. "I thought he made some strange calls. So when I got the deal about midnight, I gave the deck a quick riffle, just watching the backs. Jack, you should have seen those spots jump when I did that, corners marked to show suits and then a sort of position code for the numbers. I had to study it on the sly for a couple of hours, but when I got it I knew I had a chance for that middle deal."

"Never saw it," Jack Murdoch said. "I knew something was happening but I never figured marked cards. That farmer is a regular, owns a place outside of town, they say. Now you expect that this guy is working out in the fields all day. Instead, he's bendin' over a deck of cards on the kitchen table, maybe, marking those cards with some daub that he got God knows where. An' doing this every night, 'cause the house starts with a fresh deck and he has to ring in his own cold deck each time."

For a moment the image was vivid for them all: the ham-fisted farmer coming to the tailor's shop every evening with a newly marked deck in his dirty denim overalls, making the switch every night for months, and no one ever knowing it.

Together the three of them began to laugh.

"There is proof, if you need it," Murdoch said when he had caught his breath. "Ever'body has an angle. Ever'body has a scheme. Don't care who, ever'body has got one or is workin' on one.'"

Their laughter had been loud. A window opened on the second floor of a building in the alley, and a man's voice shouted for them to be quiet.

They said nothing for a while, listened to the silence and felt the shared mirth there in the darkness.

"A daubed deck," Murdoch said. "Not enough you spot it, Josh, but you know how to make it work for you. You are good at this dodge, young fellow."

"I suppose," Burgess Putnam said, "that this is how you'll start to get back where you belong."

"I belong here, time being," Joshua said.

"You stick out here like a bottle of milk on a barroom shelf. I was referring to your social status."

"I don't know what you mean."

"One of my gifts, Josh, is a memory that won't stop working. I have a mind like a cluttered closet. First day on the train, you mentioned your name and something about a business, and I recollected a newspaper blurb I'd read the day before in a Boston newspaper about a crazy old coot who died and left his fortune to some religious fanatic. The fortune was supposed to include a thriving shipping business. Shut his son out of every penny, the story said. I found the issue there on the train, looked for the piece, and saw that the dead man's name was Belden. Simple."

"I didn't want anybody to know. I'd had advantages but I knew that now I'd have to be like everybody else. I've worked at it. I've tried."

"You did it well," Putnam said. "Everybody knows there is something different about you, but we're all different in our own ways there in that show. It's not as obvious as it used to be, either. Used to be you were either acting like you expected something out of us or else were trying too hard to show you didn't want anything special, that you would earn what you got. Lately you have evened it out. Nobody'd know now that you had lost a few million not so long ago. I told Murdoch the story when you started in with the cards. Nobody else. It is your affair, is the way I look at it."

"I appreciate that. I'm not ashamed. But as you say. It's my affair."

Putnam had reached for one of his cigars. Now he struck a match, which flared momentarily in the darkness.

"Your own affair. So true." Putnam made sounds of sucking on the cigar, then expelling the smoke. "You know I claim to be a student of the human animal, an astute observer. Having read that newspaper article and seeing what a proud sort of fellow you are, I watched you. I'll be truthful, Joshua. I saw you for the young strong bear that's been kicked out of his den. That bear will be angry. If he can't fix to get back in his own cave, then the next best thing is to find some other bear and take his cave away from him. I waited for that to happen. I just didn't see you staying out in the cold. I surely didn't see you suffering this life as long as you have."

Putnam pulled again on the cigar.

"Especially," he said, "since you have all the means to regain your status as a monied individual."

"I never thought I could," Joshua said.

Putnam giggled.

"Did you hear that, Jack? Did you hear your *wunderkind*? You're precious, Joshua, you are. Maybe you're not that bear after all. Maybe you are more like an eagle that lived on the back acreage of my parents' farm when I was a child. I saw him first when he was very young. He would try to roost in a tall pine on the edge of the forest, but two crows badgered him unmercifully, swooped down at him and pecked at him every time he strayed into what they regarded as their own domain. This went on for nearly two years, well after the young eagle had gained his mature strength. It was quite a ludicrous sight, as you might imagine, to see the two crows lording over this magnificent creature. But he didn't realize that it never had to be. He simply assumed that he must run away from them because he had been doing it for so long. That is you, Joshua. You don't realize your own power and what it can do for you."

Murdoch spoke.

"Burgess is full of words, but what he says is true, Josh. You got a talent. No, *talent* ain't exactly the word. It is a gift, Josh, first to be able to work the cards like you do and then to keep a cool head whilst you're about it. The way you did tonight. You think just anybody can do that? You think a few thousand sharpers, myself included, wouldn't kill to be able to do what you do? Not to mention with just two years' work, an' accomplishin' more in that time than most of us ever did in ten or twenty. Hell, Josh, I'm good. I mean I am *good* at sharpin'. And at that, we're past the point where I can teach you anything. Last few weeks, I've been learnin' from you. The little man here speaks the truth. There ain't no limit to the heights you could take yourself."

Joshua thought: I'd like to be rich again. I belong rich, was born that way and would have stayed that way except for the intervention of Gault. And what was he? A sharper with big ideas.

He said: "Well, I've pondered it, being rich again. But I thought it would do no good, that I ought to concentrate on living without millions because that was how things would be with me."

Putnam puffed, and the tip of the cigar glowed red.

"Joshua, the sharping is only part of it," he said. "You can work people. You can make them do what you want 'em to do. Like the way you work the tips before each show. When you are really working, they crowd up at the ticket booth as though you were giving those things away. And the few of them that you don't reach, why, they crowd in with the others anyway, because they don't want to be left out there alone. It's a natural talent, and yet it needs cultivation. But you have it, Joshua. It's in you, boy. And if you have it but don't use it, you will never be a happy man. Gifts like yours can be delightful burdens, Joshua. They are fine to have, but they don't leave you a lot of choice. You follow them to their logical conclusion or else die hungry and unsatisfied."

"I wouldn't know where to begin," Joshua said.

"You've begun already, Joshua. I've kept count, last few weeks since we organized this little campaign of ours to take a gamblers' tour of the hinterlands. You must be three or four hundred ahead since that. That is without trying hard. That is playing against bricklayers and mechanics and farmers who will go without tobacco for a week if they have two bad nights running at the table."

Putnam clambered to his feet, and the others followed. They walked toward the railway station.

"Now imagine," Putnam said, "the possible rewards if

you did this sort of thing for a living. Playing against men who can drop five hundred in a hand without flinching. Those men aren't any smarter or harder to sharp than anybody else you've stared at across the poker table these last few weeks. But they are a damn sight richer."

They walked on, their feet scuffling along the boardwalk.

"You might be interested in the conclusion to that eagle story. It was a summer day and the crows were after him again, and I suppose that bird was a little irritable and more than a little disgusted with himself. What he did then must have surprised the devil out of him. Not to mention the crows. He was flying off and the two crows were flying right atop of him, trying to poke at him with their beaks. Very suddenly he rolled right over on his back, and just as quickly he had his talons sunk into those crows' breasts. Then he rolled upright again, practically as though he had never missed a beat of his wings, and as he flew across the field he shook those two birds until there was a rain of black crow feathers fluttering down to the ground. When he was done, he let go of them and flew to his roost on the big pine tree.

"And nobody or no thing ever chased that eagle off that tree again."

CHAPTER TWENTY

When Joshua left Hemingway's troupe, in January, 1858, Jack Murdoch pressed into his hand a folded piece of paper. The erratic script on it read:

How to Stay Healthy and Wealthy While Sharping
(Jack Murdoch's Six Commandments)

1. Stick to greedy men when you sharp. The others are too much trouble and greedy ones are easy to find. The greedy man will sell himself if you give him half a chance.
2. Leave a little bit behind. This is not so much charity as plain smart thinking. Even a dumb greedy man will get suspicious if you try to pluck every penny from his pockets. Give him the comfort of at least a pittance and you will take his mind off the rest. Also, observing this commandment will keep you from becoming a sucker for somebody else who knows Commandment No. 1.
3. Cheat only when you must. The world is full of opportunity in the form of pure luck or outright stupidity on the part of others. You need not stack the deck or fabricate a lie to take advantage of this opportunity. This is true at the card table and in the

rest of life. Take what the breaks give you first, and if that is not sufficient you can help the breaks along.

4. Remember if a man has a gun on you he don't have to prove you was cheating. That means that in a tight spot where you have no allies and no handy exit you can't even look like you are sharping. In fact, whether you actually are or not makes no difference. (Putnam says to remind you of Caesar's Wife if you don't understand the foregoing.)

5. Bear in mind that anything can be faked and that there is no such thing as too big a lie if it is told right. In other words, think big. Bigger the better, especially if you figure the other guy ain't going to think you capable of such a grandiose scheme. When telling big lies do not spare the fine details, scientific if possible, to support your story. This appeals to the sucker's vanity, and it is a rare man indeed that has the nerve to speak up and admit he don't understand a word of what you are saying. You should not be trying to sharp such a character in the first place.

6. Never admit nothing. Even if they catch you with one finger in a daub box and a holdout up your sleeve, never admit that you are a cheat. This goes back to No. 5. Keep lying and eventually people will start to believe that it is just colored snuff in the box and the holdout is just to keep your cuffs straight.

That is all, I guess, Josh. If you haven't figured it out already, I will set down in closing the main function of a sharper. A sharper changes life and fortune around to suit himself. That is all. It is not so much different from turning forest into farmland.

> Yr. Tutor,
> John J. Murdoch

He left the troupe in Yazoo City, Mississippi, and made his way over to the river. He drifted south, knowing that New Orleans lay before him. In Vicksburg he won three hundred dollars in a single hand of poker by changing the crimp and the weave that another sharper had put in the aces. In Natchez he worked three-card monte for the first time, bilking the sports who had arrived for the annual race meet outside the city. He grew a moustache. He ordered boots custom-made of glove leather, and wore loose-collared linen shirts and tailored black pants. In Baton Rouge he bought a gold stickpin that embraced a pearl at its head, to wear in the lapel of his new black broadcloth coat. He liked this wardrobe so, he had it triplicated.

The wife of a cotton speculator in Biloxi became his first lover. She came to his cabin one night while her husband played euchre in the social hall as the riverboat churned toward Memphis. He was twenty-three, and he gave her his stickpin. For all his confidence around men, he had always been reticent around women, but the cotton speculator's wife changed that the moment she wiggled herself out of her skirts as he looked on from his bed. He had been practicing a new method of dealing seconds when she rapped at his door.

He came to New Orleans by riverboat in the spring of '58, hired a porter to help him with his trunks of clothes, and rode a *faicre* to the French Quarter. He took a room at the St. Charles, and by the time he had stayed there three weeks, and had eaten in the best restaurants, and had bought a new stickpin with a larger pearl and a Juergensen watch with a heavy gold case and a diamond in the stem, and had sampled the prostitutes on the second floors of the houses on St. John and Gravier Streets, he had spent all his gambling winnings and was living on his savings from the salary Hemingway had paid him.

That was enough inducement to make him look for work. He found it as an artist in a first-class skinning house on Chartres Street that catered to wealthy visitors from upriver. The game was faro, and it was rigged. Joshua worked for a few weeks as a dealer, but the mechanical gaffs built into the dealing box made the job routine, so he began to work outside the house, making the rounds of the best restaurants and the lobbies of the expensive hotels, finding men with money and steering them to the house.

Yes, the food is good here, but it's nothing compared to the meal I had last evening. And free, too, if you can be-

lieve that. Yes, yes, it's true. It was at a gambling house
not far away, a true gentlemen's club. I ate and drank until
I was full and then bucked the tiger for a while. Won a
couple of hundred on top of it all. Well, no, it would do no
good to give you directions to the place. Admission is by
reference only, I'm afraid. I suppose I could bring you
there. Wouldn't mind having another go again myself.

He was both a steerer and a capper. He brought the victims to the skinning house and then stayed with them,
playing as a shill while they gambled. If the man insisted,
Joshua would take him into one of the private dining rooms
—the motif of this particular place was blue plush carpet,
oak paneling, chandeliers, and gold-leaf filigree—but usually Joshua would nudge him to one of the tables to try
his luck before the meal.

Joshua's cut was ten percent of the take, so he was careful to choose only the most obviously wealthy victims.

He met Thérèse at a Quadroon Ball that June. She wore
a single camellia behind her right ear, and though her
gown was red satin, it was less gaudy, being cut more simply, than the others. He noticed that. The other women
were in a contest of plumage and jewelry and finery, so they
seemed to be interchangeable except for minor differences
in detail, but this girl with the single flower set off by her
black hair stood apart from them. She danced with three
different men during the first hour, he noticed, and more
than once when he turned his head to find her, he saw that
she was looking his way. He tried to watch her after one
quadrille, but when the dance ended and the pattern collapsed, she was lost in the crowd. He was scanning the floor
for her when he heard a voice behind him, speaking to him
in French.

"You aren't dancing, sir?"

He turned and she was there, a small young woman,
smaller than she had seemed at a distance. Her hair was
absolutely black, pulled back straight, and it shone with
highlights from the gas jets on the wall.

"I don't dance," he said.

"Not at all?"

"I have never learned. But when I saw you, I regretted
that."

She laughed lightly, and somehow the sound of it and the light in her eyes hit him in the chest. It was a physical sensation, and his lungs seemed to work against the constriction.

"You are so beautiful, you take my breath away," he said.

She said only: "I've never seen you here before."

They spoke during the next dance. He watched her face and saw nothing else. In Boston a woman might have chided him for that, would certainly have averted her own eyes. But this one met his look and returned it. She was nineteen years old, and her name was Thérèse Latour. Her mother was across the room. He could come to meet her, if he wished.

Mother was taller than her daughter, with a straight back and a slim waist and skin the shade of walnut wood that has bleached in the sun. Her own dress was unadorned white. She sipped punch from a crystal cup while her daughter introduced Joshua. They spoke for a while—she wanted to know about his family and his upbringing—and when Thérèse excused herself to find a friend, her mother put the cup of punch down on a table.

"Madame Latour, I would like to come to your home to visit your daughter."

"How long have you been in New Orleans, my young man?"

"Less than three months."

"This Quadroon Ball, is it your first?"

"Yes."

"Perhaps you haven't been in this city long enough to understand all of its customs. So I'll tell you that although Thérèse is as pale as any proud Creole woman, and certainly as beautiful and well educated, she is restricted in some ways. There are some things to which she cannot aspire. Her chances of marrying a wealthy and respectable white man like yourself are regrettably poor, and she will not even consider a free man of color. As her mother, I'm naturally concerned for her well-being. To be most blunt, her best chance for happiness is to find a liaison with a man who can support her and care for her adequately. I want to arrange that, as my mother did for me, as every other mother in this hall wants to do.

"She is not interested in frivolous affairs, for her reputation is admirable now and that is one of her great advantages. Do you understand all this?"

"Yes," Joshua said.

"And do you still wish to visit Thérèse in my home?"

"Yes."

"Excellent," she said. Her face softened for the first time.

He found that Thérèse could cook. Thérèse could play the coquette or the caring mother. She had been to Paris. Sometimes she smelled of lilac, sometimes of jasmine, sometimes of orange blossoms. She was accomplished at the pianoforte, and she had read more books than he had. Her feet were small, and she sewed her own dresses.

It was done this way: When Thérèse agreed to be placed by Joshua, her mother presented him with a list of demands. Thérèse was to have a furnished house in her own name. He would place a fund of five thousand dollars in her name at a local bank. He would provide a monthly stipend for household expenses and necessities. For her part, she would be his faithful lover and his mistress forever. She would be discreet. He could live with her in the house, and she would perform all the services of a wife.

He sent to Boston for his savings, bought a small white cottage for her along the ramparts and filled it with furniture. It's only money, he told himself. With his skills he could get more anytime he needed, and a few thousand made little difference against the millions he had committed himself to regaining. Besides, he was saving money by having a woman to cook so well for him, to wash and mend his clothes. He had taken an apartment in the French Quarter. Now he could give it up and save the expense.

For a year he was free of care. He spent his time and his money lavishly, without thought of return. It seemed to him then that he would be forever young, and there would always be money. Maybe Murdoch had prepared him for more difficult work than capping in a skinning house, but he was good at this and the income was steady. He slept until noon most days, and somehow, though she rose early in the morning, Thérèse always anticipated him and was there beside him when he was ready. She brought him a meal and they ate together and drank wine, and then they made love, for hours sometimes, their bodies sweaty in the humid afternoons. Sometimes he put his head on her breasts or her stomach and talked while they both lay naked and waited for a breeze to blow past the lace curtains and cool their clammy bodies.

I am something special, he might say. My father used to tell me that, and now I know that he was right. I feel a destiny. I feel a part of great acts and momentous happenings. Myself in particular, I am meant to be wealthy. I'm not doing so badly in that regard already, with this house and the good food we eat every day, and my woman with her expensive tastes. But I mean wealthy the way I used to be. I think I would like to go back to Boston when I am rich again, Thérèse. Go back and walk along the wharves and greet my friends there again as an equal. Boston is different from New Orleans. For one thing, it does not have shit running in the open culverts, at least not where I grew up. The attitudes are different. Money is different. In New Orleans you cannot tell the difference between a monied gentleman and some smelly *maquereau* on Tchopitoulas Street. Both dress the same. A man of wealth in Boston, there is no mistaking. He dresses quietly, as though he is holding something back, but all the same you know that he has it, the money. That is how the cities are. Boston is always holding something back. New Orleans knows no bounds.

Thérèse listened to this and said nothing. She thought the ambition of which he talked was incongruous with the lovely lassitude of their life now, but she said nothing. She didn't think that she would like Boston from the way Joshua talked, even if she could pass for white there. She was sure that she wouldn't care for ice and snow in the winter.

That autumn she saved his life. The city was in the midst of one of its periodic epidemics of yellow fever— "the Saffron Scourge" was the term the English-language newspapers liked to use—and one evening after he had been feeling weak all day, Joshua began spitting up black blood. Thérèse sent for a French doctor. But the man who arrived spoke English, and it was an accepted custom among the English-speaking physicians to treat the fever by anticipating the symptoms and then matching them, as though the effects of the illness might be lost in the rigors of the cure. First they bled the patient unconscious, and then they administered calomel, a compound of mercury, until the patient salivated. Thérèse let the man in the door, but when he produced a scalpel and began to make the first incision, she screamed and drove him from the house with a chef's knife. She kept a cold cloth on Joshua's head, and tried to make him take orange juice, and sat with him until the fever broke.

They had one good year together before Joshua grew unhappy. Thérèse was as loving and as dutiful as ever, but where he had once admired her for her solicitude and her fealty, he now condemned her as meddling and constricting. After a year and a half in New Orleans, he was no closer to his fortune. The house was too small, the job was drudgery, and New Orleans was making ready for war. There was talk that young men would be pressed into service. No telling how badly that might sidetrack his plans.

Mostly he resented the rich suckers he steered into the club. He cursed one of them one night, and the man wanted to duel him. One week afterward, at the dueling oaks, Joshua found seconds. He even enlisted at a fencing academy, and discovered that he was hopeless with swords or pistols. To Thérèse and to his employers at the skinning house, this made no difference; if it was a choice between dying and losing honor, then Joshua ought to be choosing his headstone.

The evening before he was to duel he told Thérèse that he was taking a long walk so as to arrange his thoughts and compose a will. He walked down to the waterfront, past where the skiffs and rafts were tied, and bought passage on a boat leaving that evening for St. Louis. He had brought his gold stickpin and the Juergensen watch and three hundred dollars.

He gambled on the Mississippi riverboats until the beginning of the war, and then he began working boats on the Missouri. But they were different. There was less gaiety, less easy money with a war going on, and the passengers tended not to be wealthy sporting plantation owners, but dour sodbusters who still worked the land with their own hands and understood how much effort they had devoted to earning each dollar in their purses. One night a slightly drunken merchant from Independence reached for Joshua's right hand as he played the shell game in the dining room. The man turned over Joshua's hand and found the pea nestled in the muscles of his palm.

It was low-stakes action, so the merchant granted leniency. He would not be arrested at the next town, but merely deposited on the nearest sandbar. Two crewmen took Joshua by the arms and lowered him into a rowboat and forced him to row toward shore. There was no sandbar, but a low-lying spit of land that had the appearance of a marsh, and that would be adequate, they judged. They patted his pockets and took his money. The rest of his stake was hidden in the false lining of a portmanteau that still sat in his cabin.

He stepped off the boat and sank into mud that covered his glove-leather boots and reached to the knees of his striped trousers. He was still slogging through mud when the steamboat began to move again, and it was well downriver when he had climbed onto solid ground and removed his boots and pants and dangled his muddy legs in the river.

He cleaned his boots and his trousers as well as he could, and then he lay beside a wild hedge to sleep. The next morning he dressed, walked to the road, and found a ride to the nearest town. This was St. Joe. He walked into a jeweler's store and sold the watch for ten dollars. Next door was a mercantile, and he begged a three-foot length of packaging twine. He tied the twine into a loop and put it in his pocket and went into a saloon on the corner, where he drank a beer. He sat at the bar, took out the loop of twine, and began to make patterns with it laced between his fingers. He held it draped over each hand and brought the hands together, and when he pulled the hands apart the twine was in a figure eight within an encircling loop. He laid the twine down on the bar with the pattern intact. He put one finger in one loop of the eight and pulled at the twine. The loop caught around the finger. He did the same thing again, but this time the twine pulled free and did not catch on the finger. He did this for several minutes as he sipped the beer, engrossed in the twine and the loops of the figure eight.

He had not drunk half the beer when a man sitting a couple of seats down the bar walked behind him to watch, then asked Joshua the purpose of the twine.

"This is a game," Joshua said. "I learned it last night. Some gent taught it to me on the riverboat. It was quite a lesson, actually, cost me almost sixty dollars before I got wise that he was sharping me. Now I'm trying to puzzle out how he did it, and I'm damned if I can get anywhere."

"I've seen that game," the man said.

The bartender had drifted to within earshot now.

"That's prick-the-loop," he said. "One of the oldest schemes going. I didn't think anybody could be fooled by that little bit of business, not any more."

Joshua looked at him.

"Maybe you can show me how it's done, then," he said. "The gentleman on the boat said it was even odds, fifty-fifty, that I would put my finger in the loop that caught. One loop catches and the other doesn't, and it could be either one. He even showed me how to make the figure so that I could try it myself."

The bartender laughed.

"The way he showed you, he was right. But the way he showed you ain't the way he done it once your money was on the line. There's three different ways to throw that loop. One is straight, fifty-fifty either way. Another is done so that either loop will catch when he wants to make sure you win, to lead you on. The third is fixed so that neither one will catch. Let me show you. It's all in which fingers you use to make the loop. When this one and this one grab here and here, you got your straight figure. But when your middle finger an' your thumb here hook the string thisaways, then you got the one that is a winner every time. Or with the ring finger here and the first finger here, you got it fixed so that neither loop will catch. See that?"

"I certainly do. I'm grateful for the explanation. At least I won't waste any money on it next time."

"My pleasure," the bartender said. "In this line of work

we see it all sooner or later. That prick-the-loop is a real antiquity, though."

Joshua picked up the twine, made a figure eight again on the bar.

"Still," he said, "I suppose it would be a fine game of chance if it were done legitimately."

"Well, sure," the bartender said, "then you have your reg'lar even-money chance, no advantage either way."

Joshua toyed with the loop of string.

"You ain't anxious for a game, are you?" the bartender said.

"I've lost quite enough at this little diversion already. I do enjoy risking a dollar now and then, though, in a legitimate proposition."

"I'll throw the loop square," the bartender said, "if that's what's worrying you. That sharper last night, he did it so fast you couldn't see what his fingers was doing, I wager. Well, that ain't square. I'll do it real slow so you can see what I'm up to. Then you can be sure I ain't rigging it."

Joshua swallowed his beer.

"You'll do it slowly," he repeated, "so that I can be sure that it's on the up-and-up?"

"I promise," the bartender said.

"Can I be the one to pull the string? Last night, the sharper let me pull the string."

The bartender considered this.

"Don't know why not," he said. "I never heard that it makes any difference who pulls the string."

"Just a friendly game, then," Joshua said. "Just a few throws."

"Just a friendly game," the bartender said, and he picked up the loop and made the figure eight within an oval, and Joshua played the first time for a dollar. He won the first time, lost the next two, won three of the next four tries. After about ten minutes, betting dollars each time, he was ahead by eleven dollars. The bartender had begun to frown. Joshua had won again, and was pulling in the money when his elbow brushed his stack of winnings and knocked the silver dollars to the floor. As he bent down to pick up the coins, the bartender was preparing to fashion the looped figure. When Joshua rose with the coins in his hand, the figure was on the bar, ready.

"You don't have to stay with the single dollars," the bartender said. "You can boost it up a bit, if you'd like. Two dollars. Five, if you'd like."

"This is just a friendly game," Joshua said.

"It can stay friendly betting five a throw. I just reckoned that luck has been running with you and it was about time it changed. I'd rather be playing for five when it does, that's all. 'Course, if you feel the same way, like your luck has crossed over the bar, then maybe you ought to stay betting singles."

"No. I have a hunch. I'm sure luck is with me for at least one more throw."

"That's the time to put money down, friend."

"So it is. I have eleven here, nine more in my pocket. I'll bet any part of that."

"Gives me a chance to get even and more," the bartender said. "I have a double eagle in my shoe. Safest place for it. Here, let me dig it out. Yep. Twenty it is."

"I wouldn't mind a side bet," the man behind Joshua said.

"And who do you like?" Joshua said.

"I go with Mike here. Your streak can't last much longer, friend."

"Unfortunately, I left the greater part of my traveling funds with the sharp-witted gentleman last night. I do have this pin, though."

"The pin's no good to me."

The bartender reached out to look at the pin. He twirled it between thumb and forefinger.

"That's the real article," he said. "I'll advance you thirty for it out of the till. You lose, it's mine. If not, then you can keep it and the thirty."

The pin was worth twice that.

"That sounds fair," Joshua said. "Eminently fair." He laid the pin beside the coins, and the bartender went to the cash box for a double eagle and a stack of ten silver dollars.

"Let me see now," Joshua said. "Right or left, I wonder." The index finger of his right hand moved above one loop, then above the other, then back to the first. "The right loop has been a winner for me more often than not, but perhaps that is the very reason I ought to pick the left. Let me see, let me see."

He threw up his hands.

"This is hopeless," he said. "Since this is an either-or proposition, I'll let the fates tell me which loop to prick. Heads I take the left. Reverse, the right."

He flipped a dollar and caught it on the back of his left hand.

"Heads. I take the left."

He put the finger down in the loop nearest his left hand. He grasped the twine.

"The moment of truth," he said, and he pulled slowly. The figure lost its form. He pulled some more, and the loop grew smaller and smaller and finally fastened itself around the tip of the index finger.

"A winner!" he yelled. "This is my lucky day. And after such a disheartening experience last night."

The bartender had no more stake and no more stomach for the game, so Joshua pocketed his money and reclaimed his pin and left the place. Before the afternoon was finished he had found five more people who knew prick-the-loop and knew that there were three ways of throwing the figure, but were totally ignorant of the fact that for every way to make the figure was another way of pulling it apart so that either loop would catch. He won two hundred thirty-three dollars. He bought a plain cotton suit, a hot bath and a haircut, and a good meal. He took a hotel room, and the next morning he walked into the ticket offices of the Overland Express Company. He paid one hundred fifty dollars for through passage to California.

CHAPTER TWENTY-ONE

Jenny and the others went into business by buying a set of scales and claiming squatters' rights to a dirt-floored cabin a few hundred yards uphill from the main camp at Hangtown. The cabin had no roof and only a single room, but the necessary repairs and modifications were accomplished in two evenings by a volunteer crew of men from the camp. Once they threw away the jeans and shirts and wore woman's dress, men followed them through the streets, though at a respectful distance. Others bowed and tipped shapeless felt hats as the women passed. There was no doubt of what they were, even with Elizabeth and Tommy in tow. But more important, they were women, of whom there were few of any kind in Hangtown. Of these few, almost all were old, or married, or too young, or were betrothed as quickly as they wished. One of the bolder miners, who had gone so far as to approach them that first evening, to welcome them to the diggings, had explained the situation:

"We have some females. We have a few grammers, an' some wives that is guarded more jealous than a cache of gold, an' a few young'uns still in pinafers. We had one sweet lass that broke our hearts when she hitched to a feller up to Coloma way. But we ain't had no single ladies here since then, an' sairtinly none in what you might call a *commercial* capacity since Mademoiselle Maryse an' her thievin' bunch a French whores, 'scuse the expression, left town for points south this spring."

There was no shortage of labor for the cabin's repairs. Jenny stood on a box in the camp one evening and announced that she and the other ladies were naturally anxious to accommodate the men, but not until suitable living arrangements had been provided. That evening a roof went up and two partitions of the cabin were begun. The next evening saw the completion of the partitions and the construction of a lean-to addition. Others brought bed frames, pine-bough mattresses, and hand-hewn chairs and bureaus. When the work was finished, about midnight, Jenny lit a bonfire that drew the men about it as it crackled and lapped up at the sky. Jenny pushed shoulders aside to reach the fire, and when she had reached the edge of the gathering she spoke loudly.

"My name is Bea," she said. "The other women up there, standing by the cabin, are Louise with the dark black hair"— this was Annabelle—"and Maggie, the tall one. We are honest women, and by that I mean in our house you will not have to look to your purses every minute and you will get what you paid for. The price is one ounce for reasonable services. That sounds like a greedy price, maybe, but gold seems to be plentiful in these districts, and I don't suppose we are robbers, considering what Peckinpaugh and Brashears and the others are getting for their goods. Maybe what we are offering will not fill your belly like dinner, but it will be remembered a good deal longer. You know we must be worth at least the price of a dozen eggs and a few mealy apples."

The men laughed. Jenny grinned and spoke again, hands on hips.

"As for the rules. Maybe this ain't a church bazaar, but it is a ladies' home and you will all be expected to behave in a fit manner. That said, I don't have to mention that there will be no spitting, no cursing, no fighting, no drunkenness, and no gunplay on the premises. I am strictly serious about this, and I hope I can count on the rest of you to discipline those few who might step out of line. The hours of business are from noon until midnight, seven days a week.

"There is one more thing that needs saying. Maybe some of you have noticed a comely young girl and her brother in our party. That girl is one of us. I mean she has decided to join our profession. Boys, we think she is something special. To begin, she is unspoiled. She has never known a man so far. I know you've heard that pitch before, but if you will speak with her for a moment you will know that what I say is true. She's seen difficult circumstances, elsewise she would never consider doing this. She is a perfect little angel and we think highly of her. The first man who takes her will pay ten ounces. But don't bother crowding in line. It ain't that simple, and I won't turn this into a lottery. Before anything happens, you will come up with a fit place for the boy. He don't belong here in this house. He needs a place with a strong and God-respecting man for as long as we stay in this camp. So talk among yourselves and come up with such a fellow. I don't expect that caring for the boy will be a hardship. He is a good-natured child and likely will do more than his share of the chores. If there is a question of feeding him, the girl will take care of his expenses.

"The first man who has his privileges with the girl will have to be approved by me. I want this to go easy on her, and I won't have her submit to just any fumble-fingered lout who strolls through the door. After her first few times she is on her own, but till then you will have to go through me to get her. Also, this will happen when she is ready for it an' not before. That covers it. Ordinarily we will be shutting down about this time, but this is an exceptional night, I guess. Nobody with a heart would turn away such stout souls who have worked so hard for her. You may all step into my parlor, gents."

Elizabeth watched from a window in the cabin. She heard Jenny talk, saw the men turn and look at her when Jenny spoke of her. Their faces were orange in the glow of the fire. She wondered: Which will it be? Which of these men, these anxious and curious faces? They don't look so bad now. These are men I know. No different, anyway, from those I've known. Will he change when he's alone with me, that first one? Will he touch as though he cares?

Jenny led the men up the hill from the fire and into the house. When she saw Elizabeth at the window, she hurried forward, picking up her skirts and running to lead them all through the door. She came to Elizabeth, held her close, and whispered into her ear.

"I was terrible direct, dear, but you'll be used to that soon. It was the only way to do it, put it out there so plain for 'em. You're on sale now, Liz, no avoiding that. If you're up to it, stay here and talk to some of them while me and the other girls entertain. It's quite a crowd, but they won't all want us, not tonight. They will want to just look at us, most of them, look at us and hear the sound of us when we talk, and smell us. Your name is not Liz, not to them. None of us uses our true names with them. I'll explain later, but think of one now."

She squeezed Elizabeth and released her. When she was a few steps away she turned back and said, loudly enough for the room to hear: "And don't suffer no nonsense, dear. Don't allow 'em no more liberties than if you were in the settin' room of your parents' home."

She walked off, drew a half dozen men to her, put an arm around one, and laughed loudly at something the man said as he bent to speak into her ear. Elizabeth felt her face flush watching the sudden intimacy. Deirdre was nuzzling one man. Annabelle was disappearing into one of the back rooms with another. Then Elizabeth became aware of men's voices. They were talking to her.

What's your name, young lady?

Why, Jacqueline, sir. (Jacqueline. Where did that come from?)

That wouldn't be French, would it, miss?

On my mother's side. She was from Paris. (Another lie. They come out so easy.)

French, one of them crowed. Hear that, boys? French on her mother's side. Oh my.

Elizabeth found herself scowling at the man as he rolled his eyes like a clown. He stopped, looked downward, properly chastened. (They are not so bad. Not so different from little boys.)

Pay no attention, miss. Some of us hain't seen a young lady for quite some time an' we fergit ourselves.

Understandable, I'm sure. (She smiles at the offender. Redeemed, he manages a weak smile in return.)

Where was your home, miss, if I might be so bold as to ask, 'fore you left the States?

Nashville, Tennessee, it was.

I'm from Tennessee, miss. You know Roper, Tennessee?

Afraid I don't.

You ninny, the lady don't care about Roper, Tennessee. 'Sides, she is too perlite to tell you what you ought to know awready. Whoever is here, what's behind is behind 'em. Past is past an' we is all Californios now.

So well put, sir. I appreciate that.

She held them for more than two hours. None even ventured a hand toward her. They looked at her with eager, longing eyes, and she caught herself pitying them. She was almost sorry when Jenny, dressed in a chemise, shooed out the last of them and closed the door behind them.

"Seventeen ounces between us in two hours. I would call that a start, ladies. I would call that quite a start."

Then she looked at Elizabeth.

"You done good, Liz. You done just the way you should. You made 'em know that you was a lady an' you didn't let 'em forget it. That's the way you always want it to be. Don't never let 'em forget that you're a lady. Always remember it yourself."

"Tell me about the names," Elizabeth said.

"It takes a bit of explainin'. I will if you ain't too tired."

"I'm not."

"Then come in with me an' set on my bed while I comb my hair."

The others joined them. They all looked at Elizabeth while Jenny spoke.

"These men," she said, "they ain't bad sorts, most of 'em. Maybe they ain't prizewinners, but they are nice enough that when a bad one happens along, you'll spot him soon enough. That's one advantage to our job, Liz. You see a lot of men, an' when the exceptional one comes along, good or bad, you know him for what he is.

"Okay. They ain't so bad, I was sayin'. Maybe you think you know what they come to us for, but you're wrong. Most of 'em want to be near a woman. The act ain't as important as our lettin' 'em be close to us. We're different from them, an' we have the power in us to make a man feel good, make him feel important, so he can walk about like he is somebody special when he leaves us. It ain't logical that ever' one of these fellas should be special, the way one follows another in an' out of the room, but that don't bother 'em. They shut that out of their minds.

"What happens in bed is part of that. You can't imagine, Liz, how important that is to 'em. Remember that. Remember that no matter how clumsy and hopeless one of these fellas is with you, you got to make him feel like he's done somethin' special, somethin' no man ever done to you before. You do, you will have them leavin' your bed with their chests puffed out for a week. An' you'll be good at this job.

"This gets into the part about the names. This is all a sham, Liz. Them men ain't special. There is too many of 'em for any one to be special. Also, there is a part of you that none of 'em touch. They are buyin' your smile. They are buyin' your time. They are buyin' your body, if they use it kindly. But they ain't buyin' what is inside of you, the special part of you that you keep to yourself. I can't describe what that is, but the first time you are with a man, you'll find yourself holdin' back somethin', and that somethin' is what you will keep to yourself as long as you are in this life. The name, Liz, is so you'll remember that this ain't for real. So you make up one, and when that gets too familiar, you find another. When these men come to your bed callin' you by a name that ain't your own, you know it's just a game you're playin' for the money they give you. It ain't nothin' else. It ain't got nothin' to do with what's inside of you, the part that is always Liz."

Some of the miners came to Jenny the next morning. There is a fella named Parker, they said, has a dry diggin's and a good cabin up-gulch a ways. Keeps to himself, 'cept on Sundays, when he comes into camp an' sets down in a shady spot an' reads from the Good Book. No preachifyin', understood. None of that. Just reads from the Good Book to those who will listen. He might be the one to keep the boy.

Jenny dressed herself in her best blouse and skirt, put on

a hat, told Elizabeth to do the same. They washed Tommy's face and his hands, combed his hair. Then the three of them walked up the gulch to where Parker was supposed to be.

They found a man shoveling gravel out of a bank and tossing it onto a wire screen. He had a long beard, and hair that grew down to his shoulders from under his hat, and his muscles were sharply defined throughout his back. When he heard them approaching and saw that it was women, he threw down his shovel, stepped behind some brush, and came out pulling a flannel shirt over his shoulders.

"Beg pardon," he said. "It is a powerful hot day. I never imagined September would be this way, 'specially as chilly as the nights are."

"We understand," Jenny said. "We're looking for a man named Parker."

"That is me," he said. He was about forty, with veins showing at each temple.

"We are seeking someone to board the boy," Jenny said. "He is the brother of this girl, and we are—"

Parker cut her off with a wave of one hand.

"I know who you are," he said. "Some of the boys come up to see me early this morning."

"If you know," Elizabeth said, "are you bothered?"

"Bothered? No, I don't suppose I am."

"Can we make some arrangements, then, to have the boy stay with you? Surely you understand why we want this."

"I understand," he said. He looked down at Tommy. "What is your name?"

"Thomas Burgess."

"Tom, can you cook?"

"No, sir."

"Can you haul water up this hill for a few hours a day?"

"I think so."

Parker looked at the women.

"This ain't an easy life," he said. "Dry diggings are three times the work. I must have the water to work this gravel, and the only way I can get it is by bringing it up the hill in buckets. It's slow and tedious."

"He is no pack mule," Elizabeth said. "But it wouldn't hurt him to lend a hand, part of the day."

Parker bent down to the boy's height, looked at him.

"Would you mind what I say, same as if I was your pa?"

"Yes, sir."

"I got one back home in Virginia. Ten years old, younger than you, Tom Burgess, unless you're big for your age. I wish to God he was here with me."

He stood up.

"I'll treat him as though he were my own. That means I'll care for him and feed him, but if he don't respect my wishes then he'll feel a strap just like my own boy used to, once or twice a year. Since he says he'll work, I'll feed him out of my provisions, or at least try to. If I run low, then I'll come to you and maybe you will help us out."

"Can the three of us talk alone?" Jenny said. Parker nodded yes and walked back to the gravel bank.

"He seems a good man," Elizabeth said.

"He does."

"Tom, you can have a say in this."

"He looks more strict than Pa used to be."

"He'll soften up," Jenny said. "Pay him heed and he will treat you well. I believe that."

"I'll come to visit every morning," Elizabeth said. "We won't be apart so much. If anything goes wrong, then we'll find another place. But I think you should try this man first."

They walked up to Parker.

"Sir," Jenny said, "we'd like the boy to stay with you. He ought to eat right, so if you are short of a decent meal we want you to come to us. The girl will be visiting him mornings to spend some time. If that is satisfactory, we'll leave him now, and his sister will return tomorrow with his clothes."

Parker nodded.

"One last thing before you go," he said. "Can the boy read and write and cipher?"

"I was in fourth grade, sir, 'fore my family left Kentucky."

"Are you Christian?"

"Methodist."

"Then we'll have something to do with our evenings, Tom

Burgess. We can both practice writing and our figures, and we'll read together from the Bible. We'll be too tired to do much else."

"Yes, sir."

Tom was standing beside Parker when Jenny and Elizabeth left them to walk down the trail to the cabin. And as she left him there, Elizabeth felt another step closer to the end of her childhood and the beginning of being a woman in every way.

There was a man waiting outside the cabin when they returned.

"It's a little early for business," Jenny said, "but if you insist, there are two girls inside, up and around."

"I've seen them already," the man said. "I wanted to talk about . . ." One hand kneaded the cloth of his shirt, and he gestured with his head at Elizabeth.

"We'll send her away, if you'd rather," Jenny said, and Elizabeth left them and walked into the cabin. From where she stood inside, the man was only quarter-profile as she looked at him through a window. He was tall and gangly, maybe twenty-five years old, sandy-haired and with a wispy failure of a moustache.

"He ain't half bad-looking," Deirdre said behind her.

"I don't know about that." He wasn't ugly, anyway. The nose was too long and slightly crooked, but the eyes as she remembered them from the moment's glimpse in front of the cabin were soft and blue. The eyes were nice.

He turned at that moment and caught her staring at him. He looked away.

"Come away from the window," Deirdre said. She put an arm around Elizabeth and led her away. "You're making the poor fellow so nervous he is likely to run and hide."

"Do you have the ten ounces?" Jenny was asking the man.

"Ma'am, two weeks ago I sank my spade into a bar and it came up half full of pure gold. That was the narrow part of the vein. Yes, ma'am, I got the ten ounces."

"That is a start. Maybe you can tell me why you think you ought to be the one to be with the girl."

"I thought on it. First I thought it was wrong, the whole idea of spoilin' a fine young lady like that. Later I thought, it's going to happen no matter what. I looked round me, ma'am, at the men in the camp. I couldn't see one that I thought would treat her nicer or more gentle. So I come up here to talk to you."

"Understand that this is no joke," Jenny said. "She has never been used by a man before. Never been kissed, so far as I know. This will be bad enough for her without her being roughed about and mistreated. Have you ever been with a woman before, when it was the first time?"

"Three years ago," he said. "My wife. Back in Pennsylvania. I love her, but we're apart six months now, an' that girl is so pretty . . ."

"Don't apologize. Men need women, is all. I just wanted to be sure you knew what was going to happen. You have to be gentle. You'll have to be kind and patient."

"I know."

"Are you clean?" she asked.

"I ain't bathed in a few days, ma'am, but I will when the time comes."

"You damn well better, but that ain't what I mean. Do you drip white in the mornings?"

For a moment he did not comprehend. Then he blushed and stammered.

"Oh, no, ma'am. Nothing like that. I ain't been with a woman since my wife."

"I'll be checking, just the same," she said.

He will be as good as any, Jenny thought. No prince, but as good as this place is ever likely to throw forward. "No reason to put this off," she said. "What do you say to tonight?"

"Tonight is good," he said.

"Since you have enough that it don't make a difference, the price is twenty ounces. You know she's worth it, and I want her to know it, too."

"Twenty," he said.

By candlelight they made her ready. Jenny chased away the customers after dinner. Deirdre found a white taffeta gown with lace about the shoulders. Annabelle had brought powders and perfumes. There was not a proper bathtub to be had in all Hangtown, so they boiled water in a kettle and mixed that with spring water in their largest cooking kettle. Elizabeth undressed herself and stood beside the kettle while the women washed her. They wanted to do this, and she did not protest. Nor did she feel any shame at being naked in front of them. They were her sisters now, and she understood why they wanted to be with her at this time.

"His name is Ralph Burwood," Jenny said.

"Twenty ounces, I hear," Deirdre said. "Twenty ounces, more than three hundred dollars. That is something to be proud of, Liz."

"I can't think what it will be like," Elizabeth said. "I can't feature him and me. I don't know what I'm supposed to do."

"Don't do anything," Jenny said. "He knows you're not Lola Montez. Be your sweet self, and if he hurts, let him know."

"You can kiss him if you want," Annabelle said. "Sometimes we do and sometimes we don't. But if it don't feel right, don't do it."

Jenny was standing, drying her shoulders.

"It will happen all right," she said. "It will. We were made for this. When it's over and done, you'll laugh that you made such a fuss over it."

When they were finished, Deirdre dusted her with powder and Annabelle colored her cheeks with a slight smudge of rouge. Jenny pulled back her hair and tied it with a red ribbon. Elizabeth raised her arms so that the thin gown would slip over her head. Her body felt warm. It seemed to glow where the taffeta brushed her skin as she walked alone into her room and closed the door behind her. There was a clean cotton sheet on the bed, and she stretched out on her back and watched the door while the candle on her bed table played indistinct shapes on the wooden walls.

There was a soft, hesitant rap on the door.

"Yes?" she said.

"It's me. Ralph. Ralph Burwood, that is."

"Come in."

The door swung open. He walked through and stood in front of the bed, looking down at her, until she pointed toward the door.

"We'll want that closed, I think," she said, and he hurried to shut it. Then he approached the bed with short, uncertain steps, his path a coy semicircle between the door and the edge of the bed, where he finally sat. She pushed herself up to lean her back against the headboard.

He wore a white shirt with a starched collar, no tie, a pair of black duck pants held up by suspenders, and a new bowler hat.

"I'm Jacqueline," she said.

"I know."

"You can lay your hat there on the chair if you'd like."

He could not stretch far enough, so he had to leave the bed to put his hat away. When he sat down again, he was close enough to her that his left hand rested on hers.

"You smell so nice," he said.

"So do you, Ralph."

"They made me wear witch hazel. The boys, I mean. And a dab of peppermint, too."

"I like it," she said. "It's very fresh."

He swallowed.

"You are beautiful," he said.

"Your hand is shaking," she said.

"I am a mite nervous. I never seen anybody so beautiful as you, Jacqueline."

She moved closer to him.

"Nothing to be nervous about," she said. She raised her free hand and touched his cheekbone. So much like boys, she thought. They are just big boys.

"That collar seems terribly tight. Does it chafe your neck?"

"It is rasping a bit. It ain't mine. I took the loan of it, and the other chap's neck was even thinner'n mine, maybe."

She tucked her legs beneath her, knelt forward.

"Let me see if I can puzzle it out," she said, and he grinned as she twisted the stays. She let her breasts brush against his arm, and she saw his chest swell with a deep breath.

"Got it," she said. She drew back and held the collar out for him to take. He looked at her and let his eyes wander from her face down to the gown for the first time. He was reaching out to her, his hands nearly girdling her waist when he put them there. He was leaning forward, burying his face in the curve of her neck, the smells of peppermint and witch hazel and lye soap strong in her nose.

Her eyes were open. She watched the candlelight dancing on the wall while he pressed against her.

"Ralph Burwood, be good to me," she said.

Jenny had opened the front door once Ralph had gone into Elizabeth's room. He had been followed up from camp by several dozen miners who had thumped him on the back and joked with him as he loped with long steps up the hill. Now they were laughing and stealing furtive looks at the closed door.

"This is practic'ly a wedding night!" one of them yelled. "That means a shivaree! We'll gather up pots and pans and any sort of music maker we can find. Them that can spare the powder and caps will serenade 'em that way."

Jenny stopped them as they moved toward the door. She stood in front of them and stopped them with a terrible hard stare.

"None of that. No damn shivaree," she said. "This ain't an occasion for celebration."

CHAPTER TWENTY-TWO

They came into his camp while he was still sleeping (though three hours had passed since first light; he had been up late) and pulled him from his bedroll. He fought against them at first, but when one of them jerked a knee into his groin and another brought a fist down on his nose, he stopped struggling and sagged, limp weight in grasping hands. They dragged him to his feet. He saw then that it was not just two or three of them, but twenty, thirty, maybe more. He was in their midst, and when they moved, he moved, punched and pummeled, stumbling, feeling hot blood on his lips and tasting it where it seeped into his mouth. They moved and he moved with them away from camp and up the side of a knoll. Halfway up they stopped and parted in front of him. There was a body face down on the matted grass, with the hilt of a knife marking center of a dark splotch on the shirt. Then he saw sandy hair and he knew that it was Buck lying there. He heard shouts, accusing tones. Hands on his back propelled him forward. Someone snatched at his collar and grabbed a fistful of it and dragged him to his knees so that the hilt of the knife was in his eyes. Look at the handle, somebody was shouting. The handle, you murdering bastard. He saw the monogram "EW" at the base of the handle, and then he knew that they were going to hang him.

They are going to kill me, Joshua thought. They are going to kill me and they don't even know my true name. In five minutes, maybe less, I am a dead man.

There were low black clouds on the horizon, and a rumble of thunder from that direction. A death knell, he thought. Queer that we should have a lightning storm so early in the season. Today is the third, no, fourth of June. June 4, 1863. Don't suppose they will put it on any tombstone. A white light slashed down through the clouds. Rain thumped, large lonely drops, into the ground. He felt one drop spatter on his head. The mob re-formed around him and began to move once more up the hill. Between moving, bobbing heads he saw two men standing at the top of the hill beside the hoisting frame of what he knew was an abandoned mine. One of the men was slinging a rope and a noose over the top of the frame, and the other was pulling loose the boards that had been nailed across the mouth of the shaft.

His mind fought against the idea. This is '63. They don't do this in the camps any more. In '49 they would slip the noose over your neck and make you stand on a single board over the shaft and then kick that board loose, but they don't do that any more. There are courts. There are judges and juries. They don't do this any more.

Joshua had come to California with enough stake to buy a horse and a secondhand faro outfit in Sacramento. He traveled the camps as tourist and itinerant gambler. His winnings were steady but small, because the gold went into company treasuries now, not into prospectors' pouches as it had in '49. The prospectors had left or had become wage producers. Joshua stayed one night or two in a mining town, never winning so much that he would be unwelcome the next time, then wandering down the road to the next place, the horse ambling along trails that were thick with mud in the winter and so dry in the summer that dust rose in lazy plumes from the animal's hooves. There were oak trees and manzanita and heavy-scented bay leaves and grass that was green in the spring when it first sprouted alive but long and dry and yellow in the summer.

He met Buck that first winter in a town called Hornitos.

He went into a saloon there to open a faro snap and found this towheaded kid with a farm boy's broad shoulders dealing a game there already. The kid wore a black clawtail coat made for somebody four inches and twenty pounds smaller. The coat had the initials "EW" embroidered over one breast, and the same initials were on the faro layout and on all the checks and on the dealing box. The layout was the finest that Joshua had ever seen, and the kid was the worst dealer he had ever known. He fumbled with the cue box, spilled checks from the rack, paid winners slowly, and was even slower collecting his own winnings from the layout. And he had the grit to be cheating. Joshua figured him for a two-card box with two tell-cards, and when he figured out which were the tell-cards he took the kid for eighty dollars. That was thirty more than the kid had when he had bought back all the checks, so Joshua told him that he would take the faro outfit instead. The kid's eyes grew big and moist, and Joshua found it impossible to imagine this boy a competitor. But he would make a fine shill, Joshua thought, so he followed a hunch and took him on as a partner.

Joshua threw away the tell-box and taught Buck to use rough-and-smooths instead, treating the backs and faces of some cards with carbolic acid and rubbing sperm-candle drippings on others. That was a lot less risky than a tell-box. He used the kid in three-card monte, too, where a shill made things so much easier because he seemed to be cheating Joshua by turning up one corner of the winning ace. That appealed to the greedy ones in the crowd, and they never blamed Buck, not Buck with his open face and easy dumb grin, when the card with a turned-up corner became a losing jack instead of the ace. Buck was not the smartest sharper Joshua had ever known, but that face was priceless.

They traveled together more than a year. Joshua kept their winnings in a Bible with a clasp. He had cut a hole in the middle of the pages and stored their gambling stake there. They were robbed three times on the trail, but the thugs got only pocket money, never stopping to unlock the clasp on the Bible. In June of '63 they heard of a strike in a place east of Volcanoville, high in the foothills where the green slopes edge into the granite of the high mountains. The place was being called Johnny's Gulch. In a region of abandoned quartz mines, some Chinese had been working gravel that had been worked a dozen times in as many years, and they found placer gold that everyone else had missed. This was accepted truth: Chinamen will work ground that a white man won't piss on. Once in a while Johnny finds pay dirt, and when that happens he gets booted downriver unless he can keep it a secret long enough to get the gold out and disappear.

The strike, as the occasional strikes did, aroused latent faith and optimism beyond all reason. Men laid down their carpenter's tools and plows and made for the place called Johnny's Gulch. Since Buck and Joshua were two days' ride distant, they went there too. Buck was a believer. They had sat beside a campfire the night before they were to ride separately into the gulch and the camp that had strung up at the diggings, and Buck had talked of hitting the big money this time, because this one had the smell of a big strike and the gold would be tossed around like ripe apples in an orchard, with so much of it around. That was foolish, of course. Joshua and Buck were going to get their share, but even if they took every ounce that every miner eked out of the gravel, Joshua told him, they still would not have enough to call themselves rich men. After a year and some months in California, Joshua wanted to leave, to travel across the mountains to the Washoe district. Now, you could find money there. If he could carve a slice out of that, Joshua knew, then he could go back to Boston the way he had always dreamed. Buck was against the idea, because they knew California and knew nothing about Nevada, and there was a lot to be said in this job for knowing your territory and feeling a part of it. But when Buck left the camp the next morning to ride ahead into the diggings, Joshua resolved that they would have to talk some more of this. Nevada seemed the next likely spot for him; he could die a poor man, an old man, if he stayed in California.

Because the clothes fitted him and because he was the

far better sharper, Joshua wore the "EW" coat and used the opulent faro layout marked with the initials. Buck had bought the outfit from a hotelkeeper who had seized it for nonpayment of room and board. Now Joshua had taken the outfit, except for a pearl-handled derringer pistol and a stiletto knife that both bore the monogram. Joshua had never worn a weapon, having decided that he would surely be less adept with them than any man he might face. Because Buck coveted them so, and promised to keep them well hidden, Joshua let him keep the knife and the pistol. Buck was a good kid, and Joshua liked to indulge him when he could.

They had had a good first night in Johnny's Gulch. There had been enough gold to sustain the foolish optimist for a few days. The prospectors were pretending that it was '49 again, and to make it all real they had tossed down bullion instead of cash, and they had laughed when a turn of the card cost them what would have been a week's wages if they had not quit their daily jobs to come to this place. As usual, Buck had come away with most of the money. He was supposed to be a shill, after all, and it looked better to have the gambler come out a loser. Buck had left around midnight, and Joshua had folded the snap a few minutes later. In the morning they would leave separately and meet a few miles down the trail.

But now Buck had a knife in his back, and the emblem on the handle was the same one Joshua wore on his own coat. They were going to hang him without a trial—determined to make this '49 again in every way—and he could say nothing because the truth would sound like the most absurd lie. They were pushing him to the top of the hill. The hoisting frame sat atop a stone base, and they had to boost him up on its edge to get him there. A man was standing there braced against one of the uprights, noose in one hand. He reached for Joshua's head, grabbed his hair, and pulled the head down so that he could slip the noose over his neck. It was rough sisal and it chafed against the skin of Joshua's throat when the man shoved the knot against Joshua's esophagus and pulled the rope snug. The sun was gone now, covered by dark clouds that cast a twilight pall

on the faces of the men as Joshua looked down at them.
Lightning split the sky again, and the report was immediate, shaking the stone base of the hoisting works. There
was a plank across the mouth of the shaft, and the hang-
man pushed Joshua out on it, out over the darkness beneath
him. He had fastened one end of the rope to the crosspiece of the frame, making sure to give Joshua a few feet
of falling slack before it would come taut under his plum-
meting weight. Joshua sucked in desperate breaths. He
wondered: How many heartbeats do I have left? Three?
Four? Oh, feel the breaths. Feel the chest rising and falling.
You have never felt that so plainly before, but feel it now,
feel it. The plank sagged under his weight. He closed his
eyes and opened them again, looking beyond the upturned
faces of the mob to the hills across the gulch where the
storm clouds roiled black and angry. This is the last sight
I will ever see, he thought. There was a buzzing in his ears,
growing louder. He shut his eyes. He felt the plank rocking
beneath him. He fought for his balance. The insane buzzing
became louder as one foot slipped. He was falling, falling
into the blackness, with a roaring in his ears.

CHAPTER TWENTY-THREE

There was a small upright organ in the parlor of Adele's house that never wheezed a note but on Christmas Eve. This year it was a girl named Emily who sat at the keyboard and picked her way through "Adeste Fideles," while two others sat beside her on the bench and tried to remember the words.

"A hell of a commotion," said Adrienne. "My head hurts already, and that ain't helping."

She was drinking rye whiskey, pouring it into a tumbler and drinking it hard. Jenny and Liz sat beside her, drinking the rye with water. The door was closed tonight and they could drink liquor if they chose. It was a good Christmas Eve: nearly nine o'clock and not one of them had cried yet. Adrienne leaned back on the upholstered couch where the three of them sat. She was a big woman with heavy hips and heavy shoulders, and the couch groaned when she gave it her weight.

"I hate this goddamn night," she said. "I would rather get plugged by two whole platoons of drunken Irishmen than sit through another Christmas Eve."

One of the singers at the piano turned to frown at her.

"Your tongue," she said.

"Look at this, the Virgin Mother over there. One night a

year we got a bunch of goddamn saints in this place. My tongue? Look to yours. At least I use mine for talking once in a while."

"We have gifts, you know," Jenny said. "Why don't we open our packages?"

Adele liked her girls to feel the Christmas spirit. Accordingly, she bought a pine-bough wreath each year and instructed the girls to exchange gifts. Each of their names on a slip of paper went into a box, and then they took turns drawing slips. In that way, each girl bought and received one gift. Adele specified that the gifts were to cost between one dollar and one dollar and a half.

Jenny carried the boxes into the parlor and handed one to each girl.

"Liz dear, you first."

Liz's gift was from Martha: a red woolen scarf. Liz, in turn, had picked Emily's name and had bought a white cotton blouse for her. Jenny was opening her package when the brass knocker sounded on the front door.

"Go away!" Adele shouted from the kitchen. She was heating spiced cider. "It's Christmas Eve. Go home to your wife and children, one night at least."

"Men!" Adrienne spat.

"Can we not start in on men right now?" Martha said.

"Yes. Look at that lovely pair of gloves, girls. You picked them, Emily? How lovely. How very beautiful."

When they had all opened the gifts, Adrienne walked to her room with the bottle of rye. Emily sat again at the organ with Nicole, but Martha sat on the couch and put her head in her hands and began to weep. Jenny left her. Better to let her be, tonight anyway. Liz came and stood beside Jenny at the front window. A hard rain splashed outside.

"The quietest night of the year," Jenny said. "Like the world stops for a few hours."

"A bad night."

"Maybe Adele has the right idea with her bottle. Five more minutes and she will be done with Christmas Eve until next year."

"It was hard, the first couple of years," Liz said. She smiled. "But you get used to it after a while. Hell, you can get used to anything."

CHAPTER TWENTY-FOUR

Joshua lay dazed and insentient for a moment in the darkness. Then he tasted blood again and smelled smoldering wood and he knew that he was alive. He put out his right hand to move his body, and it touched fire. He saw then the ember edges of a piece of wood, a chunk from the crosspiece of the hoisting frame, the hanging rope still twisted around it. He raised himself to kneeling and looked above him, and against a patch of gray sky he saw the shattered frame, flames licking at the wood. The noose was tight around his neck. He jerked slack into it, felt the soreness where it had cut into the skin, pulled the loop over his head. He rose to his feet, took a step and then two forward. The light from the hole above him cast an uncertain glow a few feet in diameter, but when he moved beyond that he was in blackness. He had his arms extended in front of him. His hands touched solid rock, and he edged slowly to his right until the rock stopped. He moved forward again, tentatively, but his hands met no resistance. He heard shouts from above the shaft. Bent into a crouch, he stumbled into the blackness with his arms out to cushion any impact, his shoulders roughly brushing the sides of the tunnel when he veered from a straight path.

Above him, the mob was stunned for a few seconds by the electrical charge that had splintered the hoisting frame with a white flash and an awesome thunderclap. The sight and the sound of it had shocked them backward, collapsing, those closest to the explosion falling with burned faces, crisped brows, moustaches and beards singed at the edges. Those farthest from the shaft were the first to recover, to realize that the frame was gone and Joshua had fallen. They ran to the shaft and looked down into the darkness. Someone went running for another rope. They would lower a volunteer to the bottom of the shaft to investigate. Then other parties broke off and ran to find the mine's exits, if there were any. Others, feeling their burns for the first time, went to find cold water, and the rest milled about the shaft, reluctant to leave so quickly, still charged by the residue of the excitement.

Joshua ran for several minutes, until he saw splotches of light at the end of the tunnel. He drew closer and saw that these filtered through thick brush that had grown over the entrance. He rested. He drew short, furious breaths that did not satisfy his lungs. His shoulders were sore from banging against the walls of the tunnel, his neck hurt from the rope, his face hurt from the punch that had subdued him when he struggled against the mob. The floor of the tunnel had been wet and muddy, for the most part, but his feet were still cut by sharp protruding edges of rock.

He knew that he had to move, had to be away from the tunnel. The mob would be looking for him, perhaps even now coming down the shaft after him, with torches to light the way. Still, he could not run far, half naked and hurt as he was. He needed clothes and boots.

He parted the bushes at the mouth of the tunnel and crawled out to the light, and saw that he was alone. He could not see the camp, but the high mountains were ahead of him, to the east. He was sure that he ought to be leaving the tunnel, though he craved the shelter of the brush. He had decided to sprint from the brush into a stand of pine trees across from the tunnel's entrance when he heard boots scraping on gravel. He tensed and waited, and in a few seconds a miner came into sight, walking a path that would bring him just a few yards below where Joshua crouched.

There was a fist-sized rock within arm's reach. Joshua picked it up and felt its solid weight in his right hand. He waited. The man sauntered toward him. Later Joshua would marvel at the detachment and cold purpose and feral savagery that he was able to summon as he waited for the man to pass him and then leaped from the bushes, the right arm swinging around and down, the rock smashing into the back of the skull just as the stranger was beginning a reflexive turn toward the sound of Joshua's springing from the brush. The man crumpled. He lay still. Joshua stood over him with the rock ready and waited for him to move again. When he did not, Joshua grabbed the body around the armpits and dragged it behind the bushes. The man moaned softly. Joshua tore off his own shirt, unbuttoned the stranger's, and slipped into it. The man was Joshua's size and weight, so the fit was good. Joshua took the man's pants. His own feet were smaller than his victim's, but the boots were tolerable.

Then Joshua knew that he had to run. If this man did not die, he would struggle back to camp or be found soon and they would be after him. He thought: I can't count on a lightning bolt twice in one morning. If I stay here they will find me. Probably they will have word out in the district that a killer is loose. But the mountains are to the east. I have the high mountains and the lonely ridges ahead of me. I can hide. And Washoe is on the other side. There is big money in Washoe.

He loped into the closest stand of trees. His legs felt strong, his mind never more active and alert. He imagined a band of pursuers behind him, closing in on him, and he ran even faster. He could not remember the last time he had run like this, but now the long strides and the rhythmic motion of the arms seemed only natural to him. When he had run nearly a half mile, to the top of a wooded ridge, he stopped. He climbed atop a large granite boulder, and from that perch he could see the open spaces and the brush that marked the tunnel's entrance. He saw the stranger that he had surprised, stumbling out of the bushes and across a clearing, toward the camp. That made Joshua jump down from the rock and run some more.

For hours, into the afternoon, he made his way eastward. Much of his progress was uphill, and through manzanita that grew so thick it left only narrow passages beneath the high limbs. Joshua had to bend down on hands and knees to crawl for hundreds of yards through the maze left by the vegetation, but this gave him security. They would need a mircle to find me here, he thought. He had put miles between himself and the camp, and he would be safe so long as he stayed away from the main roads, where he might be recognized. The mountains were both goal and barrier. They might be difficult to cross, but on the other side he would be safe. He was sure of that. The mountains were a wall between two worlds.

The rain had fallen through the day, but being wet was no problem as long as he stayed moving. By evening, though, his legs were tight and rebellious, so he had to rest. He had found an old Miwok trail that followed the tops of lateral ridges, above the arroyos where the brush grew so thick, and when the trail brought him past a granite ledge with a low overhang, he decided to stop for the evening. He felt safe. They could never trail him here, and he had not seen human signs since he had left the camp. Somewhere north of him was the road from Placerville to the south end of Lake Tahoe, and somewhere south the road from Jackson to the Carson Valley. But either one could be twenty miles distant. He was alone. The gray granite peaks of the Sierras were straight ahead of him now, easily visible from the ridge. On the highest of them he saw streaks of snow left over from the spring melt, the last glow of the setting sun tinting them salmon. I will be there tomorrow, he thought. Nobody will touch me there.

The coming of night brought a wind, and he was cold under the wet clothes. He searched around the rock for tinder and firewood, gathered an armful of damp sticks, and found pine needles that had stayed dry in a corner protected by the overhanging rock. There was a package of lucifers in the pocket of the pants, so he used the pine needles for fire starter. The wet wood smoked and popped and sputtered, but he huddled close to it while the rain came down. The water dripped down off the overhang and into puddles, and he moved as close as he could to the bosom of the rock. He curled around the dying fire and slept an unsatisfying sleep, his body a sodden prize in a struggle between soporific exhaustion and teasing, tormenting cold. He realized at one point during the night that the water no longer dripped into puddles, and he thought, that at least is a blessing. But when he woke at dawn, his teeth chattering, he rolled over and saw that the rain had turned to snow during the night.

The flakes were wet and large, some of them the size of two-bit pieces, some of them in even larger clumps, which rocked gently and without haste as they fell, like dry maple leaves, so large that Joshua imagined for a moment that he could hear the sound of their hitting the ground, the only break in an otherwise total silence. They melted quickly on the damp ground, but there was an ominous purposefulness to these flakes, their size and the quantity. They were thick enough to obscure vision beyond a few hundred yards, but still Joshua thought he could see the outlines of the next line of hills. They seemed to be covered with white, and he was frightened.

He thought: You have three ways to go and you have to choose one of them now. You can go back toward where they tried to hang you yesterday morning. You can stay here and get cold and hungry. You can head east to where you really want to be.

He decided that June was too late for a bad storm, that what lay ahead could not be much more rigorous than what he faced now, so he rose and made tracks toward the suffused glare in the gray clouds that marked the rising sun. He climbed higher, the ascent more obvious now, for he had left behind the foothills and was clambering up the steeper approach slopes. Gone were the manzanita and the buckbrush that had impeded him the day before. Gone, too, were the thick stands of pine. The trees now were wider spaced, and larger, the trunks of some so large that no two men together could encircle them with their arms. The footing was thick-grained granitic sand, into which his feet sank to the ankles, and when he climbed the steeper hills he slid backward two steps for every three he put forward. By mid-morning the snow was six inches deep, and the flakes, though smaller, were even more plentiful than they had been before. Joshua's lungs were struggling for air, and when he sucked it in, it was cold and the back of his throat felt raw from it. His pants were wet as high as the knees, and the dampness had long since soaked through the seams of the boots. His limbs were stiff from exertion the day before, and he was more than hungry; he had not eaten since dinner two days earlier.

One by one his mind registered these discomforts, and catalogued them, and ignored them. Around midday he dragged himself up the side of a coarse-surfaced boulder, the facets of the mica and quartz gleaming wet, and he saw above the treetops the angular peaks of the high mountains, so close now that it seemed to him he could reach out and take hold of their chiseled knife-edged sides. They were white with snow. He slid off the boulder and down a ridge, then across a narrow valley and up the steepest hillside yet, up toward the peaks. He chose what seemed to be a gap in the fortress walls and scrambled up toward it. The snow reached to his knees in spots now, but his feet were touching loose scree that shifted beneath his weight. He twisted his right ankle when the foot came down awkwardly on a large stone beneath the snow. He kicked his boots straight into the snow so that they would not slip beneath him, and he put hand over hand to reach the top. And when he had reached the top of the saddle between two peaks, he stopped, his feet wet and numb from the cold.

He had expected a downhill slide from here, straight down from the crest and into the Nevada valley. Instead, he looked out over what resembled nothing more than a far-stretching wind-whipped sea of granite. But he did not look back. He plunged down the slope, sliding on the snow, then trudged on toward the next gap in the series of peaks and ridges. The wind blew harder, and instead of wafting down gently, it streaked horizontally with the gusts, and stung his face. Now he was truly cold. He pushed forward, but held his arms close to his chest as he walked. He could no longer feel toes or fingers. His face burned from the wind and the snow. The wind ended for a moment, but that was worse than before, because he was able to see more clearly the snowfields that lay before him. Then, for the second time in two days, he knew that he was going to die. He did not stop walking, to let the cold take him, because stopping would have required more of an effort than mechanically pushing ahead, one step after another. But he knew that he would fall short of his goal. The storm and the mountains are too much for me, he thought. They are too strong and powerful, and I am too weak. One of these steps will be the last I have in me. Then it will be finished, and the mountains will have won.

His mind seemed bored with the cold and the pain now. He found himself thinking of the house on Beacon Hill, and of the fires that always blazed in the hearths, and of warm afternoons on the Common. The cold and the snow did not exist any longer. He was, in fact, hot, uncomfortably hot. He felt sweat on his forehead, and reached up the back of an arm to wipe it away. Hot. So hot he could barely breathe, oppressively Boston-muggy hot. He had to shed his shirt. Nobody around to be offended. And he was hot, so hot. The trousers, too. They would have to go. He was simply too hot. Then the underclothes, and then the boots. That was a little better.

He was on a steep downslope now. His clothes marked his path of descent, arrayed behind him. He could see the valley, the valley green because the storms were not cold enough to bring snow to these lower elevations. He could see the valley, and he stumbled forward, but the snow was still too deep up here. He fell forward on his face. That felt good. That was cool on this day of impossible heat. He was naked. He reached forward and dug a hand into the snow to pull himself forward, forward and down to the green valley. But he had no strength to spend except to keep his chest heaving, the lungs working. He was losing consciousness when he heard voices behind him. He could not understand the words, and he did not have the strength to turn and look at the bodies that went with the voices. He was tired. He wanted to sleep. He was quite unhappy with them, the way they treated him so roughly, hauling him up when all he really wanted was to lie on the cool white bed and sleep.

CHAPTER TWENTY-FIVE

"Mushege!"

Mouse spat out the word: Crazy savage. They were no longer White Faces to him now, but savages, totally erratic and unwhole. They were capable of any atrocity against nature, any folly against true humanness. And, as if to prove his belief, here was this one, naked and face down in the snow.

His first impulse was to let the idiot die there. Then a softer voice inside him reasoned that he would not let any other helpless animal freeze to death, so he and two of the other men of his bunch skittered down from where they watched high on the ridge and they picked him out of the snow. The strongest of them slung the body over his shoulders and carried him down to the dwellings where the bunch was making its winter camp.

The women cooked a broth of powdered dried rabbit meat. When the stock had been poured into a drinking basket (the weave so tight that it held water without a coating of pitch), one of the women used wooden tongs to reach into the burning fire and extract hot stones, which warmed the liquid when they were dropped into the basket. The women tilted back his head and forced him to drink. The soup was nutritious, and the basket had power symbols woven into the pattern with black-stained reeds. (The crazy savage needed all the help he could get.)

He was incoherent for two days, and the skin of his hands and feet peeled away to red during that time. The Washo fed him for a week and cared for him and kept him warm in their blankets. He tried to speak to them after a while, and when they did not answer, he watched them with uncomprehending eyes. The first time he stood up and hobbled outdoors to crap, Mouse knew that the savage was healthy enough, so he sent one of the youngsters down into the valley to find someone to bring him down to the whites.

Joshua was bundled up in a rabbitskin robe when the new Indian crawled through the door of the dwelling. This one was dressed differently from the rest. He was wearing white man's clothes, not in piecemeal fashion, like most, but a full wardrobe. He squatted in the entrance and said nothing, only stared at Joshua. He rocked gently on the balls of his feet. His body blocked out the sunlight that came through the crawl space, so Joshua's eyes had to adjust to the new darkness. When they had, Joshua saw a wide, self-confident grin on the visitor's face. Then the Indian spoke:

"Christ's sakes alive, boy, you had yourself a close one there. And you get found by Injuns that would as soon kick your ass into the nearest lions' den as help you the way they did. You are a lucky man. You don't dabble in games of fortune, do you? 'Cause if you do, I would stay away from them for a few years. I reckon you have used up about a lifetime's ration of good luck just by being here."

When the boy came down from the hills with news about the sick white, Jim threw clothes and boots into a sack and saddled two horses and rode to Mouse's winter camp. He had his reasons. It did not hurt to ingratiate himself with the whites. This one might be a bum, but he might also be a wealthy and grateful man, so the clothes and the boots and the effort of bringing him down to the valley were just a minimal investment. When he saw the man lying there with his raw feet and hands, Jim knew that he needed caring yet, so he decided at that moment to expend a little more. When they had ridden down to the valley, to the town called Genoa, where he lived now, Jim brought Joshua into his cabin, gave him his bed, and found food for him. Jim was a town dweller now, having used some of his money from Longstreet to buy a lot and build a home, and this gesture of friendship toward a white man could only earn him the admiration of his neighbors.

For two days Joshua accepted the generosity without a word, except mumbled thanks with each meal. The morning of the third day he was eating porridge and watching Jim try on a new hat. It was wide and stiff of brim, with a high crown. Jim had lifted it out of a red hatbox and set it experimentally on his head. He was examining it in a mirror, cocking his head at various angles with one pose after another, when Joshua spoke.

"Who the hell are you, anyway?"

Jim turned.

"I was wondering when you would regain the use of your vocal apparatus, pard. The name is Jim, designation captain. I am a Washo Indian."

"I never saw an Indian like you. Granted, I have never been on speaking terms with many, but I never heard an Indian talk the way you do, either."

"I am a prodigy."

"You'll get no dispute from me. For an Indian, you're doing well for yourself."

Jim's tone became sharper.

"For almost anybody I am doing well, pard. I have money in an account in the bank down the street. I own six horses, which is at least five more than any Washo or most of the pitiful emigrants that pass this way. I can wear a different shirt every day for two weeks. Used to be that I was a performer, but now I am a broker. Farm labor a specialty. Also, I supply fresh fish to the restaurants here and in Virginia, caught by my Washo with hooks instead of the spears they used to use, so that the appearance of the meal is not spoilt. I negotiate contracts between your people and mine, as when an express company wishes to put a station on a meadow that is a favorite of the Washo. There was a time when the company would simply take the land, but now I have got those grabby folks into the habit of coming to me first so that I can negotiate a settlement. I don't get much money out of 'em, maybe, but it is more than the Washo would have got a few years back, which is nothing."

"And you take a percentage."

"That is my job."

"I'll tell you straight out that I can't pay you for what you've done for me."

"Not a dime?"

"That is ten cents more than I have. If you are unhappy and want to toss me out, I'm ready to go."

"No," Jim said. "You stay. You'll be stronger in a couple more days. I had my hopes, I admit. You could have been John Jacob Astor. But you weren't, and there's no changing that."

"I'll give you something later. Once I've established myself."

"What do you do?"

"I'm a gambler. A sharper, too. There must be fifty clubs in Virginia, and I know one of them will be able to use a good man on the dealing box."

"Maybe."

"I'll pay you then. If things go well, maybe one day I can be generous."

Jim turned back to the mirror and adjusted the hat to a rakish angle.

"You intend to make a big killing, I suppose."

"I do, as a matter of fact. Something wrong with that?"

Jim studied the image in the mirror.

"I just hope that you are different from every other young blackleg that comes into that town expecting to walk out with his pockets full of Comstock silver."

Joshua did not answer. Jim put his back to the mirror, put the hat carefully on a table, and looked again at Joshua.

"Let me tell you about that silver. I don't know that it will last, pard. Some say it is endless and others disagree, but regardless of that, it is fabulous anyway. They ship it out of the mills in express wagons, every day, at least one wagon loaded to busting with pure silver, and a few pounds of gold every now and then just for variety's sake. That kind of money, it draws hungry men the way stinking meat draws vultures. Every one of them figures there is so much of it around that they can get rich and nobody will notice that they have taken a bit more than their share. They figure to do it with the cards, the cards being the obvious way. But it doesn't work that easy. Me, I nibble at the edges, pard. I try not to get in anybody's path. You might say I work the tailings, but in this country even the tailings are a good enough living. Being Injun, I figure the big gouging is out of the question for me. I have to know my limits. But if I was white, and I was hungry for a big slice of what is coming up out of the mines, I wouldn't do it with the cards. Not right off, anyway.

"What I would do is, I would learn those mines. I would know as much about 'em as any man in the town. I would learn about the rock and the ledges and the leads. This is the way I figure—without them mines there wouldn't be any Virginia City. To try to become a rich man in Virginia by playing cards would be like drinking water from a mudhole when there was a clear spring a few feet away. That is what I think, pard."

Three days later a couple of Washo came to Jim's door with a wooden crate that had holes bored in the top. Inside the crate was a badger that they had captured that morning. The animal grunted and snuffled and scraped its claws against the sides of the crate. Jim paid the Washo ten dollars for the badger, and when he told them that he would pay two more for a stray dog, they left and returned about an hour later with a skinny, wide-eyed, terrier-muzzled brindle on the end of a rope.

The next morning Jim and Joshua rode the ten miles into Carson City, with the badger in its crate strapped to the empty saddle of a third horse and the dog trotting at the end of a lead. When they had climbed a hill and were looking down on the town, Jim jumped down from his horse. He walked to the dog and pulled a corked bottle from one pocket. He splashed liquid from the bottle onto the dog's coat. Then he gave Joshua five dollars and told him to ride

BIRTHRIGHT   227

ahead into town, have lunch, and then go to a street corner
on the east side of town in the afternoon. There would be a
badger fight there, in a pen. Joshua was to bring the dog
and pay three dollars' admission for the fight, and when four
or five dogs had been whipped by the badger he was to insist
that his be given a chance.

Carson City was small and dusty, set in a three-sided basin
of sagebrush and brown earth and boulders. When he had
eaten a saloon lunch on the main street, Joshua walked east
four blocks. On one corner there was a corral, and at one end
of the corral a chest-high solid wooden fence that enclosed
a circular area perhaps thirty feet in diameter. At the gate
of the corral a man was collecting money from everyone who
passed through. Joshua paid him three dollars and joined
the crowd that was filling around the wooden fence.

Inside the pen was the badger crate. Joshua heard the
animal clawing at the wood. Around him the men sucked at
whiskey bottles and speculated about the size and tempera-
ment of the badger and joked about the last baiting contest
they had seen. Dog and badger had fastened their jaws into
each other and had died that way. There had been fistfights
among the bettors over which animal had expired first.
Joshua had been standing at the fence nearly a half hour
when some of the men began to yell at the cash taker at
the gate, and when more of them yelled, louder, the man left
the gate, went into a shed, and came out holding a hammer.
He opened a door in the high wooden fence, walked to the
crate, and stood with one foot resting on it. He spoke:

"Bill Williams says that mangy coyote he calls a dog is
recovered from the scrap last month, so it will be first into
the pen. So as to give you boys a good show, I will do as
usual, just knock one side off the box and let the dog try
to draw the badger into the open."

He lifted the hammer and struck twice at the board that
made up one narrow side of the rectangular crate. On the
second blow the board pried loose from the rest of the crate,
and a third swing broke it loose completely. The man
stepped back, away from the open end of the crate, then
vaulted the fence. The door of the pen opened wide enough
to admit a shaggy, barrel-chested dog with one ear erect, the

other torn and ragged. The dog walked stiffly into the pen, with a limp at a hind leg, hackles raised, staring into the open crate. It walked a semicircle around the crate, wheeled, and crossed in front of it again in a circling path that brought it a few feet closer. It did this once more, but when it passed before the crate the fourth time, the dog raised itself on rigid legs, yapped twice, and began a stunting dance, a series of hops back and forth that gradually brought it closer to the open end of the crate.

There was a sweet stink from the pen now, the badger's musk. The men whooped and threw down money for bets without moving their eyes from the dog and the crate. Three to one that he drags it out. Ten to one that he finishes it in five minutes. The dog hopped close enough to stick a nose into the crate. It jumped back, hopped forward again in a crouch that put its head into the crate. It jumped back and then forward again, and this time the head stayed, the crate sliding in the dust as the dog jerked and pulled at the animal inside. There was muffled growling for a few seconds, followed by the dog's whining, then a yelp as it pulled away, blood streaming from a long deep cut that showed the animal's white skull.

The second dog in the ring was a skinny-haunched black-and-white mongrel, which died in the ring from a slashed neck. The third, a pit bull, dove into the crate and pulled the badger out, and died doing it when the badger fastened teeth on a back leg. Joshua could hear the bones splinter. The dog released its grip and howled, but the badger held and shook and twisted its head until the dog lay still.

With the badger finally exposed, the fourth dog, a Dalmatian, had to be pushed into the ring. And then it stayed against the fence, nervously circling with its tail between its legs, looking alternately at the badger and at its owner, who cursed it from behind the fence. Finally the man, red from shouting and from the taunts of the crowd, drew a pistol and shot the dog in the head.

The badger was spread flat and motionless in the afternoon sun, red streaks on its black-and-white fur. There were dark moist patches in the dust, and some of the men shouted for two dogs, three, to finally get the best of this badger.

Joshua yelled so that his voice would carry around the pen.

"My dog is the match for that miserable creature!" he said. He bent and picked it up, lifted it so that they all could see it.

"That dog is no match for a sage hen."

"This dog is a battler," Joshua said.

"The dog looks like a fighter to me." This was Jim's voice from across the pen. Joshua had not noticed him until now. "She is wiry enough, and she has vinegar in her eyes. I say give the scrawny bitch a chance."

"Who is this red man?" Joshua said.

"Oh, that's Digger Jim. Jim is a square fella, for an Injun."

"I'll back the yellow bitch," Jim said. "I like the build of her. Who'll give me odds that the dog walks out alive and the badger is belly up?"

"Five to one."

"Six, Injun. Six to one."

"Hell, I'll go seven."

Jim bet twenty dollars at seven to one and fifteen more at six. The dog had to be prodded into the pen—at that, Jim immediately got another five-dollar bet, at ten to one—but once the gate was closed, it bared its teeth and growled, feinted twice, and then leaped at the badger. It buried its teeth behind the badger's neck. It snapped once and then twisted its head back to grasp the dog's front shoulder. The animals rolled in the dust, writhed, and held. For about a minute they were still, then rolled and twisted again. One of the men who had bet with Jim yelled at the badger, but the others were quiet, and then he was silent, too, as he watched what had become a single, panting, growling, dust-caked animal in the middle of the pen.

Then the dog let loose its grip, and yelped.

"She's done," somebody said.

The dog rose to its feet, the badger still fastened, and walked a few steps across the pen.

"Hell she is. That badger is dead."

"Can't be. That dog don't bite hard enough."

The door opened.

"Come here, dog. Here, girl."

"She bites hard enough. Oh, yes. This badger is dead. Hanging on, but dead just the same. We'll need a bar to prize it loose from here."

"I never seen such a thing. Dog must a busted its back, is all I can say. You sure that dog ain't poisoned?"

Jim had a hand out at that moment. The first man with whom he had bet was counting out gold coins into his hand. But he stopped when he heard that.

"Poisoned? Why, it do seem odd that the badger should c'lapse in such a fashion. You, mister, you ought to taste that dog. I got a right to ask. You're the owner, you get down and taste that dog."

He was talking to Joshua.

Someone else spoke.

"Now wait. That fella didn't bet on his own dog. It's the Digger here that is tryin' to walk off with all the hard chink."

"Maybe the Injun ought to taste the dog."

"Go on, Injun. Down on your knees. Go down and taste that dog."

Jim walked slowly around the fence until he stood beside the dog. A man was working with a knife to crack the badger's jaws. There was a snap, and the dead animal dropped away.

Jim looked at Joshua.

"This dog is square, ain't she, mister?" he said. "Just tell me that."

"She's square."

Jim bent down over the dog, hesitated, then put his face to the dog's shoulders and stuck out his tongue. He ran his tongue over the dog's dusty coat.

"Get your tongue on there, Jim. I mean I want to see your tongue flat on that hair."

"He is. He's tastin' her, for sure."

"Now down the back and round the belly. Cover her good."

Jim licked at the dog a few seconds more before he looked up to see that the men were satisfied.

"Okay. If there was anything on 'er, it's in you now, I s'pose. A wager is a wager, boys. Jim's skin is red, but the tint of his money is good enough that you all would have taken it fast enough if it was the other way around."

Joshua tied the rope around the neck of the brindle bitch and led it away. It was bleeding, but not badly. Joshua walked west two blocks toward the center of town, expecting that Jim would follow. He waited, and when he did not see Jim, he walked back toward the corral. The others had left. Joshua walked around the corral until he heard a retching noise behind the shed. Jim was there, spitting into the ground. He put two fingers into his mouth, forcing them in until he gagged, and he spat once again.

"The dog was a fighter," Joshua said.

"She was braver than I thought she would be."

"I didn't think she was that strong."

Jim spat again.

"She ain't, by far. It was tincture of arsenic that killed the badger. The dog's coat was full of it. I put it there myself."

"You licked the dog's coat, Jim."

"I was afraid all day somebody would want that dog tasted. But I spat it all out, I think. I tried to save it all up in my mouth without swallowing, and then I spat, first chance. Then I went to the horse trough and rinsed out with water. I got it all, I think. I've done it before, without getting too ill."

"They wanted me to do it, first."

"I'd have spoke up, if nobody else did. If you'd got sick and died, I'd have lost my winnings. This was some day. I'm three hundred up, counting the thirty I got for the badger. Here, you take forty. You got it coming. We'll make up a bill of sale, like I bought the dog from you, and in a couple of days I'll be able to sell her to somebody else. Everybody will know her after this, and I'll get good odds betting against her next time."

He opened the drawstring of a leather pouch and reached inside for four ten-dollar pieces. He gave them to Joshua, then dumped the rest into the open palm of his left hand. They rang against one another as they cascaded out of the bag.

"That is pretty," he said. "That is worth tasting poison for. I've been thinking I could use a nice little buckboard."

He looked up from the coins, into Joshua's eyes.

"In case you ain't realized," he said, "I'll tell you now. I learned the white man's ways real good. For enough of this stuff, I will do about anything."

The coach from Carson brought Joshua into Virginia City that evening. The road led through Silver City—just a suburb, though it was the largest settlement Joshua had seen since Sacramento—then into Gold Hill, bigger yet, built up a steep canyonside without street plans or resort to reason. Each dwelling had a separate staircase that led down to the street; when the rains came, debris and garbage washed down the hillside and into the road, so the Virginia City newspapers called the place Slippery Gulch, and sometimes Slumgullion Alley. The canyon narrowed to nothing at the north end of town, the road going up a hillside and over a saddle. Virginia City was at the other side of the Divide. Before he saw the town, Joshua heard it: thumps and rumbles from the stamp mills, whistles and chuffing from the hoisting whims, a runaway drift of melodeon music, and, as the town itself hove into sight, a bellow of explosion from down in a mine, followed a second later by a pistol shot somewhere along the road. He had heard mining noises in Silver City and Gold Hill, just minutes earlier, but somehow those did not have the concentration and urgency that issued forth here at the top of the Divide. The sound of the city struck him with its purposefulness, but the sight of it astonished him for its audacity. Sun Mountain, known otherwise as Mount Davidson, was high and steep, yet the town not only clung to the hillside like lichen on a rock, but retained a stubborn orderliness of rectangular blocks as it spread itself over the contours of the mountain. The place seemed proud and vain, as though refusing to yield to the exigencies of nature, determined to retain the outward signs of normal urban habitation even if it had been set down in an inhospitable and inconvenient place. Some accommodations had been necessary. Buildings two stories high in the front were four stories in the rear, for the grade was that steep in some places.

The evening crowd was in the streets when Joshua stepped from the coach. Sharps and swells and dirty miners and starched-collar speculators swirled around him. Virginia was coming alive for another night. Joshua got directions to a rooming house off B Street, left his bags in the room, and

walked the streets until midnight. The sidewalks were as
crowded then as they had been five hours earlier. He walked
and let the city's rowdy life fill him. He listened to the jokes
and the rumors of new dips and widening leads in the
mines and the bragging about stock coups. He told himself:
This place knows why it is here. That night he fell asleep
satisfied that he was where he belonged, sure that he had
reached the place of his reckoning.

CHAPTER TWENTY-SIX

They laid Jenny out in a virginal white smock. The other girls had found it in her trousseau, fresh and never worn. They had pulled it over her head to cover her body as she lay in the pine coffin.

Elizabeth Burgess sat beside the coffin from the afternoon of Jenny's death to her burial, two days later. Jenny would not be alone in death. She had been through too much for that.

They had traveled the mining camps together. After a while the camps turned into family towns, and the men who had been so willing before now listened to their wives and made laws against the girls' presence. Fair enough, Jenny said. Nobody ever guaranteed us a place to live. Show me where it is written down, Liz dear, that the men have to give us a place to live.

A couple of years in Sacramento. A couple more in San Francisco, hired as pretty waiter girls in a Barbary Coast dive. Pretty waiter girls wore short shifts without any underwear and had to tolerate and even encourage the groping hands of the sailors and the roustabouts as they served drinks. When they were not waiting tables, the pretty waiter girls sang lewd songs and danced dances in which they always kicked their legs high. And when they were not serving drinks or singing and dancing, the pretty waiter girls were with the sailors in private booths that lined the walls of the hall.

It is not so bad, Jenny told her then. I have seen worse. You just have to make yourself understand that it is somebody else they are touching and laughing at and leering at. That is somebody else, and you are on the outside looking in. You don't feel it a-tall.

Then, in San Francisco, they had vaulted together that big step from the music hall to a parlor house. It was not one of the fanciest, but it had a regular, sober clientele. They worked only six nights a week and ate well most of the time. She made enough money to send Tom to a boarding school and, when he had finished there, to a college run by Jesuit priests in a town called Santa Clara, about sixty miles south. Tom was going to be an engineer. He was going to build bridges.

It was in the parlor house that Jenny met the lawyer who said that he was going to take her away. He was going to marry her and make her a respectable woman. He was in love with her.

Now of course I know better than to set store by such wild promises, Jenny had said, but I think I may buy me some new clothes anyway. Just to be on the safe side. Why, this may all happen. It would be a wild chance, I know, but strange things do occur in this world. 'Course, I ain't banking on it.

A week before this was all to have come about, he came to visit and told her that he had changed his mind. He had found another, he said.

Liz had heard Jenny shout: But you promised. You promised!

And his reply: What is a promise to a lousy whore?

She came out of the room smiling, laughing. That night she drank a bottle of cleaning fluid. She lingered two days before she died, drugged so against the pain with morphine and laudanum that she did not even recognize Elizabeth.

Now Liz sat with her as she lay in her pure white smock, and together they waited for the funeral time.

Damn men, she thought. Damn the life of a whore.

CHAPTER TWENTY-SEVEN

In the tumultuous Tertiary period of the earth's geologic formation, within a minor range of mountains of limited breadth and extent in what is now the western side of the state of Nevada, a fault fissure about four miles long opened on the face of contact between the east face of that range and an overlying wall of igneous rock. Thousands of years passed, and during that time the earth spewed forth great quantities of mineralized water in the form of superheated steam. The steam worked into the cracks of the fissure and cooled, and gradually the minerals were deposited in solid form. During the passage of time the fault slipped and ground the mineral deposits to dust, but that opened new branches of the fault, to be filled with more mineralized steam. Most of what was deposited was common quartz and sulfur compounds, but in places gold and silver were impregnated into the rock, too. The ore grew richer as time passed. Some spots along the fault were barren of what would be precious metals to man, but other portions, thousands of cubic yards in volume and many hundreds of tons in weight, were high-grade ore, and these were scattered randomly—"like plums in a pudding," one man who knew the mines would later describe the setting—above the supporting ledge and within the matrix of igneous rock above

the fault fissure. This rock eroded and exposed outcroppings of gold.

In 1850 a wagon of Mormon emigrants camped beside a
stream that flowed down from the deposits and discovered
traces of gold in the streambed. But the wagon moved on
the next day. That autumn a prospector bound for California
wandered out of camp beside the stream, walked up a
gulch to follow the stream to its source, and dug gold nuggets
out of a hillside with a pocketknife. Word of the discovery
brought some miners to the gulch, though the workings did
not measure up to the pound diggings, sixteen ounces of gold
per day per man, that most prospectors expected to find in
California. At first the placer diggings paid about five dollars
per day, though the ground could be worked only when the
streambed was wet. The workings provided subsistence for
a community of miners for nine years. When earnings
dropped to just two or three dollars per day, many of the
miners drifted away for other areas and left the gulch to a
few who were bound to the place by optimism or by simple
inertia. One of these was James Finney, known as "Old
Virginny" after the state of his birth, who worked high up
the gulch to the head of what became called Gold Canyon.
Where the ravine ended, he climbed to the top of a rise to
work a new location. He took on two partners, Pat Mc-
Laughlin and Peter O'Riley. In the spring of 1859 these two
were digging a water hole about a mile and a half north of
Finney's placer location when they struck a black stratum
sequined with flakes of native gold. They chucked the ore
into their wooden rockers and began taking away gold by
the pound, instead of the fractions of ounces they had been
earning down in the gulch. Henry Comstock, who had mined
for some time in the gulch, learned of the find that evening
and, by dubious claim to the land itself and to the water that
McLaughlin and O'Riley were using to wash the ore, forced
a share of the workings for himself and for a friend, Em-
manuel Penrod. All began to mine the deposit. If there was
a drawback to the operation, it was the nuisance of dealing
with the heavy blue-black substance in which the gold was
found. It sank to the bottom of the rockers and spoiled the
mercury amalgamation process with which the miners col-

lected the gold from the rockers. They cursed the dark stuff and tossed it away for several weeks. As the partners dug deeper, the blue-black ore became heavier and firmer, and had to be pounded and pulverized before it could be worked to extract the gold it contained.

By now the partners had been joined by other prospectors, who had staked claims adjacent to the original. A visitor to the diggings picked up a chunk of the heavy blue ore, brought it to an assay office in Grass Valley, in the California goldfields, and discovered the rock was a rich sulfuret of almost pure silver. This was the stuff that Comstock and the others were throwing away. Three men knew this and pledged to keep it secret until they could travel to the Washoe district to stake a claim of their own. But the word leaked, and the great rush was on.

Comstock, bully and braggart, sold his one-sixth share in the mine for $11,000 on August 12, 1859, and supposed that he had struck a magnificent bargain.

About a month later, McLaughlin sold his share for $3,500. The buyer was a miner from Grass Valley named George Hearst, who had heard the rumor early, borrowed money, and sold his interest in a California placer mine to make the purchase.

Penrod sold his share in November of that year, for $3,000.

O'Riley held out longer than any of the original partners and got $40,000 for his interest. The sum was considered extravagant.

Within a few weeks the mine, named the Ophir, was yielding ore that paid $2,200 per ton. In the next eight years the location would be exploited for 70,700 tons of ore worth $5 million.

Comstock became a merchant in the area, went bankrupt, and committed suicide in 1870, near Bozeman City, Montana.

McLaughlin lost his proceeds and became a cook at a sheep camp.

O'Riley spent his share boring a tunnel through unpromising granite, went insane when the venture was a failure, and died in an asylum.

A camp grew up at the site where Finney had worked the first placer gold claims. This became known as Gold Hill. A similar camp, around the Ophir mine, got the name Virginia Town in 1859, when the resident miners chose to honor Finney.

When the first outcroppings were worked out, the prospectors and mining companies sank shafts into the crumbling earth. In 1860, prospectors discovered two important ore bodies in a line that lay between the Gold Hill claims and the Ophir. These became the Chollar-Potosi and the Gould and Curry. But work on the mines below the 50-foot level—where the ledge of paying ore was as wide as 175 feet—became impossible because of the soft, crumbling rock that was in danger of cave-in whenever the miners enlarged the stope. California miners, working in harder rock, had never faced the problem. It was solved in 1860 by a German engineer named Philipp Deidesheimer, who came to the mines and observed the problem and invented a system of sets of timbers, laid atop and across one another in squares. The square-set principle effectively ended the danger of cave-ins of Virginia City's mines and created a new industry that put millions of board-feet of Sierra Nevada pine into the ground beneath the city.

The town grew up directly above the main ore ledge. From California gold camps came anxious miners and the transient flotsam. At first Virginia was no different from any one of a dozen boom camps in the West. It was sybaritic and lawless except for those unlegislated standards of conduct that were by common consent universally and harshly enforced. It was a beacon and a haven for the shiftless, the greedy, the opportunistic, who connived under the desert sun while other men tore open holes beneath the surface and created caverns by shipping up rock in bucketloads.

What they found down there made the difference for Virginia, and the difference was simply one of quantity. Nobody had ever found this much rich ore in one place before, and there was no doubt that more would be found with the proper expenditure of time and money. Never were a place and a time so perfectly matched as were strutting, spreading, sweating Virginia City and the mid-nineteenth century. The earth held all (the theory went) and waited for man to come and take. There was no limit to what nature provided if man reached out and grabbed hard enough, often enough, with enough vigor. It was all there for the taking, and the only limit to the yield was man's reluctance to commit full effort to the struggle.

CHAPTER TWENTY-EIGHT

His day began at five-thirty. He rose earlier than he needed so that he would not have to stand in line to use the toilet at the end of the hall. His first few nights in the rooming house, he had not slept well. He had been kept awake by the incessant, grating, hacking coughs from one room or another off the hall. Some of the men were tubercular, and almost all suffered in one way or another from chest colds or pneumonia or some other respiratory infection. The worst-afflicted coughed until they spat up blood into their wash-basins, then tossed the clotted mess out the nearest window, so that during a long dry summer the rooming house gradually was surrounded by a ring of dried blood and sputum that became wider and darker until the next rain. The coughing had bothered him at first, but now he paid it no more heed than he did the gunshots he heard at least a couple of times a week down in the street. Living in Virginia City meant these things, and Joshua had promised himself that he would quit the mines before he himself became a rasping Washoe tenor.

When he returned to his room he had time to dress without haste in black cotton trousers and a white shirt. Breakfast in the dining room was ready by six, and after he had eaten he picked up his lunch pail and walked out onto B

Street and down toward the Ophir. The landlady was the widow of a Cornish miner who had died in the Mexican mine two years earlier. This woman had never sent her husband off to the mine without a mid-shift meal, and her boarders got the same consideration. Every evening she baked each of them a meat-and-vegetable pie that she called a pasty and set it out to cool, wrapped in a white linen napkin and placed inside one of the identical tin lunch buckets that she lined up on a table beside the front door. She did this for three shifts of miners every day.

Joshua walked down B, then downhill a block and along C, the main street. The road and the sidewalks were already filling. An ore wagon had stopped in the middle of the intersection at Union and C with a broken rear axle. Other teamsters were shouting at the driver, he was shouting back, and traffic was stopped in all four directions. On the west side of C Street, an auctioneer was chanting the description of a lot of mining stock being sold for payment of delinquent assessments. A background to all the noise was a steady hammering from sites a block to either side of C Street. Virginia City was growing, and the wheezing of saws and the crack of hammers on nailheads were constant in every quarter of the town from first light to sunset. Joshua stopped at a fruit stand and paid a nickel for a pear. The markets put goods out on the sidewalks, and butchers did the same. Slabs of bacon and beef, sausages, and dressed poultry hung from beneath awnings, and flies already were buzzing.

He had fifteen minutes before the start of his seven o'clock shift when he walked through the doors of the hoisting works at the Ophir, and got the full din of the steam engine. The pumps worked constantly to relieve the flooding that had occurred in January, below the three-hundred foot level, when a miner had stuck his pick into a clay seam and a stream of water had poured through. Beside the engine room at the top of the main shaft was the dressing hall. Joshua pulled off his pants and his shirt and hung them on a peg. He tugged himself into a short-sleeved woolen union suit and fastened over it loose cotton trousers (cut off just below the knees) and a shirt of the same material. Shirt and pants were streaked by sweat and dirt and tallow drippings on this

Saturday afternoon. Fresh ones were piled in the middle of the room every Monday morning.

When he had finished he walked toward the shaft and gave his name to the timekeeper. The other miners were beginning to gather at the mouth of the shaft. It was possible to descend into the mine in one of the two big counterbalanced ore buckets that were pulled by the steam whim, but Joshua in his first week of work had noticed that not a single Cornish miner ever rode the bucket. This was supposed to be just superstition, but once already in the six weeks he had been working in the mine, the manila rope pulling one bucket had snapped and the load and bucket had fallen down the shaft. So every day Joshua waited for a chance to climb backward down the ladder that led to the first level of the workings. Then it was through a crawl space on hands and knees to another gallery, and from there down a winze to the third level. Only candles lit the darkness, though the eye grew accustomed to the weak yellow light after a while. In not too many minutes after he had reached the fourth-level gallery, Joshua could again make out details with which he was already familiar: rough-hewn timber sets stacked and butted against one another in a honeycomb that somehow kept the soft rock from falling on their heads, lunch buckets collected in a corner, shovels and newly sharpened picks and steel hand drills laid uniformly against one wall, beside crates of blasting caps and Bickford fuses and drums of black powder. There were iron plates laid on the floor, beginning where the rails of the ore cars ended. These were turnsheets, so that the cars could be moved in any direction, over to the shaft, shunted off to one side, then back to the tracks.

Joshua was a mucker, a common laborer. Occasionally he wrestled the ore cars on the turnsheet, but usually, as today, his job was to shovel together the ore that had been blasted and drilled loose, then to load the rock into an ore car. The first few days in the mine, the work had seemed impossibly difficult. His hands had blistered from the shovel, the blisters had rubbed raw, then had hardened into calluses, and Joshua had wondered whether he would ever be able to handle the cards again. (He waited two weeks and tried; the hands were stiffer than they had been before, but that was no impediment, for the fingertips were still soft and full of feel.) The morning after his first shift he had been tempted not to return. He knew how strenuous the work was, and he was sure that his aching joints and inflamed muscles would never be able to take another eight hours of it. But he remembered what Jim had said, and a day down there in the tunnels and caverns had proved it to him. There was something happening in this place, and the heart of it was below the ground. To know the city you had to know the mines, and trying to coax this place to give up some of its wealth without first learning the mines was like trying to seduce a woman by telegraph. So he had climbed out of bed that morning and walked stiffly to the Ophir and picked up the broad-bladed D-handle shovel to fling the chunks of ore into the heavy car. The next morning was even worse, but the one after that was not as bad. He shoveled harder and faster. And he was becoming accustomed to the subterranean world, the darkness and the dampness, the air that hung dank and heavy in adits and winzes where ventilation had not yet been achieved. He learned to flatten himself against a wall when a car came through, and after raising some bumps on his skull, he learned to bend low enough to miss the overhead timbering of some of the less spacious excavations.

This morning he chose a shovel from the row along the wall of the gallery, and with some of the other muckers who were starting their shifts, he walked down a main drift. The steel rails, polished smooth by the ore cars' wheels, made two parallel receding strips. They reflected the glow of the candles that sat, sputtering lumps, in spike-ended holders that had been driven into timbers at intervals of twenty or thirty feet. This close to the flooded lower levels, the air was damp and musty, a not-unpleasant change from the surface in mid-July. As they walked the miners spoke above the ring of hammers on drills and the thunk of picks into rock faces that came from all sides. They spoke mostly of mines and their investments in them. Almost all of them had bought stock in one or several mining companies. They made four dollars a day, worked every day of every week, and on the first day of each month collected a pay slip that was good for one hundred twenty dollars in cash at the company cashier's office. From this they paid their living expenses, drank and gambled and got roostered on D Street, and found enough left over to buy stock in mines. Some might save enough to buy a share or two in the big producers like the Gould and Curry or the Ophir, but most of them splurged on wildcats located off the main ledge. So when they hefted picks and shovels and began another eight-hour shift, the talk was almost always of good indications and a rich drift and the certainty that this location or another would tap a vein of the main deposit. After three years of tunneling and excavating, there was still debate about the size and shape of the lode and its direction of travel, so a miner found it easy enough to believe the best when he stopped at a brokerage house to buy some shares or to check on the latest quotations before beginning another eight hours of digging somebody else's ore. And in a way, being there in the mine made believing that much easier. These men had seen veins as wide as Market Street in San Francisco, had shoveled tons of ore that paid a dollar a pound. They thought: If here, why not a half mile away?

Two hundred feet down the drift, Joshua and the others turned down a crosscut. They had been excavating here for three weeks and probably would be for some time to come, following a vein that had been four feet wide at its narrowest point and was widening into a sizable horse of ore. It was becoming both wider and higher as they followed it. Now it was as tall as a two-story house and about twenty feet wide, and the foreman had decided that instead of simply following the course of the vein, the company ought to widen the excavation to find the configurations of the deposit. So now they were breasting the stope, using first powder and then picks to break the ore, working mostly from platforms set across the timber sets so that they could attack the top and the upper side of the stope. The previous shift had shot the lower part of the excavation just a few minutes earlier, so now, as Joshua and the others reached the workings at the end of the crosscut, the floor was littered with chunks of rock, and where the blast had been set was a jagged concavity ready for the pick. Joshua used his shovel to brush aside the loose rock from the newly laid rails. When he had finished this he called for an ore car, and when it was trundled into position, he dug the shovel into a mound of rock and hefted his first load of the day. It clanked against the metal sides of the car. A few minutes later the Cornish drillers arrived, followed by a tool nipper, a teenage boy with an armload of sharp drills. There were two drillers and a third man, the shift boss, who carried an oil lantern and held it against the walls of the stope as he slowly paced its circumference. He climbed atop the second series of timbers and again shone the light on the rock face as he edged around the timbering. He grunted for a pick. He took the one that was handed up to him, set the lantern on a timber close to the wall, and gripped the tool near the throat. Deliberately, he swung the pick three times, and each time the tip of it made an indentation in the rock, vaguely describing the corners of an equilateral triangle. The drillers climbed into the timbers, the nipper reached up to lay the drills one by one at their feet on the nearest cross-timber, and then the drilling began. Here, on the upper portion of the stope, they were not restricted by the muck pile, so they had room for double-jacking. One man knelt on the timber, held a drill in both hands, and placed the point on one of the three pick-marks that the shifter had left. The second man stepped close and swung a long-handled maul. The sound chimed in the cavern—as the drill worked into the rock, the sound would be dampened—and then chimed again a second later. The hammer swung pendulumlike, the target the size of a two-bit piece. Fifty beats a minute was the standard, the holder each time twisting the drill slightly while the hammer rocked on the back stroke. After a few minutes the holder flung away the steel drill, gathered up another, inserted it into the hole, so deftly that the hammer did not pause in its motion. Steel rang on steel, the shovels scraped against the floor of the stope and sharp-edged ore, and the men grunted when they lifted an especially heavy load at the end of the shovel. And they talked. The Sacramento and Meredith has hit a rich lead, likely will be paying a dividend this month. The Lady Bryan is letting out a contract for a new tunnel; that is something to watch out for. Did you notice the price on the Overman yesterday afternoon? Got me ten feet of that mine, and may just buy another five when I get up above the grass this afternoon.

A fully loaded ore cart carried about two hundred pounds short of a ton. The muckers in the stope filled six cars while the drillers punched out the holes in the stope face. This was good ore, bringing six hundred dollars a ton. The cars rumbled in and out of the stope, and past them on the main drift, and sometimes several of them were backed up on the turnsheet while the trammers waited to unload them into the giant buckets.

When the three holes had been drilled, the muckers and the drillers left the stope and the shift boss sent in a blasting crew. This would be a carefully done job, the shift boss tamping black powder into the holes with a wooden mallet that would not raise sparks if it struck the rock. Joshua and the rest of the crew were sent to the third level to muck out a new crosscut. They heard the rumble from below them about a half hour later, and a few minutes after that they were back in the stope again, the muck pile from the explosion as large as ever, the air gray with smoke and full of the smell of burned powder. The shift boss marked drill holes again, several of them in a circle around the new concavity, and the drillers came in again, single-jacking this time, each man holding the drill in one hand and swinging a short-handled hammer in the other, the hammer released after impact and swinging back on a leather thong around the wrist.

And the rich rock filled the ore cars, and the cars rolled up to fill the yawning buckets, and the buckets filled the ore wagons, and the wagons wore a grooved path from mine to mill, and the mills spewed forth ingots that had express wagons riding low on their springs as they rolled out of town three times a day.

Joshua worked until the drillers had finished their second round. Then the crew ate lunch while the shift boss prepared the charges. They all picked up their tools, and since the main gallery was shelter from the blast, they stayed there to eat. When they were leaving the stope Joshua picked up a chunk of ore and held it up to a candle stuck on a timber upright. One of the Cornish drillers was passing him, and Joshua turned to get the man's eye.

"What do you think, cousin?" he said. He gestured with the chunk of ore. "Is this pay rock?"

The Cornishmen knew mining, and ore, and would talk freely about either. This one took the rock from Joshua and glanced at it and handed it back.

"'Ee's a bloody hawful rich," he said. "Five 'unnert the ton she pay, hor I hain't a rocker."

The driller walked past. That left Joshua alone in the stope. He slipped the chunk of ore into his shirt, held it there with the pressure of an elbow, walked down the drift and into the gallery. He sat with the others and ate his pasty. When he finished his meal, he bent at the waist as though examining his shoes. His left hand slipped into his waistband. His right brought up the bucket, and then the chunk of ore was in the bucket and Joshua was covering it with the napkin. He put the bucket against the wall and rested on his haunches until the second round of charges in the stope. When the shifter was sure that there had been no misfires, the crew trooped back to the excavation. By the end of the eight-hour shift they had loaded thirty tons of high-grade ore, most of it blown from the upper part of the stope. They had widened the excavation enough that a timbering crew had come in to add two new sets of supports. They had not yet reached country rock, the end of the deposit.

When his shift had ended, Joshua picked up his lunch pail and climbed through the upper levels. He had to shield his eyes against the light when he emerged in the hoisting room. He gave his name to the timekeeper, stripped off the outer clothes and union suit. He washed his face and hands in one of several tubs in the middle of the room, and he put on his trousers and his white shirt. His eyes were still sensitive to the direct afternoon sunlight. He walked up Carson Street to C, and down C Street to the Sazerac. He drank a beer and then walked to the rooming house. With his pail in his hand, he went to his room and stretched out on his bed. He lay there for a few minutes and dozed until he heard footsteps outside. He heard the door across the hall open and then close. That is Mackay, he thought. Time to get my lesson. In the corner of the room was a steamer chest. He walked to it and opened the top. The chest was full of pieces of rock. He took the chunk of ore from the lunch pail, tossed it into the trunk, and closed the lid. Then he left the room and crossed the hall and knocked on the opposite door.

A voice with an Irish accent invited him in. Joshua opened the door.

"It's me, John," Joshua said. "I have a few more questions."

CHAPTER TWENTY-NINE

He had a plan. It had begun working inside him the first day, not so much definite details as a conviction that there was a way it could be done. That was the first essential of a scheme, and he had had it from the first five minutes after he crossed the Divide and entered Virginia City, and sensed the palpable energy and recklessness and optimism of the town. Rules of reason seemed suspended here, and understandably—to behold this place burgeoning in the middle of the desert, on the steep side of one of the world's ugliest heaps of dirt and rock, was to shake loose from logic's firmest hold. Any ordered mind would reel at the sight. If this is possible, the spectacle implied, then there are no impossibilities. Virginia City, dizzy and demented, embraced the notion.

That, at least, was a start. It could be done here, if anyplace. Next he needed details. Working in the mine was fine, but shoveling ore guaranteed only rough hands and a strong back, not an education. Talking to the Cornish miners helped. Then he found John Mackay living across the hall in the rooming house. Mackay was quiet. Mackay was thrifty. Mackay was untouched by the frenetic craziness of the town, seemed undisturbed by the proximity to all the wealth. But mostly, Mackay knew mining. The books he read were not cheap novels, but treatises on geology and chemistry and engineering. Other miners might operate on intuition and experience. They might with some reliability predict the dips and angles and narrowings of a vein. Mackay could do that, it seemed, and better than most. Most important, he could give reasons why these things should occur.

He was a pick-and-shovel laborer who worked the same morning shift as Joshua. Because they lived in the same boardinghouse and kept the same hours, they saw each other often, nodded, spoke a few polite words. One night during supper, one of the boarders was bragging that he had bought delinquent stock in the Pride of Washoe mine. The workings had paid well three years earlier, but when the surface croppings had pinched out the mine was deemed worthless and was abandoned. Now the owners were levying assessments to finance the sinking of a deeper shaft, and the boarder at the dining table had bought stock that had been abandoned by shareholders who refused to provide the capital.

Mackay seemed not to listen as the man spoke. He carefully spooned soup from the bowl into his mouth and kept his eyes on the table. The man's voice was loud. There was a real killing to be made, the man said. Everyone knows that the ledge tilts west toward these diggings, so it is simply a matter of getting a shaft down there deep enough. Problem is that the last superintendent was the cautious type. Surface croppings disappeared and he got the shakes, the crazy old duck. Drew down when he should have pressed his bet. Didn't want to spend the money to get down to where the real ore was to be found.

Mackay blew on a spoonful of soup to cool it and then put the spoon into his mouth.

But now things are different, the man said. We got a boss miner who knows his job, and he is going to go after that ledge. He says we got to get to the three-hundred-foot level, is all. He guarantees we will hit the ledge 'fore then.

That was too much for Mackay. He looked up from the bowl and looked at the man and said softly: "At three hundred you will be well in syenite."

"What's that, mister?"

"At three hundred feet you will find nothing but syenite.

That is the stuff that Sun Mountain is made of, and there is not a dollar's worth of silver in a ton of it. That high up the mountain the footwall is close to the surface, and that is why the croppings worked out so shallow."

"Well, indications are good enough, I reckon, mister. The shaft is down to two hundred feet, and the assays look promising."

"Likely it was salted, then."

"Salted? Now that is a fine hoo-raw. I got a four-dollar-a-day expert here sitting two miles from the shaft, probably has never been down in these particular diggings, and he has the gumption to tell me what is down there in the mine. Don't even have to leave the supper table to do it, neither. That is what I call a real marvel."

Mackay did not answer. He looked down at his bowl of soup again.

"I'm telling you," the man said, "that there is a considerable load of rich ore down there, and I am counting on it making me rich so I do not have to tolerate such fools as you any more. There is plenty enough ore down there that my share will buy me the best house in San Francisco."

"Probably you are right," Mackay said.

"Certainly I am right," the man said. "Those croppings that was worked out three years ago wasn't dropped down from the sky, you know. They come from down below, was percolated upward, one might say. Now answer me. Is it sensible to suppose that the croppings alone was shoved to the top without leaving nothing behind? 'Course it ain't. The process ain't like cream rising, mister. That gold and silver that cropped out on the surface had to be pushed to the top by something. And by what?"

The man leaned across the table, thrust his jaw at Mackay, slammed an open hand on the table so hard that the dishes rattled.

"By more gold and silver, is what!" he yelled. "It figures by the easiest stretch of logic that where there is croppings on the surface there has to be paying ore underneath. It can't be no other way. 'Twould be like finding a deer in the middle of a dewy meadow without any tracks leadin' to it."

Mackay's face was impassive.

"Yet there has to be an end to it somewhere, wouldn't you think?" he said.

"I don't see where that follows, mister. I truly don't. I reckon there is a source somewhere down miles and miles in the bowels of the earth, you might say, where all these riches sprung from. And beyond that it would stop, naturally. But I can see us working a hundred years from now to get down to that place. I mean three shifts a day, seven days a week, maybe ten times the number of hard rockers we got on this lode now, still without reaching the source, but all the time following the ore down, down, down into the ground. Miles and miles, like I say. Likely the trip down to the workings will become so long that it will be more convenient to build a city down below. Keep the boys that much closer to the job. And even with all that, I don't suppose we will get to the fountainhead. Talk is that in the deepest diggings now there is some increase in temperature, and that will be the rule as we go deeper. More heat, bad air. That is what will stop us, mister. Our own frailties. The limits of the human body. That is what will put an end to these diggings."

The man seemed satisfied with his point, and when Mackay returned to spooning his soup, the man resumed his lecture on the merits of the Pride of Washoe. Mackay ate steadily and without speaking again. When he had finished his meal he pushed his chair away from the table, gave thanks to the housekeeper, and left, walking up the stairs to his room. Joshua hurried to follow him, and caught Mackay as he was stepping into his room.

"Friend, could we talk? Just a moment?"

Mackay nodded.

"The name is Joshua Belden. You're Mackay, I know. Christian name John. I heard them inquire of the landlady after you left the table. I was hoping that we could talk awhile about mining."

"If you were planning to invest in the Pride of Washoe, you already know my opinion."

"No. I'd hoped that we could talk in more general terms. You spoke as though you know something of this business. You talked with your head, where that other fellow was talking from the heart."

"Probably his shares in that mine are all that he has to show for a year's hard labor. You would take it to heart if that were so. Probably I would, too."

"But you do know mining."

"I'm a student. I try to learn and remember all that I can. Then I go down in the mine and I attempt to make what I see fit with what I have gotten from the books. Sometimes I think I know a considerable amount and other times I'm not so sanguine about my prospects. Look here, Joshua. I came to California in 'fifty-one. I've worked placer diggings and hard-rock mines. I came to Washoe three years ago, when this place was rats' nests and coyote holes and sage. The place has made millions for at least a dozen men since then, and I am still bringing my pay slip for one hundred twenty dollars to the payroll office every month. So you can judge for yourself how much I know and how much it has benefited me."

Mackay had spoken quietly at the table, but now he spoke more quickly and stammered as the words piled up.

"But you know a great deal," Joshua said. "That is true, isn't it?"

Mackay breathed deeply.

"True enough," he said.

"I want to learn. I want to make my fortune here, and I want to know all that I have to know."

"We are not so different, maybe," Mackay said.

They went into Mackay's room. He took a pencil and a paper and drew a cross section of the mountain. You need to understand the shape and the lay of this lode first, he said. This is the mountain, Sun Mountain. *Syenite* is the name for what it is made of, and it is useless as far as we are concerned. Except that you know when you find it that you are out of paying ground. Then there is this stuff, porphyry. It lays atop the east side of the mountain, starting about halfway from the top, and it gets deeper as you go farther east. Some would dispute that, but it's true just the same. And that's important, Joshua, because the paying ore is in the porphyry, the country rock. That fellow downstairs speaks nonsense when he talks of the ore going straight down into the earth. The town is here, about where the upper veins dip to the west. But that's an illusion, see, it's misleading. The syenite wall dips east under the porphyry, and that is where the ore lies. Farther west you go from town, up the mountains, the thinner is the skin of the porphyry before you hit the syenite.

That evening and most evenings for the next few weeks, they sat in Mackay's room and talked mining. Mackay was patient and a good teacher. Sometimes he told Joshua more than Joshua wanted to know, but Joshua listened anyway, and reminded himself: You can never know too much. It can't hurt, all this drivel.

And every day, Joshua went into the mines to work, and saw the evidence of what Mackay had explained the night before. He saw the rich veins, and knew what a ton would bring. He saw the ore cars stringing up at the shaft. He heard the miners talking of their speculations. East of the town, west, made no difference. They ought to know what Mackay knows, he thought. The evidence is plain enough. When he mentioned this once, Mackay looked up from a book, shrugged.

That is the way with us, he said. We want to be happy and we need only a little encouragement to believe what pleases us.

And he had gone back to the book.

Mackay knows more than rocks, Joshua thought then. Murdoch had part of the answer: There is no such thing as a lie that is too big. But Mackay understands the rest. Making somebody believe the lie is not such a chore, either, if they are inclined that way, if believing makes them happy. Now I need somebody with money, who is ready to believe.

The next day he was working in the fourth level of the Ophir when he was knocked flat by a dusty billowing blast of air that boomed through the main drift just behind the splintering of timbers and the roar of collapsing earth. The concussion blew out every candle on the level, and Joshua had to walk in darkness to the gallery. When he reached there, crews were already stepping off the cage with lanterns. A cave-in at the Mexican, somebody said. The Mexican was the first mine north of the Ophir. The

place was a scandal, the only major workings on the lead
to spurn Deidesheimer's square-sets. Now one end of the
Mexican had collapsed and sheared off the north end of
the Ophir with it.

Joshua sat against a wall and drank from a canteen that
one of the relief workers had given him. He was safe here,
where the wooden skeleton frame held strong against uncertain rock. He drank the water and looked up at the
timber cubes stacked higher than the light of candle or
lantern would reach, climbing into the blackness.

A hand touched his arm. A voice was asking his impres-
sions of the catastrophe. Joshua tried to explain the sudden-
ness and the fury of the thing, though he had been more
than a hundred feet from the disaster. He tried to describe
the force of the blast and the terror of finding himself on
his back in the dark, with timbers popping and cracking
and earth sliding not far down the drift.

He stopped.

"Why do you want to know?" he asked.

"This is for the *Enterprise*. We are the first newspaper
down here at the scene."

The man beside him gave a name and stuck out his right
hand. Joshua did the same, found that his hand was trembling.

"You seem shaken," the reporter said.

"It appears that I am."

"Can I do anything for you?"

"I would like to get up into the light and have a couple of
good swallows of tarantula juice."

"I think that could be arranged," the reporter said.

CHAPTER THIRTY

His name was Dan DeQuille. That was his literary name, at least, and as they sat at the bar at Almack's, he apologized for the transparency of it. But one has to have a nom de plume in this line, he told Joshua. His born name was William Wright, but Joshua would oblige him mightily if he would forget that and stick to Dan.

Each drank three whiskeys in an hour. Then DeQuille said that he had a story to write. He would be pleased to have Joshua come along, he said. Joshua could check his piece for factual errors, and might interject a note of color now and again where the narrative dragged.

The *Enterprise* would soon occupy an expensive brick two-story on C Street, but at the moment the office and the presses were in a one-story frame building with an adjacent lean-to that ran the length of one side. The lean-to housed bunks for the reporters, a kitchen, and an eating table. DeQuille sat with pen poised over a pad of paper that sat on a scarred and pitted oak desk. The top of the desk was covered with loose papers and old back numbers of the *Enterprise* and the *Union* and the Gold Hill *News*. In this early afternoon the paper was between editions, so the old Washington press was still. But the wet smell of printer's ink hung over the place, and when Joshua sat in front of the desk, in a chair that DeQuille had pulled from across the room, he touched a finger to an exposed triangle of oak within the scatter of papers and brought back a fingertip smeared black.

DeQuille hunched over the pad and began to scribble. He wrote for a couple of minutes, pausing only to dip the pen into an inkwell, until he stopped and asked the spelling of Joshua's name without looking up. The pen scratched a few seconds more, and then DeQuille lifted his eyes from the paper.

"Was there pandemonium?" he asked. "Squeals and panic and such?"

None that he could recall, Joshua said.

DeQuille twisted his mouth, pursed his lips, shook his head.

"But it would only be natural to call it a horrifying and chilling experience. That would be a fair description, would it not?"

Some would have found it so, Joshua said. It had been frightening, at least.

"Good," DeQuillle said. "Because it wouldn't do to intimate that this was any Sunday picnic under the pines. The public figures that such a catastrophe would scare them witless if they were involved. They'd be let down by any other point of view."

It was certainly frightening, Joshua said. Most stimulating.

"Stimulating. You sure you can't come up with a stronger word? It ain't stupendous enough, if you grasp my meaning. Wouldn't you say terrifying, at the very least? An awesome and terrifying shock? 'Cause if you don't favor such strong words, I'm sure I can go back down there in the Ophir and find some that would."

Awesome and *terrifying* would suit fine, Joshua said. Dan could even throw in *nerve-shattering* if he cared to. DeQuille was off again at that, his head nodding slightly as the pen jumped across the paper. Joshua sat in his chair and watched a compositor walk to a rack of type, pick out a few lead slugs, and drop them into a chase. DeQuille ran through six sheets of paper. Then he told Joshua that he had one negligible chore to do, to fill a column and a half of nonpareil type with local news. He attacked with the pen again, and after he had written a few more pages, he asked whether Joshua was aware of any excitement in the city. Excepting the catastrophe of which he had just been a part, of course.

No, he had seen nothing, Joshua said. Then: Wait. There was a scuffle below my window last night. A Chinaman and a Paiute, grappling for a few scraps of wood that had dropped off the Chinaman's pile that he carried lashed to his back.

"Now that is the stuff I need," DeQuille said. "Local color. If it is a Chinaman and an Injun, so much the better."

He went back to the pad of paper, and it was late afternoon once he had corrected his copy and given it to a typesetter. Then Joshua and DeQuille walked together out of the office. He would be needed before the edition went to print, DeQuille said, but that left him a few hours anyway. The Almack had been convivial enough before.

They drank whiskey again. After his second glass, DeQuille began to brag about the power of the Fourth Estate in Virginia. They could make a mine's stock jump ten points in an hour on the exchange. They could close a play before the end of the first act. You could say what you wanted about Bill Stewart or the mine supers or the big capital that was beginning to flow into the mines. It was the Fourth Estate, particularly the *Enterprise*, particularly DeQuille of the *Enterprise*, with his salary of forty-five dollars per week, who really held the scepter in Virginia.

"Then maybe you will be able to get me a job," Joshua said.

"A job? You have a job in the Ophir, unless they must lay you off for a few days on account of the cave-in. More likely they will want you there to clean up the mess tomorrow."

Joshua laid one hand on DeQuille's left coat sleeve.

"Dan," he said. "I am not a thickheaded sort. I don't need a second intimation like the one today to convince me that my place is up here in the sunlight. My career as a hard-rock miner is finished. I have hefted a shovel in anger for the last time."

DeQuille had a long brown beard. It hung down nearly to his chest and came readily to hand now, when he fingered its wispy ends.

"What is your line of work?" he said.

"I am a card man. A damn good one. My hands have hard pads on them now, but they will disappear directly and my digits will be as soft as a baby's derriere. There ought to be somebody in town who can use a man of my talents."

That was how Joshua, two whiskeys later, found himself in the back room at the Occidental, riffling a pack of cards on a bare wooden table while DeQuille and the owner of the place stood across from him and watched his hands. He concentrated against the effects of the alcohol. There seemed to be a barrier between his head and his hands. He cut the deck and shuffled, and shuffled again. The owner looked at his face and noticed the perspiration on his brow and told him that any time now would be fine.

So Joshua bit his lower lip to keep the top of his head from floating away and fanned the cards out on the table in a crescent. He flipped a card at one end, and every card in the crescent followed. He caught the last card as it turned over and turned it back, so that the wave was arrested and then the action reversed. It was a cheap trick that he had learned early from Murdoch, but it was flashy enough, and it gave him confidence. He gathered up the cards in a single sweep and then told the owner that he would show his second-deal. It was passable. The cards talked more than they should have, but they talked for almost everybody. Which was the problem with showing off a second-deal. Every sharper did the sleight, and it was a rare observer who knew when it was done just passably or superbly.

The owner nodded but stared into Joshua's face, and Joshua knew: He is getting away from me. I'm showing him nothing he hasn't seen before. I need something different. Something that will set me apart from every other card man who comes here looking for work.

"Cut the deck," he said, and he shoved it across at the owner.

"Now the top card is, what, the four of hearts, am I right? Now I take the top card and place it in the deck. In fact, sir, why don't you do it? Yessir, just take the four of hearts off the top of the deck and put it somewhere in the middle, wherever suits you. Fine. Now watch. I tap the top of the deck and the top card is, you bet, the four of hearts again. Now I'll try it again, do it a little different this time . . ."

Under a gaslit chandelier, seated in the notch of a horse-shoe table covered with green felt that showed enameled representations of the thirteen denominations of playing cards, Joshua held forth at the Occidental, his manner easy and friendly but unmistakably professional. At first he was both dealer and casekeeper, but it was as dealer that his confident mien and his quiet patter showed best, so after a while the Occidental let somebody else drive the hearse. Joshua could deal faro as much as he pleased.

A new deal, gents, a square deal every time. Twenty-five winners stacked in here and the first is . . . a deuce. Seven wins for the bank. Pay the winner three on the deuce. And who is this that coppered the two? Charlie? Charlie Alexander? Wouldn't you know. Ye of little faith. Now a queen wins, who's on the pretty lady? Four wins for the bank. Ouch. That is fifteen, eighteen, twenty on *la biche royale*. Nothing on the four. You gents are hot as a pepper-mill pistol after target practice.

Not that he was an incessant gab. He knew when to shut up, too, seemed to sense when the mood shifted and they would take no more of his puns and cracks and jabbering. And when he did talk, he edged along that uncertain line between annoyance and amusement. He knew his audience, knew what liberties might be taken. When he was right, which was most of the time, he could make a loser grin as he pulled his money off the layout. Now that was good. Not another dealer on C Street could do the same.

The fact was that he was something of a celebrity. Nothing on the order of blustering Bill Stewart, who ruled the city with his fists and his bullyragging ways. Not even to be compared with DeQuille or his notorious colleague,

Clemens, he of the acerbic asides and penchant for trouble-making hoaxes, both of whom were known by sight and by reputation in every quarter of Virginia and Gold Hill and in most of Silver City besides. Joshua was not even to be stacked against one such as Tom Peasley, broad-shouldered and splendidly handsome, who would have The Mencken's arm wrapped about his own when he escorted her to her suite at the International after her nightly performance at Maguire's (following which they both would disappear into her rooms, not to be seen again until morning); and who surged into the fray swinging an axe handle that memorable day when his laddies from Engine Company No. 1 tangled with the hard-noses from No. 2 when they collided on Taylor Street while rushing to a fire in a carpenter shop. Peasley was everywhere in evidence that time as the firefighters battled with pistols and brickbats while the city burned, four square blocks and nearly a million in improvements being consumed before No. 2 retreated, having suffered the first fatality of the donnybrook from a well-placed .44 round.

By no means was Joshua the popular equal of any such as these. But he had his coterie of admirers, just the same. Virginia City was that way, embracing fad and fancy and fashion with senseless passion. Of a moment (seemingly) and as of a single mind, the sports decided that faro was not properly played unless Joshua Belden was dealing out of the box. They crowded about his table, reached over heads and shoulders to put down bets when other layouts were half empty. They were convinced that Joshua dealt a square game. That happened to be mostly true. Policy at the Occidental dictated a square game, because the percentages were with the house anyway, and if the volume of money crossing the table was high enough, then a reasonable profit was assured. Overriding mere policy, of course, was the common sense that if you have water nearby, you use it to put out a fire; and if you have a sharper of Joshua's talents, you let him do what he can to cool off a hot player. If Joshua could do that, with the sports all the while believing in his honesty the way the Seceshes at Jacob Wimmer's Virginia Hotel believed in the divinity of Jeff Davis, then so much the better.

He had a following of another sort, too. They were as

charmed as anyone else by his wit, these others, but he used it little when he was in their company. This was the town's new money, which (there being no old money to fill the traditional roles of standard-setter and spiritual guide) found itself in a curiously insular and undirected state. Wealth, these sudden patricians were discovering, has a way of imposing responsibilities that no four-dollar-a-day mucker ever need face. They were obliged to escape their humble origins, and they tried to do so with vast and frantic expenditures. They succeeded mostly in embarrassing each other with their gaudy displays. There was a right way of doing this, but none was exactly sure what that was.

They discovered Joshua dealing private games of *vingt-et-un* and poker in the mahogany-paneled upstairs room at the Occidental. And they knew immediately that he was what they were supposed to be. It was a short, quick, and totally natural step, then, from the upstairs room at the Occidental to the card rooms in any one of the dozen various and ridiculously appointed mansions above B Street. Virginia's money embraced Joshua with as much warmth and faith as did the pikers who snowballed the faro layout with their two-bit white chips. They liked to have Joshua around. Josh knew how to talk and how to dress. You could ask Josh which wine to order with the squab at the dining room of the International. Josh could (and did) sit down with a pen and write up the names of two or three hundred books that ought to be ordered for a properly outfitted library. A man could learn a lot just by sitting back and watching Josh.

Mostly, Joshua lent a genuine patina of class to any card game. He won, of course. Won most of the time, but not in the grand and spectacular fashion that he might have. Enough that he felt compensated for his time and effort on their behalf (they had all been wage producers themselves, not many months ago, and believed in fair play), but not so much that they would be obliged to notice. This led to some memorable moments, as late in a game one evening when Joshua, having already raked in a goodly share of the hands that session, felt compelled to throw in four kings while a ninety-dollar pot sat before him on the table.

Most nights, after working his shift at the Occidental,

Joshua chose from among three or four invitations to play poker. The choice mattered little, for his opponents in any case would be five or six of the several dozen newly rich men in the town, who, almost without exception, regarded Joshua with a restrained and careful awe.

The exception was "Lucky" Ames. The nickname was supposed to be ironic; it was commonly known that conniving and cheating had had as much to do with his success as good fortune. He himself attributed it to simple hard work and foresight and some genius. He believed that money made the man, recognized no excesses, would have scoffed at the proposition that wealth imposes any responsibilities beyond the spending. He had twenty-four-carat-gold doorknobs in his seventeen-room home on Taylor Street. He picked his teeth with a diamond-headed stickpin. The gold studs of his shirt were encrusted with diamond chips, and he rode the streets of the city—never walked, never even a half block—in a black lacquered brougham that carried a gold-leaf coat of arms on the doors. The brougham was pulled by two matched sets of white horses.

Naturally, he despised Joshua with his fastidious table customs, his precise speech, his status as unofficial social arbiter.

No matter. Joshua was happy. He was in striped trousers and clawtail coat again. He was close to the ineffably sweet and satisfying fragrance of real money.

CHAPTER THIRTY-ONE

He wanted a woman, natural enough. It had been some time. Usually he could ignore the yearnings, and he had been trying to save what he could of his wages. He had spent a lot on new clothes for the job, and his first week's pay from the Occidental wasn't due for two days. But this evening he had been keeping cases for a game when a strutting swell brought a woman to stand with him while he played. She had stood beside Joshua's chair, a delicate woman with long glossed nails at the end of slim fingers, hair piled in careful curls atop her head, a stomach flat and slim between the loose skirts and the fullness of her breasts, tight against the fabric of the dress. She had smelled of lavender. She had made Joshua ache. He watched her hands move as she talked, watched her hold the swell's left arm and lean toward him so that one breast pressed against the sleeve of his coat. Once as he studied her she turned her head as though he had called her name, and met his eyes for a moment. She read him, no trouble doing that, smiled, and turned away. She left with the swell a few minutes later, but the ache stayed on. When his shift ended, Joshua walked down the hill to D Street, where the white bungalows lined both sides of the road. Some of them had red paper lanterns glowing outside the door, and others had red lamps in one of the two windows that uniformly flanked

the front door of each place. This was his only choice, if
he wanted a woman. There were none of the other kind.
None, at least, to be found as he pleased in some restaurant
or shop, to be approached on the street and flirted with and
courted. This was a town of males, and for every daughter
or widow there were thirty hungry men in the rooming
houses. They all had their needs, and tonight he had his.
He had pushed out of his mind for a while the thought of
how pleasing a woman could be, the strings that her voice
and her curved eyelashes and her full lips could pluck
inside him, the resonances and nervous harmonies she
could create within him by being *there*, close, attentive.
Now he remembered, and he walked D Street, wondering
which whitewashed cottage held the woman for him tonight. For no reason except that his desire would no longer
wait, he turned and walked up the nearest path, took the
two steps up to the small porch with a single stride, and
rapped on the door. A window opened in the door. A woman
was behind it.

"Hello, sport," she said. "Do I know you?"

"No, ma'am," he said.

She laughed, and the door opened.

"No need to be formal," she said. "I don't believe the
Queen Mother is seeing callers here tonight. You can come
inside. My name is Clarisse. Yours?"

She stepped back and pulled the door with her. He
walked into a dark hall, moved forward when she gestured.
On the right side of the hall were four closed doors, to the
left a parlor that opened into a dining room and kitchen.
The woman closed the door, put a hand at his elbow, and
walked beside him into the parlor. A single lamp burned
on one table. There was a carpet in the middle of the floor,
two marble-topped tables in opposing corners, two plush
armchairs and a matching settee of embroidered broadcloth. Joshua sat in one of the chairs; the settee was occupied by a man who sat with his legs crossed while a girl
in a fringed camisole nibbled at an ear.

The woman who had met him at the door wore a long
dress. It swished as she walked to the couple and spoke to
the girl.

"You know the rules, Caroline. No exhibitions here. The gentleman can take you to your room if that's his pleasure. But no displays here."

The girl looked at the man. He nodded. They left the parlor and walked down the hall, leaving the woman alone with Joshua.

"I don't want to seem hypocritical," she said to Joshua. "But there is something to be said for decorum, no matter what the circumstances."

She was standing in the entrance to the kitchen.

"I am steeping some tea now, Chinese tea from a shop down the road. It has a more subtle flavor than the India kind, I think. Would you like some? I have more than enough for two."

"I would."

"Good." She walked into the kitchen. It was better lit, and Joshua watched her through the curtains as she walked to a cupboard, reached for cups and saucers, bent to open the top of a teapot and sniff inside. She was tall, lithe where he could perceive the outline of her body in the dress. He guessed at long trim legs moving beneath the folds of the skirt. Her hair was tied up behind her head, but he knew from the size of the knot that there was a lot of it, and he imagined her back naked and white, with the long hair brushed free and trailing behind her.

She was standing before him with the tea and the cups and saucers on a tray.

"The couch is ours now, if you'd like," she said. "It will make conversation easier."

He sat at one end, took the cup and saucer that she offered, and held it while she poured the tea. She put the tray on a table, poured her own, and sat beside him, at a distance that was somehow between discreet and inviting.

"I have sugar," she said. "Personally, I take Chinese tea without."

"This is fine."

"You haven't visited us before," she said. "I'm sure I would remember."

"No," he said. "I haven't had the pleasure."

They sipped at the tea, simultaneously clinked cups into

saucers. Joshua watched her. She was lovely, no debate. She could have sat down to dinner in any house on Beacon Hill, just as she was right now. Long arms in the sleeves of her dress. A graceful slope of the neck. She looked at him and then looked away, in a movement that belonged as much to bashful virgin as to coquette. She drew details out of him, wanted to know his name, his occupation, how long he had lived in Virginia. His mouth formed the words when he answered, but his eyes and his mind were busy with her, with the set of her head, the way she looked at him and then away, so confident, as if to say: I know what you want. No need to stare you down or snare you with my eyes.

"I apologize for the delay," she said. "We are short one girl and another is abed with the chills. But we'll accommodate you shortly."

"You would be perfect," he said.

She smiled in a way that did not commit her. She told him to stay where he sat, laid a hand on his nearest knee, rose, and left the parlor. Joshua heard a hollow knock, a squeak of hinges, a few words, a light thunk of wood against wood, a click of lockworks. Then she was back, standing before him.

"I hadn't intended to see visitors tonight," she said. "This is my establishment, and that is my prerogative."

She looked down at him.

"But maybe this single exception," she said. "No need to hurry. We can finish our tea, if you want."

"No," he said.

She took his cup and saucer from him, put it with her own on the tray, and took the tray into the kitchen. He was standing when she returned. She put both hands around the crook of his left arm and led him—rather, directed him without perceptible effort—out of the parlor, down the hall, to the last of the row of four doors. She left his arm, stepped forward to open the door, waited until he had crossed the threshold into the darkness. Then he heard her skirts rustling as she left him. A match flared. He saw that she was holding a lamp and touching match to wick. She refitted the globe, placed the lamp on a table in a corner, moved toward the bed. It was a large bed with a brass frame, spread with a comforter. She turned down the spread, sat on the edge of one side, and motioned him closer, patting a spot beside her on the sheet.

"Sit here," she said. "Don't be nervous, Joshua. No need to be nervous with me. Sit here and talk to me for a moment."

He sat. She shifted slightly, and their hips were touching when he settled his weight into the yielding mattress. She reached toward him, took his hands in her own, looked at him. He found his breathing short and shallow and labored.

"I'm not nervous," he said. "But it has been some while since the last time."

"That is good. Then you will feel it all. Just like the first time, isn't that so?"

He nodded. She knows, all right, he thought. She knows men.

"Tell me what you want," she said.

"I want to pass some time close to a woman."

She tilted her head and breathed a nearly silent laugh.

"You've come to the place for that," she said. "How much money do you have?"

"I have money. Enough."

"Do you have fifteen dollars?" she said. "You could spend the night with me and have breakfast here in the morning. I don't make a practice of that, but you seem to be a gentle sort, and I don't think it would be an unpleasant evening for either of us."

"Fifteen," he said. "Fine."

When he did not move, she said, "If you give it to me now, Joshua, we can put it behind us for the rest of the night," and he reached into his pockets for the money. She took it from him, left the room, returned a few seconds later. She knelt in front of him, tugged off his boots and his socks, looking up at him as she did it, the same assured and knowing face.

"I will knead the muscles in your shoulders," she said. "We can do what you like, but we have the night ahead of us, and that might put you more at ease."

She took his shirt from him when he pulled it off. She

hung it on the back of a chair beside the bed, and when he was prone, stretched out on the cotton-covered comforter, she drew her legs up beneath her on the bed, leaned forward, laid her fingers on his shoulders.

She worked the muscles.

"Your shoulders are so tight," she said. "So tense. No reason for that, not here with me."

Her hands worked down his backbone. Her thumbs pressed for a few moments in the depression at the base of the spine, and then she reached under and around him and unbuttoned his trousers. She pulled them off. He felt motion on the bed, and when he turned he found her with the dress coming over her head, leaving a short petticoat behind. He rolled onto his back. She leaned forward and laid her hands, softly, on his chest, and the sensation forced his eyes closed. Her hands moved over him like warm shadows, here and gone, now there and now gone again. He felt transported, the walls and the ceiling and even the bed itself part of a faraway tableau, as though in a doll's house, no longer part of his world. She was gathering him up and compressing him into a tight little universe that had his skin for a boundary. Nothing existed beyond what he felt and touched.

It was over fast enough. She left him when he rolled away from her with his eyes so heavy, his body so deliciously warm, and began to doze. When she returned she slipped in beside him, and since the nights had been chilly, she pulled the comforter over them both. She lay her head on his near shoulder. They slept for a while, and then he woke her, wanting her again, and he did the same about dawn, too. She slept again after that third time, but he lay awake and watched her, watched the slow and measured rise, fall of her chest as she breathed in sleep, watched a quiver of her eyelids, noted the symmetry of her high cheeks and the straight line of her nose and the arch of her brows.

She is a fine looker, he thought. Quite a beauty at this angle, in repose this way.

He thought: With those looks, and her quiet way, and the peacefulness of her sleep, she seems almost innocent.

He thought: You would never guess the truth.

She had been ready for sleep, boiling water for the tea that she always sipped before retiring, when he came knocking. It had been a quiet night, nothing like the rowdy evenings of the past summer, when the customers had clogged D Street, tramping up and down the road until well after midnight, sometimes even stacking up outside the door to wait to get in, one man entering for each that departed. She could never have handled such a night being two girls short as she was now, Louise having bolted from the house and disappeared two days earlier, and Amy still bed-bound, alternately shaking with chills and sweating out a fever. Ordinarily she would have had one of the others open the door and do the honors while she let the tea steep. But this was her establishment, and nobody else would treat it right if she didn't.

So she went to answer the knock. The face in the cutaway window seemed friendly enough, anxious and bashful and a little hesitant, too, the way most of them tended to be. It was a rare man who could approach this as the purely business arrangement that it actually was. She greeted this one as though she had been waiting for him all night. You had to do that. No matter that he might be the last item you would want to find on the front porch five minutes before closing time. No matter that he might be carrying half the dirt on the Comstock with him on his shirts and pants and under his fingernails. You treated him courteously and with as much friendliness as you could muster. Any other way was bad business. And for what it was worth, this one was not at all filthy. He was right sharp in his gambler's outfit, sitting there in the parlor. He was not bad-looking, either. Not by half. A little on the smallish side for her tastes, but with fetching features, a pleasant voice, and (she noticed when he reached for his cup of tea) long delicate fingers. Somehow that last detail appealed to her most of all. Not that it made much difference. Handsome or not, she shut them out at the crucial moment anyway. But given the choice, she would naturally prefer to look up at a decently pleasing face while the fellow puffed and sweated over her, trying to finish.

That was one of the nice things about owning the house. She had the say-so on who she took, and when. She couldn't afford to retire from the active end of the business yet, since her cut of the other girls' take would barely meet rent and expenses, but at least she could say no when she wanted. Now this one was anxious, seemingly didn't want to wait for one of the other girls, and said he wanted to go with her.

She left to check on Alice; Alice was busy and expected to be that way for a time. Caroline would be occupied for a while yet. So good business dictated what she did next. She walked back into the parlor and told the sport he could have her if he still wanted. He wanted. For sure he wanted. Didn't even wait to finish his tea.

It was a queer thing he said when they reached her room and she asked him what he wanted. To pass some time close to a woman, he said. The queer part was that what he said was true as sunshine. That was what they all wanted, but they rarely knew it. Few of them ever went quite so directly to the heart of the matter. So she came back with the invite to stay the night. There was a fixed price for almost anything else a fellow might want, but this was negotiable, and she figured him for a man who had not been that near to a woman for some time.

Fifteen dollars, she said. It was a lot. She couldn't recall how much dealers in the clubs were paid—this one's new outfit gave him right away—but she knew it was more than the miners got.

Fine, he said. Fifteen. She wished she had said twenty, he agreed so fast.

She had him take off his coat and his shirt and lie face down on the bed so that she could do her back-rubbing routine, the way she did with her all-nighters. It softened them up nice, made them real friendly. Since this was her room, and her home, friendly was the way she wanted them. Rubbing their backs somehow took the starch out of the feistiest of them.

This one was mercifully quick the first time, as she had expected. Second time around in the middle of the night was no surprise, but he did catch her unawares when he wanted thirds around dawn. Still, he had paid for it. It still worked out to five dollars a throw, if you didn't count bed and breakfast.

She awoke in bright daylight to find this fellow poking around her cabinet. She spoke up harshly.

Mister, she said, this is my room here. You are my guest and nothing more. That fifteen dollars you paid buys what you already've gotten, not sightseeing privileges too.

He looked at her, startled. Didn't mean any harm, ma'am, he said. (She disliked that *ma'am*. She was no old lady.) Just noticed your books in the cabinet here and wanted to get a closer look.

I read some, she said.

So you do. Poetry, I notice. Longfellow. Tennyson. Byron. Browning.

He said it in a wondering tone that irked her.

Goddamn it, she said, whores can read, too, y'know.

He looked surprised and a little hurt at the way she said it.

Look, she said. I'm sorry. I broke one of my own rules just then. I don't normally express myself in so coarse a manner, but I get a mite thickheaded, mornings. I am not so good in the morning.

It's okay, he said. I understand. (He hesitated.) There is another fellow, a poet, you might be interested in reading. I met him once when I was a child. He used to live at a small lake in Massachusetts. That is where I grew up, in Boston. A friend of my family's used to cut ice in the winter at the pond where this fellow had a cabin.

Walden, she said. Walden Pond.

Why, exactly, he said.

Thoreau, she said. I have read Thoreau.

They dressed and went into the kitchen together for breakfast. She visited Amy, found that the chills and fever had broken. Then she went into the kitchen and tied an apron around her waist. She was stoking the fire in the stove, throwing in a couple more sticks of wood to heat the griddle, when she noticed the fellow studying her with a quizzical sort of look, as though she were some sort of museum freak.

Something wrong with me? she said.

Nothing, he said. Nothing wrong. Just watching.

She boiled water for tea. She sliced some potatoes into a cast-iron skillet and cracked four eggs and dumped them in, too. The fellow was still looking at her in that strange unsettling way. She made the tea, slid the eggs and potatoes out of the skillet onto two plates, set one of the plates in front of him, poured tea for him. She pulled a couple of biscuits from the warmer and put those on his plate, too, and gave him butter and marmalade.

When she sat down across from him she asked him to tell her about Walden Pond. Anything to get those eyes off her, distract him from whatever he was looking at. He went on for a while about the changing seasons in Massachusetts.

We have nothing like that here, she said. We have summer and winter, nothing in between. I miss the trees changing color, sometimes. I miss trees in any condition, as a matter of fact.

This place is beautiful in its own way, he said. It has its attractions.

I've been here only a short time, she said. I haven't seen much of the area. (The truth was that she rarely left the house.)

You know Washoe Valley? he said. On the other side of the mountain, it lies. It is brown and rocky on the near side of the valley, just like here. But on the far side, the west side, it slopes up into pine trees. There are springs there and lovely meadows.

It sounds beautiful, she said.

Would you care to drive there with me tomorrow morning? he said.

Her answer jumped out before she had a chance to stop it.

I would, she said.

CHAPTER THIRTY-TWO

~~~~~~

Jim watched the Washo as they plodded down Genoa's central street, advancing on his cabin. Such a ragged conglomeration, he thought. Next time I will tell them to meet me in a field somewhere. They are a disgrace to the town. For a moment he considered leaving by a back door so that they would not find him at home. He had bad news for them, and getting it past them would not be easy. But it would be just like them to set up camp in front of the house and wait for him to return, whether it was an hour or a month. His white neighbors would never forgive him that. So he sat in a chair beside the door and waited for them.

The knock came directly, a sonorous full-fisted thumping. Your knuckles, he thought. Use your knuckles and you won't beat the place down. But he said nothing, only opened the door and smiled at the delegation that clustered around the stoop.

"Friends," he said in the Washo tongue. "Brothers and sisters. I've been hoping that you would be here soon. I have your *money* for you." He held up a cloth sack, shook it so that the coins within jangled. He glanced from one side to another, at the houses that flanked his cabin. "Let us walk away from here, to the meadow outside town."

They said nothing, so he closed the door behind him

and started down the street. The town was small yet. The meadow was less than a half mile away, and the Washo followed him silently, their feet making nearly imperceptible swishing noises in the dust. When he reached the meadow he sat in the middle of a patch of sunshine—these October afternoons were chill and brittle—and the Washo sat in front of him. When they had settled themselves, he spoke.

"As I told you," he said, "I have your *money* for working in the fields. It makes my heart sad to tell you that there is not quite as much as we hoped."

There was a grunt or two, some quiet whispering, but most of them took the news impassively, stared at him.

"The crop was bad this season," he said. In fact, the crop in this area was always bad. "The whites cannot afford to pay you *ninety cents* for a day as they usually do. They have told me that they can give only *eighty-five cents* a day this time. The difference is not great."

Still they stared at him. That was not necessarily a good sign. He drew from his shirt pocket a sheet of paper, unfolded it.

"I have your names and the number of days you have worked and the *money* that is yours. You may each come forward to get your *money* when I speak your name."

He was reading the first name when a voice spoke up from the crowd, using English words.

"Wait," the voice said. "Tell me again. How in hell can white man pay eighty-five when he say ninety?"

Jim looked up from the paper. The speaker was a boy of sixteen, one of Grub's children. Jim had noticed him before. A smart boy.

"Don't use white man's words," he said. He had stopped encouraging them to speak English. "You don't say them the correct way, and the whites will only laugh at you if they hear you. Leave me to speak the whites' words. I understand them.

"You want to know about what the whites promised you. They are just men, these whites. They cannot look at the field and know for sure how much is there. When you finished your work they saw that there was not enough and they would not be able to give you as much *money* as they said. Listen to me, young man. The white man has to make *money*. If he does not, then you will not. And where would you be without *money* to get you through the winter?"

"Can we buy enough food with this money?" the boy yelled. "Can we buy clothes, too? We did not work enough days and we are not getting enough *money*."

The boy was impertinent, but Jim noted with some satisfaction that at least he had dropped the English. That was good. He didn't need any other fast-talking Indians moving into his territory or into the affections of the whites. Things were bad enough already. He decided to let the remark pass. They all knew the answer to the questions anyway.

He read the names and the numbers from the list, and each came and took the money sullenly and returned to the group. He was paying out the last of the coins when the boy spoke once more. This time it was English again.

"Since you so damn close to the whites, maybe you tell us why the barbwire is being strung around the fields."

He had hoped to save that for later. Maybe months later, if he could. But there was no avoiding it now. The others in the group were nodding, murmuring, yes, we want to know that.

"The crops have been poor lately," Jim said. "The ground and the sky have been harsh. Some of the whites think they can do better by putting cows in the fields."

He turned and walked. Maybe that is the best way to tell them, he thought, shove it in their faces and hope they will not recognize what it means. But the boy spoke again.

"What about us?" he said.

"What do you mean?"

"If the whites have cows in the fields, there will be no crops. No crops for us to plant and to cut."

"That is true," Jim said. "But don't be angry. The whites tell me that maybe you will be able to work with the cows. You would not work during the winter in any case, and by spring something will happen. Believe me. You need not worry, brothers and sisters."

Then he walked, and did not stop until he reached his cabin. He shut and barred the door behind him.

Crap, he thought. Things are going to hell all around me. There won't be a penny in the cows for me. Not a penny. This fall had been bad enough. His agreement with the white farmers had been to take ten cents of the daily dollar that the Washo were paid, in return for providing their labor. That was his private arrangement with the whites. But ten cents a day for just three weeks and fewer than thirty Indians, well, that was just not enough. So on his own he had taken another nickel of each dollar. At that, it was barely worth the effort.

Got to find me a new line, he thought. Something that pays big and steady. After all. A fella has to make a living.

CHAPTER THIRTY-THREE

He would come calling at nine in the morning, he said. If that was agreeable. If that was not too early. Yes, she told him, that would be agreeable. But after he left she sat sipping her tea and she scolded herself for not getting his address. Already she was thinking that this running off into the countryside with a customer was a poor notion. No way it could be good for business, she thought. A poor notion all around, but now she had no way of finding him to call off the appointment.

I suppose I will have to go, then, she told herself. Wouldn't be proper for him to show up at the house tomorrow morning to find that I've changed my mind. Nothing good can come of this, though. Don't understand whatever possessed me to say yes. He did know of Thoreau. That was it, Thoreau. And he was a model gentleman. That didn't hurt his cause, either, his shy and courtly way around me. Still, nothing good can come of this. Finally, there had been the absolute and total surprise of the question. No man had ever come straight out and asked her to go for a drive in the country.

That night was another quiet one, and with Amy well again, she had to service only two customers. Each time, annoyingly enough, she found herself looking at their fingers and comparing them (one's were short and stubby, the other's long but quite thick) to Joshua's. When she turned in alone for the night, she warned herself against the dangers that this man posed. Nothing good can come of this, she told herself again. Probably I would be doing us both a favor if I refused even to come to the door tomorrow. That is what I will do.

But she was awake early with no thought of turning him away. Instead, she stood before the open doors of her armoire for a quarter of an hour, pulling out one dress and then another, holding them in front of her and studying the effect in the mirror. Red satin. No. That is wrong for a drive in the country. Royal-blue velvet wouldn't be right, either. She wondered: What does a woman wear for such a day, driving into the hinterlands with a young man? She tried and rejected each dress in the main wardrobe at least twice. She was ready to ask Amy for help when she remembered an old gingham thing that she had not worn for years. She found it in a bottom drawer, painfully plain. It was checked blue with white lace cuffs. She hung this one before her as she had the others, but this time she also pulled it over her head. You are no young girl any more, she thought. He will laugh when he sees this. But it is better than any of the others.

She brushed her hair more than she had in months, and after she washed her face and dried it, she had to decide on perfume. She dismissed the idea of using most of the ones she put on in the evening. He knows what I am already. Certainly it's not necessary to remind him. Then, defiantly: I am what I am, and he can take me that way or not at all. Don't see why I ought to make concessions for this stranger, and it matters little anyway, because I surely won't repeat this folly. This one adventure will be quite enough. Eventually she chose a few drops of a light eau de cologne that she found in a corner of her cosmetics drawer.

She dressed and walked out into the parlor. Caroline and Amy both were there. Caroline made a remark about a church social and Amy laughed, but she walked past them without a word, to have biscuits and tea for breakfast. Shouldn't have told them what I planned to do, she thought. They will tease me without mercy, but no matter. Likely they are just jealous, anyway. He is a handsome fellow.

He arrived seven minutes early. She had gulped breakfast, and was ready. He waited at the door with a bowler hat in his hands, nodded a good morning as she draped a shawl over her shoulders, and as they walked side by side down the walk told her that the blue of her dress matched the morning sky.

"How long will we be gone?" she asked him.

"Most of the day. The drive down the hill and across the valley is an hour and a half, at least."

"I didn't think to bring lunch," she said.

"In the hamper," he said. There was a wicker basket on the floor of the carriage that he had left outside the front gate. He put a hand out to steady her as she climbed the single step up to the seat, and then, without a word and without even glancing at her, he chucked the reins and the carriage moved forward, the wheels riding in the parallel grooves that were worn and baked hard in the clay of D Street.

They rode north out of town, along the ridge of Sun Mountain, then down the Geiger toll road to Washoe Valley. Wagon traffic was heavy pulling up the grade, but once they reached the flat and started down a side road that would skirt them along the west side of Washoe Lake, they were alone. When they reached the lake he turned down another road, this one rutted and chucked. He slowed the horse to an easy canter so that the jolts would not shake the carriage so badly. At the far side of the valley the road became less distinct as it sloped up into the mountains and entered a forest belt. She breathed deeply of the pine smell. They drove another mile before he stopped the wagon in an open, grassy patch that lay beside a trickle of a stream.

"This is lovely," she said.

"Taste the water." He had opened the wicker basket to pull out a goblet, had dipped the goblet into the brook and now held it before her, brimming and so clear that except for the drops of water that clung to the sides, there was no indication it held anything at all.

She took the goblet in both hands and put it to her lips. The water was cold. It also had no taste. That was a novelty in Virginia, where the only drinking water seeped out of the mines, full of sulfur and iron and arsenic.

He spread a blanket. She sat at one corner, he at another. They looked up at the sunlight that streamed through the gaps in the tree cover.

"Do you often bring women here?" she heard herself saying.

"No," he said quickly. "This week I had a new job that gave me my mornings and afternoons free, so I rented a carriage and followed the roads and found the place."

"It doesn't matter," she said.

"You are the first woman I've brought here."

"I was trying to be humorous. None of my affair anyway."

"You are the first, all the same."

"Good," she said.

There was a period of uncomfortable silence, which she ended by asking him about his job. He had been dressed in gambler's clothes the other night.

Yes, he said. But he was not just a gambler. He was a card man. As good as any, better than most. (His back stiffened and his jaw jutted when he said that, as though he were waiting for somebody to challenge him on that point. She liked that.) That led to talk of Murdoch and Hemingway's show and Mississippi riverboats and New Orleans. He talked until they were both hungry. They ate the cold chicken and potato salad that he had brought, and drank the wine he had put to chill in the stream. When they had finished, he produced a half-dollar piece and showed her coin tricks. He made the silver piece dance from elbow to napkin to jacket lapel, to the overhanging branches of a sugar pine, to a spot in her loose hair, just behind one ear. That was as close as he got to her all day, reaching with one hand behind her ear to pluck out the coin. Then he packed the hamper, and they drove down the road and around the lake and joined the slow-moving wagons on the road up the Geiger grade.

They were nearly to the top when he turned to her and said, "You know, with all the palaver I was making, I never did get to find out a thing about you. Not a blessed thing."

"Maybe another time," she said.

"Tomorrow?"

"Yes," she said.

Amazing. He thought it was purely stupefying, the way she looked when she came to the door. That blue gingham dress. She looked like a farm girl, every inch of her. Once she was out of the doorway of that bungalow and in the carriage, there was nothing to suggest that she whored for a living.

Now, most people might have figured (he told himself as he sat in his room and considered the events of the day) that, having laid with her just two nights before, I would find it easy to be with her this time. As though I could say, Well, I've been as far with this gal as a man can go, and so I don't have to worry what I say to her or what I do. But it didn't hold that way. It was like she was not the same woman. She didn't even look the same. It was like starting fresh. I was nervous as hell, and none of what happened before meant a damn.

He was smitten. Not enough that she was so lovely, but she had to behave like such a princess, to top it all. The next day, when he came to call, she took him with her on shopping errands, buying food for the week. He carried the goods (the bulk and weight of packages growing greater with each stop at grocer, at butcher, at apothecary) up and down the length of C Street while she led him along. He found that he didn't mind being seen with her. He liked being beside her. When they returned to the house she cooked a meal for him, and the two of them ate together while Caroline and Amy entertained. Again he did not so much as touch her hands. Every morning for the next week he came to visit, and they talked. One day she told him about her childhood and how she had come to Virginia City.

They were on the settee in the parlor when she described these things. She wanted him to know, she said, because he ought to understand that she was no different from other women. They might not agree, she said, and laughed, but the only difference between them and me is circumstances, nothing more.

"I know," he said.

"Does it bother you," she said, "that I run this house, and do what I do?"

"It does when I think about it."

"I see."

"I don't think about it much," he said. "When you bring it up, mostly, or when it's forced on me so that I can't avoid it.

But there's nothing about you that makes me think of it. I'd find it hard to believe, if I didn't for certain know different."

He skipped a shift at the Occidental, and they went out together at night for the first time that evening. She left Amy in charge and went with him to a performance at Maguire's. She watched him play billiards in the foyer. She sat with him in the orchestra section to watch Junius Booth play Hamlet. They went to the Sazerac and drank champagne and gulped down smoked oysters with DeQuille, who had sat in the front row, reviewing the performance. He swallowed an oyster and allowed that he would go easy on old Booth this time.

The house was dark when he brought her to the front door. He would be sleeping late, he told her, but probably he would call about noon, if she approved.

"No," she said. "Don't leave now. Stay for a while, anyway. For some reason, I don't want to be alone now."

He followed her inside. They walked through the door, and he was about to turn for the parlor and the settee when she stopped him with a hand at his right elbow. She stood, still. He turned to face her.

"You have been so considerate these two weeks," she said. "A woman could not ask for a kinder man at her side."

She reached out, put a white-gloved hand on his cheek.

"You could be bolder," she said, "but no less kind at the same time. Do you understand?"

He took her to her room and to her bed. He unfastened every button and every stay of her clothing. When she lay naked on the bed, he undressed and stretched out beside her. He ran his hands over her body. He kissed her, and she put her arms around him and held him against her when he did.

He was moving over her, moving and panting. She clutched at his neck. His head was beside hers. He was whispering.

"Clarisse," he said. "You are so beautiful, Clarisse, so lovely."

And her lips were against his ear, forming words without breath.

"My name is Elizabeth," she was saying. "Call me Liz. Please call me Liz."

CHAPTER THIRTY-FOUR

He was dealing faro in the Occidental one October evening when Jim walked through the doors. A drunk at the bar spotted him first and shouted as he climbed off his stool: Hey, get your red ass out! This is a white man's establishment, and we don't want no Injuns smelling it up. Joshua told the casekeeper to watch the table, and reached Jim before the drunk did with a drawn pistol.

"Hello, pard," Jim said. "You wouldn't let that crazy man plug me, would you?"

"No. Say, friend, he didn't know any different. I know this one. He's not a bad Injun. He just forgets himself, is all. Go on back to the bar. Next round is on me. Just a little misunderstanding."

The drunk glared at Jim and Joshua, slowly holstered the gun, turned, and walked back to the bar. He ordered a drink and watched with narrowed eyes as the two of them walked outside.

"Seems we are about even, youngblood. Don't know that I could have talked my way out of that one."

"You ought to be careful, Jim. You know he wouldn't need a reason to ventilate you if he pleased, not in this town. You are a good enough reason all by yourself."

"I do my best to stay invisible. But I had to talk to a fella about some firewood—I got my Injuns felling dead trees and splitting them for stove wood these days—and he wanted me to meet him here."

"You wait outside. I'll get him and bring him out."

"That will do, Josh. Considering that I ain't ready to go south just yet."

He told Joshua the man's name. Then he grinned.

"You skinned the world yet, pard?" he said.

"No. Not even a small part of it."

"Sticking with the cards, I see. Wouldn't listen to what your benevolent Injun sage had to tell you."

"Oh, I listened. I did my turn down below."

"You wasn't impressed, huh? Least not enough to get any ideas."

"I got ideas. Got a couple of good ones, Jim. But it's not enough, somehow."

"You want to talk about it?"

"I might. My shift ends at eleven."

"Make it eleven-ten, then. In front of the smitty's on C Street, near Sutton."

In October, once the sun dropped behind the mountain, the wind blew harsh and cold. Earlier that week, Joshua had bought a heavy woolen overcoat, and he buttoned it up to the neck when he walked out into the darkness to meet Jim that night. Joshua found him in front of the blacksmith's shop, wearing a buckskin jacket and blowing into his hands.

"Gone soft, I guess," he said. "I used to run naked, nights colder than these. Gotten too accustomed to setting beside a good hot stove, is my problem. How you been wastin' your time, pard?"

"I learned how to use a pick and shovel. I almost got mashed in a cave-in. I know more about rock and mining and veins and hanging walls than any human being ever needs. I have developed a positive itch to set a scheme to working, but I lack some essentials yet."

"You need somebody to work it on."

"That is exactly right. Somebody who is ready for what I have in mind. The place is right and the idea is right, but every time I look at a sucker something tells me that he is wrong. I have to listen to myself. It has to feel right, you know. You have to believe in it or it will be a misfire for sure."

"I know."

"I figured you would, if anybody."

"I don't know your plan, Josh, but I can tell you this. Sometimes it's easier to work it on somebody you disenjoy in the first place. Myself, I don't have that peculiarity. It don't have to be personal with me. But maybe you are different. Maybe it would give you that little push into it."

"Maybe. I also have gotten myself into a situation here. A lot of people know me in this town. The sports at the tables are no problem. But the kind of man I might be trying to skin would have his suspicions, maybe. There's no hope if the sucker doesn't have confidence. I am cozy with some big money now, but it only goes so far. They might back off quick if I started talking a business deal, me being a gambler and such."

"You think your sucker might smell a one-eyed man in the game and draw down from the bet just about the time he ought to be throwing it on the table with both hands."

"It could be. I've been thinking that I need to go about it another way, sneak through the back door instead of trying to get through the front."

Jim blew on his hands.

"I'll remind you, Josh," he said, "that in this region there is nothing dumber to a white man than an Injun. And that includes sure-enough prodigies like myself."

"But a white man won't trust an Injun."

"A white man won't trust an Injun to carry ten cents across the street, or to walk past a fruit stand without making off with a few apples. But let the matter be a slight bit complicated and we don't get a thought. We cause no more worry than a gelding in a pen full of mares."

Joshua looked at Jim. He remembered the Indian kneeling in the corral at Carson City, licking poison from a dog's coat to win a bet.

"It will be warmer in my room," he said. "I have a small stove there. Also a crateful of rocks that you ought to see."

He visited Liz most mornings, and some evenings, too, through the end of summer and into autumn. She was working less and less, and one night she told him that she had decided to stop seeing customers. She had saved some money, and that would get her through until spring, anyway. Ordinarily she would take on another girl, but there wasn't enough traffic for two already. All the houses said the same, and the business on C Street was hurting, too. Weeks had passed since the last big discovery on the lode, and Virginia had turned sluggish, lethargic, dejected.

So, she said, there is no point in my seeing customers when Amy and Caroline are only knitting, themselves, most of the time.

The next day he asked her to marry him. She would, she said.

"Not immediately," he said. "There is something I need to do first. There is a good deal of money in it, and I won't have you marrying a poor man."

"You're not poor," she said. "You have a fine job."

"I won't be there come spring, I hope."

"That suits me fine," she said. "But the money isn't important. We'll get by."

"It's important," he said. "I'm not putting you off, but I must see this matter through. Then we will have money and you will have all of me."

She was sitting with him in the parlor one afternoon in early November when Amy answered a rap at the door. She came back with an envelope and gave it to Liz.

"The boy says he will wait for an answer."

Liz tore open the envelope and scanned the single sheet of notepaper. She looked up at Amy.

"Tell him," she said, "that the answer is the same as it has been for the last month."

She looked at Joshua.

"It's a man," she said. "I used to see him in his home, some evenings. A business arrangement. He has money and he treated me well. I suppose he is quite taken with me, because he won't take my no."

Joshua looked through the curtains. A black lacquered brougham waited in the street.

"Lucky Ames," he said.

"He wouldn't let me call him that. His name is Charlie. He is pleasant enough sometimes, but I don't care for him now.

I suppose I'll have to see him personally to tell him that I want no part of him any more."

She glanced at Joshua; he seemed not to have heard. He was gazing out the window, his tongue running across his upper teeth as he stared out at the black coach and the matched horses prancing nervously in place.

CHAPTER THIRTY-FIVE

Joshua's opening came when Albie Noble asked him to join a poker game, evening after next. The reg'lar crowd, Noble said. Me and Bowers and Fisk and Finn. You'd make a fifth. Oh, yeah. And Lucky Ames said he would be there, too. Maybe you'd be so good as to filch a few packs of pasteboards from the club, the way you usually do.

Somehow Joshua had known all along that the cards would launch him. Knowing the city and knowing the mines would be indispensable for what was to follow, but the cards would be his start. He hadn't wasted the hours alone in front of a mirror, studying the cards and his fingers, first getting each move perfect and then doing it that way so often that he knew no other way. If all went well tonight, he'd soon be paid back for the hours. After tonight, he would be setting in motion a series of inevitabilities that would practically proceed of their own momentum, with just a helpful nudge along the way. And the cards would be the start of it all.

Not that Jack Murdoch would be especially proud, Murdoch so cautious, such a purist. Jack would faint dead away if he knew: Joshua was going to cold-deck them.

After he spoke to Albie Noble on C Street, Joshua walked around the corner and up a block to a machinist's shop on B. He had a special order that he needed by tomorrow afternoon, he said. It was a spring-loaded clamp with an eyelet, the spring to be heavy enough to let the jaws grip a deck of cards but not so strong that the clamp would snap back and make a noise as soon as the cards were released. The machinist nodded. He did custom work for the mines and the mills; this would be simple. The piece would be ready by four tomorrow.

Joshua was there waiting the next day as the machinist fitted the spring to the clamp. He gave it to Joshua to test. Joshua paid him two dollars and a quarter, walked down to C Street to a notions stand, and bought a spool of heavy black thread and a card of needles. He went to the Occidental and gathered up a handful of sealed decks from an open carton in the back room. Then he walked to his boardinghouse room, spread his broadcloth clawtail coat on the bed, and poked the end of the thread into a needle's eye. He sank the needle into the lining of the coat, below the collar, pulled the thread through, and looped the thread and punched the needle into the fabric again, and again, until the strand was sewed securely to the lining. With his teeth he nipped the thread at the eyelet of the clamp. He dropped the clamp into the right sleeve of the coat. It hung there, near where his right elbow would be. Then he broke the seal on a fresh deck of cards.

This was the best part. He relished this, sitting in a boardinghouse room and creating a tempest that would blow havoc in a few hours, but in a calculated, exact way, just as he ordered it up. If six players sat at the table and if Joshua sat three seats to Lucky Ames's right, then it would happen. There was no uncertainty about Joshua's ringing in the cold deck. If all depended on his getting the cold deck into the game at the right time (and all did), then it would be there.

Joshua turned the deck face up and picked through it for cards. Might as well get some money in the pot while I am about it, he thought, so in a pile he placed three tens and two fives. In the next he put five cards without a hope for anybody: a bust hand. Into the next pile (the piles beginning to form a circular pattern) went three queens and a nine and a trey. That would be the start of Lucky's hand. And in succeeding piles: a nine-high flush and another bust hand. Finally his own. He pulled four aces from the deck and laid them down with an eight of spades. Then he picked cards off the stacks, moving about the circle in a clockwise fashion, until they were all in a single pile in the order in which they would be dealt. At the bottom of this pile he placed a deuce and Lucky Ames's fourth queen. He would get them on the draw. When those cards hit the table, he thought, there will be a riot. It will all work as long as I make certain that mine is the last raise before the draw. To be sure of that he would have to raise each raise before the draw until they all got tired of that and just called. And raising will be no unpleasant chore, he thought. Not with four aces in my hand.

He placed the pile on top of the rest of the deck and squared it, then tied a piece of thread lengthwise around the pack and another about its width. He opened the clamp and let its jaws grip the cards and dropped it into the sleeve. Then he put his arms into the coat and sat at a chair. He pressed his right elbow to his side, felt the clamp open, the cards drop free. Then he slowly let the clamp close, then straightened the right arm. The cards fell into his right hand, open to receive them. He could hide them in his palm, and the thread would shake away, easy enough.

The game was to be early, at seven. He already had told them at the Occidental that he would be missing his shift that evening. When he had finished with the clamp and the thread and the cards, he had less than half an hour, so he pulled on the clawtail and the woolen greatcoat and wrapped a scarf about his neck. He walked out of the boardinghouse and into a storm of small hard snowflakes that, driven by the wind, pelted his face as he climbed Taylor Street up toward Noble's house on A.

Most of them were gathered in Albie's front room, smoking cigars and drinking whiskey from etched brandy snifters. Ames was the last to arrive. That made six. And the last uncertainty of the night was resolved when Ames hurried to a chair at the big circular table and Joshua was able to pick a seat on Ames's right with two chairs between them.

Joshua had brought three hundred in cash but he knew he would be needing more when they played the cold-deck hand. And since this was the last poker game he would play with this bunch, he itemed his hands, and second-dealt, and used the reflective curved side of a brandy snifter as a shiner, and did all the rest of the things that he had been holding back these weeks. In the first hour, he took a pot for seventy, another for ninety, a third for more than two hundred, and a fourth for at least twice that. The last two times he went head-to-head with Ames and won each time. He noticed a red flush creep up from Ames's starched collar when he pulled the money in from that fourth hand, and he thought: So much the better. He wants me now.

The timing had to be right before he could try the cold deck. The deal had to belong to the player at his left, and they had to be using a new deck, since the cards in the clamp were fresh. With the game two hours old, and more than warm and loose now, Joshua called for a new deck when Finn, at his left, took a pot and won the deal. Finn shuffled the stiff cards and passed the deck to Joshua.

Joshua cut the deck that Finn had slid to him on the table. But the deck he pushed back at Finn was the cold deck that had dropped from the clamp. The other was palmed in his right hand, then hidden in his coat pocket when Joshua shifted his weight in his chair. It was tough, a switch like that. But it could be done. And it was so much better this way, because Finn was dealing, and nobody suspected Finn. They would be too stunned in a few minutes to remember that Joshua had ever touched the cards. Like a butterfly crawling from a cocoon and spreading its wings for the first time, like a green rosebud bursting open to reveal perfect red petals that slowly peel away from the clump, the hand unfolded (or so it seemed to Joshua, who could view it with a certain reflective detachment while he caressed the four aces he held in his hand) with a natural grace and orderliness. There was Noble checking, Ames opening for fifty, a call from Bowers. Fisk threw in and Joshua raised. Finn called and Noble threw in and Ames raised and Bowers called and Joshua raised again. After Joshua's third raise, Finn hesitated—he wouldn't dare, Joshua thought, not with a full house, the moment of panic subsiding when he saw that Finn was only forcing up a belch before he made the call—and when Ames called and Bowers did the same, it was over.

Last raise was Josh's, Finn said. How many you want, Josh? The voice seemed to quaver. They were millionaires, most of them, but had not been so rich so long that the sight of this much money in the middle of a table did not make them choke a little.

Pat, Joshua said. Fisk and Noble grinned.

Dealer is pat, Finn said. Lucky?

Two, Ames said. He tossed away his discards and lifted the two new ones singly from the table. He got the fourth queen on the last of the two cards. Joshua knew it because that was how he had stacked the cards, but Ames's face told it all anyway. His jaw set, and he stared across at Joshua for a long moment, and then he looked back at his cards and his back straightened in the chair.

Bowers's pat call only meant more money in the pot. Joshua opened for two hundred, and Ames jumped in with his raise of three hundred before Finn could even call. Bowers called, but folded next time around when Joshua raised five hundred. Ames's raise of five more exhausted his cash, and Joshua could not cover it.

He could give a draft, Joshua said. But Fisk shoved back his chair, looked over Joshua's shoulder, and said, No need. I will back Josh for ten percent of the pot, if he thinks that is fair.

So it was Ames dropping a draft into the pile on the table, twice, for a total of two thousand, and when he finally called, it was not so much from a lack of confidence (Joshua thought) as to escape the drudgery of having to scribble out another bank note.

He had his hands in the pile of paper and gold pieces when Joshua turned over his four aces.

When the gasps and the exclamations and the curses were finished, after Ames had walked away from the table, after Joshua had paid Fisk his ten percent and had stuffed the rest into the pockets of his clawtail and his overcoat, he walked to where Ames stood by a window.

"About these drafts," he said, holding them out.

"They are good as gold. I have so much anyway that I

won't notice the difference when the bank pays them."

"I'm sure," Joshua said. "But they are such an inconvenience. I have a suggestion. I've been wanting to get into the mining business for some time, Charlie . . ."

He wanted the Fireball. The Fireball, of all the misbegotten properties. Belden had two drafts totaling two thousand dollars and he wanted to swap them for the Fireball.

Lucky Ames had to subdue a grin. He had to appear to deliberate, to agonize, to weigh carefully all the ramifications. But not for too long. The young fool might be struck by some sense and change his mind.

Done, he said.

He would need Liz's help, Joshua knew. She knew Ames. The small details could make the difference in a blind like this one. Liz could supply the details. Liz could make it work.

He would have to tell her the truth, though.

The morning after the game he met Ames at Atwill's to sign the papers. Joshua gave Ames the two drafts, and Ames tore them into a dozen pieces and dropped the scraps into a trash basket.

Young fellow, he said, you have not only become the owner of one of the most ridiculous pieces of property on this lode. You have also taken title to a certifiable curse. I took out a few thousand in surface croppings for about six weeks back in 'sixty-one, but I spent four times that in running a shaft and two drifts to find that that dirt is as barren as a wrinkled-up old woman. It was always good for a laugh when somebody in town wanted a poke at my expense. They can laugh at you now.

"I'd wish you luck," Ames said, "but it wouldn't do you no good, anyways."

Joshua left Atwill's and went to Liz's place on D Street. He built a fire in the stove and they sat beside it, silent. Joshua clasped her hands while he chose his words. Liz was funny about these things, he was learning. He would have to approach her just the right way.

"I want us to be happy together," he said.

"We will be, Joshua. We are already." She squeezed his hands.

"I won't be, not for long, unless I have money. You say it's not important to you, but it means a lot to me. I have had it and I have been without it, so you can believe me when I tell you that a rich man is a free man."

"I've told you before that I don't understand."

He drew three breaths, and was silent, before he spoke again.

"I have a way of getting some. It will be a good start toward what I want. It has to do with Lucky Ames," he said.

As plainly as he could, he told her his plan. It lacked some refinements yet—that was where she could help—but the workings were there.

"And there are things that you can do for me, knowing him as you did."

"This is beneath you," she said. "It is beneath both of us."

"Would Lucky have such compunctions?"

"I wouldn't marry Lucky."

"You won't want to be married to me if we are constantly struggling with finances. You think it doesn't matter now, but you will feel different in another year or two."

She said nothing.

"If for no other reason," he said, "then do it for me. Do it because it is as important to me as anything I have ever done."

He waited for her answer.

"Tell me what you want to know," she said finally.

From the *Daily Territorial Enterprise*, November 18, 1863:

We can safely state that nobody is immune to Washoe fever and its deleterious symptoms. This statement is occasioned by our learning that Joshua Belden has paid two thousand dollars to "Lucky" Ames for full and total interest in the Fireball mine, with all its improvements, dips, angles, and appurtenances, such as they are.

Until now we had considered Belden a *rara avis* in this community. That is to say he struck us as an exceedingly levelheaded individual of excellent judgment who had somehow managed to stay aloof from the speculative fringes of the mining industry with all its excitements and alarums. Evidently we were mistaken.

Belden has jumped with both feet into a black and possibly bottomless pit. Of course we wish him well, but we hope he understands that he is more likely to find truffles than silver there in his new acquisition.

His cook stared up at him with unblinking, dispassionate eyes when Lucky Ames gave her his dinner order for the evening. She was a Chinese woman who never had smiled or frowned at him once. She took his commands, and his occasional insults or compliments, with an expressionless stare that unnerved him. Whenever he had finished what he wanted to stay, she would nod slightly and then look away, return to what she had been doing when he had interrupted her. It disturbed him that she would not even pay him the deference of anger, much less an ingratiating smile. He would have dismissed her long ago if she had not had the singular talent of listening once to his dinner menu and then producing it exactly as he wished a few hours later, actually in far richer and more imaginative detail than he had specified. She knew what he wanted.

Tonight he would have capon, he said. Mushroom sauce. Glazed carrots. Fruit compote. Liver pâté. A fancy fresh pastry. She could buy these last two ready-made if she could find them somewhere.

She was kneading a lump of dough when he spoke. She worked the dough and spread it flat on a table.

"Any questions?" he said when he had finished.

A tic of the head. It could have been an involuntary gesture.

"No? Good. Then I will expect it about six this evening."

"Mistuh Ames," she said. "How you feel?"

He needed a moment to answer. He was startled. In a single breath she had practically doubled the number of words she had spoken to him since he had hired her, two years earlier.

"Feel? Why, I haven't felt better."

She slapped the dough, pounded it with open palms. She looked up.

"You lose sumepin, maybe?"

"No. I haven't lost a thing."

She nodded and went back to the bread.

"Why do you want to know? What brought on such a question?"

"Last night," she said, "fix rabbit. Shop no dress rabbit. Got to cut myself. Cut stomach of rabbit, read guts when they fall out."

"How do you read a rabbit's guts, woman? Explain that."

"Guts tell story, way they fall out. Chinee people long time read guts. Tell future. Tell truth, what happen."

"And what did the rabbit guts say last night?"

"Say Mistuh Ames lose sumepin, plenny valuable, make lots money for somebody. You not lose nothin'?"

"No. No, I ain't. I ain't in the habit of lettin' go of what I have that is valuable. You can tell that to the next dead rabbit you cut."

He left the kitchen and tried to force out of his mind what the old woman had said. The Fireball was barren. Everybody said so. Rabbit guts. Such an idea. You couldn't (could you?) possibly see past, present, future in a mess of bloody entrails.

Alone in her room, Liz Burgess stared at the ceiling and considered what she had done.

He talked me into it, she thought. I let Joshua talk me into something I wouldn't have considered a week ago. He has some power over me. Maybe that is the way it is with love, but it is frightening all the same.

She thought: He has power over other people, too. Likely he will get away with what he wants to do, because he seems to have that talent, making people do things they wouldn't think of ordinarily.

And that, she told herself, is something to ponder.

CHAPTER THIRTY-SIX

Joshua banked his poker winnings and rented a deposit box for the safekeeping of deed and title to the Fireball. He went to the Occidental and said that he would be gone for a week. He bought a valise and took it to his room. He would need clothes for a week, he had decided, so he packed the valise full. He carried it to the International, where there was a stage depot and ticket office in the lobby. Twenty-five dollars bought him a ticket on the next Overland to Placerville.

From Virginia to San Francisco was unalterably a minimum two-day trip. He was fortunate, the ticket agent told him. There hadn't been a decent snowfall in the mountains yet, though the nights had been cold enough, so the driver would likely be able to stick to schedule on the trip over the passes.

It was late afternoon when the stage attacked the grade up the old Johnson Route, and twenty-two miles later Joshua saw the big lake for the first time as the coach crested the summit. Lake Bigler was the popular name for the place, though there was some sentiment for calling it Lake Tahoe. An Indian name, he had heard. By any name, it was stunning, azure in the evening light, placid and unsullied.

The night was mercifully dark, the moon late in rising, as the stage climbed up from the lake toward Johnson Pass. The coach rocked and bounced, but that was merely unpleasant. He had heard that to be in that careering coach in the daytime and to see the precipitous cliffs along which the road edged on one side was enough to terrify a brave man.

He changed coaches twice during the night. The second got him into Placerville for breakfast. Then it was a local stage to Folsom, a short run on the railway to Sacramento, and a three-hour wait on the docks at Sacramento for a riverboat. With all the delays before each connection, it was night again when he boarded the boat, so he paid an extra dollar for a cabin and a meal ticket. There were card games in the main hall, poker and faro, but he was tired, and anyway, he sensed that he had gotten all that he wanted out of cards for a while. He would leave them alone for some time, and maybe the feeling would pass. For now they were a tool that he had used too long and too hard.

So he slept to the muffled thrumming sound of the engine and awoke the next morning. The boat was out of the Sacramento River now and booming across the bay. He stayed inside, because high waves were pounding against the prow and splashing spray across the deck, yet even from inside he could smell the ocean salt and feel a hint of the chill over the water. He had not known these things since Boston. They might have made him sad ordinarily, but today they seemed fitting. Today, remembering Boston was not all bad.

Just after noon, he stepped onto the dock in San Francisco. He knew that he would have to wait until after business hours, anyway, to do what he wanted to do. So he ate lunch and walked about the waterfront, and after a few hours he stopped a strolling policeman to ask directions to an address on California Street. He had last seen the address eight years earlier, on the flap of an envelope. But he was sure that he remembered it, just the same.

"That is near the top of Nob Hill," the policeman said. "You'll want to walk three blocks this way up Sansome, then turn left and up the hill. It is quite a climb if you ain't prepared for it."

He walked anyway, lugging the valise. On its stretch up the hill, California Street passed through a commercial district, a Chinatown that was far more cluttered than the one in Virginia, then a residential section. The houses became bigger and more opulent as the top of the hill grew closer. The streets were numbered in the hundreds, by block, and as the numbers became higher, the houses were set farther apart, with trimmed lawns and hedges and rows of flower beds beside the sidewalk.

The house that he was seeking was just below the crest of the hill. It occupied one quarter of the block. The lot was surrounded by a black iron fence. A stone wall had been built around the lower section of the block so that the yard could be filled in level. Joshua paused at the gate in the iron fence. The house was immense, bigger than the family home in Boston, three-storied, with wings jutting in three directions from the main structure. It was designed in what would later be known as the Victorian style, with ornate filigree marking the line between each story, with overhanging cornices, and with dormer windows and gables in the roof.

He would build a house like this, Joshua thought. So different from what he had known. He would do such a thing.

Joshua passed through the gate, walked up the brick path, strode to the door, and tapped the brass lion's-head knocker twice. There was a pause of a few moments. The door opened and disclosed a man in a white shirt and starched collar and black vest with a watch fob. He had a moustache. That is new, thought Joshua, but little else seems to have changed.

"Joshua?" the man said. "Is that you, Joshua?"

"It is," Joshua said. He stepped forward, and the man opened his arms, and they hugged and clutched each other.

Joshua hadn't expected it to happen quite this way. He'd thought that in a house so large, a butler would come to the door first.

But he might have expected John Belden to open his own door.

John brought him into the house, one arm around Joshua's shoulder. Brought him into the dining room, where a woman and a boy and girl sat. They seemed puzzled.

"Father is crying," said the girl. "Don't cry, Father."

"This is my brother, Joshua. Your uncle, children."

The wife's name was Anne. The children were Matthew and Annie, aged six and four, John said.

"They know of you, naturally," John said. "Though I'm not sure that they were convinced that you ever existed, Josh. Eight years without so much as a letter. I began to doubt your existence myself. When my letters were never answered, I wrote to the company. I learned about Father and what he had done to you. This charlatan, this Gault, sold the place quickly, but my letter reached someone who had been retained. But of you, Josh, not a trace. Not a word."

"I was traveling."

"You must have traveled far."

"I did. You must understand, John. I was ashamed to have had the home and the business taken away from me. Ashamed to be poor. Can you comprehend that? I felt that a part of my life had ended, and I wanted to be as far from it as possible."

"I can understand. Tell me, then, what you have been doing for eight years, the places you have seen and what you have been about."

"Later. It is nothing to be especially proud of, but I do have stories, and they would take up half the night if I told them properly. I want to hear about you, John."

There was so little to tell, John said. Anne, of course. He might have mentioned Anne, in passing, in one of his last letters. His voice took on a joking tone. Marrying her made sense, if for no other reason than that living alone in such a great house would have been a terrible waste. Of course, the two children had the same justification. Money from the gold mine—the first one, near Sutter's Creek—had built the house and made him a rich man. The others he developed later had provided capital for business. Lumber up the coast. A couple of foundries. A newspaper. A ranch near a town called Gilroy.

And an import-export business here in San Francisco, he said. He laughed. Father got his wish, after all.

Anne Belden and the children left the room. Bedtime for them, she said. She was happy to meet her children's uncle, she said, but now she would leave the brothers alone.

The room was quiet after they left, and John and Joshua looked across at each other.

"Now tell me your story," John Belden said.

He had been in the West nearly three years, Joshua told him. He had wanted to see John, but pride held him back. Yes, yes, it was vain and stupid, but this was how he felt. Now he had come because he was about to change that, about to regain some of his wealth. Not on this scale, maybe, he said, glancing around the dining room, but close enough, anyway, to give him a start. And he had come, too, because he needed help in what he was doing. Not money, but help that John could give.

He told of Hemingway's show and Jack Murdoch and the riverboats and California and Virginia City. He told about the mines and the stock excitements. He told about Lucky Ames, and he told about the Fireball.

Then he told John what he needed.

"I've never done such a thing," John said when Joshua had finished.

"But you can do it. It shouldn't be so difficult."

"Surely someone else could do it better."

"I have nobody else. And you are perfect. You know such men, their talk and their manners. I need that if this is to come about."

"But you'd have found someone, wouldn't you, if I hadn't been here? You'd have found someone else to do this for you."

"Perhaps," Joshua said. "But you'll do it, won't you?"

"I'll do it," John said. "For you. For my brother. Especially if it will give you the money you seem to need if you are to come around here again."

They talked until the middle of the night. John showed Joshua to a room and then went to his own bedroom. His wife awoke when he climbed into bed.

"I will be going to Virginia City for a few days," he said. "Joshua is staying here a day and then is leaving. I will follow him shortly after that, when he sends for me."

"Business?"

"Not my own. Joshua has a venture there, and he has asked me for some help. I can hardly refuse."

"What does he do?"

"I suppose one would call him a speculator, for want of a better term."

John Belden thought of Boston. He thought of Joshua and himself in the room where they took instruction from their tutor, and Joshua painstakingly copying the names of the states and their capital cities on a tiny square of paper that he could hold in his hand during a quiz. It would have been far easier simply to memorize the list, but Joshua would not be persuaded. He would do it no other way.

"Has he changed much, your brother, in fifteen years?" Anne Belden said.

John turned to her, kissed her on the cheek.

"Not so much," he said. "Not much at all, now that I consider the matter."

CHAPTER THIRTY-SEVEN

He met John Mackay at the door of the rooming house, Mackay coming off his shift and Joshua having just returned from San Francisco.

"Joshua, I've been trying to find you, to talk to you. What is this that I read about you and the Fireball? Is this true?"

"It is."

"But you know, Josh, that it is worthless. After all the time I have spent with you, you must know that."

"Everything has value to someone. Believe me, John, when I say that somewhere there is a man who values that mine a great deal."

They climbed the stairs up to the second floor, Mackay following Joshua.

"But there is no silver in the mine," Mackay said when they reached the landing. "The Fireball is west of the lead. You will be in the hanging wall soon, if the shaft hasn't struck it already. What possible value could such a mine have? What are you doing, Belden?"

"I can't tell you that, John, as much a friend as you've been to me. But I can say that what you've taught me has been of great help. You've been indispensable. And I intend that when I get my money out of this speculation, you will have a share of it. You deserve it."

He left Mackay standing there in the hall.

Joshua changed his clothes and walked out into the street again. At a tobacconist's on B Street he bought an *Enterprise*. He leaned against the front wall of the store and turned to the stock quotations. He read the mining news and the notices of delinquent assessments. When he had finished, he folded the paper under his arm and walked briskly around the corner to C Street and the office of Wilson, the stockbroker.

The place was a single large room with four desks behind a single waist-high counter that ran the width of the place. On the wall behind the desks was a slate board that reached the ceiling, so high that there was a stepladder in front of it to allow access to the upper edges. The board was full of the names of mines. Some, like the Savage and the Ophir and the Chollar-Potosi, were painted on the board. Others, smaller and far less certain of survival beyond each afternoon's work, were simply chalked in. Beside each name was a series of three chalked numbers under columns that read: BID, ASKED, RECEIVED.

Three of the four desks were empty, but when Joshua entered, the one man in the place pushed the chair back from his desk and walked to the counter. He wore a leather eyeshade and a garter around his right sleeve.

"May I help you, sir?"

"I wish to open an account," Joshua said. The clerk picked up a pen, dipped it in a well, poised it over a form. "My name is Belden. Yes, e-l-d-e-n. Tomorrow morning I will transfer two thousand dollars to your firm's account, to be used as my purchasing fund."

"Very good, sir," the clerk said.

"I have a list of stocks I would like to purchase," Joshua said. "I know that the exchange is closed for the afternoon, but I'd appreciate prompt attention early tomorrow morning.

"The New Carolina was up at two bits today, I see. No takers. I wish to bid twenty cents for the first lot and then to buy as many shares as I can without pushing the price above fifty cents."

The clerk was bent over another form, dipping and scratching.

"I see that the Byzantine traded for ten cents yesterday."

"Yes. A small lot of two hundred shares."

"I will bid ten cents for as many as I can buy at that price. Go to thirty-five cents if need be."

The clerk crooked his head and peered past the eyeshade at this strange bird, obviously bent on tossing away his money as surely as if it were chaff thrown into a howling Washoe Zephyr.

"Last week there was some trading of the Cleopatra, though I don't see it listed today. I understand that there are five hundred shares extant. Bid fifty cents a share, and go to six bits if necessary.

"Finally, there is the Underwood. I haven't seen it listed for a month or more. I'll bid ten cents a share and see what develops."

"Yes, sir," the clerk said. "You realize that this may take a few days to execute. What I mean is that these aren't exactly the mainstays of the exchange. The truth is that most of them are pretty well dormant, sir."

"But when it's known that there is a buyer for them, I think I'll find some takers, don't you think?"

"Oh, yes, sir. You certainly will. I can about guarantee that."

Joshua hurried from the broker's office through the afternoon sidewalk clutter. Two blocks away, there was supposed to be a stock auction. He reached C Street and Union just as the auctioneer was climbing onto his barrel. The man held a printed circular in one hand and read from it, shouting, in a voice that was all boredom despite its volume.

Joshua listened until he concluded: "Whereas these parties have declined to meet the financial obligations legally imposed on them by the board of directors of the Steaming Warsaw, I am authorized to offer for public bidding the shares of stock on which they have defaulted."

He looked up from the circular. He saw Joshua standing beside the barrel, looking up at him, but the rest of the sidewalk was a swiftly moving current. He sighed.

"The first lot," he said, not as loudly as before, "is one

hundred shares of the aforementioned Steaming Warsaw. Assessments are one dollar per share and must be paid immediately."

"How many lots are you selling?" Joshua said.

"Please," the auctioneer said. "Let me do this according to form, sir."

"I don't think anyone will notice the difference," Joshua said. The men on the sidewalk still bustled past.

"I suppose you're right."

"How many lots, then?"

"Six lots. A total of three hundred sixty shares."

"And how many shares extant?"

The auctioneer looked around him, jumped down from the barrel.

"Four hundred," he said. "The other forty belong to the board of directors." Softly, leaning toward Joshua: "The dollar per share is to pay their annual salaries."

"I seem to remember that the mine hasn't shipped a ton of ore in two years."

"Unfortunately, correct."

"I bid five cents a share for every share that you have to offer."

"You'll have to pay the assessment. No avoiding that."

"I know. The total comes to three hundred seventy-eight dollars."

"And a small transfer fee."

"Naturally."

"We need to find a notary. You, my friend, have just become the proud majority stockholder in the Steaming Warsaw silver mine."

The paperwork required less than five minutes. When it was finished, Joshua crossed the street to the telegraph office. To his brother's home in San Francisco he sent this message:

JOHN   TUESDAY AFTER NEXT   JOSHUA

Sun Mountain's shadow was long and black against the desert when he walked from the telegraph office and down Taylor Street. On D Street he continued north past where the bordellos ended and the Chinese section began. He liked being here, liked the cooking odors, familiar smells, somehow slightly out of kilter, liked the ringing of wind chimes, liked catching a vagrant whiff of joss stick. Or was it opium? He was never sure. It was even nicer in the summer. The people grew gardens. Grew gardens in this grainy, barren devil's wastepile. The Chinese in Virginia did more with less than the thriftiest and most imaginative whites. They made houses out of junk from the whites' trash, and when they were finished the places did not seem salvaged. They had the look of homes.

He walked into a grocery store, through to the back, where some men played fan-tan, squatting on their haunches. He walked up a narrow set of stairs and down a short hall. He knocked at a door at the end of the hall.

A woman's voice spoke to him in Cantonese.

"Come," she said again, and he pushed aside the door.

She was seated on a cushion in one corner of the room, wearing loose pajamas, dipping chopsticks into a wooden bowl of rice and steamed vegetables. She stared up at him. The room had a bare cot along one wall, and the cushion on which the woman sat, and a small carved table that held a statue of a bare-bellied idol. With Joshua standing in the middle of it, the room seemed crowded.

It was Liz who had mentioned her and had helped him to find the woman. Liz had told him: Charlie is very superstitious. A sure believer in any sort of that drivel. He believes in spirits and fortune-telling and bad omens. He sees bad omens every time he turns a corner.

"Did you talk to him?" Joshua asked the woman.

"I talk."

"Did you tell him what I said? About the rabbit guts?"

"I tell."

"About how the guts told you he had lost something valuable?"

She raised her voice.

"I tell. I tell," she said.

"Good," he said. "Let me give you something extra." He reached into his pocket and gave her a silver dollar. She peered at it closely and stuck it somewhere in the folds of her pajamas. She looked up at Joshua and then stuck her chopsticks into the bowl and pulled out a mouthful of food. She chewed and looked at him.

"Well," he said. "I should be leaving. Thank you. Thank you again."

There was a piece of paper under his door when he reached his room at the boardinghouse. It was from Jim. Jim wanted to meet him at seven, along the road at the Divide. Joshua didn't like that. Too many men tried to cross the Divide after dark and never made Gold Hill with heads and purses intact. It was a favorite of the footpads. Jim could walk there with impunity, his safety probably assured by the assumption that no Indian, no matter how dressed, would have anything worth stealing. But if it was to be seven at the Divide, then Joshua would be there. He gobbled his supper at the rooming house. Mackay was there. He said nothing, but stared at Joshua with eyes both hurt and puzzled.

The Divide was just a couple of minutes away. Joshua walked beside the road. Traffic was spare: two men on horseback, wearing sombreros and speaking Spanish; the omnibus from Gold Hill, on the first of its shuttle trips to Maguire's. Joshua stood at the top of the ravine and looked at Gold Hill blinking beneath him, and at that moment a shadow emerged from the darkness.

"Hello, pard," Jim said.

"Next time we meet someplace safer."

"I recall nearly getting plugged the last time I tried to meet a white fella in one of your places. You got your safe spots and I got mine."

"I went to a lawyer before I left," Joshua said. "Bill Stewart, as good as they get in this region. He thought I was moonstruck but that what I wanted to do was legal and proper. He says the union may fuss but there's nothing wrong with the owners of a mine going down to do some work, that it's different from hiring cheap labor and under-cutting union wages."

"What about the rest?"

"He says it will hold. Three years ago a miners' court wouldn't have let it stand, but now we have real judges who go by law books and there won't be a problem."

"That's it, then. I'll have my boys here and ready by the afternoon."

The next day Joshua visited the notary's office. He wanted to transfer ownership of a mine, he said.

"Very good," the clerk said. "I'll need the second party if I am to witness the signing."

"Coming right behind me," Joshua said.

Through the door walked Captain Jim. And forty more Washo Indians.

From the *Territorial Enterprise* of November 27, 1863:

The Comstock has seen some unlikely partnerships in the past but we have the topper now. Lately we reported on the optimistic Mister Joshua Belden, who paid two thousand in specie of the realm for that notoriously worthless parcel of mining property, the infamous Fireball. Now Belden has passed the Fireball on to a consortium of more than 40 Digger Indians from the area of the Carson Valley.

Ordinarily we should castigate Belden for taking advantage of these poor savages in order to recoup his losses. But it seems that in payment of the property, Belden received no money. The Diggers obviously know a fair deal when they see one.

In compensation, Belden is to receive 50 percent of everything that is taken from the mine in the next 10 years. Also, he is to be given one half the proceeds of any sale. In total, then, Belden is to have one-half share of all the disappointment and frustration that surely will be the mine's sole dividends.

We learn from Belden that no assessments will be made. No money will be spent apart from the tools necessary to outfit a work crew. The actual labor will be performed by the Diggers themselves. The union may howl at that but the Indians are all owners and thus are perfectly entitled to work their own property.

On first reflection, this seems to be a splendid move on the part of Belden. He guarantees himself free labor and the lion's share of the riches. But before we congratulate him on his sagacity and cunning, we remind ourselves that 50 percent of *nada* is still *nada.*

"Dan," said the typesetter, "you'll want to see this, I think."

DeQuille glanced up from his writing pad and frowned at the interruption. He was gathering full steam just now, and the distraction annoyed him. The Gold Hill *News* in its latest edition had chided Virginia for the deplorable condition of C Street since the last rainy spell; a riposte was mandatory. DeQuille had decided to remind the residents of Slumgullion Gulch to pull in their trash and garbage before each storm, lest it be carried down the hillside. If that municipality had fewer problems with mudholes and bogs in its thoroughfare (and he wasn't for a moment conceding that it did), it was only because the depressions had been filled in by refuse matter of the most deplorable type.

But how was a man to maintain such perfect bombast under these conditions?

The typesetter handed DeQuille a folded sheet of paper. It bore the letterhead of a San Francisco hotel, and a message that specified type sizes for the copy that lay below.

"It's to be a paid notice," the typesetter said. "Payment enclosed for three days' publication."

"Yes, yes," DeQuille said.

He read the message through once and then read it again, audibly, as though that might make the implication more clear.

Mister Elisha Woodcock, representing monied interests from the Eastern Seaboard, will arrive in Virginia City on Tuesday, Dec. 1, and will remain for a period of not less than three days. Mister Woodcock's purpose is to evaluate the developed and undeveloped properties on the Comstock on behalf of his employers, who are seeking capital investment opportunities in the region.

Mine owners and directors desirous of contacting

Mister Woodcock are advised to leave their names and addresses on a list that will be maintained by the head clerk at the International Hotel.

DeQuille rested his feet on the top of his desk and leaned far back, with the chair balanced on its two rear legs.

"Well now," he said. "Well now. The fellow wants this set in twelve-point lightface with a fourteen-point head, in a puny one-column box. But an announcement like this one deserves far better. It is likely to be passed over by nine readers out of ten.

"We will run this in a two-column box on the front page. Make the body twenty-point and the headline thirty-six. No, wait. We will do that, but we'll also give our advertiser what he specified."

DeQuille yanked the sheet from the pad and crumpled it. Gold Hill's garbage would be an eternal target. This was news.

He stared at the paper for two minutes, and then his fingers moved.

"The nay-sayers and merchants of gloom who have had their way in Virginia for the last few weeks are advised to head for the hills with all dispatch," he wrote. "The doldrums which have afflicted Virginia and the entire Washoe region since the end of summer seem to be near an end. A notice received by this journal and reproduced on this page indicates that, outside Washoe, at least, there seems to be no lack of optimism about future prospects for bonanza."

DeQuille grinned. He was a happy man.

Joshua visited the stockholder's office at least twice daily. For the first couple of days the stocks he had specified had been hard to find. But rumor that somebody in town wanted these dregs had brought the owners to the exchange with their certificates. As Joshua had instructed, the broker bought all the shares available.

At the end of each day Joshua visited the broker's office once more, to take away the certificates that had accumulated during the day's transactions. He took them to his deposit box at the bank. At the end of five business days he had a thick stack of engraved sheets of paper that represented: ninety-six percent of the outstanding shares of the New Carolina Mining Company; eighty-nine percent of the Byzantine; eighty-four percent of the Cleopatra; and ninety-eight percent of the Underwood.

CHAPTER THIRTY-EIGHT

The Washo worked twelve-hour shifts in the mine, digging two new crosscuts. Joshua had bought picks and shovels, and a used fifteen-horsepower whim to replace the old windlass at the top of the mine shaft, and blasting powder and timbers. The pile of waste rock grew larger every day for a week. The *Enterprise* made note of the sight:

> We know now how the Diggers earned their name. They are tunneling madmen, and seem to have no peers in the human race when it comes to moving dirt. Their only competition in that department comes from moles and badgers. It is unfortunate that such industry should be expended on the Fireball, but all is not hopeless. We understand that there are some fine prospects in the Reeves River region. That is only a couple of hundred miles distant, and if the Diggers turn their drift to the east they will probably reach the area in four or five months at their present rate.

Late one night, Joshua and Jim met at the boarding-house. Joshua opened the steamer trunk and filled his valise with the ore that he had pilfered from the rich stope in the Ophir. Jim threw pieces of the ore into a leather bag that he held over one shoulder. They carried the load down the street and to the mine. They dumped the ore into a car, half filled with waste rock, that sat at the entrance to one of the new crosscuts.

Joshua held a candle close to the ore and selected four fist-sized chunks.

"These are likely pieces," he said. He gave them to Jim. "Any will suit our purposes. You know what you're to do now."

"It's simple."

"Your boys understand that they're not to speak to anyone about their work in the tunnel?"

"They aren't like Paiutes. They don't speak to whites. They leave that to me."

"And you know what you're supposed to do if we get our visitor down here?"

"Not exactly. I will figure a way of getting him to do what we want."

"You ought to have some idea. It has to be done."

"Leave it to me, Josh. When the time gets here, I'll make sure that he does it, and without his knowing that I've had a hand in it."

"Good, then," Joshua said. "We are close, partner. This thing is starting to get tight. Before long, we'll be playing on velvet."

The next morning Jim visited each of the three assay offices in the town, and one in Gold Hill. To each he brought a specimen of blue-gray ore that had sat in Joshua Belden's steamer trunk for several weeks.

DeQuille was eating lunch at Almack's when the printer's devil from the *Enterprise* tapped him on a shoulder.

"Dan," the boy said, "a fellow from Ruhlings, that chemist, was at the office to see you."

"Yes?" DeQuille said. He was interested. The man was a source, had tipped him earlier in the year to the discovery of the big rich ledge at the Yellow Jacket. That had been front-page stuff, had earned DeQuille a ten-dollar bonus.

"He says he has an assay report to show you. Says you will for sure be interested. But he couldn't stay, and he told me after I found you to tell you to come around the back door."

DeQuille sent the boy to the office. He stuffed his mouth with a wad of roast beef and gravy and bread, threw a few coins on the table, and hurried out into C Street. This would be a rich new stope, he was certain. No other reason for the man to have gone to such trouble. And he would get the story. This one would be his. It would be the biggest thing in Virginia for several weeks. This Eastern financier was big, but a new strike would be even more sensational. That would be something to quicken the community's pulse again. Virginia needed that kind of excitement now.

"Dan. Stay in the back, out of sight," the chemist said. "This costs me my job, if I'm seen dallying with you this way."

DeQuille leaned back into the shadows.

"But this is something you ought to know about," the chemist said. "This is a copy of the one I gave the customer."

It was an assay report that listed the composition of a sample of rock. Sulfides of silver, 17 percent by weight, it said. Traces of gold. Value per ton $950 in silver, $30 to $40 in gold.

"That is nice rock," DeQuille said. "Must be the Savage or the Chollar, or the Ophir, maybe, to produce ore like that."

"They have their own assayists. You know that. They don't need us."

"Well, to spot-check their own people. They do that sometimes, don't they, use you for that?"

"They do, sometimes," the chemist said. "But not this time."

"Who, then? Not a wildcat?"

"A wildcat in every way."

"Tell me, damn it."

"It was an Injun, Dan. One of the ones from the Fireball, had to be. This one spoke the white man's lingo as well as you or I, and I've heard that he is the one in charge of the diggings up there."

DeQuille squinted at the piece of paper in the shadows.

"Can't be," he said. "Can't possibly be."

"It does seem unlikely. I visited Kuhn's office, and a friend of mine said the same Injun brought in some rock there, too. This one assayed out to just seven hundred a ton. He told me he heard from Gold Hill that the Injun was down there, too, and the rock processed out to about twelve hundred a ton. It was good stuff, Dan, I could tell by looking at it. Nice color, you know. You can tell by color, the real high-grade stuff."

Only one way to find out, DeQuille told himself. Only one way to know for sure. The Indian might have stolen the rock from a passing ore wagon, though he didn't know what purpose that would serve. But there was one way of knowing for certain.

The Fireball's hoisting works sat on a swell of ground above A Street. DeQuille walked to where an Indian stood at the controls of the steam engine, with two others waiting beside the shaft to empty the bucket.

"Where is your boss?" DeQuille said. "Where is your foreman?"

The Indian at the engine looked at him and looked away. A bell rang twice on the hoisting frame above him. He yanked twice at a lanyard and then pulled a lever on the machine. The engine hissed and boomed white steam, and the reel on the crossframe moved slowly, winding up the rope.

The noise was impossible. DeQuille stood silent until the bucket had reached the top of the shaft and the engine was more quiet. Then he shouted down the shaft:

"Anybody here speak English?"

The return voice was hollow and distant as it filtered up from the hole in the rock:

"Be up directly, pard. Soon as they get the bucket down to me."

Jim rode the bucket to the top.

"Now, sir," he said when his feet were on the ground, "what can I do to help you? You'll excuse me for shielding my eyes this way. That sun is pow'ful bright for the first few minutes."

"I know. I'm DeQuille, of the *Enterprise*."

"I read you when I get the chance."

"You flatter me."

"My name is Jim, captain of the Washo tribe."

"Jim, I'd like to go down into your workings. I do that regularly, inspect the new operations on the lead and then report on them for the benefit of the public."

"Beg your pardon, sir, but I don't know why you would want to do that. It seems to me from reading your newspaper that the *Enterprise* has already decided what is inside the Fireball and don't want to know any different."

"We tend to be a bit sarcastic sometimes, I admit that. A touch too much for our own good, too."

"You boys have been riding old Josh pretty hard. Now me, bein' an Injun, I am used to that sort of thing. But Josh is a sensitive fella, and I don't take kindly to what you have been doing to him."

"Well, actually, the rough pieces, they were the work of Twain."

"Mark Twain is in Carson, covering the constitutional convention. I told you I read your paper, remember?"

"I suppose I ought to find Joshua, then."

"You do. You have him give you permission to go down in the workings and I will take you down personally. But not till then."

He had to wait until Joshua began his shift at the Occidental. It took some talking, some backtracking, a good lot of apologizing. Nothing personal, Joshua. I feel kindly to you, always have. Why, I was responsible for finding you this position here, wasn't I? Now all I ask is a chance to go down in the mine. A quick trip only.

It was evening and the crew was ending its shift, crowding three and four at a time into the ore bucket for the trip up to the top, when Jim heard DeQuille shouting from above. Jim rode with the next bunch up to the top and waited there with DeQuille while the mine emptied and the Washo laborers walked to the camp they had made on the side of the mountain.

"I have a note here, from Joshua," DeQuille said. "It says you are supposed to let me down there."

Jim took it. "I can read as well as anybody," he said. "Okay, that is Josh's writing." He spoke a few words of

Washo to the Indian who waited at the controls of the steam engine. Jim and DeQuille climbed into the bucket and rode it to the bottom. It stopped with a jerk, and the bucket swung for a time.

"He ain't exactly a sure hand on the controls," Jim said, "but he is learnin'. We're all learnin'."

Each man swung one leg and then the other over the side of the bucket and onto the floor of the drift. Jim pulled a burning candle and its holder out of a timber, and he walked with DeQuille down the tunnel.

"This is the old drift. Runs a couple hundred feet in all, from where it's bisected by the shaft. We figured there was no use in extending it any further, so we decided to cut an adit off to the side here, about seventy-five feet along. We've been making real good progress, from all I can tell. The rock is not too tough, and the boys are nothing but willing. You can walk down to the end, if you'd like."

DeQuille walked inside the freshly tunneled cut. He walked to the end and saw no change in the color or texture of the rock. They left the adit and walked along the main drift again.

"Since we had such a big crew and couldn't work 'em all in the same crosscut, we decided we would start a second one down at the other end of the drift. This is it, right here."

They were standing beside a nearly filled ore car. It sat at the entrance to the second new adit. DeQuille tried to look at the rock in the car. He had no candle, and Jim held his at such a distance that it cast only a dim light on the rock. But DeQuille's eyes were becoming accustomed to the darkness, and he guessed that the rock was darker than the walls of the drift.

He took a step down the new adit. Surely the ore in that cart would have come from the end of the new excavation, and he could look at it better down there.

"Sorry, pard," Jim said. He put out a hand, grabbed him by the sleeve of his coat. "Don't want to be impolite, but we're not allowing anybody down there for a while."

"Why?"

"Bad timbering. We ain't sure of our timbering down there, and we don't want to take chances."

"I don't mind. I'll tread easy."

"No. Sorry. That is our decision. You don't mind, do you? I mean, I sure hope you understand."

"Yes," DeQuille said.

"Say, excuse me a minute, pard. I been swilling water all day and it is getting to me. Don't think I can wait until we get topside."

Jim left DeQuille standing beside the ore car. He walked a few steps away and urinated against the side of the adit. He turned around to find DeQuille waiting for him, ready to go back to the top, he said. Jim walked behind DeQuille and made note of the new, heavy bulge that hung, pendulous, in the outer pocket of the white man's coat.

CHAPTER THIRTY-NINE

With winters so lengthy and so harsh, Virginia needed diversions. Bare earth and sage were never so bleak as when they were coated by a thin, hard layer of snow that crunched under boot, and the blasts that swept down off the mountain froze the spirits of men and of the town. Both needed warmth. Any excuse for a bustout would suffice, but for a legitimate reason like the arrival of Eastern capital there was no holding back.

The gala for Elisha Woodcock was spontaneous, the spark being provided by the head clerk at the International, who for two days after DeQuille's exclusive was occupied with listing and pacifying and assuring those who wanted some part of Woodcock's time. Not enough that they showed their faces once to have their names registered. Most would stop at the desk later that day, and again the next morning, and probably once or twice more, to make certain that the name was still legible, the address still obvious, to express concern that the list was growing so long that Woodcock surely would be unable to devote sufficient time to all.

The clerk took this for two days and then revolted.

"What you all ought to do," he said, while a cluster of the anxious pressed against his counter, "is to sponsor a civic function for this Woodcock. Make him a banquet right here in the main hall of the hotel. Show him what Virginia is made of. There is an advantage to that, you know. Come on like a bunch of street urchins and he will figure that he can buy you cheap. But put on a good show for him and he'll know that he must pay big money to buy in the game.

"Best of all, you can every one of you attend the affair and introduce yourselves there. Take turns standing up and telling him what properties you've got and what your prospects are. That way you can make yourselves known in orderly fashion."

He was only trying to rid himself of a bad job, of course, but he had an idea there, all the same. The city mobilized, threw itself into the task. A lot of energy had been stewing away in front of fireplaces and faro tables. Now it would go to some good use. They would give him something to tell his high-blooded Eastern friends about. Maybe their ore was just an ugly lump, but the city itself could glitter, given the incentive.

It would be at the International, fair enough. But no single restaurant had enough fine chefs for this occasion, so others were drafted, too. One for the dessert pastries alone, another for the dinner rolls and breads and croissants. One chef for the soup, another for the appetizers, another for the side dishes. A crew of three would handle the two entrees, and were forbidden to disagree over methods or ingredients. Wine cellars in every mansion were plundered for their rarest and most prized vintages.

The International knew only that this Woodcock was due from San Francisco sometime on Tuesday afternoon. That meant only that he would be arriving on a stage that passed through Carson City. An envoy was sent to Carson to greet every stage of the day, to ask for Woodcock, then to shoot off a telegram when he found him, so that the town could be poised for a properly rousing welcome.

Finally the message clicked into the office in Virginia City. The four o'clock from Carson, it would be. Those who had been standing vigil by the key rushed outside and shouted. The crowd, choking C Street and only grudgingly allowing the passage of ore wagons and freight carts, gave up a shout, but returned to frustrated milling. It would still be more than an hour before the stage passed through Devil's Gate in Silver City and began the climb up the canyon.

The stage was on schedule, the telegram said. At a quarter of an hour before four, the dense gathering in front of the International, where the stage would stop, began to disintegrate at the fringes and form up along the sidewalks lining C Street. When the walk was full, the people slopped over into the road. In front of the greeting stand—occupied by the town's five members of the Board of Trustees, and the superintendents and principal shareholders and boards of directors of the major mining companies, all in frock coats and high stiff collars, ruddy-faced and shivering now that the shadows had reclaimed the town—the bodies were as thickly packed as ever. Across the street was stretched a canvas banner reading WELCOME WOODCOCK, which had been painted by an itinerant artist, who, having been caught trying to skip out of a bill at the Union, had opted for civic work over jail. A ripple of shouts and cheers and yelling went up at the south end of C, near the Divide. It carried along the street, slightly in advance of the Overland as it moved into town. The crowd in front of the International separated, and the coach poked into the opening and stopped in front of the greeting stand. The first passenger out was a bearded man with the look of a miner. He grinned and waved and stepped into the crowd. Then a gray-worsted trouser leg appeared, slowly, deliberately, almost tentatively. The rest of the outfit was as low-key and yet obviously well appointed. The high stiff hat was the clincher. That had to belong to Boston or New York.

The president of the town trustees stepped forward.

"Woodcock?"

"Yes."

The president of the board stuck out his hand. A cheer spilled out from the crowd, and Woodcock smiled, shyly, and crooked his neck to take in the banner and the legs that dangled from eaves and balconies above him. The president of the board urged him forward. One by one the dignitaries stepped forward to greet him. Then his bags were lifted from the stage and he became the centerpiece of a phalanx that pushed into the hotel.

Dan DeQuille followed the official party into the lobby. He needed to do an interview. This was his story and the *Enterprise* must stay with it. But it would not lead the front page tomorrow morning. Eastern capital was one thing, but a new extension of the lead was even bigger. The evidence was there: an assay report on the rock that he had taken from the Fireball. Eleven hundred dollars a ton in silver. It would need some exploration but the prospects were there. Virginia was ready for that. New capital from the East might excite the big money, but a rich new deposit touched everybody who bought or sold in this town, the thousands who had built the place up from nothing, who now grew depressed or elated as the mining stocks fell and soared on the exchange. They wanted to hear this news.

DeQuille pried Woodcock loose from the clinging civic leaders. He would like to go to his room, wash some of the dust off, Woodcock said. He could grant DeQuille a few minutes.

No, he couldn't disclose the identities of the potential investors, he told DeQuille, splashing water on his face. They'd remain anonymous until the proper time. But they were important, and notable, be sure. Of course he would look into the established mines while he was here, but their possibilities were already recognized and proven. His investors were more intrigued by the potential of some of the undeveloped properties. This was not some distant plan. His employers trusted him and had deposited money in a San Francisco bank. He was prepared to do business immediately if he found prospects to his liking. The decision was his.

Lucky Ames waited in the foyer of the dining room. He held a glass of champagne in one hand and watched the staircase that Woodcock would be descending. He thought: I'll do well to get close to the fellow. We'll work something out, he and I. When he saw Woodcock coming down the stairs, Ames hurried across the lobby. Wanted to introduce himself proper, he said. Charles Ames, owner of some of the more important mines and mills on the Comstock and also in the Silver City and Flowery and American Flat districts. You're a stranger here under trying circumstances. Everybody'll be wanting your ear, with you just trying to do a job. I can be of assistance, sir. I know the area and its personalities. I can point you toward some of the promising quarters and away from the losers. No, no, I'd be glad to do it. Glad to be of assistance. Matter of fact, why don't you consider making your headquarters in my home? No, no trouble at all. You're far too accessible here, if I may say so. At my place you'll be far less at the mercy of the crowds. It'll be a more serene place to conduct your business. Let me send for my coach now. We can transfer your baggage immediately and then go back there later, when this little affair has run its course. Let me do this for you, sir.

Woodcock smiled. That would be a friendly gesture, he said. He would like that. He had seen too much of hotel rooms and, no offense, this place was not exactly up to first-class Eastern standards.

So Ames established himself at Woodcock's side and did not leave. He directed Woodcock to some, and just as deftly touted him off others. Trust me, dear sir. I do know my way around this little menagerie of ours in Virginia, and I can tell you that that rascal is not worth a half minute of your valuable time.

They drank champagne from four until eight and then sat down to eat. The courses streamed out of the kitchen. The white tablecloths became spotted and rumpled. Men tottered and later staggered away from the dais and the flanking tables. When dessert was finished and coffee had been poured and after-dinner liqueurs set out in thin-stemmed crystal, Woodcock was called on to make a speech. He did. The others then did the same, one by one, every man in the room. The first few were short enough, and to the point, briefly describing their properties and their plans. But soon one man spoke longer and more vividly than those who had preceded him, and the contest was on, each succeeding speaker describing more ornately than the last the unique qualities of his development. Midnight came, and passed. The speakers droned on. Woodcock drank coffee and tried to keep his eyes open while one man after another rhapsodized on the superbly conceived excavation plan, the marvelous hoisting works, the unequaled morale of the employees. And when they finally had finished, it was time for informal drinking in the bar. Well, Ames told Woodcock, a gentleman can hardly refuse.

They were laughing and drinking brandy and smoking cigars, about forty of them, when a boy lugged in a bundle of the morning's edition of the *Enterprise*. He set it beside the locked door of the newsstand and novelty shop in one corner of the lobby. It was Albie Noble who walked over and produced a penknife and cut the twine, pulled one newspaper from the stack, and flipped two bits into a jar beside the door. Some others did the same.

Lucky Ames watched them. They were at the other end of the bar from him, so he could not hear what they were saying. But they were excited. Men were leaving the bar and congregating around the newspaper. They were looking at him, reading the newspaper, and laughing.

"That was some stroke you pulled off, Lucky," Fisk was saying beside him. "Two thousand dollars for the Fireball. You showed Belden a thing or two about business, yes indeed."

The talk at the other end of the bar was more distinct now. Silver in the Fireball. A half dollar a pound at least.

Ridiculous, somebody said. There wasn't enough ore there to fill a gopher hole.

DeQuille has gone off the tracks, another agreed. That is barren ground.

Oh, said a third. When was he last wrong about something like this?

"Did you hear, Lucky? You was sitting on a bonanza all these years and never knew it. All it took was a sharper and a few red-skinned savages to find it."

There was laughter at that. Ames felt his throat tighten. Woodcock was looking at him, showing a faint bemused smile.

I don't care what the newspaper prints, someone was saying. I don't believe there is any silver in that area.

Lucky Ames bit his lip and said nothing. There was

nothing to be said. They might doubt it, these others, but for him there was no denying the truth. He had been taken. He knew. He knew the truth.

Now he had to salvage what he could. If there was silver in the Fireball, then it would inevitably be in the adjoining mines, too. Ore was not simply deposited in random dots; splotched and smeared was more the way. There would be a run at the exchange tomorrow, but he would have a man there first thing, buying all he could of the stocks of those satellite mines. They would cost him plenty, though he could have had them for pennies anytime during the last two years. The Underwood, the Byzantine, the Steaming Warsaw, the New Carolina, the Cleopatra. Amazing. Who'd have thought?

After the last Washo had left the mine that evening, Jim and Joshua nailed heavy planks across the mouth of the Fireball's shaft. They waited there until the two armed guards that they had hired appeared for work. Nobody was getting into that mine tonight.

Jim left to join the laborers in their camp, and Joshua walked down to Liz's house on D Street. Dozens of times he had walked this same path to the house, but never with the dread and apprehension in him that he felt now.

She had told him, quite casually, the last time they were together: I'm not certain any more that I want to be your wife. I may not be going to San Francisco with you when you leave. She'd given him no reasons, told him that if he didn't realize what made her feel this way, there was no hope for him or for them together.

Now where did she find these crazy notions? he wondered. Why today, of all days? Why must she spoil what ought to be the most important moment of my life, when I'm about to accomplish what I've worked so hard to do?

Amy answered the door and sent him to Liz's room. She was putting dresses in a trunk.

"Liz," he said, "I'm so happy."

"Why would that be?" He walked to her and took her in his arms, but she was not returning the embrace, as she usually did.

"You're gathering up your things. Making ready to leave with me."

"I am making ready to leave, in any event," she said. "I have decided to leave this life. Amy is taking over the business and will make monthly payments to me in San Francisco for as long as she stays."

"Do you intend to marry me, then?"

She pushed away from him.

"I don't know, Joshua. In all honesty, I don't. I thought for weeks that this was what I wanted to do, that I wanted you for a husband and that I could set the direction of my life with some assurance. But I can't be so confident now. I am not certain that I want to spend the rest of my life with you."

"I wish I understood."

"You don't? No, no, you don't. I can see that. Sit here beside me on the bed while I try to explain. You frighten me, Joshua. I thought I knew you and had seen the best and the worst of you, but since you've started this scheme I've begun to doubt that.

"Joshua, this is no way to make a fortune. There is no honor or dignity in what you are doing to Charlie Ames. You were made for better. I'm not one to criticize professions, perhaps, but at least I've never lied except to protect myself, and always gave full value for what I got.

"You are a cheat, Joshua. You are a fraud. I wouldn't mind as much, maybe, if you weren't so good at it. But you lie so well that I must wonder whether you'll be deceiving me. I don't know that I'll ever be able to stop wondering whether you're skinning me just as you did Charlie Ames. And that is no way to live, my love."

She wept. He rose from the bed and walked to the door.

"This is Tuesday," he said. "If all goes well, I will be leaving here before noon on Thursday. Maybe by then you'll know what you want. We can travel together to Carson, at least."

CHAPTER FORTY

After sleeping past nine and then breakfasting with Lucky, Elisha Woodcock toured the mines of the Comstock. Lucky insisted on showing him his own properties first. That occupied the day past lunchtime. Then Woodcock descended into the workings of the Ophir, the Gould and Curry, the Savage, the Hale and Norcross. Ames was with him constantly, dour after learning from a messenger the morning rumor in the exchange: Joshua Belden had been buying every share of every mine around the Fireball for a week now. There was almost nothing to be had, and prices were exorbitant for what was available.

Woodcock spoke little. Ames and all the mine superintendents each pointed out the advanced hoisting machinery, the sturdy construction of the square-set timbers, the admirable profit figures for the last three years. Woodcock took it all in, and nodded in a way that made him seem interested but noncommittal. When he left the Hale and Norcross, Ames pointed out the Chollar, the next in line on the lode.

"Later, perhaps," said Woodcock. "Now I want to see this Fireball."

So they rode in the black lacquered brougham up beyond A Street. They found Jim there with a crew of Washo, sitting at the mouth of the shaft. Jim stood up and approached the coach as the door opened and Woodcock and Ames alighted.

"I am the foreman and part owner of this mine," he said. "My name is Jim."

"I am Elisha Woodcock. I would like to inspect your mine to explore the possibility of investing money in its improvements. Do you understand?"

"Naturally I understand. Been expecting you, as a matter of fact. Kind of thought you would be here sooner."

He gave a command in Washo, and the laborers set upon the planks, prying them loose. Another fired the steam engine. When they were ready, Jim showed Woodcock to the cast-iron bucket, steadied it for him as he climbed in, then vaulted into it to join him. Ames started for the bucket, but Jim held up a hand. This is a private affair between this gent and me, he said, then motioned to the operator of the engine, and the bucket and the two men dropped out of sight.

Ames waited and fidgeted. He pulled out a pocket watch. Ten minutes he has been down there. Fifteen. Twenty. Half an hour. Woodcock had not devoted so much time to the Ophir. Finally, the bell rang on the hoisting frame and the operator shoved the lever and the bucket rose to the surface. Woodcock climbed out, face showing nothing, and walked to the brougham. Ames hurried beside him, and the laborers replaced the planks and sank nails into the wood again.

He would like to go and have dinner, Woodcock told Ames in the brougham. He had seen enough today. Possibly he had seen enough to be able to terminate his trip sooner than he had hoped. But he said no more.

Ames pressed wine on him during dinner. Please, drink up. We don't want to waste the bottle, do we? The wine seemed to loosen his visitor. Ames was encouraged.

"Elisha," he said, when they had finished dinner and sat in Ames's study, sipping brandy, "I admire directness in others. I try to practice it myself, and I credit that trait for much of my success. So I will come out and tell you. I would like to get in on some of your investments. I know that this is irregular, but your employers are far from you now. You have a chance to make some capital of your own, right now, just by sharing with me some of the things you know. I can be generous."

Joshua Belden sat in his room at the boardinghouse and waited. It should happen now, he thought. Sometime tonight. If not now, then probably not forever. I will have to find some new town and start over again.

He was staring out the window at the empty street below when there was a rap on the door behind him.

"Come in," he said.

John Belden came into the room.

"I've been waiting," Joshua said. "I was hoping that you were late only because you had trouble finding the place."

"No. Your directions were admirable. But I hadn't yet concluded my negotiations."

"And how did they go?" The question nearly choked Joshua. He was tight, tense, almost afraid of the answer.

"Not badly, once I grew accustomed to being called Woodcock. I have been enjoying myself."

"You know what I mean."

"He is envious of you, Joshua. Best of all, he wants to try to get back at you. He said he wanted to go partners with me, but I have my doubts. More likely he will try to buy you out cheaply before I get a chance to make my offer. Then he will sell to me at the price I quoted, just to spite you."

"And what did you say?"

"I said that you had run into a stope of rich ore and that from the length of your crosscut, the stope was as wide as anything I had seen today on the main lead. I told him that I had fifty thousand dollars on account in San Francisco and that tomorrow I was going to offer it to you and the Indian as down payment for your share in the Fireball and all the adjacent mines. I said that the mines were probably worth millions but that I was going to get it from you for half a million. Or at least try."

"A half million."

"I know. More than we talked about. But he was ready

for it, Joshua, I felt that. I felt he wouldn't gag on a half million."

"No. You did right. That's what you're supposed to do, go on your feelings. A half million, by God."

"I should be leaving. I told him I wanted fresh air. He'll be sending for you here, shortly, I know. Josh, he bribed me ten thousand to tell him that. Ten thousand."

John was gone. His departure was followed not five minutes later by the arrival of one of Ames's men. Mr. Ames would like to see him soon as possible, matter of the utmost urgency.

Joshua spurned the brougham. He would walk, he said. Tell Lucky he would be there before long. He put on his overcoat and wrapped it tightly around him as he walked up the hill. A nervous joy spread through him, and he felt for a moment that he could not contain it. He fought against it. Not yet. Not quite yet. Stay calm and you will be able to enjoy it even more.

Ames met him in his study. He began by congratulating Joshua on his skills. Nobody else could have predicted ore in the Fireball, he said. Not the best geologist in the territory. Joshua had nipped him, square, and that move of getting the Indians in there as part owners, to develop the mine without capital, that was genius. Now Joshua would have a chance to see some material reward for his effort. He would pay Joshua one hundred thousand dollars for his shares in the Underwood, the Byzantine, the Cleopatra, the New Carolina, and the Steaming Warsaw.

That would not be enough, Joshua said.

Without much haggling, they settled on a quarter of a million dollars in cash. They signed a contract there, Ames having summoned a notary, the cash to be exchanged the next morning.

Twelve hours later, Joshua and Liz were leaving town in Jim's one-horse chaise. In a pocket of his greatcoat he carried a receipt book showing two hundred fifty thousand dollars deposited in a Wells, Fargo account.

CHAPTER FORTY-ONE

Jim brought the forty Washo into town on Thursday morning. They went to a notary, who witnessed their marks on a document that transferred their shares of the Fireball to Jim. They were to be paid one hundred dollars each, set aside earlier that morning by Joshua after he had done his business with Ames. Jim already had a notarized letter with which Joshua relinquished any claim on the Fireball. That had been part of their agreement. Now Jim owned the Fireball whole, and Ames wanted to buy. Ames had come to visit him personally that morning after finishing with Joshua. Ten thousand, he had offered at first. Fifteen. Eighteen thousand. Twenty, my final bid, Ames had said. It was more money than Jim had ever imagined. But he wanted to think on it, he said. That was another part of the agreement. He was to give Joshua and his girl and his brother time to clear town before he sold the mine and gave Ames a chance to look at it.

Now Joshua and the girl were three hours gone and the brother had left town on a stage to Placerville, having first, just for effect, thrown a tantrum at Ames for undercutting him on the deal. He would make certain, he had shouted, that no Eastern money ever made its way to this devil's playground.

So Jim had nodded when Ames came calling again, offer-

ing twenty for the final time. He would take it, he said. He
signed the deed and title and watched Ames fix his signature
to a piece of paper that was supposed to put twenty thousand
on account with Wells, Fargo. Just like that, he thought, I
am the richest Indian who ever lived.

He had given Joshua his carriage so that he and Liz could
start the trip to Genoa. The three of them were to meet there,
in a meadow outside town, before traveling across the
mountains to San Francisco. Jim could get his money in
cash from Wells, Fargo there, Joshua had said, just as he
himself intended to do.

Jim left Virginia on foot. He climbed the side of the hill
until he was at the edge of town. Then his pace increased.
Ames might at this moment be ripping away the planks to
look at his new investment. He would be angry enough to kill.
Jim walked through the desert, on the west side of Sun
Mountain now. As always, there was wind. A brittle tumble-
weed bounced past him; a dust devil twisted a few hundred
yards away, touched earth briefly, then rose and vanished.
A few years ago, he thought, that would have frightened me.
I'd have seen a spirit in it. But now I know it is only dirt and
wind. I have changed. I have traveled a long way from where
I started.

He passed through Carson City in the evening and turned
south, staying away from the road, into the Carson Valley.
It was night and he was tired of walking, so he decided to
rest. He stopped beside the river, where bulrushes grew along
the bank. That would be good. The rushes would cut the
wind, and hide him, too. He sat surrounded by the rushes
and looked at the sky. He thought about San Francisco and
twenty thousand dollars. And that would be just the start,
Joshua had told him. There was no limit to what the two of
them could do together. It's a miracle when you consider
it, Joshua had told him as they talked two nights earlier. One
white man and one red, born a continent apart, and yet so
much alike in so many important ways. We are two of a kind,
Joshua had told him, cast from the same mold. We both
have an eye for a greedy man, and the touch to take him the
way he deserves to be taken. That is a talent, Jim, he had
said.

Jim heard a noise in the rushes. A deer, he thought. No, too heavy for a deer. The steps were coming closer, measured, purposeful.

His father's father was standing a few feet away, wrapped in his rabbitskin robe. Of course. The night was cold.

Jim rose to take him in his arms. He stopped short. The old man was not smiling, as he usually did when they met. Then Jim realized that the old man was dead. He'd seen the body go up in the smoky flames of a pile of sage, a funeral pyre. I myself smeared my face with dirt, he thought, and mourned for a whole year.

Talks Soft looked at him steadily, eyes unblinking.

Yet he is here, Jim thought. No denying that. That is him, standing here before me. But he seems unhappy. Displeased.

"What have I done to anger you, father of my father?" he said. The old man's face softened. He said nothing, but this was just like him, never able for very long to keep his love for the son of his son from breaking out.

I am dreaming, Jim thought. Then, with the shock of sudden realization: No. I am not dreaming. I am *dreaming*.

The old man's face was happy now. He was smiling in earnest. Jim rose to embrace him, but for each step forward he took, the old man moved backward a pace. Jim stopped, and the old man turned and walked through the rushes the way he had come. He was moving quickly, so quickly that he was receding even as Jim watched. No. Can't let that happen. Jim ran, and the old man looked over his shoulder, grinned at him, kept moving.

Jim ran. The rushes slapped against his legs. He looked down and saw that it was not rushes against his legs but yellow-topped sagebrush. His legs were bare. His body was bare, except for a breechcloth. It was daylight, and he was walking down the draw that led to the mouth of the big canyon where the wagon trains passed. There ought to be a road here somewhere. And Adam Longstreet's ranch is here. This puzzled him. He knew this area and knew that Adam's barn was here, right here, on this spot. This place looked as it had before the first white man had ever seen it.

He walked. He had lost sight of Talks Soft, but there was no indecision in his steps. I am walking the right way, he thought. This is the way I am supposed to be going. At the end of the draw was a stream. He walked beside the trickling water for a while and then he saw his wife and his son. It was a woman and a baby. He had never seen them before. But he knew. This was his wife. This was his son. He knew. The woman knew, too. She looked over her shoulder at him and her eyes were full of light and love. She rose and held the baby up for him, fat and brown, reaching out a chubby arm. He also knew.

The baby was in his hands, in his arms, warm, alive. The baby put a fat hand on his nose, gripped and twisted.

"Are you hungry?" his wife asked.

He discovered that he was. Yes, he would eat.

She had raw shoots and rabbit meat and pig weed and pine nuts for him. He ate and watched his son crawl in the dirt and let the sun warm his back. It was an afternoon made for that. He had nothing to do. A strange sensation for him, nothing to do, no place to be. Since he had lived with the whites he had forgotten how that could feel.

Then he remembered Talks Soft.

"Have you seen my father's father?" he asked her.

"He passed by just ahead of you. He said he was walking to the river to spear some fish."

"I will go to find him," he said. He walked away a few steps and turned back to look at them. He knew that he ought to stay. He knew that if he left now he would never see them again. They watched him, and he felt within himself that already he had gone too far away, that they were too distant to be reclaimed, as ephemeral and intangible as a reflection in a still pond, which is destroyed by the touching.

The path led downhill to the river, but he found himself rising higher with each step. He was floating. He was high above the river and the canyon, higher than the highest mountain, so high that he could see the range of the people from north to south, east to west. He could see behind cliffs and into arroyos, could see every person in every bunch as they harvested greens and speared fish and swam in the lakes and knocked pine nuts and copulated and prayed and basked in the sun and froze and were born and bore children and starved and ate their fill and mourned their dead and died themselves. He could see these things in progress, could feel the passage of time on a grand scale, which was the only scale that the people acknowledged, and which therefore was the only scale of time that existed for them. He was high above them all, and yet he could see the details of their lives and could feel their individual joys and disappointments, and most of all, could sense within himself the subtle, magnificent orchestral harmonies that the living and the dying created.

He knew: It never ends. It never changes. If you listened well, the tones and their sequence had an eternally repeated pattern. There are changes of shading, and rises and fallings like the shifts of season, but it goes on all the same, just the way the seasons do. With their lives the people create music, and they have that ceaseless music in their hearts.

The clarity of his vision blurred. He was too high now, maybe, to see the people as he had moments earlier. His eyes were filled with liquid. He was in the clouds and the clouds were obscuring his vision, making his eyes water.

No. It was not clouds, but smoke, stinging and acrid. There was a fire upwind. He could see orange flames in the midst of the tumbling gray. White men were throwing rags on the fire. White men. And him mostly naked. He felt ashamed. He was about to cover his body, to run and hide until he could find proper white men's clothes, when he saw that he already was properly attired in pants and shirt and boots. A white man's hand was pulling at an arm.

"Jim, get out. Move out away from that smoke, boy." The hand pulled him into clear air.

"Them clothes are diseased, Jim. You don't want to breathe the smoke. You'll get the fever too."

Behind him he heard a woman's voice, shrieking and wailing, anger in it and distress, but mostly misery. He turned. The woman was behind a three-stranded barbed-wire fence. She was naked. He recognized her as a woman he had put to work cleaning the white women's houses. But she was older than he remembered. Now she was naked, and grabbing the barbed wire so tightly that streaks of blood ran from her clenched fingers and down the undersides of her forearms.

Behind her he saw more Washo. Some were naked and others were dropping their clothes into a sorry pile, and a few were struggling against white men who were trying to strip them. All the Washo were in a barbed-wire enclosure, and Jim somehow knew without asking that they were ill, had been taken with a contagious fever that would kill most of them. They were being quarantined so that the whites would not contract the fever. To one side, outside the compound, two Washo were dropping the body of a third into a shallow strip grave. There were other bodies in the grave, and a couple more Washo stood with shovels, ready to begin flinging dirt on the bodies.

The woman saw him. She screamed for help, in Washo. She stretched a bloody hand toward him. And she was not alone. There were others at the fence now, weeping and wailing, calling out to him for help, help us please, tell the whites to let us leave this place. The Washo were pasty-faced, with flaccid muscles and flat eyes. Even in blatant supplication, they could not find a spark of life inside. He listened for music, but heard only a dissonant grating jumble of painful grunts and moaning and shallow breathing.

Their eyes were on him. They called his name and cried out to him. He recognized some of them, men and women for whom he had found work in the fields of the whites, now stripped naked and begging.

The wind seemed to have shifted. His eyes were wet again. This time he could not stop crying. The bitter smoke and the painful harsh cacophony of human misery without counterpoint were too much.

He was on his knees in the bulrushes, crying without a sound, when the sun came up over the Pine Nut hills. Without a thought, he straightened unsteady legs and waded into the river. When he walked out, he left to keep his rendezvous.

CHAPTER FORTY-TWO

"Where do we go from here?" Joshua said.

"I guess the question is Liz's, mostly," he said. They were standing in the meadow outside Genoa, Joshua and Liz in Jim's chaise, Jim standing beside it. "I mean, Liz is the one with the uncertain future. You and me, Jim, we're headed to San Francisco. Maybe our plans are uncertain beyond there, but we know that much."

"No," said Jim.

"You don't want to go to San Francisco? You want someplace else?"

"I am staying here, Josh."

"Now, don't joke that way." But Jim's face was solemn. No joke.

"I am staying," Jim said.

"What has got into you, Jim? You can't stay. Ames will kill you personally if he knows you are still about."

"No," Jim said. He knew that he was not going to be killed. He could not explain to Joshua how he knew this, but he had seen himself alive in his dream in a time that was still off in the future, so he knew that Ames would not kill him.

"You'll never be able to work another scheme, even if he doesn't. No white man within thirty miles will buy or sell or trade with you again."

"I don't intend to."

"But this is your life, Jim. This is what you do best."

"I got people here who need me. I can help them, maybe."

He looked at Joshua and saw that he would not understand. A month of talking would not get through to Joshua.

"You can keep the horse and carriage, if you want," Jim said. He turned and walked toward the grove of trees at the fringe of the meadow.

"You've got money waiting for you in San Francisco!" Joshua yelled at him. "You'll never be able to get it if you stay here!"

Jim did not stop. He strode into the trees, and in a moment Joshua could not see him or hear him any longer.

"You never know," Joshua said. "I never expected him to start acting like an Injun, was my problem."

He turned toward her.

"And what about you?" he said. "You leaving too?"

She is, he realized. She wants to leave, but for the moment the words won't come for her.

He spoke quickly, before she could.

"At least we'll go to San Francisco together," he said. "Better that you don't stay here alone any longer than you must. From San Francisco you can go where you please."

She hesitated. Then she nodded slowly, yes.

He slapped the reins. The horse trotted forward. He slapped the reins again, and the horse broke into a canter. Two days by stage to San Francisco. He would have some talking to do.

But he would find a way.

POSTSCRIPT

The histories of John Mackay and Virginia City after 1863 are inextricably entangled. The town's mining industry underwent a depression in 1865, after the boom year of '63. Mackay took advantage of the lull in the stock-trading madness to buy a large interest in the Kentuck mine, between Gold Hill and Virginia City. The mine had been unproductive until that time, but discoveries north of the Kentuck, in the Crown Point mine, made a sizable ore body in the Kentuck almost a certainty to Mackay. On January 1, 1866, a shaft being sunk in the Kentuck struck a seam of ore ten feet deep at the 275-foot level, and Mackay was on his way to becoming a rich man. The Kentuck paid $1.142 million in dividends during the next four years and provided the capital for Mackay to invest in other promising properties on the Comstock lead.

For the next decade Mackay would be struggling with William Ralston and Darius Ogden Mills, manager and president of the newly formed Bank of California, and their representative in the Washoe territory, William Sharon, for control of the major mines and mills in the area. Until 1873 the competition was one-sided. Sharon had the overwhelming leverage of massive capital.

In 1871 Mackay and his partners, James Fair, William

O'Brien, and James Flood, bought a controlling share in the Consolidated Virginia mine, which sat on the north end of the Comstock lead. The property included 1,000 feet along the main ledge that had been one of the most prized sections of the lead during the 1860s. But in the summer of 1870, after years of fruitless efforts by a number of different companies, some of the 11,600 shares in the mine sold for as little as $1 per share. Mackay and his partners acquired control for about $50,000 and immediately began work on the lower levels. One of the first excavations was a drift cut from the 1,167-foot level of the Gould and Curry mine, controlled by Sharon, who gave permission for the excavation, confident that the quarter-mile length of tunnel would carry into barren rock. In September, 1872, the drift struck a fissure of low-grade ore, and the mine superintendent decided to cut the drift to follow the northeasterly dip of the vein. In March, 1873, the drift struck a wall of high-grade ore, the upper reaches of what in succeeding months would be revealed as one of the largest rich bodies of silver ore ever discovered. This was the Big Bonanza. Stock in the Con. Virginia climbed to as high as $800 per share. It was an inflated price that could not be sustained. The market plunged in 1875, the Con. Virginia dragging down most of the other properties with it in its descent to realistic levels, though Mackay was unaffected, since he did not play the market. Just as stocks began to climb in October of that year, Virginia City was devastated by a fire that destroyed most of the city and the hoisting works of the Ophir and the Con. Virginia. But the heavily timbered workings were saved. Mining operations were resumed after sixty days.

In the ten years through 1882 the Con. Virginia paid $43 million in dividends, and Mackay became one of the world's richest men. In 1884 a company he had formed laid two cables across the Atlantic and successfully challenged the transoceanic telegraph monopoly of Jay Gould and Western Union. Mackay's estate was valued at $50 million after his death in 1901.

Mining continued in Virginia City through 1920, but was difficult and expensive because of the intense heat and problems with flooding in the deep levels. Finally the ore was too poor to pay the cost of extraction and milling, so the last mine was abandoned. Virginia City became nearly deserted but survived as a tourist attraction, and in the mid-1970s experienced a minor boom in real estate development.

Dan DeQuille remained at the *Daily Territorial Enterprise* as reporter and editor until the newspaper folded, in 1893. Encouraged by his friend and former colleague, Mark Twain, DeQuille in 1875 wrote *The Big Bonanza,* a history of the Comstock Lode that now is considered the primary source book for the place and the period. DeQuille died in 1898.

Washo tribal history identifies at least two men who took the name Captain Jim. Both were respected and admired for their ability to deal with white settlers, and one of the two attained legendary status in the tribe.

The effects of poverty and cultural disruption and several virulent epidemics reduced the Washo to fewer than five hundred survivors by 1870, and the U.S. Commissioner of Indian Affairs predicted the tribe's extinction. Today the Washo number more than two thousand, some of them in communities in Carson City and Reno, Nevada, and others in rural colonies scattered throughout the tribe's original range. Though many Washo still exist on the edge of poverty, tribal identification is intense, and the language and many of the religious beliefs are maintained. In 1970 the tribe was granted an eighty-acre reserve near Woodfords, California, and $5 million indemnification for the loss of traditional land in the Pine Nut range. Part of the tribal income is derived from the proceeds of a trailer camp on the Carson River, and there are plans for a Washo cultural center at the site of one of the original fishing camps at Lake Tahoe.

005634523

Finch
  Birthright.

C. 2